THE LEAGUE OF GOVERNORS

BY WENDY M. BARNHART

(Formerly Wendy Terrien)

The Adventures of Jason Lex Series
Chronicle One
THE RAMPART GUARDS

Chronicle Two - Jason
THE LEAGUE OF GOVERNORS

Chronicle Two - Sadie
THE CLAN CALLING

Chronicle Three
THE FORGE OF BONDS

"The Fate Stone"
A short story originally published in the anthology
TICK TOCK: SEVEN TALES OF TIME

"Light"
A short story originally published in the anthology
OFF BEAT: NINE SPINS ON SONG

THE LEAGUE OF GOVERNORS

CHRONICLE TWO - JASON
IN THE ADVENTURES OF JASON LEX

A NOVEL BY
WENDY M. BARNHART

CAMASHEA PRESS | DENVER, CO

THE LEAGUE OF GOVERNORS
Chronicle Two - Jason in the Adventures of Jason Lex
Copyright © 2017 Wendy M. Barnhart
(also known as Wendy Terrien)

Published by Camashea Press.
All rights reserved. All logos are owned by Camashea Press.

First printing, August 2017.

Hardcover ISBN: 978-0-9969031-4-1
Paperback ISBN: 978-09969031-5-8
Ebook ISBN: 978-0-9969031-6-5

Camashea Press
PO Box 631444
Littleton, CO 80163

Library of Congress Control Number: 2017908108
Printed in the United States of America

For Vincent
May you forever welcome adventure in your life

ONE

Trouble

Jason's first few weeks back at school were weird. Carrying the secret of his mom's death and how she'd tried to destroy every person at his school, actually every human on earth, made him feel like he wore a neon sign flashing: "I'M HIDING SOMETHING." Questions from friends like, "What are you doing this weekend?" made him anxious, and interest in how his burned hands were healing made him cautious. Did people know more than they were letting on? Did they know he was now a Rampart Guard and could shoot electric bolts out of his hands? Were they testing him with questions? In time Jason settled into the fact that he, Sadie—his best friend at Salton High School, and his brother, Kyle, were the only people at school who knew anything about the Rampart and Jason's role in saving it.

And Jason was good at keeping secrets.

Jason met Sadie at their lockers. "From Mamo." She handed him an apple from her grandmother's garden.

"All this healthy stuff is going to kill me." Jason grinned, took a bite. "Tell her thanks, as usual."

"I will. And she'll be glad to hear you are actually eating what she sends." Sadie snapped her locker shut.

"Hey, if it's good, as in tastes good, I'll eat it."

Sadie and Jason headed to the lunchroom where Jason tossed the apple core in a trash bin near the door. They grabbed seats and Sadie unpacked her lunch. Jason pulled a protein bar out of his bag and peeled back the wrapper.

"Seriously, that's all you're eating?" Sadie asked.

"I had an apple."

Sadie rolled her eyes. She looked across the room. "Ugh. Here comes Derek Goodman."

Jason looked over his shoulder. His lip curled.

Derek sneered. "What are you looking at?" He and two of his friends stopped behind Jason.

"I was trying to figure out what smelled so bad," Jason said.

Derek sniffed the space above Jason's head. "It's you, the slime-ball that beats up his own weakling brother."

Jason bolted out of his seat and stood inches away from Derek. "Take that back."

"Or what?"

Jason pressed his fists into his thighs. His chin jutted. "Take—That—Back."

"Not—Gonna—Happen. For all we know, you've done something to your sister, too. I heard she hasn't been in school for like a month."

Sparks zapped inside Jason's hands. He battled the urge to singe Derek Goodman. And to slug him hard in the gut.

"Jason?" Sadie's voice was half-anxious, half-warning.

Jason shook his head. "You're not worth it."

"No? How about now?" Derek shoved Jason into the table.

Jason sprang into a fighting stance. Sadie rushed to his side of the table.

"What's going on here?" Coach Martel grabbed Derek's shoulder from behind. "You. To the principal's office."

Derek moved toward the exit. Coach turned to Jason. "Are you all right?"

"Yeah. Fine." Jason straightened and relaxed. His hands cooled.

"Okay. Good man." Coach patted Jason on the back. "Don't forget basketball tryouts are in a couple of weeks."

"Thanks, Coach." Jason wouldn't be trying out for the basketball team. He wanted to stay focused on his training for the Guards.

Coach Martel nodded. "Now, if you'll excuse me, I have a problem to escort to the principal's office. Again." The last word he said under his breath.

Lunch period was almost over and most of Jason's classmates left for their next period. His adrenaline eased and he gathered up what remained of his lunch.

"Della's still having a hard time?" Sadie asked.

Jason wadded his trash and hooped it into the nearby bin. "Yeah. She's awake half the night, she starts crying at the weirdest times. She was playing fetch with Shay yesterday and lost it when Shay wouldn't drop the ball for her."

"Is there anything I can do?" The bell rang and Sadie picked up her lunch bag.

Jason looked at his hands. The skin on his palms was shiny and tight, newly healed from being burned when he'd tried to save his mom. "Nah. Dad's trying to figure it out. Thanks, though." He turned toward his next class. "See you later."

"Yeah, see ya," Sadie said.

After school, Jason and Shay headed to Uncle Alexander's. Jason opened the front door. Shay rushed in and tackled Finn. They rolled and lunged and growled like they wanted each other's blood.

Jason checked their body language. This was all fun and games. Reading the dogs' signals was one of Jason's early lessons as a Rampart Guard, along with how to consistently summon the right amount of power for whatever repair the Rampart needed. Too much energy directed at a small problem meant a small problem became a big one. And a big problem meant severe damage to a segment of the Rampart, and risk to humans from the energy of cryptids living among them. Nothing like that had happened for more than two hundred years, and Jason wasn't about to be the Guard that ruined that record and helped the rest of the world discover that the cryptids they'd thought were myths, like Loch Ness, the Dover Demon, and Skyfish, were real and living among them.

Shay and Finn continued their wrestling match with a slam into the leather couch.

"Hey, Uncle A." Jason collapsed on the couch.

Uncle Alexander poked his head out of the kitchen. His brown hair looked windblown. Jason figured he'd been riding his scooter.

"Did you study the League's guidelines and laws?" Uncle Alexander asked.

"Yep. Until I fell asleep. Which took about five minutes."

"I know it's not the most riveting read but you have to learn it. It's important to understand how the League oversees the relationship between cryptid and human populations worldwide."

Jason tipped his head back and closed his eyes. "I promise I'll get to it. Maybe this weekend."

"What about Morse code?"

"I almost have the full alphabet down, but I still think it's a waste of time. We have messaging apps, you know. And phones. And paper and pencil," Jason said.

"Your protest has been noted. Keep studying the code."

Jason huffed. "Fine. And maybe next you can teach me smoke signals."

Uncle Alexander tapped Jason with a water bottle. "No smoke signals. But definitely the Rampart distress signals."

He sat up. "Those are much more interesting. I'm now on the lookout for sun dogs, moon dogs, rings around the sun, changes in electromagnetic field noise, extra-bright double rainbows, and a few more things I can't remember. And Sadie's going to keep an eye on the internet for any hey-look-here's-a-picture-of-me-with-Bigfoot or whatever postings."

"Good. I'll quiz you while you work the bag. Let's head down to the gym." Uncle Alexander clasped Jason's arm and pulled him to his feet.

"I'm on board with the training, but I still don't get why so much of it is self-defense when we can shoot electric bolts out of our hands," Jason said.

"As I said when we first started training, it's part of the code of the Rampart Guards. No using powers against those who are without powers."

"Right, but if they attack you first—"

"No using powers against those who are without powers." Uncle Alexander rubbed his temple.

"You okay, Uncle A?"

"Yes, just remnants of a headache from earlier today."

Thanks to dear old Mom. Jason wondered if Uncle Alexander would ever be one hundred percent healthy after being poisoned by her for so long.

Gotta work harder. Gotta be ready.

In the gym, Jason kicked and punched, defended and attacked, and practiced methods to escape choke holds and bindings. During breaks, he rehearsed Shay's basic commands and started her on cryptid scent identification. Finn assisted when Shay was stumped.

When he and Shay got home that evening, like every evening after training, they headed to the kitchen. Kyle sat at the table doing homework. Shay bee-lined to her water bowl, slurped up a sloppy drink, and caved onto her kitchen bed—one of several dog beds placed around the house.

"Must be nice." Jason plunked a pile of books onto the table. "No homework for you." He bent down and rubbed Shay's cheek.

"Seriously nice," Kyle said. He stretched his arms overhead.

Dad walked in. "I'm glad you're both here. We need to talk."

"What's up?" Kyle asked.

"Della . . . the League of Governors. They're worried."

"What do they have to do with anything?" Jason took leftover chicken out of the refrigerator.

"Because of the Guards. Because of the remaining power she still has," Dad said.

"Okay." Jason bit into a chicken breast, not bothering with a plate.

"I'm taking her to them."

"What? Why?" Kyle asked.

"They may be able to help."

Jason shifted his weight and swallowed. "I don't get it. Why them?"

"She needs to talk to someone but she can't meet with a regular therapist. Since the League is fully aware of cryptids and the Rampart, Della will be able to speak freely about what she's been through. Plus . . . the League is worried she might be going down a path like your mother's."

Jason straightened. "Della is not crazy."

Dad shook his head. "No, I know. But she needs help dealing with everything she witnessed, what your mom did."

Dad always referred to her as "your mom" now, never by her name, Adrienne.

"You two and Shay will stay with Uncle Alexander, okay?"

"C'mon, Dad. I can watch Jason," Kyle said.

Jason huffed. "Hey. I don't need watching. You do."

"Whatever, dude. I'm practically sixteen—"

"Enough." Dad used the voice you didn't question. "You both need watching and you're both going to Alexander's."

"Yeah, fine." Kyle shut his notebook. "When are you leaving?"

"Tonight. Three-hour drive to the airport then we catch the red-eye. GQ is picking us up at Heathrow."

Dad's uneasiness quashed the amusement Jason usually found when he heard Grandad Quentin's nickname. "Wow. Okay. I'll get my things together." Jason snagged an apple and scooped his books off the table. He headed toward the hall.

"Me too." Kyle followed.

Shay led them upstairs and leaped onto Jason's bed. Jason tossed shirts and pants and underwear into a duffle bag. He packed his bathroom stuff. At the last minute, he remembered socks. He yanked open the drawer and scooped a few pairs into the bag.

He noticed a balled T-shirt stuffed in the corner. "I forgot all about this." Jason pulled it out and a broken chess piece—a rook— and an old metal coin fell to the floor.

Jason set the coin on his dresser and examined the two parts of the rook. It was from the antique chess set his dad gave him for his fourteenth birthday. The piece broke when he'd handled it, and he'd found the metal coin inside. Not wanting his dad to know he'd damaged the set, he'd tucked them all in his drawer, out of sight.

Jason examined the two pieces and slid the notch into its matching slot. The pieces locked like they'd never been apart.

What the . . . why didn't that work before?

He twisted the rook, trying to remove the base again. He pressed on the bottom, he pressed on the top, but the pieces held fast.

Weird. Jason returned the rook to the chessboard and glanced at the coin with the letters L-E-X embossed on the surface. He slipped the coin in his pocket.

"Ready, Jason?" Dad called from downstairs.

"Yeah. Coming." Jason grabbed his bag. "Let's go, Shay."

Shay jumped off the bed and trotted downstairs. Della, Dad, and Kyle waited in the hallway with their suitcases. Della's eyes were puffy.

"Lucky you, Dell, going to London." Jason dragged his duffle behind him as they headed to the garage.

Della sort of smiled. "Yeah. I guess."

"Well, I'm jealous. You get to have fun, and I get to go to school."

Della nodded. Jason wondered if she was about to start crying again. He wanted to say something to make her feel better, but everything seemed to make her feel worse.

Dad loaded the bags into the van. They arrived at Uncle Alexander's a few minutes later. He and Finn greeted them in the driveway.

Dad got out and helped unload the bags. "Thanks, Alexander. I appreciate this."

"Not a problem. It gives us more time to train." Uncle Alexander winked at Jason.

"I can help toughen him up." Kyle smirked and punched Jason in the arm.

"So not funny." Jason faked a punch at Kyle's chin.

"Boys, please behave yourselves and don't torture your uncle. I'll call you as soon as we arrive." Dad hugged Kyle and Jason then stroked Shay's chest and gave Finn a quick scratch behind her ears.

An October wind whisked into Jason's shirt and goosebumped his skin. "Okay. Have a safe trip." He reached into the passenger window and mussed Della's hair. "Talk to you soon, Dell. Have fun."

She batted at his arm. "Not the hair again. Now it's going to be all staticky." She raised the window.

Dad backed out of the driveway. Jason, Kyle and Uncle Alexander waved them away.

Jason shoved his cold hands in his pants pockets. *Crap. I meant to ask him about the coin.*

✳✳✳

The next day, Jason woke early and ran with Shay, a ritual he practiced as part of his personal regimen. When he got back to Uncle Alexander's house, he texted Sadie to let her know he couldn't walk to school with her since Uncle Alexander's house was off the route they usually took: "See you at school. Staying at Uncle A's. Dad and Della headed to London."

Jason wolfed down a protein bar and chugged water, then jumped into the shower.

Later in the day after completing his afternoon training, he and Kyle sat down to dinner with Uncle Alexander.

"Have you heard from your dad?" Uncle Alexander passed a bowl of roasted veggies to Jason.

"No. I thought maybe he'd called you or Kyle."

"Nada on my phone," Kyle said.

"I haven't heard from him either. He probably got sidetracked with something. The League has a way of doing that." Uncle Alexander held up a serving plate. "Salmon?"

"Yeah. Thanks." Jason's mouth watered at the scent of the maple glaze. He dug into the meal and tried to ignore the weird jitters in his stomach.

"Do you want more? How about some bread?" Uncle Alexander picked up a loaf of garlic bread wrapped in foil.

Jason waved. "Nah, I'm good."

"Jason, you're in training and doing even more than I've asked. You need to increase your calories, get more nutrition." Uncle Alexander took a piece of bread for himself. "I'm concerned about your weight. And your energy levels."

"I'm fine. I'm strong." Jason admired the veins on his forearm.

"Looking strong and being strong isn't the same thing. Plus, if you don't keep your energy levels up, your health could be compromised. Please eat something more."

Kyle dropped his fork. "And besides, don't you want guns like these?" He flexed both of his arms.

"Only if I'm entering a scrawniest arms contest." Jason smirked.

"I'll show you scrawny. Later. When you're busy trying to walk your skinny ass down the hall or something." Kyle picked up his fork and took another bite of salmon.

Jason rolled his eyes, but he'd be on alert the rest of the evening. "Seriously, Uncle A. I'm fine. I feel good. Eating plenty, I promise." He took a drink of water.

Uncle Alexander sighed.

Jason changed the subject. "Hey. Did you ever find out anything about the guy Mom kept talking about when she was trying to destroy the Rampart? Sewell Kendrick?"

Uncle Alexander shook his head. "There is a Sewell Kendrick in the system, but records show he passed away some years ago." He stabbed lettuce and tomato with his fork. "I suspect the Sewell Kendrick your mother mentioned was fabricated, a way for her to do the things she was doing without taking full responsibility. Perhaps she read about the real Sewell Kendrick in some League documents and took a liking to the name."

"So as far as we're concerned, she made him up," Kyle said.

"I think so." Uncle Alexander ate the bite of salad. "And the numbers of disruptions in the Rampart have dropped significantly, back to normal levels. That's another indication Adrienne was the driving force behind the attempted destruction."

Jason picked out the green beans and pushed them around on his plate. "Well, great. She was the big bad all along." He shoved back from the table and took his plate to the sink, rinsed it and put it in the dishwasher. He rubbed the new skin on his palms. "I guess we can stop worrying about it and all go back to normal."

✸✸✸

The rest of the evening passed without a call.

Jason dialed Dad's cell. It went straight to voice mail. "Hey, just checking in. Hope the flight went well. Give me a call . . . whenever. Love you guys." Jason pressed "end call" and crawled into bed. Shay curled up close.

"They must have gotten busy with something, huh girl." Jason stroked Shay's fur from nose to forehead. "He'll call tomorrow. Right?"

Shay wagged her tail.

"Good girl." He switched off the light.

✸✸✸

Heat broiled Jason awake in the middle of the night. He kicked off the covers. His T-shirt clung to him, sweaty and soaked. Shay panted hard.

Intense light nearby caught the corner of Jason's eye.

Fire?

He grabbed Shay's collar and scrambled away.

He turned back. Shielding his eyes, he saw the source of the heat, the light. But it wasn't fire. At least not yet.

It was the coin.

The coin with L-E-X embossed on its surface, sitting on the nightstand next to Jason's bed.

It glowed bright red.

TWO

The Coin

Jason rushed from his basement bedroom, Shay tight on his heels. "Kyle! Uncle Alexander!" He launched up two flights of stairs. "Wake up."

Finn met them at the landing, Uncle Alexander right behind her. "What's happening? What's wrong?" He scrambled into a bathrobe, his cell phone in hand. "Should I call the police?"

Kyle ran out of his room. "What's going on?"

Jason spun and he and Shay headed down to the main floor. The other three followed. "It's red. And hot. I think it's going to catch fire."

"What are you talking about?" Uncle Alexander asked.

"The coin, the Lex coin. We have to get out of here." Jason dashed toward the door to the garage.

Uncle Alexander stopped. "What Lex coin, Jason?"

Jason yanked open the door. "C'mon we've gotta go."

Uncle Alexander held firm. "Show me the coin."

"But—"

Uncle Alexander moved toward the stairs to the basement. He sniffed. "I don't smell smoke."

"Yeah, I don't smell anything either," Kyle said. "I'm going back to bed."

"No, Kyle, this is serious," Jason said.

"And I'm seriously going back to bed."

Kyle went upstairs and Uncle Alexander went down. Finn bounded ahead of him.

Jason released the door to the garage. "I can't believe no one is listening to me." He and Shay scrambled after Finn and Uncle Alexander.

His bedroom glowed red like the cheap set for a cheesy movie about Mars. The green chair looked red. The brown furniture looked red. The blue carpet looked red.

Heat waves undulated above the coin on the bedside table.

"It's like a Turkish bath in here." Uncle Alexander stepped inside the doorway.

"I guess I'll take your word on that." Jason wiped sweat from his brow with the back of his hand.

Uncle Alexander stared at the coin. "Where did it come from?"

"The chess set my dad gave me. The one that's been in the Lex family forever." Jason inched closer to the coin, squinting against the glow.

"That's why you called it a 'Lex coin.'"

"That and it says 'Lex' on it." Jason took another step closer. The coin grew and flared. Jason jumped backward. Shay pressed herself into his legs.

The light from the coin pulsed once, twice, three times. Then doused. Black filled the space.

"What just happened?" Jason asked.

14

"Good question." Uncle Alexander flipped on the light. The right colors were in their right places.

Jason flapped the front of his T-shirt to cool his skin, and walked to the coin. It was a little bigger now but otherwise didn't look different—no tarnish, no blackened edges, no scorch marks.

He hovered his palm over the coin. "It's not even warm." He picked it up and handed the coin to Uncle Alexander. "How did it grow?"

"Another good question." Uncle Alexander bounced the coin in the palm of his hand, then scraped his thumbnail across the ridges on the edge. He brought it up to his face and examined the markings. He licked it.

"Ugh. Did you have to do that?" Jason shook his head.

"All the senses provide you with information. Don't fixate on one or two dominant perspectives or you'll miss something important."

"How are you always in teaching mode? And did tasting that thing reveal something important?"

"As a matter of fact, no. But that in and of itself can be valuable."

Jason flopped onto his bed. "Right. And let's hope it doesn't later tell us you're allergic to whatever that thing is made of." He covered his eyes with his arm. "Jeez, I wish Dad was here so I could ask him about it." Jason sat up and glanced at the clock. "What time is it in London right now?"

"A little after eleven a.m." Uncle Alexander bit the coin and sniffed it.

"I think you have cereal upstairs. Or I'd be happy to make you some pancakes if it will stop you from putting that thing in your mouth."

"It's important to—"

Jason waved his hand. "I get it, I get it. Investigate using every tool at hand, blah, blah, blah." He picked up his cell phone and tapped Dad's number. He put the call on speaker, and after one ring Dad's voicemail message began.

And the coin glowed.

Uncle Alexander dropped it on the bed and Jason leaped up. They backed away. The voicemail beeped.

"Dad I need to talk to you. This Lex coin is glowing red and it looks hot, but it's not and where are you guys and why haven't you called and jeez please call me now as soon as you get this seriously." He ended the call.

The coin stopped glowing.

Jason eased forward and dialed Dad again. As soon as the voice-mail message started, the coin glowed. When Jason ended the call, the glow faded.

"Well, that's that," Uncle Alexander said.

"That's what?" Jason asked.

"We're going to London."

✳✳✳

Less than twenty-four hours later, Jason and Uncle Alexander were in the air. Jason lowered the tray table and laid his head on his folded arms, crashing to sleep as soon as the plane reached altitude. Between the freaky incident with the coin and the race to pack for London, Jason was wiped.

Something nudged his shoulder. "Shay?" He jolted up and blinked, glanced around. Clouds floated outside.

"Not as furry as Shay. At least I hope not." Uncle Alexander smiled. "We're starting our descent soon."

Jason had texted a note to Sadie and said goodbye to Shay at the airport when Kyle and Grandma Lena dropped them off. Kyle and the dogs would stay with Grandma Lena while they were gone. He already missed Shay. She was his first dog, a pit-mix rescue puppy, now closer to full-size than puppy-size, and they did everything together.

"It's stupid we can't buy dogs plane tickets and let them ride in the cabin." Jason rubbed the stubborn sleep from his eyes.

"I agree. But I don't see that rule changing any time soon." Uncle Alexander set a cardboard box on Jason's table. "You slept through the food service, but I saved one for you."

Jason opened it and tore into the wrapped cheese and crackers. "Thanks. I'm starving." He put a whole cracker and two slices of cheddar in his mouth. "Mmm . . . bust chuz evuh."

"I don't like seafood," Uncle Alexander said.

"Huh?"

Uncle Alexander turned away. "Seafood. As in S-E-E-food. Meaning don't talk with your mouth full."

Jason chewed and swallowed. "Sorry. My bad." He bit into an apple.

"I've been wanting to ask, how are you feeling?"

Jason swallowed again. "A little wigged out about Dad and Della and the creepy coin, but okay, I guess."

"I'm wondering more about how you're feeling physically. Any soreness? Tiredness?" Uncle Alexander tilted his head.

Jason knew that look. "What're you getting at, Uncle A? Spill."

He sighed. "I'm concerned about your mental and physical health. As I said, I think you're overtraining. The additional workouts and runs you've added—it's too much."

Jason squeezed a packet of peanut butter onto pita bread. "How is that even possible? I wish I had more time to train." He popped the food in his mouth.

"Well, it is possible, and it's dangerous. When you're training, you're breaking down muscle fibers and building them back up to make them stronger. But if you don't give your body what it needs to build and repair, you end up doing harm. You're more prone to injury, to exhaustion. You can damage your system."

Jason shook his head and ate more of his airline meal.

"This is serious, Jason."

Jason jerked his head to face Uncle Alexander. "In case you forgot, I know all about serious. When Mom let you and Kyle get hurt, that was serious. When she tried to destroy the Rampart and kill us, that was serious. When I couldn't stop her, or save her, that was serious. So yeah, I get serious." He sucked a breath into his lungs and forced it out slowly.

"Jason . . ." Uncle Alexander put his hand on Jason's forearm.

Jason's muscles twitched and he pulled back. A passenger across the aisle cleared his throat, reminding Jason of their close quarters. He glanced around and noticed the plane wasn't full, and the passengers near them were wearing headphones or sleeping. Relieved, he calmed his voice. "I have to be prepared. I have to be ready." He scrunched the wrappers and stuffed his trash into the box. "I'm not gonna be that clueless again. Or that stupid. Or that weak."

"You are none of those things. And I don't believe there is any immediate threat to the Rampart. But if you don't listen to me about overtraining, you'll be at an extreme disadvantage when there is one."

Jason smashed in the lid of the box. "If things are so threat-free right now, why are we rushing off to London?"

"This is simply a communication issue."

"Dad and Della are missing, some funky old coin seems like it wants to burn us alive, but it's all a communication issue?"

"The coin would never inflict harm on you."

"Oh, now you're an expert on the coin?"

The flight attendant stepped up to their row. "May I take that trash for you?"

Jason relaxed. "Yeah." He handed over what was left of his meal. "Thanks." He leaned back and shut his eyes until he heard her a few more rows away. He looked at Uncle Alexander. "You do know something about the coin."

Uncle Alexander pinched the bridge of his nose. "I thought they were a myth."

Jason waited.

"The Lex family has been part of the League of Governors and its administration of the relationship between humans and cryptids for centuries," Uncle Alexander said.

"Right. Another one of the many secrets Dad and everyone else kept from me."

"Do you want to hear what I have to say or not?"

Jason glanced down. "Sorry. Go ahead."

Uncle Alexander leaned close and kept his voice low. "For most of the League's history, the Lex family held leadership positions, and in fact were a founding family in the League. Isadora Lex is a signatory on the governing document, the Declaration of Solidarity, written when the League was created. She was largely responsible for negotiating the terms, principles, and precedents established between all parties, human and cryptid alike."

A flight attendant announced their descent into Heathrow Airport. Jason and Uncle Alexander raised their seat backs.

"To commemorate the occasion, a craftsman from each signatory family created a chess set for the person whose name was listed directly above theirs on the Declaration. The gesture draws from the symbolism of chess around intellect and heart, and is meant to demonstrate the link between all parties involved. The chess sets also incorporate aspects unique to each family, and consequently, no two sets are alike. The Lex set came from the Bayard family whose representative on the Declaration was Elymas Bayard — a Yowie."

"Wait—I know that cryptid. The Yowie are like Bigfoot, right? But Australian."

"Exactly right," Uncle Alexander said. "Like many cryptids, Yowie are shape-shifters. Some are also capable of magic, and the legend around the Lex chess set is that Elymas Bayard infused it with magical properties including a coin capable of communication with Lex family members."

Motors whirred and the wheels of the plane unfolded beneath them.

"Capable how? Like its own Morse code or something?"

Uncle Alexander shrugged. "That's one possibility. It's said the coins—as the legend states there are a number of these coins located throughout the world—interact using vibrational energy. They can also shift images on the face of the coin, and change the color, size, or surface temperature. Or at least give the illusion of these things."

"So when it was so hot in my bedroom . . ."

"An illusion. Our perception made it so, but it was an illusion manifested by the coin and the message it was communicating."

"Which was what?" Jason asked.

"Well, I don't want to speculate. I can't possibly be certain of anything I've heard about the coins." Uncle Alexander tightened his lap belt and brushed his pants like they were covered with crumbs.

"Your speculation is about a million times more accurate than anyone else I know, so go ahead and speculate."

Uncle Alexander kept his gaze fixed forward. "I think it's best we find Della and your dad first."

The plane's tires squealed on the runway and the reverse thrust engaged. Jason waited until they were taxiing toward their gate.

"You're holding something back, Uncle A. Just tell me."

Uncle Alexander ran one hand through his hair and sighed. He turned toward Jason. "If the legends are true, your dad and Della are in serious danger."

THREE

Searching

Jason's mind reeled while they waited in line at Customs. What if the legends about the coins are true and his family is in danger—again?

He turned toward Uncle Alexander. "How are we going to find Dad and Della?"

"If we can't reach them by phone we'll go to League headquarters. That's where your dad was taking Della. Where is the coin?"

"My suitcase." Jason gestured to the rolling bag on his left. "Thought it was better to keep it there than in my pocket."

"And do you have your cell phone? You didn't leave it on the plane, did you?"

"I've got it. I put it in the outside pocket on my suitcase."

Uncle Alexander nodded. "As soon as we get through Customs we'll figure out our next step."

A Customs agent's window opened and Uncle Alexander stepped forward. Jason heard the agent asking all the standard questions Uncle Alexander had mentioned when he described the process on the plane. Seemed simple enough.

The agent waved Jason up. "American as well?" He reached for Jason's passport.

"Yes, sir."

"Anything to declare?" the agent asked.

"No, sir."

"Please put your bag on the table."

Jason lifted his suitcase onto the metal table smeared with fingerprints. A second agent unzipped it and began digging through Jason's shirts and pants and shoes. A phone rang.

Jason leaned toward his bag. "That's my phone. It's in—"

"Step back." The agent held up his hand.

"But that might be my dad."

Uncle Alexander grabbed Jason's shoulder. "Leave it, Jason. Let them finish." Jason moved back.

The agent paused another moment and the phone rang again. He returned to pawing through Jason's things. Jason bounced on his toes, wishing the guy would hurry. *There's not even that much stuff in there.*

The phone rang one more time then went silent.

"We're finished here. Welcome to the United Kingdom."

Jason dashed to his bag and unzipped the pocket. The phone's screen said, "Missed call. Dad. New voicemail message."

"It was him." Jason scooped his stuff off the table without closing the suitcase. He shuffled over to a bench with Uncle Alexander, hitting play on his voicemail. He put it on speaker.

"Jason, it's Dad. I'm sorry I didn't call sooner. GQ got called out of town so a rep from the League of Governors met us at the airport and we went directly to headquarters. They took Della for tests, and I haven't seen her since. All they'll say is that the tests take time, but I'll see her soon. I'm back at headquarters now and about to start breaking down doors until I find her." He sighed. "I'm sorry. Hey, don't worry. I've got this, and I'll be in touch when I know more. Thank Alexander again for letting you stay with him, okay? Love you guys."

Jason tapped Dad's number. The call went directly to voicemail. "Dad, it's me, I just missed your call. We're in London, me and Uncle A. Did you get my messages? Things are weird and we need to talk to you."

Uncle Alexander took the phone. "Zachary, we're going to League headquarters. Maybe I can help with Della. We'll see you there shortly." He ended the call and handed the phone back to Jason. "Let's go."

A few minutes later they were seated in a black cab.

"Where to, sir?"

Jason liked the cabbie's accent. "Sir" sounded like "suh."

"Tower of London," Uncle Alexander said.

"All right then." The cabbie pulled away from the curb. "Make yourselves comfortable. It's a bit of a drive, an hour at least. That's if we're lucky."

Jason leaned into the window, watching the scenery pass. It wasn't the first time he'd been to London, but it was the first time without his parents. The family had visited seven years ago when they'd come to see GQ. Jason remembered how weird it was to sleep in the same room his dad had slept in when he'd lived there as a boy. Same bunkbeds and everything.

"We're really going to the . . ." Jason glanced at the back of the cabbie's head, then to Uncle Alexander. ". . . The Tower of London, the *actual* Tower of London?"

"Yes."

"Because . . ."

"Because that's where your dad is."

Jason furrowed his brow. He opened his mouth to ask another question but stopped. No need to stress about things now. He'd learn soon enough about the link between the League and the Tower of London. For now, he just wanted to try to stop worrying.

The River Thames came into view and followed along the highway for a while before curving away. A short time later they passed the Victoria and Albert Museum.

Jason recognized Buckingham Palace. He searched for a changing of the guard, hoping to catch a glimpse, but only tourists moved around the gates. Soon they were cruising along the Thames again and Jason verified that London Bridge had not fallen down.

A moment later the cabbie pulled off the road. "Here you are. Tower of London."

Uncle Alexander swiped his credit card and paid the fare as Jason exited. "Thank you."

"Enjoy your stay. Cheers." The cab moved back into traffic.

Uncle Alexander directed Jason to follow the signs toward the main entrance. Their suitcases rattled as they rolled along the sidewalk.

"Do you have a special pass or something?" he asked Uncle Alexander.

"No. We need to buy tickets."

"Wait—are we doing the tourist thing or are we going to League headquarters?'

"We're at League headquarters, but we're not expected, nor am I on staff, so we need to get in the standard way. Or at least the first part is the standard way."

Jason shook his head. "Are you sure we're in the right place?"

"Of course I'm sure. Get in queue."

"In queue?"

"In line. Get in line." Uncle Alexander gestured to the line of people waiting to buy tickets.

A few minutes later they were inside the grounds. Uncle Alexander's pace quickened and he looked up and down the greens and pathways as they moved.

Great. He has no idea where we're going. "Are you looking for something?" Jason asked.

"Someone, actually."

They turned left and neared a sign that said Ravens' Lodgings. "Ah, there he is," Uncle Alexander said.

Ahead of them was a tall man wearing a long, dark blue coat with red piping and a red crown on the chest. He had a matching top hat, blue with a red band.

Uncle Alexander hurried to him. "Are you the Raven Master?"

"Yes, sir. How may I help you?"

"Odin and Thor request news from the Owl Sanctuary."

"Excuse me, sir?" asked the Raven Master.

"Odin and Thor request news from the Owl Sanctuary," Uncle Alexander repeated.

The Raven Master pursed his lips. "I don't have time for jokesters, sir, so if you'll excuse me." He turned away.

Jason cringed. This was a waste of time.

Uncle Alexander grabbed the Raven Master's sleeve. "No. I need to get into the League. My brother-in-law is here with my niece."

The Raven Master jerked his arm free. "First it's ravens you want to see, now it's something called a League. I don't know what you are talking about sir, but I suggest you move along or I'll be forced to call security."

"But the entrance—"

"Sir, last warning. On your way." The Raven Master gestured toward the main path.

Uncle Alexander hesitated a moment then yanked on his rolling suitcase. "Let's go, Jason."

Jason hurried to catch up, his bag rattling along the path next to him. "That's it? We're leaving?"

"Yes."

Jason stopped on the path, forcing tourists to dodge around him. "Where is the League?"

"We'll talk about it later." Uncle Alexander kept moving.

"We'll talk about it now," Jason said, his voice raised.

Uncle Alexander stopped short causing people to bump into him. "Sorry, sorry." He waved Jason off to the side and lowered his voice. "Something is off."

Something is off with you. "Uncle Alexander, you sounded crazy back there. Are you sure we're in the right place?"

"Yes. But they've changed the pass phrase or something."

"Then we're stuck, right?" Jason asked.

"I have an old friend who works with the League. We'll go see him."

"Can't you call him or something?"

"He can't tell me anything over the phone. It's not secure," Uncle Alexander said.

Jason ran both hands through his hair. "I need to help Dad and Della."

"That's why we're here."

"But we can't just keep running around."

"We're hardly running around. What's going on with you?"

Jason breathed deeply. "If they're in trouble, it's my fault. I should have stopped Mom before she ever got to Della in the first place."

Uncle Alexander pulled him further away from the crowds. "None of this is your fault. You did everything you could. We all did."

"It wasn't good enough," Jason said.

"You stopped the Rampart from falling and saved millions of people. I'd say that's better than good enough."

Jason shook his head and looked across the path toward the Thames.

"Listen. We don't know yet that anything is wrong. After all, your dad's message was recent and he sounded fine. He's likely with Della by now," Uncle Alexander said. "We'll go see my friend, find out the proper protocols for entry, and take it from there, okay? Plus, we can leave our suitcases at his place for now. I don't know about you, but I'm tired of dragging this thing around."

"Yeah, okay," Jason said.

They moved back into the flow of foot traffic. "How's your energy? Are you feeling jet-lagged?" Uncle Alexander asked.

"No, I'm fine."

"Eat this anyway." Uncle Alexander pulled two protein bars out of his jacket pocket, one for each of them.

Jason peeled the foil wrapper and bit into the bar. They exited the Tower of London and hailed a cab. As they pulled away, Jason noticed someone staring at them.

It was the Raven Master.

FOUR
Friends and Foes

Jason watched the Raven Master and the Raven Master watched them until they were out of his line of sight.

He must have really wanted us out of there.

Jason took out his phone. "Did you let Grandma Lena know we landed? She reminded me like eighteen times to tell her."

"Yes, I sent her a note when we were still on the tarmac," Uncle Alexander said.

"Okay. I'm texting Sadie." He tapped Send Message under Sadie's contact info.

"What about your brother?"

Jason waved his hand. "Grandma Lena can tell him." He typed the message to Sadie: "Landed. Saw Tower of London sort of. Secret pass code didn't work. Cabbing to some friend of Uncle A's. Still looking for Dad and Della."

His phone beeped with Sadie's response: "Huh? Landed I get. And still looking I get. Confused about the rest."

Jason replied: "Sorry. Complicated. More later."

The cabbie wound through the streets of London, negotiating roundabouts, waving at other cabbies, and driving on the opposite side of the road.

They pulled up in front of an old brownstone and got out. Wrought iron railings ran along the steps up to the door. An arched window on the right was covered with black construction paper. Gaps showed where yellowing tape failed to keep the pieces tight. Uncle Alexander rang the bell.

A brass peephole opened, then quickly shut. From inside came the sound of a chain unhooked and swinging, one deadbolt sliding, then another. The door opened a gap and a man's face peeked out. He stepped back and opened the door wide. "Come in, come in."

Uncle Alexander followed Jason inside. He'd barely pulled his bag through when the man shut the door and reset the locks.

"Alexander, so good to see you." The man and Uncle Alexander embraced. He was tall like Uncle Alexander but older, with gray hair and a close-cropped gray beard. He wore brown pants and an argyle sweater.

"Great to see you. It's been too long." Uncle Alexander gestured to Jason. "I'd like you to meet my nephew, Jason Lex. Jason, this is Sir Bartholomew Ainsworth."

"Oh, now please. You certainly could have left the Sir out of it." He reached for Jason's hand. "Just call me Bartie."

"Are you sure?" Uncle Alexander asked. "I haven't seen you since you were knighted. Are we allowed to address you in such an informal manner? And should we have bowed when we entered? Or is it a curtsy?" Uncle Alexander chuckled.

"Haven't lost your sense of humor, I see." Bartie walked into the room with the construction paper window coverings.

It was lit with lamps in every corner. Another light hung from the ceiling. "Let's get comfortable, shall we? I've made us some tea."

"Seriously?" Jason asked.

"Would you prefer something else, young man? A fizzy drink perhaps?"

"A fizzy drink?"

"Soda," Uncle Alexander said.

"Oh. No, tea's fine. I just meant I didn't know tea was really a thing here. I thought that was only on TV." Jason sat on one of two light blue tufted couches that flanked the unlit fireplace. On the coffee table was a tower of three plates displaying small sandwiches and mini pastries. Next to the tower was a pot of tea and flowery cups.

"I assure you tea is very much a 'thing' here. I fear if it ever stops being a 'thing' here, then London will surely have fallen." Bartie poured tea into three porcelain cups. "Milk?"

Uncle Alexander nodded.

"Uh . . . okay," Jason said.

"There's also sugar," Bartie added, "but I'll leave that to your discretion."

Uncle Alexander passed on the sugar. Jason added three cubes to his cup and stirred. He eyed the sandwiches and desserts.

"Please, help yourself, Jason," Bartie said. "It's all part of enjoying this 'thing'. And I believe I'll have you quite converted to our little tradition without much effort at all." He smiled.

Jason popped a small square sandwich into his mouth.

Uncle Alexander rolled his eyes. "Would you like a plate? And a napkin?" He took a napkin off the stack and set it on Jason's thigh.

Jason swallowed. "Sorry. I guess I'm kind of hungry." He sipped his tea. *Not bad.*

"Thank you for seeing us on such short notice," Uncle Alexander said to Bartie.

"Not at all, not at all. What is it I can help you with?"

"It's the League. We went to the Tower today, but the Raven Master didn't recognize my pass phrase. I presume it's changed and I missed the communiqué." Uncle Alexander bit into a small tart.

Bartie set his teacup in its saucer. "I'm afraid I can't help you."

Uncle Alexander's brows furrowed. "What? Why not?"

"I'm not at liberty to say." Bartie added a second splash of milk to his cup.

"I'm not asking for information regarding a secret mission or anything," Uncle Alexander said.

Secret mission? Jason redirected his focus from the cookies to the conversation.

Uncle Alexander continued. "I'm simply asking for the current pass phrase so we can get inside. My brother-in-law is here with my niece, Jason's sister. And we came to help."

Bartie shook his head. "I'm sorry, it's not possible." He stood and walked to a hutch on the other side of the room, his back to Jason and Uncle Alexander.

Uncle Alexander glanced around the room. "What is going on, Bartie?"

"I don't know what you mean." He turned toward them.

"C'mon," Uncle Alexander said. "Something is off with you. There's no sign of Elizabeth here, no pictures of your kids or grandkids. You have paper taped to your windows, and more locks on your door than one really needs in this neighborhood."

"So?"

"So what is going on? Are you all right?"

"I'm fine, I'm fine. Please stop asking questions." Bartie put his hands in his pockets. "I can't help you. That's all. That's everything I know."

Uncle Alexander stood and walked over to Bartie, placing a hand on his shoulder. "We've been friends for a long time. Talk to me."

Bartie shook off Uncle Alexander's hand and returned to the couch. "What grade are you in, Jason? You do well in school?"

"Uh, yeah ... I uh—"

Uncle Alexander crossed the room. "Tell me what's going on." He sat next to Jason, opposite Bartie. "Where's Elizabeth?"

Bartie lowered his face into his hands. Jason pushed farther into the couch.

"Where is she, Bartie?" Uncle Alexander's voice was firm.

"I ... she's ... They took her." The words sounded strangled.

Uncle Alexander switched seats, moving next to his old friend. "Who took her?"

"The League. Or whatever it is the group calls themselves." He ran his hands through his hair. "I found out what was really going on, and they took her. Told me to stop talking about it. Told me they were watching me. Said they wouldn't stop watching me, and if I didn't stop talking they said they'd hurt her."

"The League of Governors took Elizabeth?" Uncle Alexander asked.

"That's just it. There is no League of Governors."

Jason leaned forward. "What? How can that be? My dad, my sister—they're there right now."

Bartie slumped into the back of the couch. "Then they're probably dead. Or soon will be."

"No." Jason sprung to standing. "That's not possible."

Uncle Alexander held up his hand.

"But—"

Uncle Alexander waved his hand down, his eyes asking Jason to stop, wait.

Jason dropped back onto the couch. His throat tightened.

Uncle Alexander turned to Bartie. "Tell me your story."

"It's not a story. It's fact."

"I apologize. Please, tell us what you know."

Bartie took a deep breath. "You know how I like to dot the Is and cross the Ts."

"Yes, I remember," said Uncle Alexander.

"On a couple of recent missions, it wasn't just Ts going uncrossed. There were loads of Ts missing completely. Nothing alarming mind you. It just seemed like sloppy work. So I decided to research the cases, some of them quite old, and knit things up. But then I found errors in those cases as well. I dug deeper, and one thing led to another."

"Which was?" Uncle Alexander asked.

"Which was that the League of Governors as a global organization hasn't existed for a long time. There is no governing body. A small faction of people, or maybe cryptids, or maybe both, have taken control, running things their way from behind closed doors," Bartie said.

"But the League is still running, still functioning as it always has," Uncle Alexander said.

"Oh, is it now? Tell me again about your experience with the Raven Master today." Bartie's gaze drilled into Uncle

Alexander. "And your brother-in-law—has there been anything strange about his visit? Is that why you're here now, because something's not right?"

Heat zinged through Jason's spine.

"You need to prepare yourselves for the worst," Bartie said.

"But they just wanted to talk to Della, to help her get better." Jason clenched and unclenched his fists.

Bartie shook his head. "There's no just wanting to talk to anyone anymore." He looked at Jason. "And your dad? If he's in their way they'll eliminate him."

Jason's stomach flipped. He looked at Uncle Alexander. "We have to do something."

He nodded. "We will. But we need more information." He turned back to Bartie. "Who's behind it? Who's taken over?"

"I don't know. And everyone I talked to about this . . ." Bartie swallowed. "They're all gone, Alexander. Dead. One supposed accident after another. I'm the only one left, and I guess that's because they took my Elizabeth instead."

Uncle Alexander squeezed Bartie's shoulder. "You can't know that for certain."

Bartie stood and walked back to the hutch. "Elizabeth disappeared a few days after one of my team members drove his car off a bridge. The report said he was intoxicated, but he'd been sober for twenty years." He opened the door to the hutch. "Shortly thereafter, I received a note in Elizabeth's handwriting. It said not to look for her, and to stop investigating. But I was hard-headed and determined to find the truth. I showed the note to other members of my team." Bartie removed a blue and white vase from the hutch.

"Not long after that, someone broke in and stole Elizabeth's favorite vase. This very vase right here. It's the only item the thieves took." He walked toward Jason and Uncle Alexander.

"But you got it back?" Jason asked.

"It arrived by post a few days later. The plastic cap you see on top of the vase? That was new. And there was a note. It read: Elizabeth will forever enjoy her favorite vase." Bartie set the vase on the coffee table, next to the tea service.

"I don't understand," Jason said.

"Oh God." Uncle Alexander closed his eyes.

"Those are Elizabeth's ashes, Jason. They burned her. They burned her and they sent me her ashes." Bartie dragged his hands down his face.

"What?" Jason gasped.

"They could have put any kind of ash in the vase, just to scare you . . ." Uncle Alexander pressed his fingers to his forehead.

"There was one more item in the package." Bartie's eyes welled. "Elizabeth's finger, her ring finger, still wearing her wedding ring." Bartie collapsed onto the couch.

Jason gaped at the two men. His mind raced. His heart hammered.

"Maybe she's still alive," Uncle Alexander said. "Maybe—"

"They're all dead, Alexander. Everyone I worked with on this project. There is no League. There's only corruption. And now that I've told you, they'll come for you, too."

Uncle Alexander stood. "I refuse to accept that. Tell us how to get in, tell us how to stop them."

"There is no stopping them. Haven't you heard a word I've said? Whoever's in power has been there for a long time.

Their tracks are covered. In fact, there are no tracks. They're ghosts," Bartie said.

"At least help us get in." Uncle Alexander reached forward, his hands upturned. "We have to try something."

Bartie sighed. "I have few connections left." He poured himself another cup of tea. "And even if I could get the pass phrase for you, I'd be sending you into great peril."

"I'm fully aware of the risks, Bartie, and I'm asking anyway," Uncle Alexander said.

Bartie clanked his teacup onto its saucer. "No, Alexander, I won't do it. I won't send you in there blind."

"Then work with us. Help us stop them."

"There's been so much loss already."

"All the more reason to get back in the game, to make a stand," Uncle Alexander said. "And if we go down, we go down fighting."

"I'd be surprised if we'd have even a one percent chance of making a difference, much less succeeding."

"That's one percent more than the zero percent if we don't try at all," Uncle Alexander said.

Bartie stared at Uncle Alexander.

"What about Churchill, what about the Monarchy? What about your knighthood?" Uncle Alexander returned to his seat next to Bartie. "And what about Elizabeth? What would she want you to do?"

Bartie's lip quivered. "My darling Elizabeth . . . she's lost to me forever."

"And you just accept that?" Uncle Alexander asked. "Is that what Elizabeth would expect you to do? To accept things as they are? To cower in your home?"

"I don't cower." Bartie glared.

Uncle Alexander waved his arm around the room. "This looks like cowering to me. I dare say Elizabeth would agree with me."

Bartie stood and peeked through a gap where a stream of sunshine forced itself into the room. For a moment he didn't move. Then he spoke, his voice soft. "She would agree with you, Alexander."

"And that's a sad legacy for her to leave behind."

Bartie stayed fixed on whatever he saw outside and didn't speak.

"I apologize if I've upset you," Uncle Alexander said.

Bartie huffed. "Compared to everything else, your little pep talk was hardly upsetting."

"Still," Uncle Alexander said, "I may have overstepped—"

"You're right, of course," Bartie said.

"And I'm sorry."

Bartie turned to face Uncle Alexander. "Not about overstepping. About the legacy being left behind, both hers and mine. I cannot let the legacy stand as it exists today. I cannot, and I will not." His face brightened a little. "So it seems your pep talk did the trick, Alexander. For Queen and country and all that. But mostly for Elizabeth, and my team."

"Excellent," Uncle Alexander said. "We have work to do, and the first order of business is to get you out of here, move you someplace safe."

"Agreed. But I need to get some things together. I've got notes, files, and contact information. Does anyone know you're here?"

"No one," Uncle Alexander said.

"Brilliant. Then we should have some time." Bartie scribbled information on a piece of paper. "I have a locker at this address. There's cash and fake IDs. We'll need them to stay hidden. Pick them up for me, would you? And by the time you get back, I'll have everything ready."

"Now that's the Sir Bartholomew Ainsworth I know." Uncle Alexander smiled. "No wonder the Queen knighted you."

Bartie shook Uncle Alexander's hand. "Thank you. Now off with you. I'll see you back here soon."

Jason and Uncle Alexander left the brownstone and flagged a cab. The locker's location was on the other side of the city.

"How bad is it?" Jason asked.

"The traffic? We should be back at the brownstone within the hour," Uncle Alexander said.

"You know that's not what I mean." Jason wiped his hands on his thighs.

Uncle Alexander sighed. "I'm not sure about anything right now. It could be Bartie's lost it, that he's imagining things. Maybe he wouldn't get help and that's why Elizabeth left him." He ran one hand through his hair. "Or everything he said is true and the League has been replaced with corruption, and murder, and cover-ups. Looking at things side by side, I have to seriously consider Bartie's mental condition. That's the more logical conclusion. Especially since he hadn't yet used one of his fake IDs to disappear rather than hunker down in his home."

"So we're just going along with him for fun?" Jason asked.

"Not for fun. I believe he can get us the new pass phrase. And maybe we can get him some help along the way."

"Wow." Jason frowned.

"What?"

"People thought you were crazy. But you weren't. Wouldn't you have liked it if people gave you more of a chance?" Jason asked.

"But my behavior truly was crazy, or so it seemed, thanks to the poison administered by your mother."

"And how do we know something like that isn't happening to Bartie then, huh?" Jason looked out the window. "It's not like I want him to be right. But it sure seems like you should give Bartie a chance to prove himself one way or the other, and not just decide he's lost it."

They rode in silence for the next few minutes. Landmarks passed the windows, but Jason hardly noticed.

A yawn forced its way out.

"You're tired," Uncle Alexander said.

"Jet lag. But I'm fine."

Uncle Alexander nodded. "And you're right, you know, what you said about Bartie. I shouldn't be so quick to judge."

"Hold on. Let me have you record that on my phone."

Uncle Alexander patted his knee. "One way or another, we're going to find your dad and Della, and figure out what's going on, okay?"

"Yeah, okay."

"And if things really are bad, it can't hurt to have a Yeti on our side."

"A Yeti? Bartie's a Yeti?" Jason asked. "But he looks—"

"Human, yes," Uncle Alexander said. "Like their cousins, Bigfoot and Yowie, Yeti are shape-shifters and often choose to live in human form."

"Huh. My first Yeti. Cool."

The cabbie pulled up in front of their stop.

"Wait here," Uncle Alexander said. "I'll be right back."

A few minutes later, Uncle Alexander emerged from the building carrying a brown satchel. He gave Jason the thumbs up as he entered the cab, and asked the cabbie to take them back to Bartie's address.

They made the return trip in good time, arriving a little less than an hour after they'd left. Uncle Alexander paid the cabbie while Jason walked up the steps to Bartie's front door. It was ajar.

"Hey," Jason called down to his uncle.

Uncle Alexander glanced up and Jason pushed the door wide.

"Wait," Uncle Alexander said. "Don't go in." He dashed up the steps and moved in front of Jason. He poked his head inside the door. "Bartie?" He turned to Jason and lowered his voice. "Stay out here. Call the police. Dial 999."

Jason pulled out his phone. "Don't go in there."

"I want to check on Bartie, make sure he's okay."

"Just wait for the police," Jason said, his voice a whisper.

"I'll be careful," Uncle Alexander said. "You wait for them out here." He stepped inside the door, setting the satchel on the floor of the foyer. "Bartie?"

Jason dialed the number and reported the break-in. He heard Uncle Alexander continuing to call Bartie's name, moving farther into the brownstone. Jason bounced on his toes, trying to hear sirens on approach. Birds chirped, a helicopter buzzed overhead but no sirens yet.

"You can come in," Uncle Alexander said.

Jason hurried inside. Chairs were overturned, the couches sat askew, the vase of ashes lay broken on the floor. He held his breath and walked toward Uncle Alexander's voice. Jason found him in the dining room.

"There's no sign of Bartie," he said.

"They took him."

"We don't know that for certain, but it's better than the alternative."

Jason's eyebrows rose.

"Meaning he's probably not dead."

Jason plopped into a dining room chair. "So now what?"

"Now we wait for the police."

A sound came from the pantry, like a canned good falling from a shelf.

Jason jumped up. "Does Bartie have a cat?" he asked Uncle Alexander, whispering again.

"Did you see a cat? C'mon." Uncle Alexander gestured toward the front door.

A second later the pantry door sprang open. A ski-masked man bounded out and rushed Uncle Alexander, slamming him to the floor. Jason leaped onto the man's back and tightened one arm around his neck. The man shifted his weight and flung Jason off, bouncing him into the wall. His head rang. Uncle Alexander kicked and swiped the man's legs out from under him.

The man rolled and reset himself, facing Uncle Alexander. Fists raised, Uncle Alexander delivered a kick to the man's chest. He buckled and Uncle Alexander slammed another kick into the man's ribs, forcing a gasp from his lungs.

Uncle Alexander charged the intruder but the man dodged right. Uncle Alexander moved in and punched. The man blocked him and connected with an uppercut to Uncle Alexander's chin. He skittered backward.

Jason shook his head, tried to clear his vision. He'd never seen Uncle Alexander fight like this. Jason pushed himself to standing, summoning his power to his hands. Nothing happened.

Damnit.

"Jason, stay back." Uncle Alexander shook off the uppercut and double kicked, connecting on the right, but the man caught the kick on the left. He twisted and threw Uncle Alexander to the ground.

Jason rushed forward and delivered a kick to the man's chest. The intruder fell backward, crushing a lamp knocked off an end table. He scrambled to his feet and braced for Jason's kick to his thigh. He reset and punched Jason's side, then grabbed his arm and spun him, swinging him into the hutch. The glass cracked. Jason sank.

Uncle Alexander grabbed the intruder in a choke hold. The man gouged at Uncle Alexander's arm, desperate to get air. He struggled, then pushed both of them backward, slamming Uncle Alexander into the doorframe. The man jerked his head once, twice, a third time, pounding Uncle Alexander's head into the wall behind him. Uncle Alexander lost consciousness and collapsed.

Jason pulled himself up into a fighting stance. The man shook his head. He swung his right fist.

Waves of black edged Jason's sight. He staggered and fell. The masked man moved in close but turned as two figures entered the front door. Jason tried to stand, to move away, but his stomach churned and he crumpled.

No sirens . . . why no sirens . . .

FIVE
Help

*B*eeps sounded in Jason's head. A light bore through his eyelids. He forced his eyes open and blinked against the brightness.

He lay in a bed with beige plastic railings along each side, and a clip on his finger registered his heartbeat, sending the signal to a machine near his head. Seventy-two beats per minute. A hanging bag next to the heart rate monitor dripped fluid into a tube attached to his arm. On the other side of his bed sat a stainless steel table. It held a pale pink pitcher and matching cup.

Jason tried to push himself to sitting. Pain stung through his ribs and he held his breath as he inched higher. He leaned back into the pillows and exhaled. He took another breath and held it, readying to move again.

The door to his room opened.

"You're awake." A girl about Jason's age stepped up to the bed. She had dark brown hair, and her right arm was wrapped in a sling strapped tight to her body. In her left hand she held out a thermometer. She swiped it across Jason's forehead.

"Where—"

"Quiet please," the girl said.

Jason snapped his mouth shut.

"Wait for the chime."

A moment later, the thermometer pinged. The girl eyed the digital display then dropped the thermometer into her pocket. She removed a digital tablet hanging at the foot of the bed, laid it in a clear space away from Jason's legs, and used a stylus to jot notes.

She was too young to be a doctor or a nurse. She wore blue scrubs with no name tag.

"Where am I?" Jason asked.

"You're in the medical unit," she said.

"Where's my uncle?"

"He's in another room."

"Can I see him?" Jason asked.

She poured from the pitcher beside the bed. "Water?" She handed him the cup.

"Thanks, but what about my uncle?"

"My assigned tasks are complete. Another member will answer your questions." She returned the tablet to its hook. "I'll be back later to complete my next assignment."

"Wait, I—"

The girl exited the room and the door closed behind her. *Okay . . .*

Jason put the cup to his mouth. A sting stopped him. He touched his skin, feeling tenderness and a scab over a split in his lip. He shifted the cup away from the wound and sipped.

He surveyed the room. The door was to the left, opposite his bed, and next to it was a steel cabinet, like a wardrobe made of metal instead of wood. To the right of the cabinet was a bathroom. The walls of his room were painted mint green, and in the corner near the door was a video camera aimed at his bed.

Jason finished the water and waved at the camera. "Hey, whoever. If you can hear me, can someone please come and talk to me?" He shifted in the bed and again pushed himself up. Less pain this time. He pointed at the IV and mimed pulling it out. "Do I need this thing in my arm?" He looked for a call button or a phone but found nothing.

He had to pee. Jason set the cup on the table, removed the clip from his finger and swung his legs from under the covers. He checked the tube running from his arm to the bag and saw the bag stand was on rollers. He clutched the metal pole and eased himself to standing. A moment of dizziness washed over him but soon cleared. Jason inched his way to the bathroom, aches and tightness revealed with every step. A breeze flowed across his butt, exposed by the open hospital gown.

He finished peeing, flushed the toilet and moved to the sink to wash his hands.

What the . . . ?

His nails were trimmed and filed, not a speck of dirt underneath them. Callouses from working the punching bag were soft. Only faded bruises looked like they belonged.

He checked his reflection and his jaw dropped. The hair on the sides of his head had been buzzed short. The hair on top was only slightly longer with no semblance of the waves he'd had before. One eye was bruised, though it was more yellow and green than purple, and the cut above his lip had stitches inside the scab.

How long have I been here?

Jason dried his hands and repeatedly pressed the scab on his lip, feeling the pain build then ease, build then ease. He floated his hand across the spiky hairs on the side of his head. He turned, looking for cuts or gashes. Unlike his face, his scalp looked healthy, pink, wound-free.

Jason shuffled toward the bed. He faced the camera. "Why did you cut my hair?" He flailed one arm and pointed to his head, frowning. Then he rolled the IV stand into place and maneuvered himself back into bed. "I liked my hair the way it was." He pointed to his head again, then blew out a breath. He closed his eyes.

I hope it grows back fast.

After a few minutes, Jason turned his thoughts to the attack at Bartie's house, replaying the events in his mind.

Why didn't my powers work? Why didn't Uncle Alexander use his?

Jason remembered being tired, hungry.

No, that can't be it. I've been training.

He scrunched his eyes and received a zap of pain from his injured face. He huffed. Uncle Alexander's warning about overtraining entered his mind.

Not possible.

A moment later the door to his room opened.

"So you're awake then. I thought perhaps you'd drifted back to sleep." A blond woman wearing blue scrubs and a white coat approached him.

Jason glanced at the camera then back to her. "Yeah, I'm awake."

"That's good news. Means you're getting better and we're doing our jobs properly." She lifted the tablet from its hook. "Simply making a note here that you expressed your bladder."

"Jeez, do you have cameras everywhere?" Jason pulled the covers up higher.

"What?" The woman looked at the bathroom door then to Jason. "Oh, no. No camera in there. The sensor on your wristband signals when you've moved from one room to the next."

Jason eyed the wristband. It looked like a typical hospital ID band, white and plastic, except this one was a bit thicker and had no markings, not even Jason's name. And it was a solid loop with no seams, no tabs, and no buckle.

"I assumed you expressed your bladder. Any bowel movement?" the woman asked.

"Uh, no," Jason said. "And yes, I washed my hands."

"We know." She smiled. "I should introduce myself. I'm Dr. Carrington and I'm assigned to take care of you. How do you feel?"

"Sore."

"That's to be expected. Do you need more pain medicine?" Dr. Carrington asked.

"I don't think so," Jason said.

"Very good. If you change your mind, do let us know."

"How do I do that?"

"Simply say so. We're always listening." Dr. Carrington pressed a stethoscope to his chest. "Deep breath."

This place is weird.

"What about my uncle?" Jason asked.

"Deep breath, please."

Jason inhaled and heaved air out.

The doctor helped him sit forward and placed the stethoscope on his back. "Again."

He repeated the action two more times.

"Very good." Dr. Carrington jotted notes.

"And what about my uncle?" Jason asked again.

She stopped and focused on Jason. "Let's start with the good news, shall we? You are recovering nicely. It was a bit touch and go when you first arrived two days ago, but you've turned the corner and there's no reason you shouldn't make a full recovery."

Two days ago?

"I only wish I had the same sort of news about your uncle," Dr. Carrington said.

Jason's stomach tightened.

A knock sounded on the door and Dr. Carrington turned toward it.

A man peeked inside. "It's time for the assigned cleaning of this room. Should I come back later?" He had a round face with brown hair and a brown mustache.

"No, that's all right, Raymond. Come in." Dr. Carrington waved him forward.

Raymond nodded once at Jason and pushed the door wide, rolling in a cart with cleaning supplies and an attached mop and bucket. He pushed the cart into the bathroom.

Dr. Carrington returned her focus to Jason. "About your uncle, first let me assure you that he's here and we're taking very good care of him."

"Okay . . ."

"And there's no reason to worry, not just yet." Dr. Carrington hung the stethoscope around her neck. "He's still unconscious, but he's suffered much trauma over the years, so it seems he's taking a bit longer to recover from this latest challenge. Still, we have every reason to believe he'll wake soon, as long as he has the will to get better."

The will to get better?

"Leadership has informed us that you're both VIPs, so you and your uncle will receive the best of everything," Dr. Carrington said.

"Wait, leadership? And how do you know Uncle Alexander's history?"

She tilted her head. "We have his medical records."

"How? I mean, what hospital is this?" Jason asked.

"You're not in hospital, Jason. You're in the medical unit at League of Governors headquarters," Dr. Carrington said.

Jason shook his head. "But I thought . . . Bartie said . . ."

She pursed her lips. "Very unfortunate, that one. If our team hadn't gotten there in time, he would have killed you both."

"Killed us?"

"Yes. As I understand it, Mr. Ainsworth attacked you and your uncle in his home and nearly finished you off. Our team arrived on scene, eliminated him and rushed you here."

Jason remembered the masked man. *He was about the same height as Bartie . . .*

"Eliminated, as in . . ."

"He's no longer a threat, to you or the League," Dr. Carrington said. "It's a shame, really. He was once a great member of this organization. But he started to unravel, becoming more paranoid, believing in conspiracy theories." She sighed. "The League offered treatment and counseling, but he refused all of it. His wife finally gave him an ultimatum, telling him to agree to get help or she'd leave him. But not even that swayed him. After she left a couple of months ago he spiraled further into his illness. Attempting to murder two people doesn't reflect a healthy mind, now does it?"

"I guess not," Jason said.

"Alright, one more test," Dr. Carrington said. "Please invoke your powers."

"What?"

"Your Guard powers. Please engage them."

"Oh. Okay." Jason raised his hands and summoned the blue bolts. But nothing happened.

"Hmm . . ." Dr. Carrington made another note on the tablet.

"Hold on. I can do it." Jason tensed and flexed and focused on his powers.

Nothing came.

His shoulders slumped. "I don't get it."

"Your system is compromised," Dr. Carrington said. "I expect your powers to return with your health."

"That sucks," Jason said.

"All the more reason for you to get better then, isn't it?" She returned to writing in Jason's chart.

"But wait. My dad and sister—are they here?" His heart beat faster.

"Yes, and they look forward to seeing you," Dr. Carrington said.

"They're okay?"

"Of course." Dr. Carrington adjusted a setting on the IV.

"Can we go see my uncle?" Relief at the news of his dad and sister loosened Jason's shoulders.

"I appreciate your enthusiasm, Jason. It's a good indication of your recovery." She returned the tablet to its hook. "But we do have a few things to address. First, we need to get you some real food and see how you do with that. And I'd still like you to rest. I'm keeping you on fluids as well. We're going to add an electrolyte and vitamin blend to your drip to help rebuild your strength. It's a serum we developed here, specialized for League members and the unique properties of our systems."

"What unique properties? Like being a Guard and stuff?" Jason asked.

"Yes. Guards, other humans with powers, cryptids, and so forth— we have specific blends for each. We'll start you on the base blend suitable for all humans, and move you to the Guard serum when you're stronger," Dr. Carrington said.

Raymond backed out of the bathroom, mopping the floor where he'd already stepped.

"I'll send your dad and Della to see you as soon as they're able," Dr. Carrington said. "As for your uncle, we're not allowing visitors right now. He needs rest so he has the best possible chance to heal himself, okay?"

"But if I could just talk to him . . ."

"We'll get there. But not yet," Dr. Carrington said.

Jason nodded.

She looked at her watch. "Colette will be here soon with your dinner. Eat slowly, see how you feel. If all goes well, tomorrow we'll upgrade you from broth and crackers. Sound good?"

"Not really, but okay," Jason said.

She smiled. "I know broth isn't too exciting. I promise we'll make it up to you with something more appealing going forward. We have excellent chefs on staff."

Raymond moved near the bed. He wiped the nobs and buttons on the machines. He wiped the railings of the bed. He moved to the other side, around Dr. Carrington, and wiped down the metal table.

"If you need anything else, the microphone above your bed is always on." She pointed to a small black device hanging from the ceiling. "And of course there's the camera."

"But, like when I'm in the bathroom . . ."

"No cameras, no microphones," Dr. Carrington said.

"That's good," Jason said. "But then how did you know I washed my hands?"

"Sensor in the faucet that monitors its use, informs if it requires maintenance, that sort of thing. And there is an emergency call button in the bathroom if needed." She put her hands in the pockets of her coat. "You're in good hands, Jason, as is your uncle. Is there anything else?"

"What about my hair?" Jason asked.

"What about it?"

"Why did someone cut it? And my nails, too?" Jason eyed the white moons of his nail beds. "Now they're kinda . . . pretty, or something."

"You were quite a mess when you came in. We followed standard procedure. Plus, cleanliness assists with the healing process." Dr. Carrington patted the bed's railing. "Have a good evening. I'll see you again in the morning." She exited the room.

Cleanliness, whatever. He picked at a dry bit of his cuticle.

Raymond mopped where Dr. Carrington had been standing.

Jason checked Raymond's haircut and his mustache. Both were short and neatly trimmed.

"So, are they kinda strict on the rules around here?" Jason asked.

"Procedures enable us for greatness," Raymond said. He gestured at the floor on the opposite side of the bed. "The path to the bathroom is dry now. No need to worry about slipping."

"Okay, thanks," Jason said.

"If you'd like, I can show you the emergency call button Dr. Carrington mentioned." He swooshed the mop in the bucket.

"I think I'm okay." Jason shifted in the bed. He picked up the controller and pressed a button to raise his back higher.

The door opened and the same girl from earlier entered, carrying a tray with her functioning arm. She nodded at Raymond. "Hello, Papa."

"Hello, darling girl. I've finished my assignment." He grabbed the tray from her and set it on the table next to Jason's bed. "I will see you back at our rooms later." Raymond opened the door and pushed his cart into the hallway.

"Oh, so you're Colette. And you're his daughter." Jason pointed to the closing door.

"Yes." Colette lifted a table attached to the bed, swinging it over Jason's lap. She moved the food from the tray onto the table and slid it closer to Jason's chest.

"I'm Jason."

"Yes, I know." She handed him a napkin.

"Can you tell me when my dad and sister are coming?"

"It is late. They'll have returned to their rooms. Perhaps tomorrow, if they are able." She removed the lid from the cup of broth. Dull crackers sat on a plate next to a bag of purple fluid.

"They're both staying here?"

"Of course."

Guess Dad decided that was easier.

Jason scanned the room for a clock, finding none. "What time is it?"

"A few minutes after seven p.m."

Not that late.

"Why can't they come see me now?" Jason asked.

"Procedure states that all members, unless otherwise engaged in an assignment, return to their rooms by seven p.m."

There are a lot of procedures in this place.

"I will now add the electrolyte and vitamin mix to your IV." Colette picked up the bag of purple fluid and hung it from the IV pole next to Jason's bed. She connected the tube to the line running into his arm.

"It looks like a funky energy drink." Jason took a sip of broth. "The blend of electrolytes and vitamins makes us stronger, happier, and healthier," she said.

"Okay . . ." Jason bit into a cracker. It was as bland as the broth. "Is my cell phone here?"

"Your personal belongings are stored in the safe. I can retrieve them for you tomorrow."

"And my clothes?" Jason asked.

"Your clothes have been sent to laundry, though some staining may prevent them from being returned to you. In the morning you will receive alternative garments, similar to what I am wearing," Colette said.

Jason eyed her scrubs. "I guess it's a good thing I like blue."

"I have completed my assigned tasks," she said. "When you are finished with your meal, please swing the table away from your bed. Someone will come by to clear it. I will return in the morning." She picked up the empty tray and exited the room.

Jeez, they sure mention 'assigned tasks' a lot. Weird.

Jason ate as much of the food as he could then pushed the tray aside and eased himself out of the bed. He dragged the IV stand across the floor, leaning on it for balance, opened the door and peeked out.

Long halls went left, right, and straight away from his room. Cameras lined the ceiling at various intervals. There was a nurses station, but it was empty. Doors to other rooms were all shut. It seemed deserted.

Jason grabbed onto handfuls of fabric around his backside, closing the gap in the gown. He stepped into the hall, but a moment later a cramp in his belly doubled him over. He gripped the IV stand and scooted into his room, making his way to the bathroom.

Procedure must have stated it was time for me to bomb the bowl. Doc will probably be happy to check that off the list.

He cleaned himself up, and was sure to wash his hands. He pushed on the soap dispenser and glanced at the emergency call button the doctor mentioned. There was something underneath it. A small bit of paper poked out.

Jason dried his hands and pulled the paper from its spot. He unfolded it:

Stop the serum. Don't trust those in charge.

I can help you.

Destroy this paper.

SIX

Trust

Jason stared at the note he'd found in his bathroom. *Who wrote this?*

He flipped the paper, looking for a name or a signature. Nothing.

Was it from that Raymond guy? He was the only one who'd been in the bathroom.

Jason heard the door to his room open. Adrenaline zipped through him. He crumpled the note, tossed it in the toilet and flushed.

Someone knocked on the bathroom door. "I'm completing my assignment to clear your dishes. Are you okay?" It was a man's voice.

"Uh, yeah, fine." Jason washed his hands again. "I'll be out in a minute."

"Do you need any assistance?"

"Nope. All good." Jason pulled paper towels out of the dispenser. "I'm just gonna get right into bed. Feeling pretty tired."

"All right. Then I've completed my assigned task. I'll leave you now," the man said.

"Okay. Thanks." Jason waited until after he heard the door to his room open, then close. He exited the bathroom and climbed back into bed.

He thought about the note. Was he supposed to trust Raymond? He didn't know him any more than he knew anyone else at the League. Then again, why would Raymond leave a note like that if there wasn't something going on? Was it some kind of test?

He'd talk to Dad about it tomorrow. Dad would know what to do.

Jason eyed the bag of purple fluid dripping into his body.

Stop the serum.

He rolled onto his side, facing the IV stand, his back to the camera. He spotted a clamp on the tube running from the purple fluid.

Jason picked up the controller that raised and lowered his bed and found a switch for the lights in the room. He turned them off, but the glow of a nightlight remained.

Still not dark enough.

He kept his back to the camera, eased his arm out from under the covers and rolled the dial on the clamp until the purple drip barely flowed.

Jason thought more about the note, about Raymond, about his dad and Della and Uncle Alexander. About Bartie. He'd seemed so nice. Why would he lie about the League?

Jason's thoughts blurred and mixed with odd images and colors.

He fell asleep.

✳✳✳

Jason awoke the next morning and stretched. Tight muscles released and bruised skin smarted but spared him harsh zings of pain. He opened his eyes.

A set of blue scrubs, his cell phone, and a charger sat on the table next to his bed. He used the controller to angle himself to sitting and reached for his phone. The screen lit at his touch and the time said nine-twenty-three a.m. The phone was fully charged but had no outside cell signal.

The door to his room opened.

"Good morning, Jason," Dr. Carrington said. "How are you feeling today?"

"Fine, I guess. I just woke up."

She lifted the tablet with Jason's data and examined the pages. "You did okay with the food last night?"

"Yeah, and everything worked like it's supposed to," Jason said.

Dr. Carrington raised one eyebrow.

"You know, bathroom stuff." Jason shifted in the bed.

"Ah, you had a bowel movement. That's very good." She made a note and checked the numbers on the machines next to his bed. "Well, let's see how you do up and about today, shall we?" She examined the bag of purple fluid. "Not as much serum in you as I would have liked but not to worry. We'll move you onto the oral application going forward. Now let's get that IV out of your arm."

A moment later, Jason was free from machines and tubes.

"You're welcome to move about the complex, but do take it easy until you feel stronger," Dr. Carrington said. "We don't want you backsliding on us."

"Yeah, no problem. Can I see my dad and sister?" Jason asked.

"I believe they are otherwise occupied this morning, but you should be able to visit with them this afternoon. In the meantime, Colette will bring you some breakfast, and afterward, she can give you a tour if you're interested."

"Yeah, sure. That'd be great." Jason raised his arm. "What about this wristband? Can you cut that off now?"

"Procedure states all members on site are required to wear the League wristband," Dr. Carrington said.

Jason glanced at Dr. Carrington's wrist. Her wristband was black. "Why? So you can keep track of me?"

"It's for your own safety, especially in light of your condition. Should you have any health issues, we'll know how to get to you quickly," she said.

Whatever.

"Plus, it enables you to enter otherwise restricted areas."

"Well, that's cool." Jason moved to push his hair back and dropped his hand, reminded there wasn't much hair to push. "And my cell phone? I should call my grandmother."

"Rest assured, the League has informed one..." Dr. Carrington swiped through Jason's chart. "Yes, here it is. The League has informed one Lena Fallon about your and your uncle's current status, and we will continue to update her as warranted." She looked up from the tablet. "Personal cell phones are not permitted according to—"

"Procedure. Yeah, yeah, I get it," Jason said. "So I can't call my grandmother?"

"If needed, we'll get you a League-issued phone and you can give her a call. Perhaps this afternoon, after you've seen your father and sister. Is that acceptable?" Dr. Carrington asked.

"Yeah. Sorry."

She smiled. "Not a problem. I understand you've been through a lot, and there's still much to deal with. It's logical that you'd feel anxious." She glanced at the serum bag again, then back to Jason. "We'll get you fixed up and feeling one hundred percent very soon. And if you'd like to connect to the League's internal Wi-Fi, you'll find guest access available on your phone. But for security reasons, there's no access to the internet."

"Okay, I guess. Thanks." He tapped the guest network and connected.

She patted his arm. "You're most welcome."

The door opened and Colette entered pushing a cart. She also wore a black wristband.

"Here's your breakfast and your tour guide," Dr. Carrington said. She swung the table over Jason's lap. "Good morning, Colette."

"Good morning, Dr. Carrington." Colette stopped the cart next to Jason's bed.

"I'll leave you to it. And Jason, I'll check back with you this afternoon." Dr. Carrington returned the digital chart to its hook and left.

"I hope there's something better than broth this time," Jason said.

"I don't choose the meals. My assignment is to deliver them." Colette set a bowl of oatmeal and a plate of buttered toast on his table.

"I know, I didn't mean . . ." Jason put a napkin in his lap. "I'm sorry. I thought I was being funny."

"If you say so." She added a glass of water along with a glass of milk. "And I guess it was a little bit funny." Her mouth tightened like she'd suppressed a smile.

"I'll try harder next time," Jason said.

Colette put a small dish of white and purple pills next to his plate. "These are your assigned medicines. Take the oblong white tablet now. It's an antibiotic. In approximately two hours you'll take the round tablet, a probiotic. The purple tablets are your serum. They will make you stronger, happier and healthier. You must always take them as instructed." She intensified her gaze for a moment.

Jason eased back a little bit. "Yeah, okay . . ."

"You understand?" she asked.

He remembered the note. *Stop the serum.*

Jason nodded. "Yeah, I got it. I'll take all the pills as instructed. But isn't serum supposed to be a liquid? Is this something different?"

"The serum starts as a liquid, and much of it is converted to pill form for easier distribution," Colette said. "But all forms are designated by the League as 'serum.' If you have no more questions, I'm assigned to return in one hour. That will give you time to eat, shower and dress."

"I don't think I need to shower since—"

"Procedure states—"

"Okay, okay. I'll shower," Jason said.

Colette nodded once and left the room.

Jason devoured his breakfast then eyed the tablets in the dish. The antibiotic made sense. The doctor wanted to make sure he didn't get an infection. And the probiotic was to replace the good stuff that the antibiotic killed. Jason swallowed the antibiotic and set the probiotic aside.

The purple pill was big, nearly an inch long. The word "Base" was imprinted on both sides.

"Whatever." He popped the pill into his mouth and headed for the shower.

Jason was ready and dressed in the scrubs before the full hour passed. While he waited, he opened the metal cabinet in his room. On the left side was space to hang clothes. The right side of the cabinet had shelving above and drawers below. Two drawers each held three sets of scrubs, all in his size. In the bottom drawer was a bag with his wallet, passport, and the coin. Also in the drawer was a pair of blue canvas shoes.

Jason took the shoes out and slipped them onto his feet. He put his wallet in his pocket. He examined the Lex coin and found it as non-glowing as the day he'd discovered it in his chess set. He puffed breath onto the face and rubbed it against his leg. A bit of tarnish wiped off, but otherwise, the coin remained unchanged. It didn't heat up, it didn't vibrate, it didn't change color. He dropped the coin into the holder with his passport and hung it around his neck.

The door to his room opened. Colette backed in with a wheelchair.

"What's that for?" Jason asked.

"So you don't overextend yourself," she said.

"I feel fine."

"It is part of my assignment to be of assistance should you feel fatigued."

Jason put up his hand. "Seriously, I mean, I appreciate it and everything. But I'm good."

"Okay." Colette parked the chair near the door. "Shall we go?"

He followed her into the hallway where she stopped.

"Right now we're in the Tower annex of League headquarters." Colette gestured left. "Heading that direction will take us across Tower Bridge where we can access the League tube to the Big Ben annex. If we have time, we'll do that later. But we begin with the Tower."

"So League headquarters is in the Tower of London, just like my uncle told me," Jason said.

Colette walked down the hall straight ahead and Jason followed.

"Not exactly *in* the Tower. That's too public for our needs. But yes, we are at the Tower of London."

"How can we be at the Tower of London but not in the Tower of London?" Jason asked.

"I will explain later. It's easier to see from the deck which is accessed from the other side of the annex," Colette said. "In the meantime, we'll start with the medical unit. As is everything at the League, the medical unit is state of the art."

The labs she directed Jason to had complicated equipment and machines he'd never seen before. They were even more complex than Uncle Alexander's lab back in Salton.

Colette showed him surgery suites and rehab centers where humans and cryptids worked to improve mobility and function. They watched for a few minutes as an Ahool worked to stretch one of its bat-like wings to its full six-foot span, then retract it and stretch it again, panting as it labored.

"I guess that Ahool is one of the good guys, huh?" Jason asked.

"Excuse me?" Colette looked toward the Ahool and back at Jason.

"Oh, nothing. It's just the last time I ran into an Ahool, he or she wasn't exactly friendly," Jason said.

"If you are afraid—"

"What? No," Jason said. "I can handle it. Or them. Or whatever." He shook his head. "Definitely not afraid."

"Okay," she said. "Let's keep going."

Colette finished showing Jason the medical unit and continued the tour with the recreation center. There was an Olympic-sized swimming pool, a track, free weights and weight machines, a climbing wall, a martial arts practice area, basketball, volleyball, and racquetball courts, meditation rooms, yoga studios, and a fancy juice bar.

"And we have an acupuncturist and several masseuses available by appointment," Colette said.

"Can I hang out here the rest of the day?" Jason stared at the height of the climbing wall.

"My assignment is to give you the full tour of the facility as time permits."

He turned to Colette. "What is with the whole assignment thing?"

"I am assigned—"

"No, I mean, I get that," he said. "But why does everyone say assignment this and assignment that?"

"It is procedure to know our assignments, to state our assignments, and to declare completion of our assignments," Colette said.

"So you have to say it, no matter what? Even if people already know what you're talking about?"

"It is procedure." She folded her arm behind her back.

"It's weird procedure but whatever." Jason gestured to the climbing wall. "Can I come back later and work out?"

"Dr. Carrington can provide you with that answer." Colette directed him through the exit. "Now I will show you the dining hall. I'm authorized to offer you a snack or meal if you're interested, though Dr. Carrington suggests you choose something light."

"I'm not really into cafeteria food." Jason stopped. "Wait—what is that smell?" His mouth watered.

"I believe that's the Italian wing," Colette said. "That is the first section of the dining hall."

"Wing? You have a whole wing of Italian food?" Jason hurried toward the scent of garlic, cheese, and tomato sauce. He stepped through double doors and halted, Colette by his side.

Five cafés circled a cobblestone courtyard. A fountain in the center gushed water straight up, and stone mermaids holding seashells caught the falling flow and poured it into the pool around them. The ceiling looked like blue sky with the occasional bird flying overhead, and an Italian singer crooned in the background.

Patrons of the cafés sat along the sidewalk, some eating pizza, some eating pasta, some eating meals that appealed to cryptids. Jason recognized a Kappa eating cucumbers.

Guessing they don't serve human flesh here.

Not far from the Kappa was a large black dog with flame-red eyes. The beast tore at a shank of meat and swallowed, then picked up a squeaky toy, squeezed it five times, tossed it aside and returned to the meat.

"Is that a Black Shuck?" Jason asked.

"Yes," Colette said.

"What about the whole 'harbinger of doom' thing? Everyone here can see it, so does that mean something bad is going to happen to all of us?"

"That particular 'it' is actually a she, and she's not on duty so you're safe," Colette said.

Huh. Maybe we could add a Black Shuck to Shay's and Finn's training.

"Besides," she continued, "the Black Shuck only delivers doom, as you call it, when it is deserved. They more often assist lost travelers, escort people home after dark, that sort of thing."

"I know, but it's cooler to talk about the scary stuff," Jason said.

Colette looked at him like she didn't understand.

"Anyway, how is this possible?" He gestured to the room.

"The League hires the best chefs from around the world," she said.

"No, I mean—it feels like we're outside. In Italy. Or at least the Italy I've seen in the travel shows Grandma Lena likes to watch," Jason said.

"Procedure states that members of the League should receive the best possible dining experience to further enable their happiness and productivity." Colette moved toward an elevator door. "Would you like to see the other wings?"

"I don't know. I think I'd like to stay here and eat everything." Jason remembered his training, his goal to stay lean. Carbs didn't fit in that plan. "But yeah, let's go see the others."

He followed Colette onto the elevator. Up one floor was the Chinese wing, as realistic as the Italian wing. Above

China was the Mexican wing, then a Japanese wing, a Thai wing, then a Greek, French, Indian, American, and finally a British wing. Each wing was as stunning as the one before it.

"A whole wing for British food?" Jason asked.

"Many at the League appreciate the cuisine of their upbringing," Colette said.

"I didn't think you could fill a whole wing with British food. Doesn't seem like there'd be that much, unless there's a lot of tea and, whatchamacallems . . . crumpets?"

"British cuisine has a long and varied history," Colette said. "There is much to choose from."

Jason turned to face her. "Why do you talk like you're thirty or something?"

She shook her head. "I do not understand."

"Well, you just use such, I don't know, serious words. All the time."

Colette shrugged. "I speak in accordance with the standards set forth by the League."

"So the League is stuffy," Jason said. "Which I'm guessing is part of the procedures, stating all members must live up to the most stuffiest of stuffy as ruled by the royal leadership blah, blah, whatever. Am I right?"

She glanced toward a camera and pulled on the hem of her top, straightening it. "Are you hungry?"

"I guess procedures don't let you answer my question," Jason said.

"It wasn't much of a question. Are you hungry?" Colette asked again.

Jason sighed. "Sure, I could eat. Is there a salad wing? Plus, why are these called wings when they go up and not out?"

"Wings are up in the sky, aren't they?" Colette gestured at one of the projected birds on the ceiling of the British wing. "And no salad wing. Though I'm certain you can find something to your liking at any of the dining units."

"Fine. Let's do Greek. I feel like looking at the fake ocean," Jason said, though he really did like the view from the Greek wing.

"Speaking of views, I promised to show you the deck. It's one flight up, so we will do that and then dine."

They entered the elevator again and Colette pushed the button for the top floor.

"This place seems huge. I had no idea the League was so big," Jason said. "How many people work here?"

"Currently there are twenty-eight-hundred League employees in residence," Colette said. "And thousands more worldwide."

"Wait—twenty-eight-hundred people work here, *and* live here?"

"The League is an historic and important international organization that demands the best people. We are happy to serve, and honored to live at League headquarters."

The doors opened onto a vast terrace covered in grass, with real sky overhead. Parts of the terrace were shielded by Plexiglas, other sections were open to the breeze blowing over London. There were picnic tables with umbrellas, and gardens growing fresh vegetables and herbs.

"As you can see, we grow much of our food up here." She pointed in the distance. "We even have a few orchard trees with their own climate control. Those are avocados."

"Seriously?" Jason asked.

"We can walk over there if you'd like, and you can see for yourself," Colette said.

"No, I believe you. It's just, seriously, this is really cool."

She nodded. "You asked me about the Tower of London earlier." She moved to a panel across from the elevator doors.

Jason followed. "Yeah, so where is it?" He held his hand above his eyes, blocking the sun while searching for the Tower.

"We're already there," Colette said. "I suggest you place your hand here." She tapped a railing next to the panel. The railing seemed to have no clear purpose.

"Okay . . ." He grasped the rail.

Colette pulled a switch on the panel. Every structure related to the League disappeared.

Jason swung his other hand onto the rail and gripped tight. "Oh my god." His knuckles whitened. Below him were the grounds of the Tower of London. No wings, no recreation center, no medical unit. His feet seemed to float in air, the ground far below him. "We're gonna fall."

He reached for Colette. She stood her ground, though it was more like she stood her air. She wasn't panicking. She was smiling.

Jason spun and checked out the other people and cryptids dining on the roof. All appeared to be floating. None seemed worried. He stomped his feet on the air. It felt solid.

"What is happening?" Jason asked.

"This is how the League appears to the world at large, meaning we aren't seen at all. Headquarters is built alongside some of London's most famous historical landmarks, and only League members are aware of its existence." Colette returned the switch to its original position. All League structures reappeared.

Jason loosened his grip. "Holy crap." *I can't wait to tell Sadie about this.*

"Um, yes. Holy crap," Colette said.

Jason's brows furrowed. He side-eyed Colette.

"I'm trying to speak more . . . teenager-y?" She shrugged one shoulder.

Jason laughed and let go of the rail. "You need practice."

"I will spend time with you and practice then," Colette said.

"That sounds good," Jason said. "Uh, I mean, do the procedures allow that?"

"I am assigned to assist in your care. Therefore, practice is enabled." She headed to the elevator.

"And, she's back," Jason said.

"What do you mean? How should I have spoken?" Colette asked.

Jason followed her onto the elevator. "Something like, 'I'll be around, so I can totally practice then.'"

"The use of the word totally in that sentence isn't grammatically correct." She pressed the button for the Greek wing.

"But that's kinda the point because—" Jason jutted his hand between the closing doors. "Hold on." The doors returned to open and he bolted out of the elevator.

"Wait," Colette called.

Jason stopped and pointed to a man at a table near the avocado trees. He was sitting opposite another man wearing a hat that reminded Jason of hats he'd seen in old movies. The two were laughing. "I think that's my dad." He hurried forward. "Dad!" Jason picked up his pace.

Colette stayed close.

Jason covered the distance, his certainty growing with each step. He ran up to the table, threw his arms around Dad and hugged him hard.

"Whoa," Dad said. "What's this?"

Jason released him and scooted onto the bench next to him. "Finally. I've been trying to reach you for days."

Colette waited about ten feet away from the end of the table, her hand at her side like a soldier at attention. Jason waved her forward.

"This is Colette," Jason said.

She took one step forward and nodded to Jason's dad. "Nice to meet you, sir." She nodded at the man sitting across from Jason's dad. "Good day to you, sir."

"Good day, Colette," the man said. He didn't smile.

"Uh, hello, Colette," Dad said. "But I don't understand."

"Oh, she's helping take care of me in the medical unit. But I'm fine. And I think Uncle Alexander is going to be fine, too," Jason said.

His dad looked from Jason to the man across the table. "Rick? A little help?"

"They didn't tell you we were hurt?" Jason asked his dad. "They totally told me you knew."

"I'm sorry young man, you must have me mistaken for someone else," Dad said.

"What? No. Kinda impossible for me not to know my own dad." Jason looked to the man, Rick, who still said nothing. He returned his focus to his dad. "It's me. Jason. Your son."

"I only have one child," he said. "A daughter. Her name is Della."

SEVEN

Backsliding

Jason's gut pushed into his throat. He gripped Dad's shoulder and shook it. "What is wrong with you? It's me. Jason."

The man named Rick touched Jason's arm. "Please, give him a moment."

Jason shook off Rick's hand. "What did you guys do to him?" He glared.

"Nothing at all," Rick said. "He took ill after he arrived with Della. We suspect poisoning, likely by the group Bartie was working with."

Jason swallowed. *Bartie was lying about everything.*

"He's had some memory problems," Rick said. "At one point he even thought we were hiding your sister from him. But we're treating him, and he's getting better every day." He turned to Jason's dad and touched his hand. "Zachary, this is Jason, your son. He's come all the way from the States to see you and Della."

Dad's eyes zoned out for a moment, then focused on Jason's face. "Jason? Oh my god, Jason!" Dad pulled him into a tight hug. "How did you get here? Where is your uncle? Is Kyle with you?" He released the hug.

Jason sat back and glanced at Rick, then his dad. "Uh, no, Kyle's still at home, in Salton with Grandma Lena. And Uncle Alexander is in the medical unit. We flew over when we didn't hear from you." He decided not to mention the coin. Not yet.

"In the medical unit?" Dad scanned the wounds on Jason's face. "Look at you! What happened? Are you okay?"

"Yeah, we're okay, I think. I mean, I'm okay." Jason inhaled. "This guy attacked us, but the League got there in time. And they brought us here. Uncle Alexander is still unconscious, though."

"He will be fine," Rick said.

"Yeah, he will be fine," Jason said. He shook his head. *Huh?*

"He will be fine," Colette added.

Jason shot a quick look at Colette then back to his dad.

Dad nodded. "Okay, well, let's go see him."

"He's not to have visitors until authorized by Dr. Carrington," Colette said.

"And you are, miss?" Dad asked.

"Dad, that's Colette. I introduced you to her a minute ago. She's helping take care of me," Jason said.

"Oh, right. My apologies, Colette," Dad said.

"No problem, sir." She looked down at the ground.

"We'll wait for word from Dr. Carrington." He looked at Rick. "Thank you for taking care of my family."

"Of course. Members are all part of the League family, and shall be treated as such," Rick said.

Colette bowed her head deeper, keeping her gaze on the ground.

"Dad, how is Della?" Jason asked.

"Oh, she's doing so well. You'll be amazed to see her progress. She's happy, she's positive." Dad looked at Rick. "It was the best thing for her, bringing her to the League."

"Can we go see her?" Jason asked.

"She is in treatment," Rick said.

"Yes, she is in treatment," Dad said. "She must complete her treatment."

"How about after that? Maybe we can all do dinner together?" Jason asked

"Not today. Perhaps tomorrow," Rick said.

"Yes. Perhaps tomorrow." Dad smiled at Jason. "But I'm so happy you're here. Have you seen all that the League has to offer?"

"Well, yeah, at least the Tower part. Colette's been showing me around—"

"Everything we could possibly need is right here, at our fingertips," Dad said. "We'll never want for anything."

"But, you know, home is good, too," Jason said. "Like, our own beds. And Shay. And Kyle."

Rick tilted his head and gazed at Jason. "Being at the League brings you happiness. Peace."

Jason's eyes flicked to Colette. Her hand clenched.

"Yes. The League brings me happiness. And peace," Jason said. He shook his head again. "Uh, right Dad?"

"So you see it, too. It's wonderful here, Jason. Just wonderful," Dad said. "We'll never want for anything."

"Yeah. And that's great, really great." Jason scratched the side of his head. "So, do you want to come with me and

Colette for the rest of the tour? We're going to get something to eat first."

Rick stood. "Your father is due for his next treatment. We don't want him backsliding, now do we?"

Backsliding . . . there's that word again.

"Nope. No backsliding. Sir," Jason said.

"Zachary, let's get you to your treatment." Rick stepped around the table, reaching for Jason's dad. "You'll see Jason at dinner."

"Oh, dinner with my son. That will be wonderful." Dad stood.

"Arrange for them to dine together," Rick said to Colette.

She deepened her bow again. "I will do so, sir."

"And Della will remain in treatment tonight," Rick said.

"Yes, sir. I will deliver that message to her team," she said.

"Very good," Rick said. "You're a good girl, Colette."

"It is my honor to serve the League, sir." She shifted her maimed arm in closer to her body.

Rick led Jason's dad away.

"Did you not say you wanted to see the avocado trees?" Colette asked Jason.

"Not—" Jason noticed Colette's eyes. They were wide, pleading. "Not earlier but definitely now, if we have time."

"We have time." She walked toward the small grove.

Jason hustled to keep up with her pace. "You're kind of in a hurry."

"It's best to see them before the light of day fades. I don't want you to miss out."

"Thanks, I guess," he said. "So that whole conversation back there was weird. My dad was freaky. Whatever happened to him really messed him up." Jason skipped to close a gap between him and Colette.

"He is receiving the best possible treatment," Colette said.

"Who is that Rick guy?"

"He's part of leadership. Very important."

"So he's Mr. Procedures?" Jason asked.

"One of several who direct us to greatness."

Jason rolled his eyes. "Still doesn't mean things are better here than at home."

Colette led Jason to the furthest edge of the grove and turned toward him. She lowered her voice. "You didn't take your serum."

"No, I spit it into the toilet," Jason said.

"I delivered the instructions. You should have taken it."

"Yeah, but there was the note...uh...do you know about the note?" *My big mouth. I'm totally going to get someone fired.*

"He shouldn't have done that," Colette said.

Jason sighed. "So it *was* your dad."

"He took too much of a risk."

"Don't worry," Jason said. "I won't tell anyone. And I got rid of the note."

She shifted her gaze to the London skyline. "He should know better."

"What's the big deal? All he said was don't take your vitamins. Just sounds like weird parenting to me."

She pursed her lips. "You should take all of your medicines as instructed."

"Okay. I'll take my vitamins. They are vitamins, right?" Jason's head ached. He rubbed his temple. "And hey—how did you know I didn't take that pill?"

"Jason. Colette." A distant voice called out.

They turned to see Raymond stomping toward them. "We must get back to the medical unit. Jason is overdue for his medicines."

"We were going to get something to eat," Jason said.

"My assignment is to return you to the medical unit immediately," Raymond said. "Colette has been assigned to bring you a meal designated by Dr. Carrington, to best support your healing. Colette will also deliver your next round of medicines."

"But Papa, he—"

"Do not question your assignment, daughter."

"Yes, Papa."

Raymond turned back toward the elevator, Colette and Jason close behind him.

"Dr. Carrington is very concerned that Jason may be backsliding," Raymond said.

"I feel fine," Jason said. *Only a little headache.*

"It is not good to backslide." Raymond huffed and increased his pace.

"Okay," Jason said. "I'll take my medicine as soon as we get back to the medical unit."

"That is good," Raymond said, slightly shaking his head. "They will help you be stronger, healthier, and happier."

"And I'm good with that," Jason said. *Did he just signal me not to take the meds? What's with him?*

They hurried through hallways, and down stairs when the elevators seemed slow. Jason worked to fill his lungs. They were almost to the entrance of the medical unit when Jason's breath shallowed. His legs jellied. Dark swirls worked into his vision.

"Hey, one second." Jason stopped and bent forward, waiting for the dizziness to pass. His headache felt like a chisel above his eyes.

"I'll get you a wheelchair," Colette said.

"No. I will help him," Raymond said. "You must get to the kitchen and dispensary. They are waiting for you."

Colette nodded and sped down the hall. Raymond lifted Jason's arm around his own shoulder, taking much of Jason's weight onto himself. "You are still suffering from your injuries." He walked Jason forward.

"But I felt really good this morning," Jason said.

"As we heal, in the morning we are rested and feel good. But the body is still working to repair itself, and activities outside of rest take their toll."

They passed the rehab center.

Jason took his arm off Raymond's shoulder. "I'm good." He continued moving forward.

"You are certain?" Raymond asked.

"Yeah, as long as we take it slow, I'm good," Jason said.

A few minutes later they were back in Jason's room and Raymond helped him get in bed. He poured Jason a cup of water.

Dr. Carrington entered. "I'm glad to see you're back." She turned to Raymond. "Thank you for your assistance. Your assignment is complete."

Raymond nodded and left.

"I'm kinda hot," Jason said. "And my head is killing me." He rubbed both temples.

Dr. Carrington pressed her hand against his forehead. "Hmm."

"Hah. That's what my mom used to say when—uh, never mind. Not important." Jason didn't want to think about his mother.

"Well, regardless of what your mother used to say, I can tell you right now it means things aren't good," Dr. Carrington said. "You're running a fever." She opened a drawer in the side table and removed a thermometer, stroking it across Jason's forehead. She frowned.

"What does it say?" Jason asked.

"One hundred and three." She made a note on Jason's chart.

"But I felt totally fine this morning." His eyes clouded a moment then cleared.

"We'll increase your antibiotics and look for an infection. Are you hungry?" Dr. Carrington asked.

"Not anymore. I just need to close my eyes." Jason scooched lower and pressed into his pillow.

I probably just need some sleep.

Nearby mumbling sounded like Colette. Then Dr. Carrington mumbled. Then Colette again. Jason rolled on his side and pulled a pillow over his head to block the light and the sound.

What if something happened to me and I'm broken? What if I'm not strong enough to be a Guard?

A door closed. A knot swelled and inched up Jason's throat. Someone shook him and yanked the pillow from his face, the sudden light driving him to scrunch his eyelids tighter.

"Jason?" It was Dr. Carrington.

"Yes, I'm Jason," he said. He pawed for another pillow. Something cold pressed against his chest. A hand pushed him from his side to his back, then pulled his arm straight.

More mumbling sounded in his ear like the funny noises parents make for their babies. A prick pierced his arm. The sounds around him were loud, then distant, then stopped.

✳✳✳

Jason tried to open his mouth. His lips stuck together like fleshy Velcro. He forced them apart, the effort tearing off bits of dry skin. He rubbed his tongue against the back of his teeth, trying to make saliva from dusty paste that tasted like sour gym socks.

"Jason?"

The voice sounded familiar. Where was he? He blinked his eyes open.

"He's awake." Colette made a note on his digital chart.

"Oh yeah. The League." He rolled onto his back and scanned the room. No one else was there. "Who are you talking to?"

"The microphone." Colette pointed above.

"Right. Always listening." He pushed himself up. A piece of metal jabbed in his arm. "Aw, not the IV again."

"It was necessary. You needed fluids and more powerful antibiotics." She handed him a cup of water with a straw.

"I just needed to sleep." He took a drink. "One good night's sleep and my headache is gone. And I don't feel hot, so the fever must be gone, too," Jason said.

"I'm happy to note that you're feeling better." She jotted on the chart.

"So can you take out the IV?"

"That is Dr. Carrington's decision," Colette said. "She is expected to arrive shortly."

As if on cue, Dr. Carrington entered the room. "Glad to see you're awake. You gave us a bit of a scare."

"It wasn't that big of a deal. I already feel way better than I did last night," Jason said.

"Hmm. Yes." Dr. Carrington took the tablet from Colette and scanned the pages.

"Hmm-yes what?" Jason rubbed sleep out of his eyes.

She handed the tablet back to Colette. "Jason, you went into shock."

He took a long draw of water. Colette stepped to the end of the bed and hung the tablet.

"You know how serious that is. It's happened to you before," Dr. Carrington said.

"Yeah, a few months ago when I . . . when I got hurt."

"And have you been taking care of yourself since then?" She crossed her arms over her chest.

"Totally. I've been working out, training for the Guards, getting really strong." Jason shifted himself higher.

"I disagree," Dr. Carrington said.

"What? No, it's totally true. I've been super-focused on my training, super-committed."

"To the detriment of your body."

"Did my uncle tell you that? He's awake?"

"Your body told me that," Dr. Carrington said. "Your system is compromised and it's having difficulty recovering from your injuries. Your muscle mass is far lower than it should be for a young man your age, and your body fat is at dangerously low levels. It's no wonder you aren't healing. Your system is focused on trying to keep things functioning, much less thriving."

"But I've been exercising. Training," Jason said.

"And restricting calories? Carbohydrates?" she asked.

Uncle Alexander's voice played in his head. *I'm concerned you're overtraining.*

"Yeah, to stay lean. But look—I'm already feeling better. I just needed a good night's sleep." Jason gestured to the normal-looking readings on the monitors.

Dr. Carrington sighed. "You've been asleep since Monday. It's now Thursday morning."

"What? I . . ." He glanced at Colette. She nodded. Jason slumped into his pillow.

"You're staying on fluids for another twenty-four hours at least, then we'll see how you do," Dr. Carrington said.

"But—"

"No discussion." Dr. Carrington held up her hand. "Your designated meals will be delivered, and you will eat them without argument, without debate, without complaint. You will not wander, you will not exercise. You will be given reading material for entertainment, and you will fill the rest of your time with sleeping. Until otherwise notified, the only time you'll be permitted out of bed is for short excursions to the bathroom. Have I made myself clear?"

"Yes . . ." Jason said.

"Following these guidelines ensures a shorter stint of bed rest. Deviating from these guidelines will extend it. Understand?" Dr. Carrington asked.

"Yes, I understand."

"Good," she said. "Once I'm assured you've stabilized, we'll revisit adding the Guard serum to your regimen. But for now, your system is too compromised. It's a shame because I'm confident the serum will improve your powers exponentially."

"I thought you said it was vitamins." Jason wondered how the procedures defined "vitamins."

"Yes, well, vitamins with specialized properties. Let's get you better, and then we'll make you stronger than ever. Deal?" Dr. Carrington asked.

"Yeah, totally. Deal," Jason said. Maybe the serum was exactly what he needed. Stronger was always better, right? "Can my Dad and Della come see me?"

"Tomorrow perhaps," the doctor said. "I want to be certain we don't see any backsliding in this initial twenty-four hours."

Jason started to say something, but Dr. Carrington gave him a look that said, "Don't you dare." He nodded.

Dr. Carrington left and Colette removed a cell phone from her pocket. She tapped the screen and paused a moment.

"There are a few magazines in the drawer." Colette pointed at the table next to his bed. "But if you tell me what else you'd like to read I'll see if I can bring it to you."

"I'd like to read my phone. Can I have my phone?" Jason asked.

"It's here, also in the drawer. Anything else?"

"Whatever. Just bring me stuff and I'll read it," he said.

Colette slipped the phone back in her pocket. "If you're hungry, I'll bring you a meal now."

"I guess I'm hungry. But can I ask you a question first?"

"Yes," Colette said.

"How long do you have to keep your arm in a sling? It must be hard whenever you want to type on your cell phone."

"The sling is permanent. And I simply use the dictation feature."

"Oh, sorry." Jason felt his cheeks flush. "But, uh, with the dictation, don't you get goofed up words that way?"

"No," Colette said. "The League has enhanced the technology to prevent such errors."

"That's cool. I hope they give that to everybody," he said. "So, what happened to your arm?"

"An accident," she said.

"Like you tripped and fell or something?"

"Yes. I'll fetch your meal now." Colette spun on her heel and exited.

Okay . . .

Jason eased out of bed and made his way to the bathroom, dragging the IV stand with him. "This again. Fun."

After washing his hands, he opened the bathroom door and jumped. Raymond was standing there, waiting.

"Yes, sir, I am happy to provide assistance." Raymond left his cleaning cart and stepped forward, grabbing Jason's arm. He directed him back into the bathroom and closed the door.

"I . . . uh . . ." Jason kept one hand on the pole of the IV stand. "I actually didn't ask for any assistance."

"I needed to talk to you, and this was the only way. But we only have a minute," Raymond said. "You know not to take the serum, yes?"

"But Colette—"

"She worries too much. You must not take it. But you must be agreeable or they will suspect you."

"Suspect me of what? Besides, it doesn't matter—they won't even give it to me until I get better," Jason said.

"Good. This is good. Are you allowed out of your room?" Raymond asked.

"No, I'm barely allowed out of my bed." Jason leaned against the wall.

"Then you must improve, and we must get you in to see your uncle," Raymond said. "It's important for you to see him."

Jason straightened. "Is he getting worse?"

"I don't know for certain. You need to visit with him."

"I'll ask Dr. Carrington about it," Jason said.

"It seems they want to keep you from him." Raymond put his ear near the bathroom door and listened for a moment. "There's no more time. I must go." He pulled a small pencil from his pocket and slipped it inside the paper towel dispenser. "We can communicate with notes. Let me know if you need my help to see your uncle."

Jason nodded. "Okay."

"And don't take the serum."

"Won't it help me with my powers, make me stronger?"

"I promise you, the price is too high," Raymond said. "Far too high."

✳✳✳

After finishing another underwhelming bowl of broth, there was a light knock at his door.

"Jason?" Della peeked into the room.

"Dell! Get over here." Jason waved her toward the bed.

She skittered across the floor. Dad walked in behind her.

Della smiled. "You look really bad." She leaned over the bed and hugged Jason.

"Yeah, thanks," Jason said. "But you don't. You look great." He reached up.

Della skipped backward. "No, you are not mussing my hair."

"But that's my job. It's in the big brother handbook," he said.

"No such thing." She climbed onto the end of the bed.

"Hello, son." Dad hugged Jason. "How are you feeling?"

"Better. Totally fine," Jason said. "Sorry if you guys were worried."

"Not worried at all. We knew you were in good hands and the League was providing the best of care," Dad said.

"Right." Jason looked at Dad's face, then Della's. Their expressions were similar, soft smiles where the corners of their mouths upturned slightly.

"It's a shame you can't start the serum yet. I understand it will improve your Guard skills exponentially," Dad said.

Sounds familiar.

"Uh, yeah, no serum yet. But soon. When I'm stronger," Jason said. "And maybe we can go home soon, too?"

"I haven't completed my treatment," Della said.

"How much longer then?" Jason asked.

"It doesn't matter how long it takes, the League is the best place for us," Dad said. "Everything we could possibly need is right here at our fingertips."

"Yeah but, I mean, eventually..." Jason shifted his weight to find a more comfortable position.

"I'm certain you'll love it here, son." Dad squeezed Jason's shoulder. "And you can't get better training for the Guards than right here."

"Well, Uncle Alexander might not feel that way."

Dad shook his head. "Things aren't good with your uncle. You need to prepare yourself." He looked away for a moment. "The doctors don't think Alexander is going to get better."

"What? Of course he'll get better. You said the League provides the best of care," Jason said.

"They do. And they are absolutely doing everything possible to bring him back to us," Dad said. "But they've seen no improvement, and in fact, he seems to be in decline."

"No, that can't be." Jason sat up in his bed. "That can't happen."

Dad's voice softened. "Your uncle has been through so much, son. From physical challenges to emotional challenges—he's overcome them all. But this time, it might be too much for him." He put his arm around Della. "The doctors suspect he's lost the will to live."

"No way. Not Uncle Alexander." Jason pushed off the covers and stepped out of bed, gripping the IV stand.

Dad held up his hands. "Hold on, what do you think you're doing?" He walked to where Jason stood and blocked his path.

"I'm going to see Uncle Alexander." Jason took one step, but Dad kept him in place.

"Dr. Carrington said you must stay in bed," Dad said.

"You can't break the rules," Della said.

"I don't care about rules or Dr. Carrington. I care about Uncle Alexander. And you can either come with me or get out of my way." Jason shrugged past Dad and moved toward the metal cabinet, opening one of the drawers where the scrubs were stored.

"Jason, I need you to get back in bed. Dr. Carrington won't be happy," Dad said.

"But *I'm* not happy, Dad. I'm not happy about Uncle Alexander, and I don't get why you seem so okay with it." Jason slammed the drawer.

"Why is he so upset?" Della asked Dad.

"He's sick, honey. He needs to get better so he can take his serum," Dad said.

Again with the serum. Jason leaned against the cabinet and pulled on the scrubs pants. "This isn't about being sick, this is about family." He rolled the IV stand and headed toward the door. "Show me where Uncle Alexander's room is."

Dad crossed his arms. "I will not. Dr. Carrington said you must stay in bed."

"Seriously, Dad, repeating what she said isn't going to make me do it." Jason glared. The door opened behind him.

Colette entered with a wheelchair. She pushed it to the side of the doorway.

Dr. Carrington followed her in. "Fine, Jason, you can see your uncle. But you must prepare yourself." She gestured for Jason to sit in the wheelchair. "Death is not far off."

EIGHT
Uncle Alexander

Colette pushed Jason's wheelchair down the hall. They followed Dr. Carrington, and Dad and Della walked behind them. The group passed through double doors labeled "ICU." Dr. Carrington opened a door across from the ICU nurses station and held it for everyone to enter. Uncle Alexander's room smelled like lemons soaked in bleach.

"I'll leave you for the moment. Colette will stay and escort Jason back to his room," Dr. Carrington said. "But please don't stay long. It's important Jason not overexert himself."

Yeah, being pushed around in a wheelchair is really exhausting. Jason moved to roll himself closer to Uncle Alexander.

Colette eased him forward. Dad and Della stood at the end of Uncle Alexander's bed.

Uncle Alexander's eyes were closed, his skin pallid, and his hair had been cut like Jason's. A white crust edged the corners of his mouth. The monitors behind him beeped off

91

heartbeats, steady but slow. Bags of fluid, one clear and one golden, dripped into his IV.

"What's the gold-colored stuff?" Jason asked.

"Dr. Carrington requested a specialized blend of vitamins and electrolytes that complement your uncle's DNA," Colette said. "She's hoping to trigger something in his system to stimulate the healing process. But she says it is hard for the body to overcome what the mind has decided."

"She thinks he's given up," Jason said.

"Yes." Colette stepped away from Jason's chair and leaned against the wall near the door.

"If this is the choice he's made," Dad said, "we must respect his wishes."

"I don't believe he'd give up. He wouldn't." Jason gripped Uncle Alexander's forearm. "Hey, Uncle A, it's Jason. You need to get better. You need to wake up."

Jason stared at his uncle's face, watching for a twitch or a tic.

Nothing.

"C'mon, Uncle Alexander. We're all here—me, Dad, and Della. And Della is doing great." Jason nodded at his sister.

"Hey, Uncle Alexander." Della waved even though Uncle Alexander's eyes remained shut. "We hope you get better. But it's okay if you don't want to."

Jason's brows furrowed. "No, it isn't. It isn't okay for you to not get better, Uncle A."

"She means we understand," Dad said. "He's been through so many challenges."

"Maybe you guys should wait out in the hall with Colette." Jason gestured toward the door.

"You must prepare yourself," Dad said. "Death is not far off."

Jason shook his head. "Seriously, Dad. Just wait in the hall, or go back to your rooms and I'll talk to you later." He turned back to face Uncle Alexander.

Dad, Della, and Colette exited.

Jason grasped Uncle Alexander's hand. It was limp and cool to the touch.

"Uncle A, please. Please keep fighting. You've gotta get better," Jason said. "I still need tons of training. And what about Finn? She totally needs you. You have to get better for her."

He scanned Uncle Alexander's face. Still nothing.

"You'll be happy to know you were right about me overtraining, I guess. At least that's what the doc says. When you get better, you can say I told you so. I know you'd like that." Jason said. "And the doc said she'll start me on the Guard serum, so that's good . . . isn't it?"

Jason paused.

"And you could take it, too. We can be like Batman and Robin or something, though I call dibs on Batman. You get Robin." Jason chuckled and cleared his throat when the chuckle morphed to a choke.

Nothing changed in Uncle's Alexander's face. The monitor beeped at the same slow pace.

"Well, I really need you to get better. If you would please—" Uncle Alexander's hand twitched.

"Uncle A? Do you hear me?"

A light pulse pressed into Jason's fingers.

"Seriously, did you squeeze my hand? Do it again." The pulse repeated two more times.

Jason yanked his hand away and pushed back from the bed. "Hey, hey—can anyone hear me? My uncle's waking up." Jason stood.

Colette rushed in. "He's awake?"

Jason dropped back into the chair. "Yeah, he squeezed my hand. Twice. I was talking to him and he squeezed it." He took Uncle Alexander's hand again. It didn't move.

Colette eyed the monitors. "No change in his vitals." She swiped a thermometer across his forehead. "No change in his temperature."

"I swear he squeezed my hand."

Dr. Carrington entered the room and Colette relayed Jason's claims and Uncle Alexander's status.

"So that's good, right?" Jason asked. "He's getting better."

The doctor turned to Jason. "If he squeezed your hand—"

"He squeezed it," Jason said.

"Alright," Dr. Carrington said. "But it was likely nothing more than a reflexive action."

"It wasn't," Jason said. "It was Uncle Alexander talking—er—telling me he's fighting."

She sighed. "I very much hope that's the case, Jason. Your uncle is a valued member of the team." Dr. Carrington handed Uncle Alexander's chart to Colette. "This is enough of a visit for today. Colette will return you to your room now."

Jason touched Uncle Alexander's arm. "I'll be back soon, Uncle A. Keep fighting." He turned to Dr. Carrington. "I can come back, right?"

She hesitated. "As long as you're progressing, yes."

Colette stepped behind Jason's chair and wheeled him into the empty hallway and out of the ICU.

"I guess my dad and Della really did go back to their rooms," Jason said.

"They didn't want to further upset you."

"They wouldn't upset me if they were acting normal," Jason said. "And stop saying Uncle A is done."

"Yes, well, Della also had an appointment for treatment."

"Like a meeting with a counselor?"

"I am not part of Della's team so I am unable to provide specifics," Colette said.

"Well, at least there's one thing here that seems to be working, helping Della get better. So that's good."

Jason paused.

"You believe me about my uncle, right?"

"I believe you felt something, yes," Colette said.

"But you think it was like Dr. Carrington said, just a reflex."

Colette opened the door to Jason's room and wheeled him inside. "Dr. Carrington is a brilliant woman." Colette set the brakes on the wheelchair.

Jason climbed into bed. "I know. I get it." He pulled the covers over his legs. "But I can't give up on him."

Colette reattached the IV. "It's not so much giving up as accepting the way things are." She moved the wheelchair into a corner. "It's important to accept the way things are."

"Sometimes maybe, but not always. Besides, it didn't feel like a reflex," Jason said. "I mean, if it was a reflex, wouldn't it have felt kind of fast? And jerky? Like when doctors tap your knee with that rubber hammer?"

"I don't know," Colette said.

"Look, I'll show you. Give me your hand."

She hesitated.

"It won't hurt," Jason said. "I want to show you what I mean."

Colette placed her hand in his.

"This is what I mean about it feeling jerky." Jason fast-squeezed Colette's fingers two times. "See?"

She nodded.

"But it wasn't like that. Uncle Alexander did this." Jason mimicked the pulse he'd felt from Uncle Alexander's hand. "Feel the difference?" He didn't let go of Colette's hand.

"Yes," she said.

"Do you want me to show you again?" Jason asked, still holding her hand. It was soft and warm.

"Uh, no, that's okay. I understand now."

Colette squeezed Jason's hand a moment then pulled it back. "Do you need anything? Else?"

He shook his head. "No, I'm good."

"Then I'll let you rest. I'll be back later with your lunch."

"Yeah, great. Thanks." Jason smiled.

A faint smile crept onto Colette's face. "You're welcome." She spun and hurriedly left the room.

✻✻✻

Colette didn't bring Jason's lunch. The man who brought it said she was busy with a different assignment.

"Will she bring my dinner?" Jason asked.

"I am not aware of her assignments for the rest of the day. But you will be taken care of," the man said.

"Yeah, okay. Thanks."

"My assignment is complete. Someone else will be assigned to collect your dishes." The man left the room.

Jason took the cover off the food. "I've been upgraded from broth to chicken noodle soup. Good times."

A few minutes later, he pushed away the remains of his lunch. He leaned over, removed his phone from the table next to his bed and unlocked the screen.

No new text messages. No new email. No new anything since they'd arrived at the League.

"What is the big deal about cell phone signals? What am I going to do? Text someone a picture of an Ahool in rehab?" He only half-spoke to himself, knowing the microphone above his head heard everything. He looked up. "I swear I won't send anything that'll go viral, so can I please have a signal?"

He knew he wouldn't get an answer, but he paused anyway.

Nothing happened.

Jason opened a game on his phone and started playing. He'd just cleared one level when the door to his room opened.

The man named Rick peered from the doorway. He wore black dress pants with a white shirt, a red tie with red suspenders, and the same old-fashioned-looking hat. "May I come in?"

Jason shrugged. "Sure." He set his phone in his lap.

Rick pulled a chair close. "How are you feeling?"

"Fine."

"I hope we soon have you feeling better than fine," Rick said. "But in the meantime, I wanted to come by and apologize for not properly introducing myself the other day."

"That's okay. I know your name is Rick, and you're some kind of bigwig around here," Jason said.

"Well, I don't know if I'd put it exactly like that." He held his hand out to Jason. "My name is Rick Shannon. I'm the director of health services for the League."

Jason shook Rick's hand. "So that's why you're all focused on everyone getting their treatments."

"Yes. It's quite important that we do the best we can to ensure our League family is healthy and happy." He leaned back in his chair. "But your family is especially important to me. Your grandfather and I were great friends back in the day."

"Grandpa Tate?" Jason asked.

"The very same." Rick smiled. "We came up through the ranks together, both of us training for the Guards."

Jason sat up higher in his bed. "You're a Guard?"

"Not at present, no. Though I suppose once a Guard, always a Guard. I served in the field for several years and very much enjoyed it," Rick said. "But I also have a gift for medicine, and I worked on research to develop medical advances and therapies, much like your uncle was doing in his lab work."

"And you decided you liked the medicine stuff better than being a Guard?" Jason asked.

"I liked them both," Rick said. "But we'd finished the base serum, and were making huge strides in developing the Guard serum. I believe Dr. Carrington told you about the Guard serum?"

"Yeah, it sounds kinda cool."

"Yes, uh, cool it is. I left the Guards to focus on refining and enhancing that serum, and the team and I had a huge breakthrough some years ago. It's enabled us to magnify the abilities of our Guards tenfold." Rick held his arms wide.

Tenfold? How strong could I be? And how far would I be able to fire my bolts? But Raymond . . .

Jason's attention snapped back to Rick.

"Others on our team have developed derivative serums for various factions," Rick said. "I'm not directly involved in their work, but they're achieving great things for the League."

"So, did you ever see my Grandpa Tate after you left the Guards?" Jason asked.

"Oh yes. Your grandmother, Lena, and my dear Margaret were the best of friends. Tate often brought Lena with him when he came to League headquarters. And we went on holiday together as well."

"You did?"

"Yes, quite often," Rick said. "I'll never forget the time we were visiting Majorca. Tate raved non-stop about your father, whom he'd met when Zachary accompanied your mum home on a break from university." Rick laughed. "The way Tate carried on made it easy for me to taunt him about being more smitten with Zachary than Adrienne was."

Jason looked down and rubbed his arm.

Rick paused. "Jason, I'm sorry about what happened with your mother. It was a great tragedy for many of us, most of all you, and your brother and sister."

"Yeah, kinda sucked," Jason said.

"I don't doubt that in the slightest," Rick said. "I met Adrienne when she was here, training with your uncle and grandfather. She had great potential."

"Did she use the serum?"

"It wasn't ready when she was training. And she declined to use it when it became available," Rick said.

"Why?" Jason asked.

"She said she was strong enough without it and didn't want to risk the side effects."

"What kind of side effects?" Jason remembered Raymond's words about the serum: *The price is too high.*

"The side effects are minimal," Rick said. "There's possible stomach discomfort, headaches, and in rare cases blurred vision. But all side effects resolve with adjustment of the dosage."

"That's it? Nothing else?"

"Correct. We've been quite pleased with the serum, side effects and all."

"And you can fix it so the side effects go away," Jason said.

"As I noted."

"Huh," Jason said.

"Why these questions about the side effects?" Rick asked.

"What? Oh . . ." Jason glanced at his phone. "I just heard people talking, ya know, like, I overheard people, or cryptids maybe, say things about the serum. Like it was tough to take or something."

Rick tilted his head. "You overheard them?"

"Yeah, like on the tour with Colette. There were a lot of people and cryptids everywhere we went, and I heard stuff." Jason swallowed. He didn't want to get Raymond in trouble.

"There's no risk with the serum." Rick's voice was stern.

"No, I totally get that," Jason said. "I probably misunderstood what I heard. You know, feverish or whatever." He swiped at the air.

"Ah, yes." Rick's tone softened. "You were having some difficulties that day."

"Yeah, exactly," Jason said. "It's too bad my mom didn't take the serum. It probably it would have made her better. And maybe less evil."

Rick's shoulders dropped back. "Well, despite how it seems, your mum was anything but evil. She loved you kids a great deal and was always sharing pictures of you with her friends here."

"Seriously?"

"Yes. She was very proud of each of you," Rick said. "But, sadly, she was also mentally ill, and we didn't catch it. I hate myself for missing the signs."

"A lot of people missed the signs," Jason said. "Including me. I should have known."

"You shouldn't have known, and you must stop that thinking. You didn't know what she was dealing with. You cannot blame yourself for even a moment. Do you understand me?"

Jason nodded. "Yeah, but—"

"No buts," Rick said. "It stops now."

Jason nodded again.

"And I'll make you a promise. We will get Della healthy and happy again. She's on her way to a full recovery. And Zachary, too," Rick said. "And in the meantime, I need you to focus on your own health so we can start you on the Guard serum and watch you develop into an accomplished and talented Guard. Agreed?"

"Yeah." Jason smiled. "Yeah, okay. But what about Uncle Alexander?"

Rick looked away then back at Jason. "I assure you we're doing everything we can, and we're not giving up hope. You shouldn't either."

"Finally. Thank you." Jason ran his hand over his spiky hair. "It felt like everyone was already planning his funeral."

"I won't lie to you. I do question if your uncle wants to carry on," Rick said. "But even if he's giving up, it doesn't mean we have to."

"Right. Exactly," Jason said.

"So we'll keep up the good fight."

"Yes." Jason sighed. "Okay."

Rick slapped his thighs and stood. "I should let you get some rest. We'll talk again soon. Oh, and rest assured I've been in touch with your grandmother, Lena, and brought her up to speed. She knows you're in good hands. And I've promised to send a League jet to bring her here, should the situation warrant it."

"Thanks for doing that," Jason said.

"Not at all, not at all. Truth be told, it's been delightful chatting with her again." Rick turned toward the door.

"And oh, hey."

Rick stopped and looked back.

"Are you a Kappa?" Jason asked.

"Why would you ask that?"

"Because of earlier when you said you have a gift for medicine." Jason thought about Haru, his Kappa friend who'd fixed his broken leg, making it stronger than before.

"Ah, of course," Rick said. "No, I'm not a Kappa, but there are Kappas working on my team."

"That's cool."

"Yes. Cool. Very good," Rick said. "Now get some rest. We need you well and strong. I'm confident you'll be one of our best ever."

One of our best ever.

Jason flopped back into his pillows and smiled but the expression soon faded. Was the serum safe?

Jason's mom betrayed them, but he didn't want her to die. He was too weak to save her.

He couldn't let anyone he cared about get hurt ever again. If the Guard serum helped him do that, taking it would be worth any price Jason had to pay.

NINE

Power

The clank of dishes startled Jason awake.

Raymond stood over him. "I was assigned to bring you your dinner. I hope you are feeling rested."

Jason pushed himself up. "Yeah, I'm just groggy. Where's Colette?"

"She has been given different assignments." Raymond raised the back of Jason's bed.

Jason rubbed his eyes.

"Shall I assist you to the bathroom before your meal?" Raymond asked. His back was to the camera.

"I think—"

Raymond's eyes were wide.

Jason cleared his throat. "I think that's a good idea." He pushed off his covers.

Raymond skittered over to the side of the bed closest to the bathroom and held Jason's arm as he swung his feet to the floor. Raymond rolled the IV stand, leading it and Jason into the bathroom, shutting the door behind them.

"Is everything okay?" Jason asked.

"I think they suspect Colette."

"Suspect her of what? Bringing me too much broth? Because she didn't even deliver my lunch today. It was some other dude."

Raymond shook his head. "No, no. It's because she doesn't take the serum. Neither of us does."

"Wait, what? She keeps telling me I should take it. But she doesn't?" Jason asked.

Raymond shut his eyes a moment. "She should not be saying that to you. She knows better."

"Okay, but you don't take the serum. Why do you have to be careful? Why does anyone care if you take your vitamins or not?"

"It is mandatory that everyone take the serum," he said. "And it's not simply vitamins. It settles the mind. It invokes compliance."

"No way."

Raymond listened at the bathroom door a moment. "We're still alone."

Jason shook his head. "Okay, back up. You and Colette don't take the serum, and that's some sort of big secret because it's against the rules. But I still don't get how anyone would know."

'The serum modifies the mind and enables those in power to dictate behavior," Raymond said. "They feed us procedures and the serum locks the mind into following those procedures without question."

"Seriously?"

"Yes. But because we don't take the serum, Colette and I must act as if we are submissive. Only when we are in our private rooms are we able to relax." Raymond rubbed his hands down his face. "Maintaining the ruse is difficult. I fear Colette may have missed something, shown her hand." He slumped against the wall. "I shouldn't have asked this of her. She's so young."

"But wait—how do you even know all this?"

"I used to work in the lab where they developed the serums."

"As a janitor."

"No, as a doctor and researcher," Raymond said. "I realized what we were developing, and I raised my concerns. I was told to stay focused on my work." He sighed. "But when they began distributing the serum, I refused to take it, and I refused to let Colette take it." He pressed his ear to the door again. "I need to go."

"Wait." Jason raised his hand. "They demoted you to janitor because you wouldn't take the serum?"

"That was one of several punishments," Raymond said.

"Like a pay cut too, I guess?"

Raymond stood tall. "The demotion, the pay cut—those were nothing. When the leadership discovered our non-compliance, they ordered Colette be punished as well. They put her arm in a vice and crushed it." A breath shuddered from his lungs. "They left her to suffer, without treatment, finally returning her to me two weeks later." Raymond swallowed hard. "And now I fear she is being punished again."

Jason felt the blood drain from his face. "No, they wouldn't do that . . ."

"They did, and they would do it again." He glanced at his watch. "I've been in this room too long. Don't take the serum. We need your help to get out."

"But—"

Raymond opened the door. "Very good sir, I'll leave you alone. Ring the call button should you need assistance returning to your bed." He closed the door and was gone.

Jason leaned over the sink. He splashed water on his face.

There's no way ... the League wouldn't do that to someone.

He finished in the bathroom and made his way back to bed.

She told me she hurt her arm when she fell.

He swung the attached table over his lap and removed the lid from his food. More chicken noodle soup, plus half of a ham sandwich. His stomach rumbled.

"Uh, thanks for the dinner," Jason said to the microphone. He tried to make his voice sound natural. "Looks great. I like ham."

Jason cringed. *I like ham. Yeah, really natural.* He bit into the sandwich. Tomato squeezed out with globs of mustard and mayonnaise.

He replayed the conversation with Raymond. What did he mean they needed Jason's help to get out? Can't they just quit their jobs and leave?

Dad and Della were acting weird ... but Della was already acting that way before she came to the League.

And, hello, Dad was poisoned and I know how weird that can make people.

Jason didn't want to think about it. He finished his meal and swung the table away from his bed. He feigned sleep until after someone cleared his dishes and shut off the lights in his room. Only the green glow of the nightlight remained.

A few minutes later, Jason slipped out of bed and went into the bathroom, rolling the IV stand next to him. He used the bathroom, washed his hands, and lathered soap to wriggle off the wristband that tracked his movement. He hung the wristband on the IV stand and disconnected the IV from the port on his arm like he'd seen Colette do earlier.

Jason turned off the light and opened the bathroom door. Hunched low, he launched the IV stand into a glide across the floor. It stopped right next to his bed.

I should totally be on the Olympic team for that sport where they slide stuff across the ice.

Jason moved from the bathroom to the side of the metal cabinet. If he could shift it forward a few inches, he could slide behind the cabinet and get to the door without being seen by the camera. Jason wedged one shoulder into the space and pushed. The feet screeched and he stopped, dropping to his haunches. He waited to see if anyone entered his room.

No one came.

Jason examined the cabinet. It was on wheels, but they were locked in place. He searched for a mechanism to release them and found it a moment later. The brake clunked loose. Jason rolled his eyes.

Jeez, not helping with the stealth factor.

He waited again until he was certain no one was coming to check on him. Then he stood, maneuvered the cabinet forward, and slid behind it.

His sleeve caught on the handle of a cupboard built into the wall that had been hidden by the cabinet. The cupboard wasn't big, only about three feet by three feet. Jason made a mental note to check it out later. He freed his sleeve, made his way to the door of his room and inched it open. He slipped into the hall.

Things were much the same as the first time he'd thought about looking around. The lights were on, doors were closed, and no one sat at the nurses station.

What if someone needs help? Are they in a break room or something?

Jason ignored the cameras, hoping whoever watched the feeds only looked at them if they had a reason to. And since his wristband was in his room, no one had any reason to be looking for Jason. He straightened and walked past the nurses station like he knew where he was going.

He tried to remember how to get to the lab. Maybe he could find out more about the serum. He wandered down hallways, then took wrong turns that routed him back to where he'd started. But after a couple more tries, he finally found it. He peered through the window on the door. The lab was empty. And the door was unlocked.

Jason walked along counters that held beakers and spinners and disinfecting ovens. The gear was much like what Uncle Alexander had in his lab back home. One wall was lined with specimens marked with names and collection dates. Several computer screens flashed awake when Jason touched the mouse. A cursor blinked, waiting for a user name and password.

That's no good.

He left the workstation and stepped into a smaller lab set off from the rest. The far wall of this lab was glass, and behind that glass, under refrigeration, were bags of purple serum. Jason scuttled closer. The shelves inside were labeled: Base serum, Guard serum, Cryptid serum. And under Cryptid serum there was Ahool, Kappa, Skyfish, Bigfoot, MDW, and on and on, listing cryptids Jason had learned about, or met, and some he'd never heard of before.

MDW . . . Mongolian Death Worm? Like they need any enhancing. He shuddered at the memory of the acid-spewing creature he'd fought to stop his mom from destroying the Rampart.

Not one label in the case said "Mind controlling serum." Not that Jason expected it would.

Unless they're all mind controlling serums? Jason shook his head. *No. There's no way.*

The door to the lab opened in the other room. Adrenaline shot through his system.

"I want nothing but the best for him." It was Rick's voice. He was headed toward Jason.

He scanned for a hiding place and ducked under a desk.

"When do you think he'll be ready?" a second voice asked. Jason didn't recognize it.

"A few more days."

Rick paused. Jason heard him mumbling, whispering, calculating something.

"Yes, good. We have plenty in stock to maintain our current dosages to the Guards on site, plus add Jason to the regimen," Rick said. "And increase production, as we discussed. I don't want to lose this opportunity with him."

"Yes, sir," the man said. "Though we will need to rush a supply order. As you know, the elements we need are rare. It will be . . . expensive."

"Not an issue. You have my authorization to acquire everything necessary," Rick said.

"You have high hopes for him?" the second man asked.

"I do. In fact, I expect Jason Lex will demonstrate abilities and power like we've never seen before."

Jason pulled in a silent breath and held it.

"Very good, sir. I'll submit the order tonight."

Rick and the man walked away, and the door to the hallway clicked shut.

Jason blew the air from his lungs.

Rick didn't act like his mind was being controlled. Dad and Della were weird but getting better.

But why would Raymond lie? Maybe he was angry about being demoted. Even Colette told Jason to take the serum, so it had to be safe, didn't it?

Jason couldn't believe he was even asking himself the question. There wasn't any such thing as a mind controlling serum. Raymond was making things up. The serum had to be safe.

Jason could handle whatever side effects the serum presented. His powers and abilities would be magnified.

He would never be weak again.

TEN

Believing

Jason returned to his room, slid behind the cabinet, and stopped on the other side, opposite his bed.

Crap. Now how do I get back into bed without being seen?

The path to his bed from where he stood was in the sight line of the camera, as was the view from the bathroom to the bed. Not to mention the fact that the IV stand holding his wristband was next to the bed, not in the bathroom. Any path he chose would be odd since he wouldn't have the IV rolling next to him.

Jason scratched at the tape holding the IV port on his arm. He glanced around, looking for some way to hook the IV stand and roll it toward him but found nothing.

Jason was stuck. There was no foolproof way to get back to his bed with everything in order. He'd have to wing it.

He scooted along the wall and slipped into the bathroom. He used the facilities without turning on any lights. The glow of the nightlight made his face ghostly in the mirror, half reflected in green, and morphing to a monotone of charcoal on the other side.

Jason smeared soap on his wrist to make it slippery for his wristband and grabbed a paper towel. He walked to his bed, slipping his wristband off the IV stand as he passed. He reattached the IV to his arm, wriggled the wristband onto his wrist, and wiped off the soap with the paper towel. He wadded the towel and stuffed it under his covers.

He waited.

At the least he expected someone to come by and ask him why he'd disconnected the IV to go to the bathroom. He was ready with a story about being tired of dragging it around. And he thought they might ask him why his wristband didn't register his movement to the bathroom. He had another story about removing it because it was itchy. He didn't know if they'd believe him, but it was the best he could come up with.

So he waited, ready to tell his stories. But no one came.

After forty-five minutes, Jason was asleep.

"Good morning."

Jason was running with Shay. *Who said that?*

"Time to wake up," Shay said.

Jason stopped running and Shay stopped next to him. *Huh? You talk now?*

Shay pressed her paw onto his foot. "Come now. Wake up."

The image of Shay dissolved. Jason felt his foot being squeezed and moved side to side. He blinked his eyes open.

"There you are," Dr. Carrington said. "Good sleep?"

"Uh, yeah," Jason said.

"Glad to hear it." She swept Jason's forehead and temple with a digital thermometer. "Temp is normal."

"So I'm better. Can I start the Guard serum?" He pushed up to sitting.

"Not quite." Dr. Carrington raised the angle of his bed. "Lie back, please."

He flopped into his pillows. "I feel good. And I'm hungry."

"Yes, well, we rushed things a bit too much before, so we're taking it slow this time. You are still on bed rest." She jotted notes on the digital chart.

Jason huffed but didn't argue.

"I've upgraded your meal plan and we'll see how you do with that. Breakfast should be here shortly." She returned the chart to its hook. "And I assume you'd like to see your uncle this morning?"

"Yeah, definitely," Jason said. "And my dad and Della, too."

"I'm uncertain of their assignments for today but will submit a request for them to visit."

Submit a request?

"Can't I just see them whenever?"

"Both are still in treatment. We don't want to risk backsliding." Dr. Carrington dropped a stylus into the pocket of her white coat.

"But if my dad wanted to reschedule a treatment or something, so he could come see me, he could do that, right?"

"He wouldn't want to do that. He understands his treatment is very important."

"Yeah, but if he did want to, he could change things around, couldn't he? And get his treatment later?" Jason asked.

"That would be highly irregular," Dr. Carrington said. "Rest assured your dad will visit you when it is appropriate for all parties."

The door opened and Colette entered with a tray.

"Here's your breakfast. I'll check in on you later." Dr. Carrington nodded at Colette as she exited.

"Good morning," Jason said. "Are you okay?"

Colette raised her eyes to the microphone above the bed then back to Jason's face. "I am good, thank you." She placed the food on the table and swung it over Jason's lap.

"I'm, um, glad you're good. I was wondering since I didn't see you again yesterday. Thought you might be sick or something." He shook his fork out of the rolled-up napkin.

"I was busy with important assignments. It is my pleasure to serve the League." Colette didn't smile. She moved her hand as if to tuck her hair behind her ear, but her hair was already pulled into a tight ponytail.

She uncovered Jason's food, revealing French toast, bacon, and scrambled eggs.

Jason's mouth watered. "Now this is a good upgrade." The aroma of salty bacon mingled with the sweet of maple syrup.

"I'll return later and take you to your uncle." Colette turned toward the door.

"Wait—can't you stay and hang out or whatever?" Jason asked.

"I have important assignments that must be completed. I will return later." She hurried out of the room.

She's back to being all formal, but at least she's not hurt. Raymond's wrong about this place.

Jason swirled a bite of French toast into syrup pooled on his plate. He put the bite in his mouth. French toast and bacon were favorites, but he had a hard time enjoying the meal. His gut nagged him, telling Jason something was off.

I'm just hungry.

He crunched into a piece of bacon and shoved the feeling aside.

✳✳✳

Colette returned an hour later to take Jason to see Uncle Alexander.

Jason watched how she walked, looking for any sign of injury. He scanned Colette's face and arms to see if anything was different, if there were bruises or marks, but she looked the same.

"So, you're good? For real?" Jason asked.

"Yes. I'm happy to serve the League." She brought over the wheelchair and set the brake. Jason sat. Colette pushed him out of the room and down the hall.

I really don't get why the League makes everyone talk that way.

Colette set Jason's chair next to Uncle Alexander. He was pale, his eyes shut, his heart rate triggering beeps from the monitor that paused too long between beats. Jason again felt Uncle Alexander squeeze his hand, but again the movements were dismissed by medical personnel as a reflex, not a sign of fighting to wake or communicate.

"No, that can't be it." Jason focused on his uncle. "Uncle A, squeeze one time for 'yes' and two times for 'no.'"

Jason felt two pulses.

"But I haven't asked you a question," Jason said. "One for yes, two for no, okay?"

Two pulses from Uncle Alexander's hand.

"Ahhh." Jason let go and gripped the arms of his wheelchair.

"He doesn't understand," Colette said.

"That's just it, I think he does," Jason said. "But I'm confusing him with the way I'm asking questions."

"But his response—" A beep sounded and Colette glanced at the tablet with Uncle Alexander's information. "His time for visitors is finished. I will return you to your room."

"I need a few more minutes," Jason said. "Please."

"It's not possible." Colette returned Jason to his room and left. She reappeared to deliver his lunch, then dinner. Jason tried to talk to her, but she responded only with brief comments about her assignments and her happiness about serving the League.

Colette was definitely more distant. But was she in trouble? Maybe there was a rule that said employees shouldn't talk to patients. Maybe she had been breaking procedure by chatting too much.

Jason didn't need to worry about her. He needed to focus on getting himself and Uncle Alexander better.

✳✳✳

Another day passed with boring meals, an unremarkable visit with Uncle Alexander and his random hand movements, and no visit from Dad or Della.

Dr. Carrington arrived after dinner. "I'm taking you off of the IV tonight, and we'll do a full panel of blood work tomorrow, and then make a decision about next steps."

"Finally." Jason leaned back. "I'm sure it's all good."

"Let's take it one step at a time, shall we?" Dr. Carrington smiled. "I'm confident we'll see good results, and then we'll design a go-forward plan."

A few minutes later, Jason was alone in his room, free of tubes and attachments. A bandage covered the spot on his arm where the IV had been, and the edges of a bruise peeked out.

He switched off the lights, turned on his side and shut his eyes, hoping he'd fall asleep. But his mind was wired, thinking about the Guard serum, thinking about Dad and Della and Uncle Alexander, thinking about Colette, and about the things Raymond had said.

What if there is something bad about the serum? What if Dad and Della are in trouble?

Jason pushed the thought aside. "I'm totally overreacting."

He cringed about saying that out loud. He opened one eye and peeked at the microphone, wondering who'd heard him.

He flipped onto his back. He took deep breaths and held them a moment, then exhaled slowly, following a meditation exercise Uncle Alexander had taught him. Jason hadn't practiced it much, but he remembered the gist of it and hoped it would calm his mind.

It didn't.

Jason didn't want to meditate. He didn't want to read. He didn't want to look at magazines with pictures of British people he didn't know. He needed to move, to do something.

Doctor Carrington said she was happy with his progress. She didn't specifically say Jason had to stay in bed. He pushed the covers off his legs, slipped on his shoes and headed out into the corridor. It was empty except for a squatty round machine floating toward Jason like a hovercraft. Silver letters on the front spelled JaS-8. The machine sprayed fluid then mopped it dry, sprayed fluid then mopped it dry.

It stopped six feet away and a yellow light flashed twice. "JaS-Eight kindly requests Jason Lex to clear JaS-Eight's assigned cleaning area." The machine said JaS like jazz.

"Oh, uh, sorry." Jason stepped to the side so the unit could pass. *How does it know my name?*

"JaS-Eight needs full clearance of the assigned cleaning area."

"Right. Uh, I'll just ... can I walk where you already cleaned?" Jason asked.

"All completed areas are suitable for passage. Floors are free of hazards," JaS-Eight said.

"Okay. I'll head that way then." Jason stepped around the machine. "Thanks, uh, is JaS-Eight your name?"

"I am Janitorial and Sanitation unit number eight. JaS-Eight. Have a nice evening, Jason Lex." JaS-Eight resumed its spraying and mopping.

Jason continued down the hallway. His first stop was in Uncle Alexander's room.

"Hey, surprise, Uncle A. Two visits in one day." Jason took Uncle Alexander's hand in his. "Don't suppose you'd like to wake up and go for a walk with me? I can show you a cool little robot janitor. Who I guess cleans up after the other janitors." He leaned closer and whispered in Uncle Alexander's ear. "I'm being a rebel and wandering around without official approval."

Jason wondered if anyone bothered to listen to Uncle Alexander's microphone since he never talked. But it made Jason feel better to whisper anyway.

A squeeze pressed into Jason's fingers.

"Yeah, Uncle A. Do that again. You're in there, I know it."

Two more squeezes, then another.

Jason tightened his hold on Uncle Alexander's hand. "I'm here, Uncle A. It's Jason. Let's try one for yes, two for no again."

Two squeezes.

Was that random?

"You've gotta get better and this can help."

Two squeezes again. *Seriously? If he's in there, he wouldn't say no to helping him get better.*

Jason removed his hand and wiped his palms down his legs. "Okay, clean slate. You squeeze my hand however you feel like it." He took Uncle Alexander's hand back in his and felt three squeezes.

Three?

A few seconds passed, then four pulses came from Uncle Alexander.

Two, three, and now four. He's counting something like my fingers. Or sheep. But counting was good, right?

Jason opened his mouth to call into the microphone for someone to come to Uncle Alexander's room, but stopped himself. They'd dismiss the pulses like they had before. How could Jason get someone to believe him, and believe in Uncle Alexander?

Rick said he hadn't given up on Uncle Alexander.

"Uncle A, I'm going to get help from someone who cares, who knows us. His name is Rick. He was friends with Grandpa Tate. He wants you to get better as much as I do."

Uncle Alexander squeezed Jason's fingers again, longer and harder.

"I know, I know. He'll make sure you're getting everything you need." Jason removed his hand. "I'll see you tomorrow, Uncle A." He said it loud enough for the microphone to hear.

Jason slipped back into the hallway. He examined a nearby directory. One listing said, "Executive Offices." He tapped the entry and a new window popped up on the display:

What would you like to do?
- *Send a message to Executive Offices*
- *See location of Executive Offices*
- *Get directions to Executive Offices*
- *View business hours of Executive Offices*

Business hours. It was past seven p.m. No way Rick would still be working.

Maybe I can leave him a note.

Jason considered choosing the "send a message" option, but he didn't know who'd receive the message. He needed to be certain he got hold of Rick.

Jason tapped, "Get directions to Executive Offices." A new message appeared: *Directions for Jason Lex to Executive Offices have been sent.*

Huh? Sent where? And how does everyone, or every thing, know it's me?

A moment later, a strip of red lights lit under Jason's feet and ran down the corridor. At the same time, a red light glowed in Jason's wristband.

Cool. And creepy.

He followed the lights, soon turning right, then left, then right one more time into a large alcove. The floor lights faded.

A desk, shaped like a C, sat in front of Jason. A sign on the edge said, "Check-in Here" but there was no pen, no paper, no digital tablet. The desk was practically empty. No computer, no telephone, nothing.

Chairs lined the walls of the alcove, all facing the desk. They were covered in light purple velvet, most of them plain, some with dark purple paisleys. Racks held magazines like the ones Jason had in his room, but here they were in perfect order, alphabetical by title.

There were three offices behind the desk. The center office had a glass wall and a sliding glass door. Etched onto the wall were dolphins jumping over waves. The name on the door said, "Rick Shannon, Director of Health Services."

Jason peered past the dolphins into the office. It was mostly dark. A few dim lights glowed, for security reasons, Jason guessed.

To the left of his view were a couch and four dark purple chairs facing a big screen television. There was a small kitchenette with a sink, espresso machine, and a refrigerator. On Jason's right was the biggest desk he'd ever seen, about ten feet wide and six feet deep. Intricate carvings of waves and dolphins crawled up the legs of the molasses-colored wood and snaked across the front panel. Two light purple, wing-backed chairs sat opposite the corners of the desk, and a low table with similar carvings sat between them. Cabinets and bookshelves made of the same wood covered the wall behind the desk. And windows to the right of the desk chair looked out over the city of London. The London Eye gleamed in the distance below.

Jason pulled on the office door. It slid open.

Yes. Now I need to find a scratch pad or something.

He hustled to the desk and pulled on the drawers. Most were locked, but the center one opened. Inside were paper clips, a stapler, scissors, and a notepad and pens. Jason scratched out a message:

Rick -

Gotta talk to you about Uncle A. He's trying to wake up and he needs your help.

Jason Lex

He placed the note in the center of the desk where it wouldn't be missed when Rick arrived in the morning. Jason returned the pen and pad and shut the drawer.

A light caught his attention. There was a door across the room, to the left of the sitting area. He hadn't been able to see it from outside the office.

The door was ajar, and a light was on inside.

"Hello? Rick?" Jason crossed toward the door. "Sorry to bug you. I didn't realize you were in here."

Jason pushed the door wide. He stepped back.

Rick lay in a hospital bed, his eyes closed. He wore blue scrubs including a blue surgeon's cap on his head. Two tubes were attached to his arm. One flowed blood out of Rick's body into a machine with filters and beakers and a digital display. One of the beakers held clear liquid, another one purple. A tube winding out of the machine delivered processed blood back into Rick's body.

Jason grasped the door handle and inched the door toward him until the gap was the same as he'd found it. He tiptoed backward and moved to exit the office.

"Jason!"

Jason froze.

Rick's voice was tight. Cold.

"I know you're out there," Rick said. "Come here. Now."

Crap.

Jason hurried over, stopping outside the door. "I'm totally sorry. I didn't realize—"

"Come in here."

Jason entered the room. He tried to keep his gaze at the floor but couldn't help glancing again at the machine and the tubes and the bed. "I'm really sorry."

"You're sorry?" Rick asked. "You enter someone's private space, without permission, and you're sorry?"

Jason looked at Rick's face. His brows were furrowed and a deep pink flushed his skin.

"I needed to talk to you. I left you a note about my—"

"Stop." Rick held his hand up. "You have disturbed my treatment. And you will suffer the consequences."

ELEVEN

Stuck

Jason's stomach flipped. "Wait, Rick. I just wanted to leave a note for you. I didn't even think you'd be here."

"Enough." Rick pressed a button on the device filtering his blood. "Return to your room. Do not leave it without permission. We'll discuss this tomorrow."

"But I—"

"Go." Rick pointed at the door.

Jason exited the room and headed toward the sliding glass door. He stopped, darted to Rick's desk and snatched up the note, crumpling it in his hand. He hurried out of the Executive Offices.

Jason barely slept.

What did I do wrong?

What kind of consequences?

What if they won't give me the Guard serum?

He thought about the machine that was attached to Rick. *Is he sick?*

He punched his fist into the mattress.

What if the League makes me leave without Dad and Della and Uncle Alexander?

He pulled a pillow over his face and screamed.

A few hours later, Jason was determined he could explain he'd meant no harm. Rick would understand. He had to, especially after Jason took him to see Uncle Alexander.

Jason was tired of thinking about it. He played games on his phone to distract himself, and wished he could surf the internet. At five-thirty a.m., the door to his room opened.

Rick stood in the doorway. He was still wearing scrubs, but instead of a surgeon's cap, he wore a black baseball cap with the Manchester United logo on the front. He had two bandages on his arm.

Heat flushed Jason's skin.

"May I come in?" Rick asked.

"Sure." Jason clicked off his phone.

Rick switched on the lights and stepped to the side of Jason's bed. "I've come to apologize."

"You have?" Jason's shoulders loosened.

"Yes. I overreacted." He sighed. "Which is not to say your actions are acceptable. They are not."

"I'm sorry. I guess I wasn't thinking," Jason said.

"We have procedures in place for a reason, Jason. They must be followed."

"Okay. It's just, I didn't know I wasn't supposed to leave my room."

The corner of Rick's mouth twitched. "Regardless, I need not have reacted as I did, and for that I apologize." He reached forward to shake Jason's hand.

"That's okay. Thanks," Jason said.

"So, let's start fresh, shall we?" Rick pulled a chair close to Jason's bed. "I understand from Dr. Carrington you've made great progress in your recovery. And I reckon your gallivanting around the League last night is a demonstration of that."

"I wouldn't say I was gallivanting, but yeah, I feel totally better. One hundred percent." Jason scooted to sitting.

"No headaches? No fatigue?"

"None."

"Any stomach issues? You're eating well?" Rick asked.

"Yeah, no problems." Jason leaned forward.

"Well, I will discuss it with Dr. Carrington, but I'd like to get you started on the base serum today, and move you to the Guard serum as soon as we see no ill effects. How do you feel about that?"

Jason smiled. "I'm totally on board."

"Excellent." Rick stood and looked at his watch. "But you must follow Dr. Carrington's instructions to the letter."

"I will. For sure."

"And you must follow all rules and procedures as are outlined by the League. If you are uncertain of the procedures, you must ask someone." Rick's lips tightened.

"I will. Starting with not wandering around after seven p.m.," Jason said.

"So you *did* know that rule."

Jason swallowed. "I . . . did. But I thought it was only for people who worked here."

"You are a Rampart Guard. You work for the League of Governors," Rick said.

"Right. Got it. I will be the best rule follower ever." Jason half smiled, hoping Rick would soften his demeanor.

Rick smiled. "I'd expect nothing less from someone of your caliber." He turned toward the door and stopped. "One more thing. You said you came by my office because of your uncle."

"Oh yeah. He's . . ." Jason's gut fluttered remembering Rick hooked up to those machines. Remembering how angry he'd been. "He's hanging in there. I really think he's going to get better. And I wanted to thank you for believing in him because sometimes it feels like not everyone does. So yeah. Thanks."

"Of course. I want nothing more than to see Alexander get well."

"Me too."

"I best get on with my day," Rick said. "The sooner I have that conversation with Dr. Carrington, the better. We'll talk more later."

"Yep. Later." Jason waved as Rick left the room.

That's a relief.

Jason looked up at the microphone. "I'm excited to start the serum." He turned to the camera and flexed his biceps. "Strong and gonna get stronger." He grinned.

A moment later, he hopped off the bed and made his way to the bathroom. He noticed a piece of paper stuck behind the emergency call button.

He unfolded it.

"Come to the hatch."

What? What hatch?

Jason remembered the cupboard behind the cabinet.

What was Raymond up to now?

Jason turned off the room lights. He moved along the wall and slipped behind the cabinet, out of sight of the camera. He turned the lever on the cupboard door and slid it open. The space inside was dark. There was no shelving, just open space. He leaned in. Small steps led down.

A light flicked on. Jason jumped. Raymond stepped from around a corner.

"Jeez, you scared the crap out of me." Jason forced his voice to a whisper.

"Apologies," Raymond said.

"What is this place?"

"Service passageways. I want to show you something." Raymond gestured for Jason to join him.

"No way. I can't leave my room."

"It's not a problem. No one is assigned to you until six a.m."

"But I promised. And my wristband—"

"I can fix that." Raymond stepped onto the bottom of three steps leading down from the hatch. "Hold up your wrist." He removed a cell phone from his pocket and tapped an app. The next screen looked like the board for a word game. Raymond arranged the available tiles to spell "manumission" and the board dissolved, replaced by graphs and digital readouts. He held the phone over Jason's wristband.

A beep sounded. The screen said: *Access Granted: Jason Lex.*

"Whoa." Jason glanced at his wristband. It didn't look any different.

Raymond tapped more items on his screen. "I'm setting it to override your location data and show you in your room. It will maintain that information until six am when live data will resume. You have to be back to your room by then anyway since someone will check on you at that time."

"Why not take it off and leave it here?"

"Sensors in the wristband register body heat. If it's removed, the data is logged," Raymond said.

"Uh, I took it off the other night when I wanted to look around." Jason scratched underneath the band.

Raymond's eyes widened. "What? Did they come for you?"

"No. Nobody even said anything. But it was late. They must not have noticed."

"That's highly unusual," Raymond said. "They always notice."

"I guess I got lucky." Jason shrugged. "Not that it should be any big deal."

"No, it shouldn't be a big deal. But the League cares very much about what their patients see and do. Their whereabouts are strictly monitored." Raymond tapped a few more items on his screen. "There. I've dimmed the nightlights in your room making the camera less sensitive. We can go."

Raymond moved down and Jason lifted one leg onto the top step, then paused. He'd promised Rick he'd follow the rules, that he'd stay in his room.

"C'mon," Raymond said. "We don't have much time."

"But I . . . I don't want to get in trouble. If I get caught . . ."

"I assure you, no one will know you were missing. And what I have to show you is important. You need to understand what is happening here."

A twinge pulled in Jason's chest. He wanted to go with Raymond, but the promise he'd made to Rick replayed in his head. How could he ignore that? Dad often reminded Jason and his siblings about the importance of keeping promises.

But maybe Raymond will show me something Rick needs to know about. I can tell him I found it on my own and not get Raymond in trouble.

Jason continued through the hatch.

They stood in a passageway with a beige linoleum floor and cocoa-colored walls. Brass sconces hung on the walls, spaced about ten feet apart. They lit as Jason and Raymond walked down the hallway then switched off behind them.

"When the League was built, these passageways were included for certain personnel to move unseen and provide service as needed, and not disturb other parties," Raymond said. "For instance, in the medical wing, supplies and medicines were delivered to rooms through hatches such as the one in your room. This was of particular importance when the patient was in a quarantine situation."

They continued moving through the passage.

"The passageways also provide access to plumbing and utility panels, as needed for maintenance and repair," Raymond said. "This is how I'm able to leave messages for you in your bathroom."

"Like the one I just found, about going to the hatch," Jason said.

"Exactly. Most of the passageways are rarely used now and have been officially sealed off."

Raymond made air quotes with his fingers when he said, "officially."

"Except in the dining areas where the passageways are used to manage events and deliver services. Quite efficient, actually," Raymond said.

"I'm guessing we're not going to the dining area," Jason said. Though he wouldn't have minded getting some breakfast.

"No. We're staying in the medical wing." Raymond turned left.

"How do you have access to these passageways if they've been sealed off?" Jason asked.

"They aren't physically sealed off. But it is official procedure that the passageways should not be accessed. And those on the serum follow procedure."

Right. The mind control thing again.

"And no cameras?" Jason asked.

"Only at the entrances from the main parts of the League. I avoid those."

A moment later, Raymond signaled for Jason to be quiet. Raymond mounted three steps on the right and eased open a door like the one in Jason's room. Jason watched from below as Raymond peered into the room, then leaned further inside. He waved Jason up.

They entered at one end of a large, rectangular room, much bigger than Jason's. There were twenty beds, ten along each side, and every bed was occupied with a sleeping patient.

Raymond whispered. "Stay close to this wall, out of sight of the camera."

Jason nodded. He scanned the room. The beds held both humans and cryptids, and each was hooked up to a machine like the one he'd seen Rick using. "Treatments?" Jason mouthed the word.

Raymond shook his head.

Jason stepped a few feet right to get a closer view of the row of beds. In the bed closest to him was a Wendigo, then an Ebu Gogo, and in the third bed was a Nandi Bear. He'd seen pictures of these cryptids during his studies, but this was the first time he'd seen any of them in the flesh. The rest of the row looked like humans, but Jason knew some cryptids lived in human form, so he couldn't be certain.

The row of beds opposite held a Dover Demon, two humans as far as Jason could tell, then a Yeti whose feet would have hung off the end if it hadn't been given an extra-long bed.

The Yeti's girth blocked Jason's view of the next bed over, but two more down the row held what seemed to be a human man, then a woman.

Wait a minute . . .

Jason stepped forward.

Raymond's arm snapped up and blocked him. "Camera," he whispered.

Jason moved back then sideways closer to the row. He inched up on his tiptoes.

Could it be him?

"I need to get closer," Jason said, his voice a murmur.

"No." Raymond's mouth formed the word. He took Jason's arm and pulled him toward the passageway.

Jason shook his head.

Raymond tapped the time on his phone. It was five-fifty a.m.

Jason rolled his eyes and scrambled through the door and down the steps, Raymond close behind him. He shut the hatch door.

"I need to know who that guy is," Jason said. "In the sixth bed over."

"Hold on." Raymond opened an app. The welcome screen said, "League Medical Unit." Raymond tapped through a few more screens. "Okay, remember this for me: YET0621-70. Got it?"

"YET0621-70, YET0621-70, YET0621-70." Jason nodded and continued repeating the string.

Raymond opened the app he used to change Jason's wristband. He typed in the digits: *YET0621-70*. A rainbow wheel spun and Jason stopped verbalizing the letters and numbers, but they still played on in his head.

The wheel faded and new information popped up.

"I have the patient's name," Raymond said. "It's Sir Bartholomew Ainsworth."

Nausea punched into Jason. "That can't be."

"We have to head back." Raymond started toward Jason's room. "You know him?"

"Yeah, he's Bartie, my uncle's friend, or we thought he was. He attacked us. Dr. Carrington told me the League stopped him, that he was dead." Jason trailed his hand along the wall. "But he's alive, and the League is taking care of him."

"Not taking care of him, Jason. Draining him."

Jason stopped. "What are you talking about?"

"Those machines—they process the biological fluids that contain the source of the individual's powers, stripping it out, and returning diluted fluids to the patient," Raymond said. "The cycle continues until the individual is no longer healthy enough to produce fluids of value." He waved him forward. "We have to keep walking."

Jason met Raymond's pace. "But why strip their power?"

"This is how they make the serums."

Jason swallowed. "So, they're like donors?"

"Not willing donors," Raymond said. "Many in the League who have questioned decisions the League has made, have disappeared or suffered sudden 'accidents.' More often than not they end up here, unconscious and used up until they have no more to give."

"And then the League lets them go?"

"There's nothing left to let go. The remains are incinerated."

They arrived at the steps to Jason's room. It was five-fifty-six a.m. His stomach churned.

"I don't get it. Why is everyone okay with this?" Jason asked.

"This is done in secret. And everyone is on serum so even if they did know, they wouldn't protest. They are compliant."

"So the mind control thing . . . that's really real."

"Yes. Cryptids with the ability of mind control were the first to be captured and drained, and others are being drained even as we speak." Raymond glanced at the time on his phone. "But there's no time to show you more. You must get into your room before the assigned medical technician arrives. Go to the bathroom first, turn on the light as you enter. It will appear to the cameras like you walked there from your bed."

"But . . . I . . ." Jason placed a foot onto the first step. "Why didn't you tell me this before?"

"Would you have believed me if I'd told you without showing you?" Raymond asked.

Jason shook his head. He took one more step and stopped. "What about my uncle? And my dad and Della? And the police? Why haven't you called the police?"

"I suspected they were draining your uncle, but he's not declining at the rate I've seen in others, so I don't know what they're doing with him. But there's no more time to talk now. You have to go." He pushed on Jason's back. "I'll be in touch."

Jason scrambled up the steps and scooted along the wall to the bathroom. He switched on the light as the door to his room opened. He closed the bathroom door behind him and slumped against it.

Every part of him felt heavy.

Are they draining Rick, too?

He dropped his head in his hands. A moment later, he took two deep breaths. He got up, washed his hands, and exited the bathroom.

Colette stood by his bed.

"Good morning." Jason climbed on his bed but didn't get under the covers.

"I'm here to take your vitals." Colette reached a digital thermometer toward Jason's forehead. Her hand quivered.

"Are you okay?" Jason asked.

"I am fine. Your temperature is normal." She tapped on the digital chart.

"That's good. I think."

"Yes. Normal temperature is good," Colette said. "Any indigestion or other issues to report?"

"No. But I am pretty tired." Jason thought he should add something that might dissuade Dr. Carrington from approving the serum. "And now that you mention it, I do feel a little queasy."

"You did not sleep well last night," Colette said.

"Yeah...how did you know that?" Jason's breath shortened. Did they know he left the room after all?

"It is noted on your chart that you were restless, that you moved around a lot."

I'm totally busted. Jason's throat dried.

Colette scrolled through information on the chart. "The only time it seems you slept soundly was from about five-thirty-two to six a.m." She turned the tablet toward Jason. A sticky note on its face read: *Have you seen my father?*

"Uh . . ." Jason nodded. "Yep, that sounds about right."

"Very good," Colette said. "I'll make a note that you confirmed that all is right with the data."

"That works. It's definitely all right." He nodded again.

She sighed. "I will return at seven with your breakfast. You are scheduled to shower now."

"Got it. Will do."

"Okay, uh, thank you." Colette scurried out of the room.

Jason flopped back into his pillows and folded his arms over his eyes. Why did everything have to be so complicated? Colette must have freaked out when she got up this morning and her dad wasn't there. And Jason couldn't do much to help her, to reassure her. He wished he could spend time with Colette like they did during the tour, talk to her more, and ask her what she thought about everything. But all the stupid procedures and cameras and microphones stopped that from happening.

And where were Dad and Della? And why couldn't Uncle Alexander wake up and tell Jason what to do?

He slapped his hands into the mattress and pushed himself up. He needed that shower.

A few minutes later Jason was dressed in a fresh set of blue scrubs. He took his passport holder out of the drawer and removed the coin. The coin was a big reason he and Uncle Alexander had traveled here.

C'mon, do something that tells me what to do next.

The coin sat in Jason's hand looking dull and tarnished. *No help there.*

Jason dropped it into the holder with his passport and hung it around his neck. He didn't think he'd be leaving the League anytime soon, but he liked having his stuff close, even if it was nothing more than a useless old coin.

I've got to talk to Dad again.

The door opened and Colette walked in with Jason's breakfast tray. Dr. Carrington entered behind her.

"Good morning. How is my star patient today?" Dr. Carrington asked.

"I'm really tired," Jason said.

"So I understand from your chart." Dr. Carrington swiped through screens. "Regardless, Director Shannon, like me, is impressed with your progress. He contacted me first thing this morning and suggested you're ready to begin the serum."

"That's, uh, great. But I am really tired so maybe I'm not ready after all."

Dishes clanked as Colette moved plates from the tray to Jason's table.

"One poor night of sleep does not an unhealthy patient make," Dr. Carrington said. "I've ordered your first dose and Colette's brought it with your meal."

Colette swung the table over Jason's lap. He had scrambled eggs, toast with butter and jam, fresh berries, and a plastic cup with two purple tablets. He glanced at Colette and she shifted her gaze to the floor.

"Director Shannon is confident you'll perform well on the serum, and he's excited to get you started," Dr. Carrington said. "We do have one checkpoint to complete first. I'd like you to invoke your powers."

"You mean make my Guard stuff happen," Jason said.

"Exactly. Nothing too strenuous," Dr. Carrington said. "A few blue bolts around your fingertips are acceptable."

So if I can't generate my powers, they'll delay the serum.

"Okay. I mean, it's been a while," Jason said. "But here it goes." He fisted his hands and scrunched his eyes. He grunted and held the position for a few seconds then blew out his breath and relaxed. "Shoot. Let me try one more time." Jason repeated the action, faking the effort and commanding his powers stay dormant. He slackened his muscles. "Wow. I can't do it."

"Hmm. We'll note that on your chart." Dr. Carrington nodded at Colette. Colette picked up the chart and tapped on the screen.

"Does that mean I'm not ready yet?" Jason asked.

"Not at all. We merely needed a baseline for future reference," Dr. Carrington said.

"Oh, that's . . . really good," Jason said.

"Indeed. And now to next steps, Director Shannon asked that I verify you've taken your first dose."

"Okay, well, here it is." Jason picked up the plastic cup and rattled the pills inside. "Consider it verified."

"After you've taken them, yes." Dr. Carrington smiled, but the smile didn't include her eyes.

"I should eat something first though, right? Grandma Lena says it's not good to take medicine on an empty stomach."

"Actually it's preferred that those new to the serum take their first few days of doses on an empty stomach so the serum has limited barriers to entering the bloodstream." She clasped her hands in front of her.

"So you want me to take these pills right now," Jason said.

"I do. Then, after breakfast, Colette will take you to see your uncle." Jason scanned his plate, his napkin, his glasses of water and orange juice, but there was nothing he could do. There was no way to hide the pills and pretend he'd taken them. He popped the pills into his mouth and washed them down with a swig of water.

"Open your mouth, please," Dr. Carrington said.

Jason opened wide like she'd asked him to say "ahhh."

"And lift your tongue."

Jason lifted his tongue.

Dr. Carrington flicked on a penlight and shined it into his mouth.

Guess she doesn't trust me.

She clicked it off. "You've taken the first real step, Jason, and it is a momentous one. Director Shannon and I both believe you'll do very well on the serum this time. Very well indeed." She dropped the penlight into a pocket on her coat.

"What about my dad?" Jason asked.

"Your dad is doing well with his treatments," Dr. Carrington said.

"No. I mean, I want to see him. Today. I want to see him and Della."

Dr. Carrington picked up the digital chart and tapped the screen. She swiped through pages. "Ah. Your father has in fact completed his treatments and is available for a visit. I'll add it to his schedule." She turned to Colette. "After Jason completes his visit with his uncle, please escort him to his father's quarters."

"Yes, Dr. Carrington," Colette said.

"And my sister?" Jason asked.

Dr. Carrington turned back to Jason. "She is still in treatment. A visit is not authorized."

"But—"

Dr. Carrington held up her hand. "It is not possible."

Jason huffed. *Maybe Dad can arrange something.*

"There are three dosages per day for the base serum," Dr. Carrington said. "You'll receive your next dose with your lunch, another with dinner, and so forth. You are to consume the dose before your meal until otherwise instructed. The League member delivering your meals will monitor your dosage and remind you to take the pills before you eat. Do you understand?"

"Yes," Jason said.

"You seem less than enthusiastic about taking the serum. Is there a problem?" Dr. Carrington tilted her head to the side.

"No, no problem. I'm still excited. Super excited," Jason said. "Just really tired, like I said."

"Ah, yes. That is understandable," Dr. Carrington said. "The serum will help with that. You should be feeling better in no time."

"Great. That's really great." Jason picked up his fork. "Is it okay if I eat now?"

"Of course. I'll leave you to it." Dr. Carrington exited the room.

Jason took a bite of eggs, but he wanted to ask Colette what he should do now. He wanted to know how soon he'd start feeling weird or different. He wanted to know how to stop it.

But he was stuck. He bit into a piece of toast.

"I'm going to return the tray to the kitchen," Colette said. "There are extra napkins under your plate." She fast-blinked.

"Thanks, but I doubt I'll need them." Jason stabbed his eggs.

"You might. In case you spill or something."

She blinked at him again.

"Yeah, okay," Jason said.

"I'll be back shortly." Colette picked up the tray and left the room.

Jason poked a strawberry and put it in his mouth. It was bland. *Is the serum changing my taste buds? What if I won't be able to taste anything?*

He dropped his fork, clattering it onto his plate. He rubbed his eyes with the heels of his palms. *How can I stop this?*

Jason dragged his hands down his face and scanned the room for an idea, an answer, something. He found nothing.

He returned his focus to his breakfast and bumped the plate as he reached for his fork. Markings on a napkin underneath peeked out. Jason slid it out further. Written on the napkin was one word: *Bathroom.*

Bathroom? Oh right—I can make myself throw up!

Jason wadded the napkin into his hand. He pushed the table aside and headed to the bathroom, shutting the door behind him. He moved toward the toilet and spotted a small packet on the floor beneath the emergency call button panel. Two words, "Take these," were written on the packet. Inside, Jason found two pills, clear in color, almost like they were made of gelatin.

"Who am I, Alice in Wonderland?" Jason examined the packet looking for anything else that explained what the tablets were and what they did, but there was no more information.

I hope you know what you're doing, Raymond.

Jason tossed the tablets into his mouth and washed them down with water from the sink.

He flushed the napkin and packet, washed his hands, and since he didn't want any more of his breakfast, he brushed his teeth.

Jason pulled two paper towels from the dispenser. *I don't feel any different. Maybe I should still try to make myself throw up.*

A second later, cramps screwed into Jason's gut. He bent forward, bracing his hand against the sink and took a deep breath. The pain subsided and Jason stood.

Maybe that's it. That was way better than barfing.

He turned toward the door. Before he reached the handle, another pang dug into his stomach. It crawled into his chest and choked off his air. Jason buckled. He dropped to all fours, then fell to his side, clutching his belly. The pain moved into his scalp, into his head, and drilled between his eyes. He tried to move, to reach the emergency call button, but the pain intensified. The light faded.

Jason wanted unconsciousness to take him. He wanted the numbness. He begged it to come. But a moment later the dark lifted and the light of the bathroom glared. Rumbles and whooshes sounded from Jason's stomach. It churned into his throat. Saliva flowed and pooled in his mouth, forcing swallows.

A spasm started in his abdomen. Jason scrambled to the toilet and heaved air. Retches jerked through him until finally, the contents of his stomach spewed into the bowl, a muddy mix of purple serum and yellow bile dotted with egg. His body relaxed, the pain waned. Jason slumped against the wall.

He flushed the toilet and watched his first dose of serum wash away.

TWELVE

Serum

Afaint film of purple clung to the toilet bowl. Jason flushed again and watched the film slough off and swirl away.

He placed his hand on the edge of the bowl and pushed himself up. He made his way to the sink where he washed his hands, brushed his teeth a second time, and spit mint foam and vomit aftertaste into the drain. He splashed water on his face.

I hope there's a better way to get out of taking the serum. Don't really want to do that three times a day.

As Jason exited the bathroom, Colette entered his room. She glanced at Jason, then the remains of his breakfast.

"Are you finished with your meal?" she asked.

Jason took a clean shirt out of the cabinet. "Yep. Don't really have much of an appetite." He turned away from Colette, pulled off the soiled shirt and dropped it on the floor.

"Then I will escort you to see your uncle." Colette held the door for Jason.

The medical unit was busy compared to how Jason had seen it in the evening. There were three nurses at the nurses station, one on the phone, one typing something into a computer, and a third organizing items on a cart.

Two people wearing white coats walked past Jason and Colette. And a machine similar to JaS-Eight scooted down the hallway. It had a basket on top that held a stack of manila envelopes and a metal lockbox. But the markings on this machine said MaE-22.

"MaE-twenty-two?" Jason asked.

"Messaging and errands, unit number twenty-two," Colette said. "Not all League correspondence can be done electronically. And it looks like MaE-twenty-two also has a cash box, likely for the dining area."

"Huh. Cool."

They turned toward Uncle Alexander's room.

Jason scanned the walls and ceiling. He didn't see anything that looked like a microphone. "So, hey, can we ever, you know, talk normally?"

Colette's eyes flicked down then back to Jason. "I believe my conveyance of information to you is always normal."

He leaned in and whispered. "I mean without someone listening."

Colette's pace increased. "Yes, you can be certain that all communications are recorded to ensure records are accurate." She didn't whisper. Her voice was almost too loud.

"Oh. Uh, good," Jason said.

A minute later, Jason sat next to Uncle Alexander's bed. He looked the same, though it seemed his hair had grown out a bit, like Jason's.

He grasped Uncle Alexander's hand. "Hey, Uncle A. It's me. Got some squeezes for me?"

Nothing happened.

"You should wake up so you can see your hair. Did I tell you they cut it totally short? Mine too." Jason jiggled Uncle Alexander's hand. "We look way dorky. Want me to get you a mirror so you can see?"

Two weak pulses then a third firmer pulse pressed into Jason's fingers.

Jason smiled. "Yes. G'morning, Uncle A. I hoped the hair thing would get your attention."

Four squeezes this time.

"C'mon, Uncle A. You're doing great."

Four squeezes again.

"That's really good, Uncle A. But you can do better," Jason said. "Do more than squeeze my fingers. How about you open your eyes?"

Uncle Alexander's eyes remained shut and didn't twitch or flick.

"Okay, no eye opening yet. How about more squeezes?" Jason asked.

Four more pulses

"Really good, Uncle A."

"I'm making a notation that he appears to be responding to you." Colette picked up the digital chart hanging on Uncle Alexander's bed.

"Yeah, good."

Another pulse, single this time. Jason squeezed in response.

No response came.

"Uncle A?"

Nothing.

"Okay, maybe you're tired." Jason turned to Colette. "I want to come back this afternoon."

"That should be acceptable. I'll request it be added to your schedule."

"I have a schedule?" Jason asked.

"Everyone at the League has a daily schedule with assignments, treatments, and appointments as necessary. Yours is active now that you are well enough."

Jason shook his head. "Whatever. Okay." He released Uncle Alexander's hand and gripped his shoulder. "I'll be back later, Uncle A. See you then." He followed Colette out of the room.

"I'll take you to your father now," Colette said.

They walked left from Uncle Alexander's room and through an area Jason hadn't seen before. A minute later they passed through double doors and the decor changed from sterile hospital to warm and welcoming. Brown and black carpeting with geometric patterns covered the floor, and the walls were painted pine green. The hallway opened onto a giant atrium with overstuffed couches under real palm trees, bean bags in front of gaming consoles and displays, a swing set and slides enjoyed by kids and adults alike, and an all-glass ceiling with a clear view of blue sky and puffy clouds.

"This is way better than the medical unit." Jason turned as he walked, spotting a food court with booths selling frozen yogurt, pizza, hamburgers, fish and chips, even snow cones. His stomach growled. "Now I'm kind of hungry. Can we get something to eat?"

"We must stay on schedule." Colette kept walking. A woman near the snow cone booth caught Jason's eye. She was talking to another woman that looked like Dr. Carrington.

Grandma Lena?

Jason hurried toward the two women who were walking to one of the League's electric cart transports. "Grandma Lena!" She was too far away to hear him over the rest of the activity. The women stepped into the cart and it zipped away.

Jason stopped. *It couldn't have been her.*

Colette called Jason's name. He turned and hustled back.

"It's important that you stay with me unless otherwise directed," Colette said. "It is procedure."

"Sorry. I thought I saw my grandmother."

"There is no note of visitors on your schedule."

"Yeah, I figured," Jason said. "She must have just looked like her. Like secret twins or something."

"Secret twins?"

"You know how they say we all have someone in the world that isn't related to us but looks exactly like us?"

"No," Colette said.

"Seriously?"

"I have never heard of secret twins." Colette picked up her pace.

Jason fell into step next to her. "Do you ever get to have fun?"

"What do you mean?"

"I mean fun, like hang out here and play video games or swing on the swing. Eat junk food and goof off," Jason said.

"These facilities are for residents only."

"Okay, so you must have a place like this where you live. What about hanging out there? Maybe we can go after I see my dad."

"That is not possible," Colette said.

"Why not?" Jason asked.

"It is not on your schedule." Colette stopped in front of marble steps about twenty feet wide, with a gold handrail running down the middle. "We've arrived at your father's residence."

Twelve steps up were two tall, frosted glass doors, etched with diamond shapes. The doors had gold handles, and gold, swirly lettering above the doors said "The Tower Residences." A doorman wearing a black coat with red trim loomed on the top step. His uniform reminded Jason of the Raven Master.

"How may I help you?" the doorman asked.

"Jason Lex has an appointment to visit his father, Zachary Lex," Colette said.

The doorman held up what looked like a mirror. A second later, Jason's wristband vibrated.

"Jason Lex is cleared to enter," the doorman said.

Colette turned to Jason. "I'll return in thirty minutes to escort you back to your room for lunch and your next dose of serum." A slight frown skipped across her face.

"Why leave? Come in with me," Jason said. "My dad won't care."

"She is not permitted." The doorman slid the mirror-thing into a pocket.

"Says who?" Jason asked. "I permit it, and I know my dad would permit it. She's coming in."

"She will not." The doorman clasped his hands behind his back.

"That's dumb. She—"

Colette touched Jason's arm. "It's okay. Procedure." She removed her hand.

Jason wished she hadn't. "Are you sure?"

"Yes." Colette cleared her throat. "The doorman will direct you to your father's suite. I will return in thirty minutes, but you have sixty available minutes for this appointment, so should you be longer than thirty minutes that is no problem. You will find me here, uh, hanging out."

Jason smiled. "Okay. Thanks." He felt like offering Colette a hug but figured that was against procedure. Besides, he didn't hug girls unless they hugged him first. Except for Della and Grandma Lena. "I'll see ya later."

He walked up the steps, his shoes squeaking on the marble. The doorman opened one of the two towering doors.

"Proceed to the elevators." The doorman gestured across the lobby. A bouquet on a round table in the center of the room made the air fragrant. They were just like the flowers Sadie's grandmother had in her house. "Your father is on floor nineteen."

"What room number?" Jason asked.

"Floor nineteen," the doorman said.

"Will his name be on his door or something?"

"Your father is on floor nineteen." The doorman pressed the up button on the elevator. The gold doors opened and he directed Jason inside.

"Okay . . ." Jason pressed nineteen and the elevator doors closed.

"Welcome to The Tower Residences, Jason Lex. Next stop, floor nineteen."

Jason didn't see any speakers. The elevator's voice seemed to be all around him. "Uh, thanks."

"It is our pleasure to serve the League." The elevator lifted, moving slowly, then slid left, shifting Jason's weight to the right. He grabbed onto a railing.

"Wait, was that supposed to happen?"

The elevator didn't answer. A few seconds later, the car resumed climbing and picked up speed.

Light inside the car brightened. Above him, the ceiling peeled back to reveal a seemingly invisible glass roof. Jason saw nothing but sky.

"What the what?" He gripped the railing with both hands and leaned against the wall. Elevator cables reached a few feet above the car and faded. Beyond that, there was no building, no elevator shaft, no structure. Jason scrunched his eyes. "Seriously, is this supposed to be happening?"

A moment later, the elevator car slowed. Jason kept his eyes shut until the car stopped.

"You have arrived at your destination," the elevator said. "Do you prefer transparent or solid?"

The doors opened and Jason peered down at the ground far below. He remembered the experience on the deck with Colette. "Oh, yeah. Uh, solid. Totally solid."

A patio appeared in front of him leading to a red door with a large brass knocker shaped like the head of a lion. Pots of petunias lined the walkway, and planted on each side of the door were dark green shrubs with orange berries. The shrubs were trimmed into spirals.

Jason stepped out of the elevator. The doors closed and the elevator disappeared. He walked up to the door and clunked the brass circle onto the lion's brass chin.

The door opened. Dad looked at him.

Oh no, he's forgotten me again.

Dad smiled. "Jason."

"Hi, Dad."

"I saw your visit on my schedule and it made my day that much better." He stepped aside and gestured for Jason to enter.

Jason found himself in a living room that flowed into a kitchen as one big space. A veranda opposite the door had views of the ocean. Waves crashed on a sandy shore that wasn't actually there. Salty breezes wafted in through open windows and doors.

"How are you?" Dad asked.

"I'm good. Better," Jason said.

"Rick told me you started the base serum today. That's wonderful news." Dad put his arm around Jason's shoulders and pulled him into a hug.

"Wow, news travels fast." *Does everyone talk about the serum around here?*

"Rick said it was important to keep me informed."

"Rick said it was important?" Jason asked. "You didn't ask?"

Maybe Dad needed more treatment.

"Well, I . . ." Dad's head tipped to the side. "Of course I wanted to be informed. I meant that Rick agreed with me about the importance of keeping me informed."

"Right . . ." Jason glanced around the room. "Nice place."

"Isn't it?" Dad's eyes brightened. "I've always thought it would be lovely to live by the ocean and now I am. It's as wonderful as I imagined."

"Fake ocean," Jason said.

"Doesn't look fake to me. Does it look fake to you?"

Jason shook his head.

"Of course it doesn't," Dad said. "The League takes care of us in the best way. And watch this." Dad cleared his throat. "JaS?"

A panel next to the front door opened and a robot floated out. "JaS-Forty reporting. How may I help, Zachary Lex?"

"Please welcome my guest," Dad said.

The JaS unit turned toward Jason. "Welcome, Jason Lex."

"Thanks, uh, JaS-Forty."

"It is my pleasure to serve the League," JaS-Forty said. "What else can I do to help, Zachary Lex?"

"My bathroom could use some attention," Dad said.

"Very good. JaS-Forty is assigned to clean the bathroom of Zachary Lex." The robot turned and moved down a hallway.

Dad looked at Jason. "Great, right?"

"That is pretty cool," Jason said.

"The League has everything we need."

"Yeah, so you've said." Jason ran a hand through his hair. "Should we sit down or something? Maybe outside?"

"Smashing idea," Dad said.

"Smashing idea? I think you've been here too long." *Or more like you've definitely been here too long.* Jason followed Dad onto the veranda.

"Nonsense." Dad slapped his forehead with the palm of his hand. "Where are my manners? Are you hungry? I have cheese and crackers."

"I could eat. Sure," Jason said.

"Coming right up." Dad spun on his heel and headed into the kitchen.

Jason sat on a lounge chair and stared at the fake ocean. Three pelicans flew low over the water, almost level with the horizon. A boat glided by in the distance, its rainbow sail puffed with air. Crabs skittered across the sand and slipped into small burrows. *How do they make this so real?*

Dad returned and set down a tray with cheese, crackers, apple slices, and two glasses of ice water. He sat on a chair next to Jason's. "So, how do you feel?"

"Dad, you already asked me that. Do you remember?"

"No, no. I mean on the serum. How do you feel on the serum?" Dad asked.

"Oh. Well, I've only had one dose," Jason said.

"Perhaps your system will take a bit longer. I felt immediate positive effects when I started it." He took a sip of water. "I came in feeling terrible. But my jet lag dissipated in what seemed like minutes. My headache faded, my energy increased—it was like magic."

"You had jet lag?" Jason asked. *They didn't tell him about being poisoned?* Jason's heart sank.

"Jet lag combined with stress about getting help for your sister. I was so worried about her," Dad said. "But you're not experiencing any improvements yet?"

"Uh ..." Jason swallowed a bite of cheese. "Actually, I ... am. My stomach hurt this morning, but now it feels better and I'm hungry." He held up a slice of apple. "So that's good, right?" He took a bite.

"Yes, it is. Very good. You'll be on the Guard serum in no time," Dad said.

"Yeah. And Della's a lot better, right? And you're good." *Sort of.* Jason took a gulp of water. "And we'll get Uncle A better soon and then we can go home."

"We'll stay as long as necessary. The League has everything we need." Dad straightened the crackers on the serving plate.

All this League stuff from him is creeping me out. "But what about your job? What about Grandma Lena?"

"Your grandmother is a very capable woman," Dad said.

"Have you talked to her?"

"Rick is keeping her informed about our status and the health of your uncle. Hopefully his situation will be resolved soon and he will no longer be an issue." Dad broke a cracker and put one half in his mouth. "You know, Rick is an old family friend."

"Yeah, I heard." A chill ran up Jason's spine. "When you say Uncle A is an issue to be resolved, you're talking about him getting better, right?"

Dad sighed. "We discussed this already."

"That you believe Uncle A wants to die?" Jason stood. "I don't buy it."

"He's been through many traumatic—"

"Yeah, yeah, I know. And I still don't buy it. He responded to me. I asked him to squeeze my hand, and he did it. Colette even noticed."

"Colette is a young girl with little experience," Dad said.

"That doesn't make sense. Why would the League trust her working in the medical unit then? Do you think she's not qualified?" Jason asked.

"No. That is not the way of the League. Personnel are sufficiently trained and follow procedure." Dad's voice was almost monotone, robotic.

The response sapped Jason's anger. His voice softened. "And does procedure allow for Uncle Alexander to get better?"

"All League members receive world-class care and treatment, ensuring the best possible outcome," Dad said.

"Okay..." Jason took a deep breath. "Dad, how long have you been taking the serum?"

"I have been taking the serum since the moment I arrived. I am happy to serve the League." He took another sip of water and stared at the ocean.

Jason counted off the days in his head. Dad had been here more than two weeks. Jason's wristband vibrated.

Dad stood. "It is time for you to go to your next appointment. Thank you very much for visiting me, son." He directed Jason toward the front door.

"But it's only been twenty minutes," Jason said.

"I have other appointments. It is time for you to go."

A choke caught in Jason's throat. "Seriously, Dad?"

"Thank you for visiting me. This was a good visit. It is time for you to go," Dad said.

Jason swallowed hard. "Okay. Good visit."

Dad pressed a button next to the front door that said: "Call Elevator." A moment later, the elevator appeared.

"Enjoy the rest of your day." Dad held his hand out to shake Jason's.

"Um, you too." Jason shook Dad's hand, then entered the elevator.

Dad turned away as the elevator doors closed on floor nineteen.

✳✳✳

Jason exited The Tower Residences, ignoring the doorman's parting message to "have a nice day." He hurried down the steps and plopped into one of the bean bags at the video game station. He picked up a controller, then dropped it. He didn't feel like playing games.

He watched the front of the residences, waiting for Colette to return. She arrived exactly thirty minutes after she'd left Jason at the door.

Jason stood and waved. "Colette."

She walked over to him. "You finished early?"

Jason kicked a piece of gravel under his shoe. "He didn't really want me there."

"Oh . . . I'm sorry to hear that," Colette said. "Perhaps he needed to focus on his next assignment. Starting a new job requires full attention for optimal performance."

"Wait—what new job?" Jason asked.

"Zachary Lex is the new facilities manager for The Tower division." She paused. "I believe it is a permanent position."

"What?" Jason dropped his face into his hands. "That can't be right. He has a job back home."

A beep sounded and Colette glanced at her cell phone. "Your schedule has been updated. You are to return to your room for your next dose of serum."

Jason jerked his head up. "It's not lunchtime yet."

"Initial doses of serum are escalated when the recipient is not responding as expected," Colette said.

"Meaning I'm not League-y enough . . ." Jason murmured.

"Your responses and behaviors are likely cues." Colette walked toward the medical unit.

Jason didn't budge.

Colette stopped and turned toward him. Her eyes widened, her mouth quivered, and she forced a smile. "Oh, my apologies if I was not clear. Please follow me." Her lips pursed.

She's afraid she's going to get in trouble if I refuse to go. Jason stepped forward and fell into pace by Colette's side. He heard her take a deep breath and blow it out.

Jason's mind raced while they walked. How could he get out of taking the serum? And if he did manage to skip it, how did he need to start acting so no one got suspicious?

Gotta remember to throw out plenty of I-am-happy-to-serve-the-Leagues. And the-League-has-everything-we-need. But what else? He wished he could ask Colette. But he'd be sure to ask Raymond if he saw him again.

I'll go into the bathroom and stick my finger down my throat this time. Or maybe Raymond has more of those magic gelatin pills. The thought triggered a gag in the back of Jason's throat.

Jason and Colette arrived at Jason's room.

A broad-shouldered orderly wearing standard blue scrubs waited next to his bed. He looked more like a security guard than a medical unit worker. "I've been assigned to administer your next dose of serum." He held out a plastic cup with the purple pills.

Jason took them. "Okay, but isn't it supposed to be on an empty stomach? I had cheese and crackers and apples like, maybe twenty minutes ago."

"My assignment states you are to take the tablets upon returning to your room."

"Even though I'm full? I ate a lot." Jason's stomach growled. *Traitor.*

"You will take your dosage now," the orderly said.

Jason tossed the tablets into his mouth.

The orderly handed Jason a cup of water and he drank.

"Open please." The orderly flicked on a penlight like Dr. Carrington had done earlier.

Jason complied and the orderly shined his light in Jason's mouth.

"Lift your tongue."

Jason obeyed.

"I have completed my assignment," the orderly said. "You are to remain in your room until after your lunch is served."

"Okay. Will do," Jason said.

The orderly left. Jason moved toward the bathroom, fighting to keep himself at a normal pace.

"I'm just gonna use the toilet," he said to Colette.

She nodded.

Jason shut the bathroom door and threw himself in front of the toilet bowl. He swiped a finger inside his mouth, between his gums and lower lip. A purple pill he'd managed to hide plopped into the water.

One out.

Jason shoved his index finger into his throat. He gagged but didn't vomit. He gagged himself again, poking his flesh far in the back. His abdominal muscles contracted twice then stopped.

C'mon . . .

He jammed his finger into his throat a third time, forcing his finger deeper and downward. A second later his stomach tightened, his body jerked, and his body heaved.

Chewed cheese and crackers washed into the bowl. Bits of apple floated on top.

But there was no purple pill. There was no purple anything.

Crap.

Jason glanced around the floor searching for a packet of gelatin pills but found nothing.

He slumped against the wall.

The serum was inside Jason, and this time it was staying.

THIRTEEN

Take Down

Jason flopped onto his bed. "I'm screwed." He cringed in the split second he realized he'd said that out loud.

"Is there a problem?" Colette asked.

Jason sat up. "No problem. I meant, uh, about my powers. They aren't working. Super frustrated." His palms heated. Jason took a deep breath and focused, settling his energy.

"But otherwise you're feeling okay?" Colette sat in the chair near Jason's bed.

He spun on the mattress to face her. "I feel about halfway good, ya know?" He raised his eyebrows. "Could be better."

"Yes, I understand." The left corner of her mouth turned up. "Is there anything I can assist you with?"

"Does the League have any magic pills to make me instantly feel all the way better?" Jason asked.

"Unfortunately, the League does not have such things." Colette stood. "I'm sorry I cannot be of help."

"That's all right," Jason said. "The League provides us with everything we need."

What just happened? How did those words come out of my mouth?

A memory flashed through Jason's mind from the day he saw Dad on the deck. Jason had said some things he hadn't consciously thought. And he had serum in his system then, too.

Colette's eyes were wide. "Yes, the League provides and it is our honor to serve."

"I am happy to serve the League," Jason said.

Colette's hand went to her mouth and she adjusted the movement as if to scratch an itch.

Jason shook his head. He didn't mean to say anything about the League. His heart rate spiked. He stared at Colette, afraid to open his mouth, afraid of what might come out next.

Colette glanced at her phone. "I will check on your lunch."

Jason nodded. He lay back on his bed, folded his arm over his eyes, and wondered how much time he had left.

✳✳✳

After lunch, Jason and Colette made a second visit to Uncle Alexander.

"Uncle A," Jason said, "I can't wait anymore. I need you to wake up right now. Right this minute." He grabbed Uncle Alexander's hand. "So we can serve the League together."

No, no, not serve the League. Not serve the League.

Jason clenched his jaw a moment then released it. "Please, Uncle A. I can't do this by myself."

Uncle Alexander squeezed Jason's hand.

"No, just wake up." Jason tightened his hold on Uncle Alexander's hand.

Another pulse from Uncle Alexander.

"No." Jason wanted to snatch his hand out of Uncle Alexander's and yell at him, tell Uncle Alexander he didn't care if he spent the rest of his life in that bed. But a haze washed over Jason and his anger dissipated. Jason added his other hand, holding Uncle Alexander's hand in both of his, and smiled.

"It's okay, Uncle Alexander. You need to heal, and the League will continue to provide you with everything you need, and the best of care." Jason patted his Uncle's hand. "If my schedule allows, I will visit you tomorrow."

Jason withdrew from Uncle Alexander and turned to Colette. "I want to return to my room now."

"Very well," Colette said.

Colette escorted Jason to his room and excused herself to complete other assignments. A short time later, the orderly who administered Jason's second dose of serum delivered a book titled *The League of Governors: A History*. It was Jason's assignment to read the tome.

Jason was reading a chapter about the League's Declaration of Solidarity when Colette arrived with his dinner. He set a bookmark and closed the book.

"The League is a fascinating and impressive organization." Jason swung his table over his lap.

"Yes," Colette said. "We are happy to serve the League." She set a plate of spaghetti and meatballs on Jason's table, along with a salad, garlic bread, a chocolate brownie, and a plastic cup with two purple pills.

"This smells really good." Jason picked up his fork. "And I'm hungry."

"Delivering your meal was my first assignment. But before you can eat, I must monitor your dose of serum to ensure you received it," Colette said.

"Right. Of course." Jason set his fork down and dumped the pills into his palm. He popped them into his mouth and washed them down with water. "All good. See?" He opened his mouth.

Colette switched on a penlight and shined it into Jason's mouth and checked under his tongue. "Very good. You are now free to consume your meal." She eyed Jason's plate.

"What? Is there a hair in it or something?" Jason stirred through the sauce.

"Oh, no," Colette said. "I was ... checking to be certain I delivered all of your meal, and I see you have received everything assigned. I'll leave you now. Someone else will be by later to collect your dishes." Colette turned and hurried out of the room.

Jason was hungry. He dug into the pasta and shoveled in bites as fast as he could chew. He bit into the bread and garlicky butter ran down his chin. He skipped the salad and dove into the brownie, washing it down with water. He pushed the table out of his way and returned to reading about the Declaration of Solidarity.

Two hours later, Jason's eyelids drooped and sleep called. He set the book aside and switched off the light.

Pain stabbed Jason awake. He scrambled out of bed and rushed to the bathroom. He flipped on the light, shut the door and scuttled toward the toilet. Then everything went black.

✷✷✷

Icy water hit Jason in the forehead. "What the?" He swiped at the air trying to block the flow.

"Wake up."

"Huh? Who's there?" Jason forced one eye partway open and shut it again against the glare of the light.

Gushes of water stung his cheek and flowed into his nose. Jason coughed and scrambled to sitting. His legs felt rubbery. "Stop."

"Are you awake?" The voice was deep.

Jason didn't recognize it. He scanned his surroundings. He was alone. "Where are you?"

"How do you feel?" the voice asked.

"Wet. And tired. And kind of grossed out from sleeping on this floor." Jason reached up for a paper towel and dried his face.

"The League requires your participation in a trial of your skills," the voice said.

"What kind of trial? To see how much water I can take up my nose?"

Jason heard something click.

"Jason, it's me, Raymond."

Jason scanned the room again. "Where?"

"I'm inside the utility panel behind the toilet and emergency call button, accessible from the passageway," Raymond said.

"But the water . . . and your voice was weird . . ."

"A squirt bottle to wake you, sprayed from behind the emergency button plate," Raymond said. "And I used a voice modulator. I could not reveal myself until I was certain you were you."

Memories of the purple pills rushed in. "Oh my god, the serum. Did you get it out of my system?" Jason asked.

"Some but not all," Raymond said. "You'll still have urges to comply. You must suppress them."

Jason sighed. "I don't know. Even when I only took one pill, I couldn't control it. It was like I was being inhabited by an evil spirit or something, like in those paranormal investigation shows."

"Hah—that's a fair description," Raymond said. "But you must be strong."

"Okay . . ." Jason pulled tissue from the toilet paper roll and wiped water running out of his nose. "But how did you get me back?"

"It was a risk, for you, and for Colette."

"Wait—what did Colette do?" Jason asked.

"She mixed pills into your food."

That's why she was looking at my plate.

"I was worried," Raymond said. "She could have been caught."

Jason's stomach flipped. "Is she okay?"

"She's fine. I don't know how she got away with it, but she did. Where there is a will, there is a way."

"What do you mean?" Jason asked.

"She was adamant about helping you and would not accept no as an answer," Raymond said. "I liked it better when she was a child, without such determination. She is very much like her mother."

Jason wondered what happened to Colette's mom, but didn't think now was the time to ask.

"But I thought she *wanted* me to take the serum," Jason said.

"After spending time with you, it seems she has changed her mind."

"Oh . . . that's uh, nice of her," Jason said. "So she mixed in more of those gelatiny pills? But I didn't get sick," Jason said.

"Different pills. Experimental. Honestly, I haven't tested it on any human subjects, and I didn't know if you'd survive," Raymond said. "And I'm uncertain if there will be any side effects."

"You guinea-pigged me?" Jason examined his hands and arms, looking for anything that might be different. He rubbed the top of his head and found the same spiky hair as before.

"Yes. Based on my research, I estimated a better than fifty percent chance of success versus inducing death. I figured you'd be willing to take the chance."

"I . . . but . . ." Jason couldn't help anyone as a League-bot, and he hated the idea of being stuck that way. "Yeah, you're right. Thanks. Especially for not killing me."

"Don't thank me yet. I've only bought you time," Raymond said.

"Right. So, I need to get out of here. Get help."

"There's no escaping, Jason. Every door, window, loading dock, even the sewer drains are monitored and guarded. Otherwise, I would have taken Colette and left long ago."

"Can we call the police?" Jason asked.

"No outside calls," Raymond said. "And what would we tell them? Please come to the invisible building above the Tower of London?"

"Yeah, probably not gonna work."

"No. We have only one option," Raymond said.

"What's that?"

"We must destroy the stores of serum. Without consistent dosing, the effects will erode."

Jason scooted closer to the emergency call button. "How are we going to do that? The League must have tons of the stuff."

"No, they don't. Their supply is limited because their number of donors is limited."

"Wait...the donors...I overheard Rick the other night. He authorized some guy to spend whatever it took to get the supplies needed for the serum. He must not have known that meant kidnapping people and cryptids and...and draining them."

"Director Shannon cannot be trusted," Raymond said.

Heat siphoned from Jason's face. "For sure? He knows about all of this?"

"I do not have proof, but I am suspicious of him."

"No. No way. He's being drained like the others," Jason said.

"How do you know that?"

"I found him in his office, hooked up to a machine exactly like the machines attached to the humans and cryptids. The League must have told him it's helping him or something. Like treatment."

Raymond said nothing.

"Are you still there?" Jason asked.

"Yes," Raymond said. "Perhaps Director Shannon is unaware, and is another victim in all of this."

"I think so," Jason said.

"How do you feel? Can you walk?"

"I don't know. I think the pills dissolved the muscles in my legs." Jason stretched his legs trying to relieve the tingle buzzing through them.

"Not medically possible. Stand up," Raymond said.

"Yeah, okay boss man." Jason placed his hands on the edge of the sink.

Raymond chuckled. "It's nice to have you back."

Jason pulled himself to standing and stamped his feet on the floor, testing his balance. "Nice to be back. Let's keep it that way."

"That is my plan," Raymond said. "It's after midnight. We have plenty of time before anyone is scheduled to attend to you. Meet me in the passageway and I'll override your wristband. Then we can go."

"You got it," Jason said.

He was ready to take down the League of Governors.

FOURTEEN

The Governess

Jason and Raymond hurried through the service passageway. "I saw tons of the serum in a lab," Jason said, "in a giant refrigerated case. It was like the frozen food section at the grocery store. It took up the whole wall."

"Do you remember the lab number?" Raymond asked.

"Uh, no. But I saw it that day Colette toured me around. It was near a rehab place."

"Yes, I know the one. That lab stores all of the customized serums," Raymond said. "There is a separate, larger storage facility for the base serum."

"We must protect it for the benefit of the League," Jason said.

Raymond grabbed Jason's arm and pulled them both to a stop. "Jason." He stared into Jason's face.

"I . . . I . . . the League . . ."

"Fight it," Raymond said.

Jason's mind fogged.

Raymond grabbed Jason's shoulders and shook. "Fight it!"

"The serum . . . it makes us stronger . . ." Jason said.

"No! Think of something else," Raymond said. "Your family, your home."

"The League is our family."

"No, no." Raymond shook him again. "Your real family. Like your Dad. Your Uncle."

Family, my family . . . Dad's face blurred in, tried to form, and blurred out.

"Your friends and family at home. They're waiting for you," Raymond said.

Sadie . . . Shay . . . the League . . .

"Me and Colette," Raymond said. "We need your help."

Colette's face formed out of the mist, then Della's, Uncle Alexander's. The dogs, Shay and Finn.

Jason shook his head. "I'm good, I'm good." He rubbed his temples. The fog faded. "I'm okay."

Raymond sighed. "Thank, God."

"That was too weird. And I feel kinda sick." Nausea swished through Jason.

"Your system is trying to purge the foreign matter. And with serum, that's an especially big challenge," Raymond said. "Hopefully it will settle quickly."

"I'm already feeling a little better."

"Good. Though you should be prepared for more such incidents."

"I don't really want to go through that again."

Raymond clasped Jason's shoulder. "But if it does, you know you can beat it."

Jason nodded, but he wasn't certain he could defeat another serum fog.

Raymond slapped Jason's back. "Let's go."

"What's the plan?"

"We'll start with the base serum since that impacts the largest group of the League." Raymond directed them to the right, down another passageway.

"But what are we going to do? Smash everything?" Jason asked.

"Too much noise."

"Well, we can't dump it. Grandma Lena doesn't even let us dump expired aspirin because she says it can affect the water supply or something."

"She is a smart woman, your grandmother," Raymond said.

"So what can we do?"

Raymond stopped next to steps leading to a hatch door larger than others. "We'll use these." Raymond removed two fourteen-inch tube-shaped items from under the back of his shirt. "UV light sticks."

"We're going to give the serum a sunburn?" Jason asked.

Raymond chuckled. "Not exactly." He handed a light stick to Jason. "The serum is produced through biotechnology. Each serum contains microorganisms that deliver the desired effect. UV light kills those microorganisms."

"But the serum, the pills and the liquid stuff, it'll still look the same?"

"Exactly."

"Cool," Jason said. "Let's do it." He started up the steps to the hatch door.

Raymond placed his hand on Jason's forearm. "One more thing. We only have the two UV lights and it takes about ninety seconds to kill the microorganism, so this will not go quickly."

"Okay. We'll just work as fast as we can."

"Start with the tablets. Most of the League receives the base serum in that form," Raymond said. "Then we'll move to the liquid supply, though we may have to come back later to finish it. And then we'll go after the customized serums in the other lab."

"Sounds good." Jason climbed to the hatch and inched it open. He listened for noise or movement and scanned his field of vision. All clear. He slid the hatch door wide and entered the room. Raymond scrambled in behind him.

A refrigeration unit like the one Jason had seen in the other lab covered the far wall. A sign inside the unit said "Base Serum," and each shelf was marked with an expiration date. The walls on either side had three-foot high metal cabinets built into them, but instead of doors, the cabinets had drawers. Each drawer was marked "Base Serum" and also had an expiration date.

In the corner above them was a camera pointing into the room.

"Holy crap, there's a lot of this stuff," Jason whispered.

Raymond nodded. "Stay low. The camera's sight line starts at the top of the cabinets. And we'll go by expiration date, starting with those that expire soonest since those will be distributed first, and then work our way forward."

"The camera will see us pull out the top drawers," Jason said.

"I don't think so."

"Do you know so?" Jason asked.

"I am mostly certain," Raymond said.

Jason rolled his eyes. "How about we start with the lower drawers, then do the top drawers at the end? Then if we get spotted, at least we'll have done all the other tablets already."

"Agreed." Raymond belly crawled to the first cabinet.

Jason scooted behind him, pulling himself forward with his elbows while he held the light stick in his hand.

Raymond slid the first drawer out of its cabinet. Keeping the light sticks facing downward, they switched them on and held the sticks over the batch. Raymond counted off ninety seconds, signaled the time, then slid the drawer back into place. They moved to the next drawer and repeated the process.

Nearly two hours passed and they still had more than half of the drawers to go when a charley horse wrenched into Jason's calf and begged him to stand. He dropped his light stick onto the drawer and dug his fingers into his leg.

"What is it?" Raymond asked, his voice low.

"Cramp." Jason held his breath. He stretched his leg. The pain tightened. A mist washed into his mind.

The serum makes us feel good, makes us strong . . . no, no, no . . .

Jason shifted onto all fours and moved to stand.

Raymond yanked him down. "What are you doing?"

"The serum . . . makes us strong." Jason fought to keep his voice quiet.

Raymond clambered onto Jason's back, pressing him to the floor. He pinned Jason's arms. "Fight it."

Jason rocked, trying to throw Raymond off. The cramp in his calf zipped up his leg.

"No way, my friend. I'm not letting you go that easily." Raymond increased his hold, yanking Jason's arm behind his back.

Pain jabbed in Jason's shoulder.

"Remember your sister, your dad, and your Uncle Alexander," Raymond said, "they need your help."

Flashes of Jason's family formed, then faded. The mist deepened. He writhed under Raymond's body.

"They're draining people and cryptids, Jason. Taking them from their families," Raymond said.

Jason bucked.

"The League took Colette's mother and they hurt her. Don't let them do the same to Colette, to you, to your family." Raymond's voice hissed.

A picture of Jason's mom formed in his mind. She'd hurt Jason, hurt their family, endangered his friends. Jason promised himself he wouldn't let that happen again. He was training hard to protect everyone. He had to be there for them. He had to.

The murk in Jason's mind rippled and dissolved. Calm returned and his body relaxed.

"You back?" Raymond whispered in Jason's ear.

Jason nodded.

Raymond rolled off.

Jason pushed himself up on one elbow. Queasiness swirled through his belly. He closed his eyes and breathed deep.

"Okay?" Raymond asked.

"Yeah. Let's get this done," Jason said.

They finished the rest of the lower drawers and were ready to tackle the top ones.

Raymond hunched low. He wriggled his fingertips under the edge of the drawer and eased it out, balancing it on his palms. He pulled it free and lowered it to the floor for its UV light bath. He used the same method to return the drawer to its spot.

They paused before moving to the next drawer, listening for alarms or approaching steps, ready to rush through the hatch.

No one came. No alarms sounded.

They continued the process on the remaining drawers. Fifty minutes later, all the tablets had been washed with UV light. It was four-thirty a.m.

Raymond tapped his wrist and gestured toward the hatch. Jason thumbed toward the refrigeration unit.

Raymond shook his head and moved toward the hatch.

Jason followed him out of the storage room.

"We can at least start on the liquid stuff," Jason said.

"The medical staff picks up dosages for their patients starting at five a.m." Raymond headed down the passageway. "And we need access to the refrigeration unit without opening the doors— they're in sight of the camera."

"So we're stuck," Jason said.

"Not necessarily. I've been working on a microorganism that might permeate the plastic and attack their counterparts in the serum...but I need to test it..." Raymond kept walking but his eyes were focused on thinking, not direction.

Jason snapped his fingers. "Yo. Are we going the right way?"

"What?" Raymond asked. "Oh, yes. Quite the right way."

"When can we go after the liquid serum?" Jason asked.

"I'm not certain. But we made great progress. Working alone, I've never been able to make a big enough dent in the supply. I need a bit more time to confirm my process will work on the liquid serum, but we're ahead of the game now," Raymond said. "Is the refrigeration unit you saw the same as the unit we saw tonight?"

"Yep."

"Alright. I'll use the time to work on a solution, and you can get some sleep."

"I am kinda tired," Jason said.

"Two nights with hardly any sleep and you're only kind of tired? Ah, I remember those days," Raymond said. "Enjoy them while you can. When you're older, like me, even one night without sleep knocks you on your backside. Today is going to be a slog of a day."

They arrived at the hatch into Jason's room.

Raymond handed Jason a packet with six of the gelatin antiserum pills. "The dose they bring you this morning, and going forward, should be from the supply we treated, rendering it useless. But you'll have these just in case."

"Should I take them after each dose?" Jason asked.

"See how you feel. You know what the effects are like. If you notice a hint of the serum consuming you, take the pills."

"Am I done with the stuff from the serum I've already taken?"

Raymond sighed. "I don't know. This is uncharted territory." He squeezed Jason's shoulder. "But I'm hopeful that is the case."

"Okay. Thanks." Jason tucked the packet into his passport holder, next to the coin. "Oh, and thank Colette for me. I can't do it in person with the cameras and everything. I'm glad she's okay."

"I will do that," Raymond said. "Get some rest."

✷✷✷

"Jason."

He jolted awake.

Colette stood next to his bed.

Tension released his shoulders. "Oh. Hi."

She swiped the thermometer across his forehead. "Your temperature is normal."

"How much longer do we have to keep doing this? Taking my temperature and recording my vitals and making me stay in the medical unit. I'm tired of it. And what time is it?"

"Until Dr. Carrington releases you," Colette said. "And it is seven a.m."

"Wow. A whole extra hour of sleep," Jason said.

"I arrived at six a.m. as assigned, but you would not wake. I requested an extension and it was approved." The door to Jason's room opened and Colette turned toward it. "Your breakfast has arrived."

"Great." Jason's stomach fluttered.

The burly orderly set down the tray and handed Jason his dose. He watched Jason take the pills, examined Jason's mouth, and exited.

Jason tuned into his body. An itch on his scalp, another on his arm. Was it from the serum? His bowels churned. Should he take two of the anti-serum pills?

"Are you hungry?" Colette asked.

"Huh? Oh. Yeah, I am hungry." *Hungry . . . I'm just hungry . . .* He removed the cover from his plate and found an omelet, hash browns, and a bowl of raspberries. He picked up his fork and dug through the berries.

"Do you prefer something else? Do you not like raspberries?" Colette asked.

"No, I uh ... I had a nightmare about raspberries." He stopped messing with the fruit.

Colette's eyebrow lifted on one side. "A nightmare about raspberries." She made a note on Jason's chart.

"Are you seriously writing that on my chart?" Jason asked. "It wasn't all about raspberries. That was just one part."

"It is part of my assignment to note anything unusual," Colette said.

"Aren't all nightmares unusual?" Jason cut off a piece of omelet and ate it.

"And all nightmares are noted," Colette said.

Jason opened his mouth to speak. He looked at Colette, her back to the camera. She mouthed a word: serum. He choked on some omelet and grabbed for his water.

Crap. I'm too normal.

He cleared his throat, took another bite of omelet, then some potatoes.

"Is your breakfast to your liking?" Colette asked.

Jason nodded. "It is delicious. The League provides us with everything we need."

"We are happy to serve the League."

"Yes. Very happy to serve the League," Jason said.

Colette smiled.

Jason pursed his lips and looked at his plate until his smile passed. He continued eating and reminded himself to keep up the act. He couldn't slip up again.

✳✳✳

After breakfast, Jason and Colette visited Uncle Alexander. Like every visit before, Uncle Alexander squeezed Jason's hand. Jason pleaded with his uncle to open his eyes, to do something different, to show Jason he was still in there, but nothing changed. Even the pattern of squeezes was the same.

Jason released Uncle Alexander's hand and slumped in his chair.

"You are unhappy?" Colette asked, her eyebrows raised.

Jason sat up. "No. I know the League provides ... all League members with the best of care. I'm only disappointed that my uncle hasn't gotten better."

Colette sighed. "It is not possible for the League to save everybody."

"I know. I get that. I just thought ..." Jason ran his hands through his hair and looked up at the ceiling. "Maybe I was wrong. Maybe he has given up."

"He has made very little progress during the time you've been here." Colette tapped the screen on Uncle Alexander's digital chart. "There's been no change in brain activity or other vital signs, no indication of healing."

Jason dropped his face into his hands. *How can I do any of this without him? I need his support. I need Uncle Alexander.*

"I apologize," Colette said. "I did not mean to provide information that would upset you."

Jason raised his head. "It's okay. I appreciate all that you and the League have done for my family." He held his breath a moment then released it. He stood. "What's next on my schedule?"

Both of their wristbands buzzed.

She checked her phone. "Our schedules have been updated. We are to report to Sewell Hall for a special event."

"Wait, did you say Sewell?" Jason remembered the name his mom had mentioned, the leader she said she served. His name was Sewell.

"Yes. The Sewell family was part of the original formation of the League of Governors," Colette said.

"Sewell was their last name, not a first name?" Jason asked. "Sewell was their last name." Colette moved toward the door. "We should go."

He followed her. "Are there any Sewells around the League now?"

Colette shook her head. "Not that I know of. The family died out some time ago. Why do you ask?"

"No reason. I'm, uh, curious about the League's history," Jason said. "It's great, great history."

So Mom got the first name of her made-up bad guy from League history. Probably his last name, too. Jason made a mental note to look for the names in *The League of Governors: A History*, when he got back to his room.

Jason and Colette stepped into the corridor. Streams of people merged into the space with them, all of them headed to Sewell Hall.

"I guess this is a big event, huh?" He walked next to Colette, moving closer to her as the hallway filled.

"Yes." Her voice caught in her throat.

"Are you okay?" Jason kept his voice low.

"The special events can sometimes be . . . challenging." She pulled her maimed arm close.

His heart skipped. "Sometimes . . . or always?"

"Sometimes."

"Are they usually good things?" Jason asked.

She gave a slight nod.

"Okay, so this will be a good one," Jason said.

Colette didn't respond.

A moment later they entered a circular corridor, like one found in arenas. Jason followed Colette to a short tunnel and they stepped inside. At the other end, they emerged into cavernous Sewell Hall.

Row upon row of red velvet seats with mahogany armrests circled the arena floor and extended upward, numbering at least two thousand. The ceiling was open to the sky, or it looked that way. In the center of the floor was something under a red velvet tarp, its edges splayed and its center tied to a golden rope running through a pulley. Near the tarp, on carved mahogany chairs, sat five people or cryptids. Jason couldn't tell for certain since they all wore black robes with hoods covering their faces. One of the five, sitting in the middle, sat higher than the other four.

"Who are they?" Jason asked.

"The Council of Five," Colette said.

"And the one in the middle?"

"The Principal Governess. She runs the League. The other four are The Advisors, appointed to assist her."

The Principal Governess. She must be the one who gave the order to kidnap people and cryptids to make the serum.

Jason wished he could get a better look at the Governess, but the hood hid everything. Instead, he watched the flow of League members move into rows and take their seats. He looked for Dad and Della but didn't find them in the throng.

Another minute went by and it dawned on Jason that most of the morning had passed without any signs of the serum in his system. He hadn't had any symptoms, he hadn't had any episodes, not even a hint of fog or mist.

They had done it. Raymond got the serum out of Jason's system, and together they'd deactivated the store of base serum tablets.

Yes. Jason clenched his fist in secret celebration. He couldn't wait to see Raymond and give him the good news.

A gong sounded and the crowd quieted.

The Principal Governess rose, stepped forward, and removed her hood. She had long, red hair and wore a golden band around her head. She opened her arms wide and the crowd exploded in applause. Jason clapped along.

As the applause faded, the Governess turned to The Advisors. They rose and removed their hoods. Applause began again. Each Advisor wore a band similar to the Governess's but silver in color.

What the . . . Jason gaped. He recognized the first Advisor on the left. It was Rick. Jason glanced at Colette. She clapped by patting her good hand against the back of her hand in the sling. But she showed no surprise. She'd already known Rick was one of The Advisors.

The Principal Governess raised her hands skyward. The Advisors clasped their hands behind their backs. The crowd quieted and sat.

"Thank you all for coming here today for this special event," the Governess said. "We appreciate your attendance." Her voice carried as if she spoke into a microphone, but Jason didn't see one.

"It is our honor to serve the League," the crowd said in unison. Jason moved his lips, pretending he was prepared with the phrase.

"As you know, the League provides you with everything you need." The Governess waved her arms above her head. The crowd nodded their heads. "The best work environment," she said, gesturing left. The crowd nodded. "Delicious and nutritious meals prepared by world-renowned chefs," she said, gesturing to the right. The crowd nodded. "Comfortable homes, excellent schools, the pinnacle of medical treatment whenever required." She lowered her hands.

The crowd continued nodding and Jason mimicked their movement.

"You know what the League does for you each and every day because you see it. You experience it," the Governess said. "But today, I want to take the opportunity to show you that our reach extends beyond headquarters, that we provide care and service to all League members. Because all League members are family." She opened her arms.

Applause erupted. Someone behind Jason muttered, "The League is family, the League is great. It is my honor to serve the League."

The Principal Governess waited and the crowd stilled.

"Not long ago," the Governess said, "we had the opportunity to save lives, to restore wholeness and well-being. To even, dare I say, rescue League members from the clutches of evil."

Murmurs rolled through the crowd.

"They came to us from the United States, desperate for care, knowing that the League would provide," she said.

Jason had a bad feeling about what was to come.

"And provide we did," the Governess said. "The League healed them from sickness, set them on the path they were seeking, and it is with great joy that I share with you today that these two members of our League family have decided to stay with us as permanent residents."

The crowd cheered.

"It is my honor to introduce you to Zachary Lex and his daughter, Della Lex!" The Governess joined the applause.

A chill settled on Jason's skin. He watched the tarp, but it didn't move. From a tunnel near The Advisors entered Dad and Della, holding hands.

Colette elbowed Jason. He wasn't clapping. He slapped a fake smile on his face and smacked his hands together.

This can't be real. They can't stay here.

The Principal Governess stepped up to Dad and air-kissed his left cheek, then his right. She did the same to Della. Dad and Della waved to the crowd with both their hands at once. It reminded Jason of gymnasts at the Olympics after winning a gold medal. A second later, their wristbands changed from visitor green to resident black, and the crowd cheered again.

Workers hurried onto the arena floor, placing two chairs off to the side. Dad and Della sat.

"I know you're all as thrilled as I am to have Zachary and Della join us at League headquarters," the Governess said. "But that's not the end of the good news."

A titter arose from the crowd.

"There is one more in our League family who we hope will choose to stay with us, and serve the League at headquarters," the Governess said. "Where are you, Jason Lex?"

Cold sweat flushed over Jason. He couldn't move.

"Jason Lex?" The Governess scanned the crowd.

Colette kept clapping but elbowed Jason for the second time. "Stand up."

"I . . . I . . ."

"Stand up now," Colette said.

Jason pushed himself up.

"There he is," the Governess said. "Please join me down here, Jason."

He glanced at Colette. Her smile was empty. She moved her legs to the side, making it easier for Jason to pass. Others in the row did the same, all of them smiling and clapping.

Jason waved at Dad and Della as he crossed the arena floor. Neither waved back. They smiled and clapped.

He didn't look at Rick. He focused on the Governess and stopped at her side.

"Welcome, Jason," the Governess said. "Thank you for joining me here." She tilted her head and smiled at him, her red hair flowing over her shoulders.

"Uh, it is my honor to be here, and to serve the League," Jason said. The boom of his voice surprised him as it carried through Sewell Hall.

"Share with your League family," the Governess said, "how you came to us at headquarters."

Jason's mind raced. *What do I say? Because we were looking for Dad and Della? No, that won't work.*

"Yes, uh," Jason said, "the League rescued me and my uncle after we were attacked. The League saved our lives."

The Governess clapped and the crowd followed. "Isn't that marvelous?" She spoke over the din and the crowd cheered louder. "Even more exciting is that Jason has healed well enough from his injuries to start the base serum, and will soon begin the Guard serum. Yes, League family, Jason Lex is on a path to become one of our best Rampart Guards."

The crowd launched into a standing ovation. Goosebumps skittered across Jason's skin and he grinned. "I am happy to serve the League," he said.

The applause crescendoed.

Workers added a chair next to Dad and Della. Jason waved to the crowd and sat next to Dad. Dad patted Jason's knee.

"Jason," the Governess said, "please know that all in our League family join me with hope that you will choose to stay with us here at League headquarters."

Jason nodded and smiled, afraid to say anything more.

"Wonderful, wonderful," the Governess said. "This is indeed a moment to be celebrated." She smiled at the Lex family then returned her attention to her audience. "But sadly, our special event today is not just one of celebration."

Dead silence covered the crowd.

Jason looked up into the stands to find Colette. Her seat was empty.

"The Policies and Procedures of the League of Governors is a vital document, and it enables us to deliver the benefits we all appreciate. Because we live by these guidelines, we are happy, we are healthy, we are proud to serve the League of Governors. Are we not?"

"Yes. We are proud to serve the League of Governors," the audience said, again in unison.

The Governess gazed up at the sky, then looked down and clasped her hands. "When one in our family goes astray and does not follow procedure, it pains me. When that League member is offered a second chance but betrays us again, it tears into my soul. And when that same League member drags others into the darkness with them . . ." She fisted her hands and grimaced, then held her fists above her head. Blood streamed down her arms.

What is she doing? Jason looked at the crowd. Their faces showed no surprise.

"This is the ultimate betrayal that cannot go unpunished." Her voice echoed off the walls.

The tarp flew up.

Raymond sat in a wooden chair, held in place by writhing bodiless tentacles. He wore an orange jumpsuit, and he couldn't speak or yell or scream because his mouth was missing, his lips erased, with nothing but smooth skin in its place. He blinked against the sudden light then scanned his surroundings. His gaze locked onto Jason.

Ice sluiced through Jason's veins. *No! No, no, no. This can't be happening.* He looked for Colette. Her seat was still empty.

"Raymond Gardner was a member of our family," the Governess said. "We trusted him. We cherished him. We loved him as we love all the members of our family." She walked forward, moving closer to the audience. Blood dripped from her hands to the floor. "But rather than serve the League with honor, he betrayed us. He disrespected our procedures. He sabotaged our systems." She turned and looked at Raymond. "He destroyed League property."

Oh god, the serum. Jason's mouth parched.

"And this is not his first offense, nor his second," the Governess said. "This is his third and final offense." She walked over and stood before The Advisors. "As punishment, I recommend the execution of Raymond Gardner to be carried out immediately."

What? Execution? No!

"What say you, Advisors to the Principal Governess?" She pointed to the Advisor on the far right.

The Advisor pressed her hands together, as if in prayer. "Your recommendation is wise. Agreed."

The Governess pointed to the next Advisor in the row.

The Advisor pressed his hands together, as if in prayer. "Your recommendation is wise. Agreed."

The third Advisor, who Jason realized was a Beast of Dartmoor, followed suit.

No, no! They can't do this. Rick has to stop it. Jason's breaths were short, almost panting.

Jason stared at Rick. The Governess pointed at him.

Rick pressed his hands together, glanced at Jason, then back to the Governess. "Your recommendation is wise." He paused.

Disagree! Disagree! Stop this!

"Agreed."

FIFTEEN
A Toll Taken

The crowd in Sewell Hall cheered the order of Raymond's execution.

Jason's gut twisted.

Rick didn't stop it. Why didn't he stop it?

Jason turned to his dad. He expected to see shock on Dad's face, outrage at the decision. He expected Dad to stand, to protest, to demand the order be reversed. But Dad remained in his seat, frowning, and clapping his support of the decision.

He wasn't Dad.

Jason's heartbeat battered his chest. His mouth hung open and he looked at Raymond.

Raymond shook his head.

The Governess raised her hands and the crowd quieted. "League family. Raymond Gardner will be delivered to the disciplinary unit where a Genoskwa, a Stone Giant, will carry out the sentence. The Genoskwa's name will be held in anonymity."

Jason racked his brain to remember more about the Stone Giant from his training.

Relative to Sasquatch but bigger ... skin like rock ... and they ... and they ... Oh no.

He shut his eyes and wished he could quash the image, wished he'd never remembered how the Genoskwa kills. But the image of Raymond's head ripped from his body burrowed into Jason's brain.

He had to stop this. He had to save Raymond.

"And it seems we have one more bit of sad business to attend to," the Governess said. "As I mentioned, Raymond not only betrayed the League, he corrupted another within the League family. He corrupted their love for the League."

Oh god, they know I helped him.

Jason's palms heated. He clenched his fists, concealing the bolts, restraining his energy until he had to fight. But how could he win? How could he escape so many humans and cryptids surrounding him?

"But I believe this member of our League family is still good. I believe this member of our League family can be saved. I believe, through our love and guidance, this member of our League family will endure their punishment and come through it stronger on the other side."

Jason braced himself.

"Present the transgressor," the Governess said.

Jason sat rigid and looked for someone moving toward him, but no one came. Faces of the crowd lifted. Jason followed their gaze. An Ahool, its batwings wide, flew in through the open roof and swooped toward the center of the floor. The Ahool retracted its claws and dropped its cargo.

Colette thumped and collapsed on the floor of Sewell Hall.

Jason's muscles jerked.

With her uninjured hand, Colette pushed herself to sitting. She spotted her dad and tears filled her eyes.

"You will stand," the Governess said.

Colette pulled her feet under her, raised herself higher, then crumpled.

Jason shifted forward to help, but Dad braced his hand against Jason's chest, pushing him back in his seat.

Colette propelled herself to standing, and tottered but stayed upright, facing the Governess. Her dark brown hair, usually sleeked back in a ponytail, hung loose and scraggly with a small bunch still snugged in her hairband. She had dirt on her shirt and her sling. She crossed her arms, her uninjured hand cupping the elbow of her injured arm, and stared at the floor.

"Do you know why you stand before us?" the Governess asked.

Colette shook her head.

"You have betrayed the League," the Governess said.

Colette shook her head again. "No, I am honored to serve the League."

"You lie." The Governess crossed her arms.

"It is against procedure to lie about one's behavior, or to betray the League." Colette hiccupped air. "It is my honor to serve the League." She glanced at Raymond.

"You look to your father for comfort, but he brought you to these depths. He corrupted your loyalty."

"No, he—" Colette paused and shifted her gaze from her dad to the Governess. "I am loyal to the League. I am honored to serve the League."

"Nonsense," the Governess said. "Your father committed crimes against the League, the likes of which he could not have completed on his own. You are in a trusted position in the League and have access to areas your father does not. And you are his daughter, and therefore likely to share the damaged genetics susceptible to disloyalty."

Colette cinched her injured arm closer to her body.

"There is no other logical choice," the Governess said. "You have aided in crimes against the League and will be punished."

Raymond yanked against his bindings and shook his head hard and fast. Tentacles wrapped tighter on his arms. Jason's skin flushed and his palms sparked.

The Governess turned to The Advisors. "As punishment, I recommend disfigurement to be witnessed by our League family today in Sewell Hall. Additionally, serum will be withheld to maximize the pain of healing and lessons to be gained therein. What say you, Advisors to the Principal Governess?"

Jason bolted from his chair. "No."

The crowd gasped.

"Take your seat." The Governess scowled. "This does not concern you."

"Yeah, it does." Jason stepped forward. "It's procedure to share information and tell the truth, right?"

The Governess tilted her head. "It is."

"Well, I have information about Colette Gardner that you want to hear. You and The Advisors," Jason said. "It should change her punishment."

"You have my attention," the Governess said.

"The information I have will prove Colette is innocent, but it will also get someone else in trouble. So I need you and The Advisors to confirm Colette will be free to return to her life in the League without any punishment. Same job, same everything. Nothing taken away." Jason glanced at Colette. Her eyes were wide, unfocused.

"Procedure dictates same," the Governess said. "Please proceed."

Jason nodded. "I can prove Colette is innocent because I know who helped Raymond." He swallowed. "It was me. I helped Raymond Gardner betray the League."

The crowd roared.

Raymond's chin dropped to his chest. Dad held his face in his hands and Della patted his back. She frowned at Jason.

The Governess waved her hand and the crowd hushed.

"What you say is the truth?" the Governess asked.

"I have no reason to lie," Jason said.

"But why come forward? Why reveal yourself?"

"Because it's the right thing to do," Jason said. "Colette shouldn't be punished for something I did."

The Governess smiled and spoke to the crowd. "And there, my dear League family, is a sign that Jason Lex still contains the qualities we cherish in our League members. He did what was right. He made a mistake, but he admitted his mistake and can learn from it. Be better. Be stronger. Be forever part of our League family."

Applause abounded.

That's it? Tell the truth and I'm good? Jason blew out a breath and raised a hand to wave at the audience.

The Governess turned to The Advisors. "I recommend the punishment as described for Colette Gardner be rescinded and assigned to Jason Lex."

What? "But I did what was right. I told the truth."

She held up her hand. "What say you, Advisors to the Principal Governess?" The Governess sequentially pointed to the first three Advisors, and each of them said, "Your recommendation is wise. Agreed."

She pointed to Rick. His gaze zeroed in on Jason. Rick's face was stern, his lips tight. Instead of moving his hands into a prayer-like position, he crossed his arms. "Your recommendation is wise. Agreed."

Jason's stomach dropped.

A split-second later, a Yeti appeared at Jason's side and slammed a kick into Jason's leg. Bones crunched, his leg caved, and Jason wailed. He writhed. He looked for his dad. Dad didn't move, didn't help.

"Jason Lex will be taken to the isolation unit where he will be left to heal as his body sees fit," the Governess said. "This concludes our special event. Thank you all for your attendance, and your dedication to the League."

"We are honored to serve the League," the crowd said. Applause sounded.

Jason's vision blurred to splats of white and black. He reached for his leg, but it hurt to move, it hurt to touch, it hurt to think. Someone lifted him onto a gurney. Agony wove into his bones and his skin.

Doorways and faces flashed by as Jason moved through space, bouncing with someone's gait. A voice directed them to a room, he was dumped from the gurney to a cot, and pain swathed Jason like a spider wrapping its prey.

✳✳✳

Jason tried to open his eyes, but light triggered drums in his head. He covered his eyes with his arm and glimpsed his wristband. Still white.

Jason scrambled to sit but stopped when pain jolted through his leg. He forced his eyes open, squinting and blinking against the light. Pounding punched in his belly and churned the contents sour. He swallowed down bile.

He was on a cot with a smashed mattress, a flat pillow, and a skimpy blanket. The walls were cinderblock painted a gloomy gray. A metal nightstand sat next to the cot, and a pair of crutches leaned against the wall. A tray on the floor had a plate with grapes, crackers, and moldy bits of cheese.

"Yeah, not that hungry."

Jason eyed the walls—no hatch door here. But there was a microphone. And a camera. Jason waved and thought about flipping the bird but decided that probably wasn't a good idea. He tucked his hands under the blanket and tried generating his power. His palms warmed but nothing more. He was too weak.

He opened the top drawer in the nightstand. He found his phone— still no signal other than the internal Wi-Fi. No surprise there. He checked the date and time. It was just before noon, but two days had passed since the event in Sewell Hall.

In the second drawer he found his passport holder, still packed with his passport and the Lex coin. The anti-serum pills were gone.

Did they really execute Raymond?

Jason clenched a sob and morphed it to anger. He had to figure out a way to stop this, to get everyone out.

He tried lifting his leg. Pain stabbed into him. Jason took three deep breaths and focused on settling his mind like Uncle Alexander had taught him. Stabs changed to throbs. Jason took three more breaths and the throbs eased. Jason lifted the blanket.

He wore only boxer shorts. His leg was ugly with bruises and blackening, bumps and welts, and his kneecap sat wonky, off-kilter. But there were no protruding bones, his foot pointed the right direction, and his thigh bone was connected to his hip bone.

Jason had broken this leg before, and Haru, a Kappa, had healed it. Since then, the leg had its own super power, able to repair damage that might otherwise need medical intervention, and heal faster than a normal leg. Jason figured another day or two and he'd be able to use it as usual.

But I'll keep that secret to myself.

He did have to do one thing first, to help with the healing. Under the cover of the blanket and out of sight of the camera, Jason pressed his hands on either side of his kneecap. He squeezed his mouth tight and wrenched the kneecap into place.

Jason suppressed a howl, avoiding an alert to anyone listening. Tears streamed from his eyes and Jason focused on calming the pain. A few minutes later, his kneecap throbbed no more than the rest of his damaged leg.

Jason closed his eyes and slept.

The scrape of metal on concrete woke Jason. The tray with the old food was gone. In its place were a ham sandwich, baby carrots, and a cup of applesauce. An empty tin cup lay on its side. It had a piece of tape on it that said, "For tap water."

Jason sat up. The movement brought pain and he cringed. He clenched his jaw and used his hands to help lift his leg off the bed. He grabbed onto a crutch and pulled himself to standing, the change of elevation making him dizzy and sick. He waited a moment then added the second crutch and hobbled to the bathroom.

The bathroom was smaller than the one he had before. The toilet and sink were stainless steel. They reminded Jason of prison cells he'd seen on television shows. But the shower was white, like a thin plastic or fiberglass. It had a metal bar on the wall.

A short lip separated the floor of the shower from the floor of the bathroom, but there was no curtain. An emergency call button was installed between the toilet and sink.

Jason shook off an unbidden memory of Raymond. He had to stay focused.

He used the facilities and returned to the tray. After three tries, he bent and picked up the cup. He left one crutch by his bed, lurched to the bathroom, filled his cup, and carried it back slopping water with each step. He sat on his cot, lifted his leg onto the mattress, and leaned into the wall that served as a headboard.

Healing might take longer than I thought.

A few minutes later, Jason scooted the tray closer, lifted the plate to his lap, and devoured his food.

"Jason, wake up, please."

The voice was familiar. Jason smelled bacon.

"Now, please," Dr. Carrington said. "Wake up."

Jason opened his eyes and shifted his weight. Throbbing thumped in his leg. He winced.

"Still painful?" Dr. Carrington asked.

"Very," Jason said.

"That is to be expected."

"Did you bring me pain medicine?" Jason folded his pillow under his head to prop himself up.

"The objective of the exercise," Dr. Carrington said, "is for the transgressor to experience pain to, one, understand that you have hurt your League family, and two, better value the serum and the gifts it provides."

Some exercise.

"Because the serum blocks pain," Jason said.

"Exactly. And you'll receive your dosages again when the Council of Five deems it," Dr. Carrington said.

Jason figured they must have started manufacturing new doses after figuring out he and Raymond had neutralized their supply of tablets. The last thing Jason wanted was fresh-batch-serum-pills, pain or no pain. The Council of Five could take all the time they wanted.

"If you're not here to give me pain meds, you must be checking to see if I'm still alive," Jason said.

"We knew you were alive. The camera and your wristband tell us that," Dr. Carrington said. "We just want to be certain you're not developing an infection."

"Sounds good to me," Jason said.

Dr. Carrington moved through the drill of temperature, blood pressure, heart rate, and oxygen levels. She asked if Jason had any discomfort in areas other than his leg, she asked about bowel movements, she asked about water consumption.

"Not a lot of water," Jason said. "I spill most of it on the way to the cot, and I'm not going to camp in the bathroom all day in case I get thirsty."

"We can't have that. I'll have pitchers of water delivered with your meals," Dr. Carrington said.

"Great." Thinking about water made Jason notice his dry throat.

"And now I'll examine your leg." Dr. Carrington moved to peel back the blanket.

Jason slapped it down. "I'd rather you didn't. It hurts."

"That is to be expected—"

"No seriously, if you touch it, I think . . . I think the pain will make me throw up," Jason said.

Dr. Carrington huffed. "Well, tell me this. Are there any especially puffy spots? Like abnormal amounts of fluid has pooled under the skin?"

"No," Jason said. "Kind of equally puffy all over."

"Any oozing of pus? Any bones protruding?"

"No."

"Hmm." She tapped on the digital chart.

"What hmm?" Jason asked.

"That leg took quite a bit of force. I would have thought I'd find at least one protruding bone." She said it like she was talking about attending an Easter egg hunt and was disappointed she hadn't found an egg.

"I guess I was lucky," Jason said.

"I'll say. Quite lucky indeed," Dr. Carrington said. "My assignment was to determine if infection was present, not to force you to allow an examination. I'll give you a pass this time. But a close examination will be conducted on my next visit."

"When will that be?"

"It depends on when I am assigned. It likely won't be for another day or two at the earliest," Dr. Carrington said.

"Okay . . ." Jason said. "But maybe you should check my nose while you're here. I keep smelling bacon."

"Oh, I almost forgot." She turned toward the door. "You can come in now."

Colette stepped into the room carrying a tray of food.

"I'll take my leave," Dr. Carrington said.

Colette set the tray on the nightstand.

"Hi," Jason said.

"It's nice to see you again." Colette handed him utensils wrapped in a paper napkin. "I hope you are hungry."

"Yeah, I am. But ... how are you?" Jason asked. "How is—is your dad ... ?"

Colette shifted her stance, placing her back to the camera. She bit her bottom lip and shook her head.

Jason's heart sank.

She took a breath. "I am good, thank you for asking. I am happy to serve the League." She smiled.

Jason copied her. "I'm glad. It's nice to see you again, too." He braced for the pain and pushed to sit higher.

"I'm sorry, I wish I could do something to help you," Colette said.

"No, I'm okay," Jason said. "Food and sleep, and I'll be better soon."

Colette set the tray on Jason's lap. The plate held runny scrambled eggs with bits of bacon, plain white rice and a wedge of cantaloupe.

"What, no fresh berries this time?" Jason asked.

"Your meal is a reflection of your assignment in the medical unit," Colette said.

Do bad things, get bad food. But at least they're feeding me.

"I'm still in the medical unit? I thought I must be in the disciplinary unit." Jason looked at the gray walls. "Or the prison unit, if there is one."

"You are not a prisoner, and are free to move about within the guidelines as outlined by procedure," Colette said.

Jason was surprised to learn his door wasn't locked. Then again, he wasn't about to go for a run or anything.

"Maybe I'll walk around when my leg gets stronger. At least I could walk to rehab."

Colette looked away. "Rehabilitation is not provided with your assigned treatment."

"Okay then," Jason said. "I see how this is going to go." Jason was on his own.

"I must leave to go to my next assignment, but I wanted to thank you." Colette's voice choked. "Thank you for stepping forward, for helping me."

"You're welcome," Jason said.

"I, and the League, appreciate your unselfish act," Colette said.

Jason nodded. He didn't know what to say to make Colette feel better. He didn't know what the League wanted to hear. And he didn't at all feel unselfish.

Colette turned on her heel and left the room.

✳✳✳

The orderly delivered Jason's lunch, clunking it onto the nightstand with a pitcher of water.

"Thanks," Jason said as the door shut.

The orderly didn't respond.

Jason pulled his lunch tray onto his lap. He'd spent most of the morning sleeping, and now his mind was fresh. Active. And lying in bed meant he had a lot of time to think.

He tried a technique of problem-solving that Uncle Alexander taught him. He could almost hear Uncle Alexander's voice in his head: *What do we know?*

Not much.

Jason knew he needed to let his leg heal. And he knew he had to figure out a plan to get his family out, and Colette, too. No way he could leave her here. But how he'd do that he had no idea. Rick wouldn't help him, Dad was being controlled, and Raymond was gone.

I need Uncle Alexander. I wish there was a way to wake him up.

Jason thought about the visits with his uncle, about the fact Uncle Alexander had made zero improvements, about the squeezes of Jason's hand. Jason had been so hopeful Uncle Alexander was in there, that he was fighting.

Jason took a bite of sandwich and chewed. Uncle Alexander's squeeze pattern played in Jason's head. Was it a beat to a song? Was it just something stuck in his uncle's head?

Maybe it was natural reflexes stuck on autopilot.

Or maybe, even in a coma, he's still trying to teach me Morse code.

Jason chuckled then stopped chewing mid-bite. What if it is Morse code?

Jason dropped his sandwich and picked up his phone. He opened the Morse code app Uncle Alexander insisted he download. He remembered telling Uncle Alexander that having an app was another reason not to learn Morse code since it was right there on his phone. Uncle Alexander countered with times Jason wouldn't have access to his phone, like if he had a dead battery and no way to charge it, or if the power grid failed.

"Or if there's a zombie apocalypse and I have to tap out a message to other humans to tell them I'm alive," Jason had said.

Uncle Alexander told Jason that was an excellent example. It wasn't the response Jason expected.

Jason tapped the pattern of squeezes into the app. First was two short, one long. It was the letter U.

U? What word would start with a U?

He tapped in the next set of pulses he'd felt. They indicated the letter P.

U, P. Up? Up . . . start? Upstairs?

Jason typed in the rest of the pattern. If it was Morse code, it spelled out UPCLE. Jason retraced the pattern in his mind, wondering if he'd missed something. Upcle?

Or did he mean "uncle" and I got something wrong? But why would he try to tell me his name? Unless he really is broken.

Jason needed to see Uncle Alexander again, and soon. When the orderly came to clear his dishes, he requested a visit.

"You have no set schedule," the orderly said. "You are free to move about before seven p.m."

"Yeah, but with my leg, it's kinda hard to walk, even with crutches. Can I get a wheelchair?" Jason asked.

"A wheelchair is not approved for you."

"Great," Jason said. "Can I at least get directions to my uncle's room?"

After receiving directions, Jason heaved himself onto his crutches and headed into the corridor.

Five minutes later, Jason was outside Uncle Alexander's door. If he'd been walking normally, he would have made it in less than a minute.

He pulled Uncle Alexander's door open and hobbled to a chair next to the bed.

"Hey, Uncle A, it's me. You've been missing out on all the fun around here." He took Uncle Alexander's hand in his. "But I wanted to come visit you because I think I figured out—"

Jason paused.

"It's just that things have been kind of hard without you, so I wanted to *talk* to you," Jason said.

Three pulses from Uncle Alexander, the same as Jason remembered from previous visits. Definitely the letter U. There was a short pause, then four pulses. The letter P. A longer pause followed.

"So, I'd tell you about the weather, but I have no idea what it is. We're inside all the time. Even when I look *up* and think I see the sky, it's usually fake."

The pulses started again. There was the C, the L, and then the E. Jason had remembered them correctly. More pulses came in patterns Jason hadn't recalled. Next was an A. Jason recognized it without the app. It was an easy one with only a dot and a dash. Next was a dot dash dot. The app told Jason that was an R.

Another longer pause.

"And I guess people even like fake weather to be nice because it's always *clear*," Jason said.

The pulses started again, and again they were new patterns. The letter D, another R, the letter I, another P, and the letter S. The pulses stopped.

Drips? Up clear drips?

Jason eyed the bags of fluid dripping into Uncle Alexander's IV, one golden, two clear. The label on one of the clear solutions read "saline." The other had a string of letters and numbers with a barcode underneath. Jason typed the string into Google.

A message popped up on the screen: *No internet connection. Please check your settings.*

Crap, I forgot.

Is that what Uncle Alexander really wanted? An overdose?

"I . . . so . . . I guess it's better to have the nice weather anyway because rainy and . . . *drippy* . . . weather can make people sad."

The pattern of squeezes started again and ended the same as before. Up clear drips.

Jason slumped. Uncle Alexander had given up. He wanted to die, and he wanted Jason to help him do it.

"I don't like rain when it *drips* all over you," Jason said.

The patterns repeated same as before.

Jason squeezed Uncle Alexander's hand hard.

I guess he's had a lot of time to think about it, lying in that bed for so long . . . and no way he'd want to stay like this forever . . .

"So, well, I'm going to focus on doing some things I think you'd want me to do. Okay?" Jason asked.

One long squeeze pressed into Jason's fingers.

"If I thought you were in there, I'd guess one long squeeze meant a "yes" from you."

The long squeeze repeated.

Jason's throat tightened. "Your pillow's kind of smushed and sliding down. Let me get you another one."

He lumbered on one crutch to the cabinet where he'd seen an extra pillow. He removed it, made his way to the side of Uncle Alexander's bed with the IV stand, and set the pillow on Uncle Alexander's chest. He turned toward the IV unit, now having his back to the camera, and pretended to have trouble leaning his crutch against the IV stand and keeping it balanced. While he fake fumbled with the crutch, he increased the flow on both clear drips. His fingers trembled and he stopped.

Up clear drips, up clear drips. It's what he wants. Jason pushed the flow to maximum.

He turned back to Uncle Alexander. He used one hand to lift Uncle Alexander's head, and the other to slide in the extra pillow. He retrieved his crutch and returned to the chair.

Jason breathed and waited for his pain to pass. After a moment, the pain retreated to a tolerable throb.

He put his hand on Uncle Alexander's arm. "I need to go back to my room and get some rest. But I'll come back and visit again if... I mean, when I can." Tears threatened, but Jason blinked fast and forced them back.

"I'll see ya later," Jason said.

Jason eased himself onto his cot. He pulled his pillow over his face and folded his arms on top of the pillow.

I killed him. I killed Uncle Alexander.

Tears came again. Jason slowed them but couldn't keep them all at bay. The pillow absorbed the stream.

Jason wondered how long Uncle Alexander would last. He couldn't bear seeing him again, but he had to be sure the clear drips stayed at maximum.

I wish I could talk to Sadie about all of this.

Thoughts about what he'd done plagued Jason through the afternoon. He considered going back to Uncle Alexander's room to return the IV to the previous settings. But a stronger instinct stopped him, told him to stay where he was, told him again he'd done the right thing.

✳✳✳

Jason woke the next morning surprised to be spared from jolting pain when he moved his leg. He mounted his crutches and shambled into the bathroom, shutting the door behind him.

He removed one crutch and inched weight onto his injured leg, prepared to quickly shift if the leg protested.

The leg ached, but the pain felt more like a sprain than the distress of major damage.

Now we're talking.

Jason rocked left and right, onto the healing leg and off. The leg tolerated the movement, and it even felt good to engage the muscles and tendons. Healing should be rapid from here on out.

Uncle Alexander flitted into Jason's mind.

No. Not now. I can't think about him. He'd want me to focus on the larger problem.

Jason used the toilet and started toward the sink to wash his hands. A folded piece of paper stuck out from behind the call button. A spike of adrenaline rushed through him. He picked up the note.

Need to talk to you. Meet here tonight at 8 p.m. Destroy this note.

The writing was similar to Raymond's. Could it really be him?

Jason flushed the note.

Maybe Raymond is still alive . . .

SIXTEEN
Seeing Red

The day couldn't go by fast enough. Jason made one quick trip to Uncle Alexander's room to confirm the drips were still set as Jason had left them. They hadn't been changed.

It's like no one is even paying attention to his care.

Jason barely looked at his uncle.

Through the rest of the day, Jason alternated resting his leg with trips to the bathroom where he spent a few minutes stretching the leg, bending the leg, and taking small steps from the shower to the sink. He did it all out of sight of the camera. He also kept his leg covered with pants instead of only boxers. The lesions were fading quickly and he didn't want that noticed on camera either.

The rest of the time, he tried to distract himself by playing games on his phone. And at one point he typed a message to Sadie, knowing it wouldn't go anywhere until his phone connected to the real world somehow: "Hey. This place is the worst ever. Tons to tell you. Uncle A not good. Wish I was home. Give Shay and Finn belly rubs for me."

Finn ... what about Finn? What would she do without Uncle Alexander?

Jason clenched his jaw. He'd take care of Finn. Everyone would take care of Finn. Uncle Alexander knew he didn't have to worry about her.

Jason tapped Send even though he knew the message wouldn't go anywhere until he had a signal. If he ever had a signal.

His dinner arrived at six and his dishes were cleared at six-thirty. Tired from his day of rehab, Jason set the alarm on his phone to vibrate at seven-fifty-eight, tucked it under his pillow and fell asleep.

Bzzz. Bzzz. Bzzz.

Jason shot awake. He reached under his pillow and silenced his phone. He threw off his blanket, affected a struggle to stand with his crutches, and doddered into the bathroom. He used the facilities and waited.

He was leaning on the wall, thinking about how he needed a shower when he heard his name.

"Jason," the voice whispered.

He moved closer to the emergency call button. "Colette?"

"Yes."

"But ... I ..."

"You thought maybe my father wrote the note?"

"Yeah ... I hoped."

"He was executed soon after the event in Sewell Hall," Colette said. "They called me to be a witness."

Jason cringed. "God, I'm so sorry."

"It was—" Colette's voice cracked. "It was really hard." She paused. "But it's done. And he wanted me to be strong. We must carry on his work."

"I don't know how. They must have made fresh serum by now, and I'd guess they've changed security so we couldn't get into the storage room again anyway."

"No, they don't know you deactivated the serum," Colette said.

"But your dad—the Governess said they discovered he'd sabotaged systems and destroyed League property."

"That wasn't about the serum," Colette said. "It was about hacking the League computer network to verify the latest formula."

"He tried to access the League network after we deactivated the serum pills."

"Yes. Before he left, he and I argued. I was so angry that he'd been doing this again after he promised me he wouldn't."

"What do you mean?" Jason asked.

"Trying to escape the League. After my mom was killed, he promised me he'd stop, that he wouldn't put us in danger again," Colette said. "And I told him if he didn't stop, I'd request a new residence, and I'd take the serum so I didn't have to be afraid of losing another parent."

"Wow."

She drew in a breath. "But I shouldn't have done that. I should have helped him. If I'd helped him, he wouldn't have gotten caught."

"You don't know that," Jason said.

"I know computers better than he did," Colette said. "But I refused to go with him."

Jason shook his head. "I totally get how you feel. But he wouldn't want you to blame yourself."

"No," Colette said, "but I do."

She paused.

"And now it's time for me to finish what he started," Colette said. "But first I need to hack into the computers in the lab."

"I'll come with you," Jason said. "I don't want you to go alone."

"I make my own decisions, and I'm going alone," Colette said.

Jason raised his eyebrows and smiled. *Smart and tough. She reminds me of Sadie.*

"Besides, you can barely move, there's no access to the passageways from your room, and there's nothing you can do at the lab. No point in putting us both at risk," Colette said.

"The passageways are still available? The League didn't know Raymond was using them?" Jason asked.

"No, they are safe for use. There aren't any hatches into the computer labs, but I can access one of the labs from underneath the raised floor," Colette said. "It's a confined space too small for my dad, so he tried an override on his wristband. He gained access to the lab from the hallway, but the override triggered alarms and led the League to him."

"He seemed so careful," Jason said.

"Not as careful as he should have been," Colette said.

Jason paused a moment. "You're still not taking the serum?"

"I take it every day, three times a day," Colette said. "And now, like you before your ... transgression ... every dose I take is monitored. But the deactivation worked. The serum has no effect."

"That's awesome." Jason was happy to know they still had one win in the mess of everything else going on. "Are people snapping out of it?"

"There are some tiny indications, but most of these people have been on the serum for a long time," Colette said. "It will take weeks, even months for the serum already in their system to lose its effect."

Jason sighed. "Hopefully we'll figure out something else before everyone gets potent doses again."

"If we can deactivate the liquid supplies, we'll have that much more time since the liquid is used to manufacture the pill," Colette said.

"What can I do?" Jason asked.

"Nothing right now. Besides, your injury is severe."

"Yeah, it's actually not so bad." Jason explained how Haru had made Jason's leg stronger and resilient. "But I'm going to milk it as long as I can so no one pays much attention to me."

"Smart," Colette said. "In the meantime, maybe visit your dad. It's possible the serum may be losing its hold on him since he hasn't been on it that long. Maybe he can help us."

"I'll do that tomorrow." Jason nodded to himself. "And I'll try to see Della, too."

"Ask your father about her, because I'm not certain where your sister is located," Colette said. "Her record is only accessible to high-ranking League members."

"What? Why would that be?"

"I don't know. It's unusual. But maybe your father knows."

"Yeah, I'll ask him," Jason said.

"I'll see if I can find anything on her when I'm on the League network tonight," Colette said. "If I can hack the secure files."

"Just . . . don't do it if it's, ya know, too hard or something and could get you caught," Jason said.

"Don't worry. I know what I'm doing," Colette said. "And I better get going. Wish me luck."

"Good luck, but somehow I don't think you need it." Jason pressed his hand on the wall close to where he heard Colette's voice.

"Hah—thanks," Colette said. "Oh and by the way, it's nice talking to you more . . . how did you call it? Normal?"

"Hey, you are talking differently."

"No microphones, less League-talk. Though I do have to work on it, especially on the League side. I can't let it slip."

"I get that. I'd never be able to pull it off, as you saw," Jason said.

Colette chuckled. "You got better. A little."

"Gee, thanks," Jason said.

"You're welcome. Meet you back here tomorrow night, same time. Good luck with your dad."

Scooting sounded from behind the wall and Colette was gone.

✳ ✳ ✳

Mid-morning the next day, Jason started the trek on his crutches to his dad's residence. The trip didn't hurt his leg as much as it did his armpits. His grimace was real as the crutches pressed into his pits, rubbing them raw. Jason forced himself to keep using the crutches and not take breaks to walk instead.

He arrived at The Tower Residences. The doorman gazed at his mirror contraption and stated Jason had been approved to visit.

Jason hobbled up the marble steps, careful to align his crutches' rubber feet so the sticks didn't slip. But he wasn't careful enough. Jason lost his balance and bumped into the gold handrail. One crutch dug deep in his armpit, like a punch into a bruise. He cringed and grabbed the rail and steadied himself.

A minute later, Jason was in the elevator riding to the nineteenth floor.

Dad opened his front door. "Hello, Jason. Please come in."

No hug, no "great to see you," no "gee I'm sorry you got your leg smashed by a Yeti."

Jason crutched his way into the front room. "Hi, Dad. How are you?"

"I'm very good, thank you. Enjoying another wonderful day living at the League."

This visit is going to suck.

"Great, Dad. That's really great."

"Would you like to sit down?" Dad asked.

Jason nodded and they moved toward the ocean breeze wafting in from the veranda.

"Have a seat and I'll get us some cheese and crackers," Dad said.

Deja vu all over again.

"Would you like some lemonade?" Dad called from the kitchen.

"Sure," Jason said.

"Coming right up."

A moment later, Dad returned with the food and drinks. He handed Jason a glass and sat across from him.

"So, you have a new job?" Jason asked.

"Yes. I start Monday. I'm managing the Facilities for the Tower division," Dad said.

"Which means what, exactly?"

"From heating and cooling, to structural and design needs, I ensure that every section within the Tower is running at peak condition and efficiency."

"That sounds . . . kinda boring," Jason said.

"It's an important position, and I'm honored to serve the League."

"And you quit your old job. Just like that." Jason popped a piece of cheese into his mouth.

"My resignation has been submitted," Dad said. "But what about you? Have you made a decision?"

"About what?" Jason added a cracker to the cheese he still chewed.

"About staying at the League with me and your sister, of course," Dad said. "It was such a joy to see them invite you during the event at Sewell Hall."

Jason swallowed. "You mean before they smashed my leg?"

Dad smiled. "Oh, that was another wonderful moment."

"What?"

"To see you admit the evil you succumbed to, and then see how the League forgave you the way they did." Dad sipped his lemonade.

"Dad, they smashed my leg. Into pieces. And left me without pain medicine."

"It was a kindness on the part of the League," Dad said. "You deserved much worse."

Jason's body tensed. "Can we talk about something else?"

"You haven't made a decision yet?"

"Let's say I'm focused on getting better first," Jason said.

"You know the League has everything you need."

"Okay, so seriously. Let's talk about something else. How is Della?" Jason chomped a cracker.

"Oh, she's thriving. I've never seen her so happy."

"Is she done with her treatment?" Jason asked.

"Her treatment will be ongoing for some time."

"Like how long?" Jason gulped lemonade.

"Until otherwise notified."

I'm so sick of this freakin' League crap.

"What does that mean?"

"The League does their very best for us and will continue to provide the pinnacle of care," Dad said.

Heat flushed through Jason. "Okay, but when is she going to be better? Have you seen her?"

"I saw her at the event, as did you."

Jason scooted to the edge of his seat. "What about before that? Or since then?"

"There is no need," Dad said.

"What are you talking about? Of course, there's a need. You're our dad. You're supposed to spend time with your children." Veins pulsed in Jason's neck.

"The League provides members with everything we need. If Della needs parenting, the League will assign me to assist."

"Assist—what are you saying?"

"You have much to learn about League policies and procedures," Dad said.

"And those procedures say your children don't need you?" Jason asked.

"If I am needed, the League will assign me to assist."

Jason looked up at the ceiling. "Fine. Don't go see Della." His jaw clenched and unclenched. "But I'd like to see her. Tell me where she is."

"I don't have that information," Dad said.

"You what?" Jason jumped up and grabbed his crutches. "Find out where she is. Right now. I want to see her."

"I cannot."

"Dad, stop it. Snap out of it." Jason hobbled a couple of steps toward his father. "You're our dad and you're supposed to take care of us and right now you really suck at it."

"The injury to your leg is causing anxiety," Dad said.

"You know what? This is bullshit." Jason looked out at the ocean view. "That ocean view you love so much? Bullshit. This fancy place you live in? Bullshit. And the League you worship is a bunch of asshats who hurt people and cryptids. But apparently you don't give a rat's ass." Jason pulled the Lex coin out of his passport holder. "And the only reason I'm stuck in this shitty place is because this stupid-ass coin lit up like some bullshit fake firework."

Jason threw the coin. It hit his dad in the chest and dropped into his lap.

"I'm done. I don't need this bullshit conversation, and I don't need this bullshit version of you."

Jason rushed toward the door, his crutches spanning distance and advancing him fast. He pushed the elevator call button and moved onto the patio. A moment later, the elevator doors opened.

"Jason, wait."

Jason ignored his dad and hurried into the elevator. He pressed the button for the lobby and the doors moved to close.

With inches to spare, Dad's hand jammed into the gap and the doors sprang open.

"Son." Dad snatched Jason into an embrace. "I'm so sorry." He whispered near Jason's ear.

"I . . . Dad?"

Dad released the hug. "Please, come back inside."

Jason looked at Dad's hand. He was holding the coin.

It glowed bright red.

SEVENTEEN

Found and Lost

Jason crutched back into Dad's home, Dad close behind him.

"We can talk here," Dad said. "All residences are free of cameras and microphones."

"Good," Jason said. "But why are you . . . you? I mean, you are you, aren't you?"

"Yes, I'm me."

Relief washed through Jason. He hugged Dad again.

"I'm here, Jason. I'm here."

"Finally." Jason stepped back. "Two minutes ago I thought you were locked in by the serum for good."

Dad directed Jason to a seat in the living room. "It was the coin. A moment after you threw it, it flared red. I picked it up and something clicked. Then it felt like fog dissolved all around me."

"That fog might try to come back," Jason shifted in his seat to relieve pressure on his leg.

"I don't think so. Not with a Lex coin on my side," Dad said. "Where did you find it?"

"It was inside one of the rooks of our old chess set. I found it a while ago but threw it in a drawer and forgot about it with everything that happened with Mom. I found it again right before you and Della left for London," Jason said. "I meant to ask you about it that night. After I went to bed, it woke me up, glowing even brighter than it is right now."

Jason glanced at the coin sitting in Dad's hand.

"Fascinating," Dad said.

"You didn't know it was in the chess set?" Jason asked.

"No. I've never seen one of the Lex coins before."

"Uncle Alexander said the coins have the power to communicate with Lex family members," Jason said. "And maybe other magic. But I think it needs to work on the communication part. Glowing isn't exactly helpful."

"I don't know about that. It snapped me out of the serum's control, so the coin seems to have communicated with me pretty well."

"But why does it have to be so complicated? If it's magic, can't it just send me a text message or something?"

"You don't have an internet connection." Dad pressed his lips together trying not to laugh.

Jason rolled his eyes. "The coin is magic. It shouldn't need the internet."

"I guess they didn't plan for that when they created it hundreds of years ago," Dad said. "But if this coin contains the kind of power the legend states, it could be a very good thing to have on our side."

"How do we activate it?" Jason asked.

"There's very little known about the coins, and before you found this one, no one knew for certain they even existed."

"Whatever it is, I'm glad it snapped you out of League-bot mode," Jason said.

"So am I." Dad sighed. "When I think back about everything that's happened . . . your leg . . ." Dad shook his head. "And that poor man . . ."

"Raymond," Jason said. "Raymond Gardner."

"The League ordered Raymond's murder. And we all cheered . . ."

"I didn't cheer." Jason cleared his throat.

"Oh, Jason, my god, what you've been through." Dad moved close and put his hand on Jason's knee. "I am sorry I haven't been there for you."

"It wasn't your fault."

"Regardless, I'm so sorry." He squeezed Jason's knee.

"No, really, I get it. I'm just glad you're here now," Jason said.

"I am here now, and we're all getting out of here," Dad said.

"Including Colette."

"Colette?" Dad asked.

"She's Raymond's daughter. And her mom is gone, too."

Dad nodded. "What about your uncle?"

"It doesn't look good." Jason swallowed. He couldn't bear to tell Dad he'd helped Uncle Alexander end it.

Dad's face fell. "Oh no . . ."

Jason felt his bottom lip quiver. He pressed his lips tighter.

"All the more reason to get out of here so we can find help and stop the League," Dad said. "Your uncle would want that."

"Yeah. Totally."

"I understand the serum is controlling everyone, but I don't know how," Dad said. "Did Raymond tell you anything?"

Jason related everything he'd learned about the serum, about the passageways, the possible way to strip the liquid serum of its power, and about Bartie, and the other forced-donors being used to make it.

"Evil fu—bastards," Dad said.

"I don't know what to do. After a few days on the dead-serum pills, you were still fully-botted. I think it's going to be a long wait for normal."

"I think you're right about that," Dad said.

Jason's stomach growled.

"Let's get some food." Dad made sandwiches and they continued talking about ideas and strategies.

"What about the Governess?" Jason asked. "Is she a cryptid? Does she have any powers?"

"She's human. No powers," Dad said. "And I'm not so sure she's the one in charge. You said Bartie didn't know who was leading the League, right?"

"Yeah."

"The Governess has been in power for years, so Bartie would have known her. But he didn't view her as the real leader, or it seems he would have said so," Dad said.

"Right. So it's not the Governess, and maybe it's not even The Advisors," Jason said. "They could all be under someone else's control."

That's why Rick didn't save Raymond or me. He couldn't.

"Which doesn't help us very much," Dad said.

"Hey—Rick used to work with Grandpa Tate, and he and his wife were friends with Grandpa Tate and Grandma Lena. Maybe the coin would work on him?"

Dad shook his head. "Everything I've ever heard about the coin is that it's attuned to Lex energy only."

Jason's shoulders slumped.

Dad's head canted to the side. "Rick worked with your Grandpa Tate? He said he was an old friend of the family, but I don't recall specifics."

"Maybe he did mention Grandpa Tate, but it didn't click," Jason said. "I mean, you didn't even recognize me when I first saw you."

"I guess it's possible, though I think I'd remember something like that."

"It doesn't matter anyway since he's on the serum. Oh, and I think they're draining him, too," Jason said. "I saw him hooked up to the same kind of machines."

"What about your uncle? Are they draining him?"

Jason shook his head. "I don't think so. All the donors have purple serum bags. Uncle A doesn't." Jason changed the subject. "What about the anti-serum? Colette might have some more of those pills. Maybe we could give Rick some. Somehow. And it might kill him. But maybe?"

"Kill him?" Dad asked.

"It's experimental. But it worked on me," Jason said.

"Has it worked on anyone else? Or the better question is has it killed anyone?"

"No," Jason said. "But I'm the only person Raymond tested it on . . ."

Dad rolled his eyes. "Let's put that idea on the back burner. Ask Colette if she has any pills when you meet with her tonight, then we'll know if it's even an option. In the meantime, I'll see what else I can find out about Rick." Dad held up an index finger. "In fact, as part of my new position, I'll request a meeting with him to discuss the medical unit facilities."

"Okay, but be careful. You still have to be all serum-y," Jason said.

"I've had plenty of practice. I'm confident I can keep up the ruse." Dad looked at the time on his phone. "You should get back, and I have an assignment to attend a meeting with human resources."

"Sounds fun." Jason smirked.

"Like going to the dentist," Dad said.

Jason stood and carried his crutches to the door.

"You're healing fast," Dad said. "Haru?"

"Haru," Jason said.

"Fifty-fifty chance and they picked the right leg." Dad smiled. "But I wish I could have stopped it from happening at all. I wish I could have stopped all of this."

"We'll stop it now, Dad," Jason said.

Dad hugged Jason. "I'm proud of you, son. I'm glad we're back on the same team."

"You don't mind giving up healthy and happy and having all your needs taken care of with the best and the pinnacle and the blah, blah, blah?" Jason smiled.

"Not one bit. Though it also means I have to do my own housekeeping, which I'd rather not." Dad chuckled.

"What does that have to do with anything?" Jason asked.

"The resident JaS units check serum levels of the occupants," Dad said. "They measure it in exhaled breath."

"No way."

"Yeah." Dad nodded. "I'll keep JaS-Forty safely tucked away in its cubby and scrub my own toilet."

"Gross," Jason said.

"Very." Dad called the elevator. "Lunch here tomorrow?"

"Sounds good."

"And here." Dad pressed the Lex coin into Jason's hand. The glow dimmed.

"No, Dad, you keep it."

"No way. It's your coin, not mine," Dad said.

"But—"

"Don't worry. I'm not going to backslide, as the League likes to say. And if by some chance I do, you throw that coin at me again. And harder." Dad winked and opened the front door.

Jason dropped the no-longer-glowing coin into his passport holder. "You got it." He tucked his crutches into his armpits and headed to the open elevator doors.

✲✲✲

A few hours later, Jason met with Colette, again through the wall in his bathroom. He told her about everything that happened with his dad.

"That's great, Jason," Colette said. "I'm happy for you. We need all the help we can get."

"No kidding," Jason said.

"And I do have a few more anti-serum pills. I'll bring them next time I see you."

"Okay good. And try to think of a way we can get Rick to take them," Jason said.

"Yeah, that will be a tough one," Colette said. "Did you visit your uncle?"

Jason paused. "Uh, I didn't see him. He's not doing that great."

"I'm sorry," Colette said. "I know how much you care about him."

"Yeah," Jason said. "But I don't really want to talk about it." He paused a moment. "Were you able to get into the computer lab?"

"I did. The formula hasn't changed, so the idea my dad had should work. We need to release it as a gas into the refrigeration units," Colette said. "But it'll be a few days before we can do anything. I need time to make enough of the formula."

"Can I help?"

"Not really," Colette said. "But Jason, there's something else . . ."

"Did you find Della?"

"Sort of. I mean, I found where she's located, but it's not a part of the League I've ever seen," Colette said. "I didn't even know it existed."

Jason's brows furrowed. "Seriously?"

"Yeah. I'm going to check it out tonight."

"Using the passageways?"

"I'll start there, but I don't know how far I'll get," Colette said.

"I'm coming with you."

"That's a lovely idea, but if you leave your room after seven p.m., the League will be on you in minutes," Colette said.

"Damnit, I wish I had that app your dad used."

"I have the app. But it won't work through the wall," Colette said. "And even if it did, the cameras and any JaS units would alarm in an instant."

"I thought I wasn't a prisoner," Jason said.

"You're not. But you are a transgressor, and you're in a part of the medical unit that is under tighter scrutiny after seven," Colette said. "There's no chance you leave your room without being noticed, day or night."

"But I need to see if Della's okay."

"I'd give her a message for you, but since she's on the serum, I can't even let her know I'm there," Colette said. "If I even find her."

Jason huffed. "I hate this."

"I'll come back tonight and tell you what I find out," Colette said.

Jason thought for a moment. "Hold on a sec."

I wonder if that would work?

"What kind of space are you in right now?" Jason asked. "Are you in one of those maintenance spaces? Close to the plumbing and electricity and stuff?"

"Yes," Colette said.

"Can you see the other side of the shower insert in my bathroom?" Jason tapped on the shower wall. "Right there. Is that exposed on your side?"

"Yeah. All the plumbing runs along there, up to your shower head and such," Colette said.

"Okay, I want you to get out."

"Excuse me?"

"Out of that space, I mean. Where you are now," Jason said. "Go back into the passageway."

"I don't understand . . ."

"I want to try something." "What exactly?" Colette asked.

"It probably won't even work."

Colette sighed. "All right, but don't do anything stupid or you'll get us both in bigger trouble."

"Give me like, five minutes, then come back," Jason said.

"Fine. Back in five."

C'mon hands, please do this for me.

Jason stood and concentrated on summoning his Guard power. His hands stayed cool. But he had to do it. He had to make it work.

Jason shook his hands and rubbed them together. He tried again.

Nothing.

"C'mon, c'mon."

He tried a third time and again failed.

"Crap." Jason slapped the wall.

His mind raced through ideas about how to jumpstart Guard powers. From his training, Jason knew of odd cases, but nothing worked consistently. And even the few things that might be worth trying weren't possible without items like industrial-size batteries and other things he didn't have in his room.

But maybe it's like Uncle A sometimes said, and I don't need force at all.

Jason eased himself back to sitting, his back against the wall. He closed his eyes and concentrated on his breathing. He inhaled, tuning into the feel of air in his nostrils. He exhaled, staying focused on his breath. He repeated the pattern four more times. With each breath, Jason's body relaxed, his mind stilled, his awareness sharpened.

Jason stood and summoned his power. His hands ignited. Blue bolts danced around his fingertips and balled in his palms. He aimed at the wall of his shower and launched the energy.

Blue flames fired into the wall, rending a gash where the bolts hit. Jason directed them up, over, and down, then stopped. The makeshift door folded down into his shower.

A moment later, Colette stood on the other side of the gap, her mouth open. "What did you do?"

"I made my own hatch," Jason said.

"I don't think that was a very good idea." Her eyes were wide.

"It's better than no idea," Jason said. "And I couldn't just sit here."

"And what happens when someone sees this?" Colette asked.

"No one comes in my bathroom," Jason said.

"Someone will be assigned to clean it."

"I can . . . hang a towel over it. Or fix it."

"Fix it?" Colette's voice changed from anxious to curious. "Your powers work in reverse as well?"

"Maybe," Jason said.

"So you don't know."

"I'll worry about it later."

"If there is a later," Colette said.

"We're running out of options, and I've barely done anything for days," Jason said. "I can't keep still any more. This way, I can maybe at least figure out what's going on with Della."

"Can you even get through there with your leg the way it is?"

Jason stepped through the space and hopped down. "Ta da."

"Very funny," Colette said. "Now if you could only make that gaping hole disappear."

"I promise I'll polish that part of my act. Later." He reached into his bathroom and grabbed his crutches. "But for now, let's go explore the secret place you found."

"You still need your crutches?"

"My leg's doing pretty good, but it's still tight," Jason said. "For now, I'm faster on these, even with aching armpits."

"Okay. Let me take care of your wristband and we'll go."

"Wait—what about the camera in my room? Jason asked.

"I'll dim the nightlight so the camera can't read as much," Colette said. She then went through the same steps Raymond had done when he overrode the GPS on Jason's wristband. A minute later, they were on their way.

Colette opened a picture of a blueprint. "I snapped this of the computer screen last night. It tells us how to get to this mystery place."

Jason and Colette followed the passageways outlined on the blueprint. They turned corners and covered long stretches of straight. Soon they were out of the medical unit and heading in a direction where no League building should be.

"The Thames must be below us now," Colette said.

There were no signs or other indications of direction or location. Jason and Colette kept following the paths on the map. Another minute in, the passageway dead-ended at a brick wall.

"This wall shouldn't be here," Colette said. "There's more League on the other side."

"Any chance the blueprint's wrong?" Jason asked.

"I don't think so."

Jason nodded. "Okay, then there has to be a way to get through."

Colette stared at her screen. "It does seem odd ..."

"Seriously, what's *not* odd right now?"

"Right," Colette said. "But I mean the brick. There isn't brick like this, or any brick for that matter, anywhere in the League. Most everything's made from natural materials, like stone and wood."

"Huh." Jason ran his fingers over the scraggly-edged blocks. "That is kinda weird."

"Maybe it's a door and we simply have to find a spot that opens it." Colette pressed different bricks with her fingertips.

"Or maybe the bricks have to be pressed in a certain pattern," Jason said. "I've seen that in movies."

Colette eyed the blueprint again. "There are no clues here. But keep pressing. Maybe we'll get lucky."

Jason and Colette spent the next few minutes trying different patterns, from pushing on the four corner bricks, to making an X, to pressing all the bricks straight down the center. They looked for off-color bricks and pressed them separately, then all at once. They tried a giant L for League. They tried a T for Tower, but nothing worked.

"It's safe to say, we've hit a brick wall," Colette said.

"And I'm annoyed enough that I want to hit it literally." Jason smacked the wall and the rough edges of the brick scraped his palm.

The sound of grating rock shocked him. He and Colette jumped. A section of bricks formed a door in the center of the wall. It opened inward.

Colette gasped. "Hurry, before it closes."

Jason followed her through the opening. "You're welcome." Colette kept her voice low. "That was luck."

"Yeah, but it was my hand that got sacrificed for the cause." He showed Colette a tiny bit of skin scraped off by a brick.

Colette smirked. "You're a regular Knight of the Round Table."

They weaved their way into the secret section of the League. Most of the passageway looked the same as the known parts of the League, with hatches leading into rooms. But Jason and Colette didn't stop to investigate. They continued following the blueprint toward Della.

"Hey, I just thought of something," Jason said. "What did you do with your JaS unit? Don't they check serum levels?"

"We . . . I don't have a JaS unit," Colette said. "After my dad lost his job, we were relocated to starter housing. Nothing nice like JaS units to clean for us, but at least we didn't have to worry about serum scans."

"But you did before that?"

"Yes," Colette said. "And you can't keep the unit locked away permanently or the League will notice. But my dad rigged a humidifier inside the JaS unit's storage cubby and that kept the unit's readings elevated."

"We can't do that for my dad. We'll have to get out of here before the League notices his JaS unit sitting still all the time."

A moment later they made a left turn and froze. In front of them was a glass door and window misty with humidity. Jason crept up and peered through spaces where drips of water cleared the view. The room inside was huge and stretched as far as Jason could see. He waved Colette up to the glass.

Row upon row of individual tanks filled the space. Each tank held a pink dolphin, its tail threaded through a Plexiglas separator that prevented the dolphin from moving more than a few inches up for an intake of air. Every tail was attached to tubes and machines to drain them of their power.

"That's how they're doing it," Jason said. "With Encantado."

"Encantado?" Colette asked. "Aren't they shape-shifters?"

"Yeah, but only between human and the pink dolphin, and they can only switch to human at night. But the more important thing is Encantado have the power of mind control." Jason thought a moment. "The Encantado is one cryptid we hadn't yet verified, but I guess we can now."

"There must be thousands of dolphins in there," Colette said.

"Yeah," Jason said. "The stories said the Encantado was rare. Maybe this is why."

One of the dolphins in a front tank thrashed. Jason and Colette jumped.

The dolphin morphed. A naked man with a hole in his forehead, his legs bound by the Plexiglas, pounded on the side of his tank. "Help! Help us!" Bubbles burst out of his mouth.

Jason couldn't hear the man's voice, but he could read his lips. A second later the man morphed to dolphin and surfaced for air. He wriggled another moment, then stilled.

Jason pulled his hands down his face. "God, they're awake. They're all awake."

"What do you mean?"

"Dolphins are conscious breathers so they're never one hundred percent asleep or they'd drown," Jason said.

"So they all know what's happening to them ... that they're trapped ..." Colette covered her mouth with her hand.

Jason nodded. He stared at the animals and wondered how long they had been there. Had it been months? Years? And what kind of freak does this to living creatures, human and cryptid alike?

"Whoever's behind this ..." Jason said, "I mean, it's huge. I don't know how you, me, and my dad can stop someone, or a lot of someones, who have the power to get away with something like this." Jason gestured toward the tanks.

"But we can't let it keep happening," Colette said.

"No, I know," Jason said. "But whatever we do, it's going to be hard."

"I have some experience dealing with hard things," Colette said.

"Yeah," Jason said. "We both do."

Colette crossed her arms. "And we're going to do it anyway."

A half smile crept onto Jason's face. "Damn right we are."

"Good," Colette said. "Our next step is to find your sister."

✳✳✳

Jason and Colette moved further through the passageway. After another minute, the passageway ended. Three steps led up to a hatch door.

"This should be it," Colette said.

Jason rubbed the back of his neck. "God, I hope we don't find something horrible like she's locked in a cage or unconscious or something."

"We won't," Colette said. "I have to believe that." She pulled her injured arm closer.

Jason nodded. He leaned his crutches against the wall, crept up the steps, and slid the hatch door a few inches to the right. Light gleamed through and Jason shifted sideways away from the opening. He looked at Colette.

She shrugged.

Jason eased back to the gap. The room was sunshine bright with blue sky above. A hedge blocked his view. He slid the door all the way open and climbed inside. Colette followed.

They stood behind a rectangular hedge about seven feet high. Through space in the branches, Jason saw a large yard with what looked like a playhouse in the far corner. To the far right was a giant oak with a rope swing tied to a branch.

Jason scanned the area above them. "Do you see a camera?" he whispered.

"No. And I think this is a residence, so no cameras," Colette said, her voice soft.

"Let's hope we have that going for us, but keep an eye out," Jason said. "And I wonder why it's day—"

An elephant trumpeted. Jason and Colette ducked.

The muscles in Jason's leg protested. "Why is there an elephant in a residence?"

Colette peered through breaches in the branches of the shrub. "If it makes you feel any better, it's a baby elephant."

"Doesn't really change my question," Jason said.

"Oh, well how about if I told you there's also a baby giraffe?"

"What?" Jason scrambled to a spot where the branches thinned. A baby elephant played with a soccer ball, kicking it with its foot, then batting the ball with its trunk. The elephant snorted. The young giraffe startled then returned to picking leaves off low branches of nearby trees.

"Hi, friends," Della said.

Della's shoes clicked on steps Jason couldn't see. She came into view. Jason stayed low.

Della petted the giraffe and it nuzzled Della's blond hair. The elephant hurried over to her and twined its trunk around Della's waist. "It's nice to see you, too. Thank you for visiting me today."

234

Della walked out of Jason's sightline, but he could still hear her voice.

"Our schedules say it's time for us to play a game," Della said. The elephant and giraffe moved in Della's direction.

"I need to get closer." Jason scuttled to the right. His leg twinged against the movement and he clenched his teeth. He moved farther down the hedge and found a spot where the hedge stopped, leaving a space to enter the yard before it started up again. Jason snuck a look around the edge.

Della and the baby animals chased each other across the grass until Della touched the hip of the elephant. "Tag—you're it." The elephant switched directions and chased Della, then the giraffe, then Della again. Its trunk brushed the nape of the giraffe's neck and the elephant tooted. The giraffe took up the chase.

Jason turned to Colette, hunched next to him. "Something's wrong. Whenever we play tag at home, she laughs her head off. But she isn't even smiling."

"She's not playing," Colette said. "She's completing an assignment."

"I can't believe that's even possible. Della, the real Della, wouldn't miss something like this for anything." He glanced at his sister again. "If this doesn't snap her out of it, I don't know what would."

"C'mon." Colette touched Jason's arm. "We should get back."

"Maybe I should talk to her."

"You definitely should not talk to her. You said it yourself—if tag with baby animals doesn't snap her out of it, nothing will."

"But I have the coin," Jason said. "It worked on my dad."

Colette paused.

"No, it's too much of a risk," she said. "Even if the coin works, you know how hard it is to keep pretending you're under the serum's spell."

"We could take her with us, and hide her."

"Where? In your bathroom?" Colette asked. "Because I promise you that will not work for—"

Jason stood.

"What are you—? Do not go out there." Colette reached for Jason's arm.

He quick-stepped through the gap in the hedge and into the yard. "Hey, Dell."

Della, the giraffe, and the elephant all stopped moving. "You are a transgressor," Della said.

"But I'm also your brother," Jason said. "How are you?"

Della tilted her head. "My brother is a transgressor."

"But I admitted my error and accepted my punishment, so that's good, right?" Jason moved next to the giraffe and stroked its back. "It looks like you're having fun with your friends. Can I play?"

"Playing with you is not part of my assignment," Della said.

"Can't we do it for fun? Like we do at home?"

"We have never played tag here."

"No, I mean like back in Salton." He scratched the giraffe's short mane and it arched its neck into his fingers.

"My home is here, and you are not on my schedule." Della tossed the soccer ball toward the elephant. It punched the ball midair with its trunk.

"Oh . . . that's weird. My schedule said to come see you and play whatever game you chose," Jason said.

Della walked away.

Jason limped after her. "Are we going to play a game?"

"I am finished with this assignment and will now sit until my next visitor arrives." Della sat on a wooden bench next to a blue spruce tree.

Gotta get outta here before someone else shows up.

"Can I sit with you?" Jason asked.

Della shrugged.

Jason sat on the bench. "I have something cool to show you." He removed the Lex coin from his passport holder and held it up.

"What's so great about an old coin?"

"It's not any old coin," Jason said. "It's special. Do you want to hold it?"

"No." Della turned her face from Jason to the animals still wandering around the yard. An adult elephant and giraffe had joined the two babies. A white bird sat on the adult elephant's back, picking bugs off its skin.

"Just check it out." He set the Lex coin on Della's leg and waited for the glow.

Nothing happened.

Maybe it has to touch her skin?

"I don't want to look at your stupid coin," Della said.

"Okay, well, would you give it back to me?" Jason opened his hand.

Della picked up the coin. She glanced at it. "What's so great about a fifty-cent piece? I've seen a million of them before." She placed it in Jason's hand.

It didn't work.

"Wait, fifty-cent piece?" Jason asked.

"Yeah, I know what a fifty-cent piece looks like." She took the coin back from Jason's hand. "President Kennedy on this side." She flipped the coin over. "Presidential seal on that side." She gave it back to Jason.

He examined the coin. He saw the same markings he'd always seen: a shield with a cross, a helmet from a suit of armor above the shield, leaves around the edge of the coin. On the other side was their name, Lex.

"But—"

"It's time for my next assignment." Della stood. "I must welcome my visitor." She walked toward marble steps leading up to the back patio of a grand house.

"Uh, okay, I'll go." Jason clenched the coin. "And Dell?"

She stopped and turned toward him.

"Best not to tell anyone I was here, okay? I, uh, my assignment was to keep our visit a secret." Jason dropped the coin into his passport holder.

"I will help you complete your assignment," Della said. "Father will be proud of me for helping you be less of a transgressor." She headed up the steps. "I must not keep him waiting."

"Wait, Dad is visiting you?" Jason asked.

"He prefers I call him Father," Della said. "Goodbye." She waved and scurried up the rest of the steps.

Jason ducked back behind the hedge where Colette waited. They climbed through the hatch and into the passageway.

"I can't believe you did that," Colette said. "Now you're caught for sure."

Jason tucked his crutches under his arms. "I don't think she'll tell."

"I hope not."

"Besides, if she tells Dad, it's no big deal," Jason said. "And her schedule must be wrong anyway since Dad doesn't even know where she is."

Colette sighed. "The coin didn't work?"

"She didn't even see the same coin." Jason took the coin out and handed it to Colette. "What do you see?"

Colette described the coin exactly as Jason saw it. He explained Della's version.

"The coin isn't revealing itself to her," Colette said. "Why do you think that is?"

"No idea." Jason took a few steps down the passageway. "Dad said it's attuned to Lex energy so—" He stopped.

Colette stopped next to him. "What is it?"

"The coin. It's a Lex coin. It's supposed to know Lex family members."

"Maybe the serum is blocking it," Colette said.

"The coin worked on my dad." Jason leaned against the wall.

"Maybe . . . because she's smaller, younger, maybe that means the serum has a better hold on her," Colette said. "Maybe she needs more than one exposure to the coin."

"Yeah, it's gotta be something like that." Jason repositioned himself on his crutches. "We'd better get back."

They moved through the passageways to Jason's room. He tried to ignore his gut, but it kept replaying one thought in his mind:

Della is lost.

EIGHTEEN
Father

Jason didn't sleep well. He wrestled with thoughts of Della and the fact that the Lex coin didn't react to her. What did that mean?

Stupid coin—worst communicator ever.

He stretched his legs then flipped onto his side. He wondered about Uncle Alexander. A gurgle swelled in Jason's throat.

I have to stop thinking about him. I can't help him, and he can't help us.

Jason thought about the Encantado trapped in those tanks. He thought about Raymond and Colette. He thought about Bartie and the others being drained.

He rubbed his eyes.

One thing at a time. Just figure out one thing at a time.

The problem was Jason didn't know one thing he could figure out. Everything was messy and broken and hard. He tried to ignore it all, to get some rest until he saw Dad at lunch. He would know what to do.

✳✳✳

The light flipped on and yanked Jason from a dream about Della.

"Good morning," Dr. Carrington said. "Have you had a nice few days of healing?"

Jason squinted against the light and pushed himself up to lean against the wall. "Uh, yeah. What time is it?" He was surprised he'd fallen asleep.

"Seven." Dr. Carrington swiped a thermometer over Jason's forehead and noted the temp on a digital chart. "No fever likely means no infection. Well done."

"Must be my good genes." Jason yawned.

"And those young cells of yours. Much easier to heal at your age." Dr. Carrington gestured for Jason to stand. "Let's see the leg. No excuses this time."

"Can I at least go to the bathroom first?"

"No. Up and strip to your boxers," Dr. Carrington said. The burly orderly stepped into the room behind her.

There was no avoiding it this time. Jason followed Dr. Carrington's instructions.

"Remarkable," Dr. Carrington said. "I knew you were healing quickly, but even with the power of youth, you've exceeded my expectations."

Jason's leg was mottled with yellow splotches where blue and black bruises showed a few days before.

"Please walk across the room and back," Dr. Carrington said.

Jason obeyed but feigned a bigger limp than the one he had.

"And can you put all of your weight on the leg?"

Jason shrugged.

"Let's try it, shall we?" She pointed. "Go ahead."

Jason shifted his weight. The leg held firm and didn't hurt, but Jason grimaced and groaned, and hurried to take his weight off the leg.

"Impressive indeed," Dr. Carrington said.

"It's really hurting now," Jason lied. He sat on the cot.

"Is it? Well, we don't want that." Dr. Carrington jotted notes.

"What are you writing?" Jason asked.

"Simply documenting information."

"And then what? Do I start the serum again?" Jason asked.

"Not yet," Dr. Carrington said. "Next on your schedule is a shower, and then I see you're having breakfast with Director Shannon."

"I am?" *Maybe Dad got through to him.*

"Yes. You are to meet him in his office at eight." She nodded toward the orderly. "Gregor will take you in a wheelchair."

"I thought I didn't rate a wheelchair," Jason said.

"A recommendation has come through from The Advisors that your situation be improved," Dr. Carrington said. "I suspect that will be the topic of conversation during your breakfast."

"Am I going back to the room I had before?"

"I do not know the details," Dr. Carrington said. "Just be certain to have all of your belongings with you."

"Yeah, that's not a problem since I have, like, three things," Jason said.

"Gregor will return for you at five before the hour."

Dr. Carrington and the orderly left, and Jason hurried into the bathroom. He examined the hole he'd made in the shower wall.

Can't leave this here.

He grabbed the Lex coin and used the edge of it to scratch a message onto the outside of the fiberglass: *Moving me. J.*

He lifted the piece into place, centered his mind, and fired his hands. High heat engulfed his palms. He followed the line where he'd separated the pieces before, melding them back together. Burning plastic smoked around his hands and filled his nostrils. When he finished, an obvious seam puckered on the wall.

Jeez, that's barely better than not repairing it at all.

Jason reignited his hands and reworked the line. He touched his fingers to the ridge and discovered he could manipulate the surface as he passed, smoothing it like frosting on the cookies they'd decorated with Grandma Lena. After a few minutes, only a hint of a seam remained. Jason patted himself on the back. "I rock." He coughed and turned on the bathroom fan to help clear the air.

After he showered, Jason put on a clean set of scrubs and hung his passport holder around his neck. He picked up his cell phone and played a few games before Gregor arrived with the wheelchair.

"What about the crutches?" Jason asked. "I still need them."

"I'll deliver them to your new residence," Gregor said. "They'll be waiting for you after breakfast."

"Residence? I'm not coming back to the medical unit?" *Maybe they're moving me in with Dad.*

"Discussing lodging is not part of my assignment." Gregor wheeled Jason out into the hallway.

The medical unit bustled with activity. Orderlies pushed medical equipment, rehab patients practiced walking, JaS and MaE units zipped between legs. "Hey, watch it," one orderly said. He grabbed the spot where a JaS unit had bumped his shin.

A couple of minutes later, Jason and Gregor arrived at the Executive Offices.

Rick sat behind his desk. He wore a sports jacket with a white shirt, and the same fedora Jason had seen him wearing earlier. Rick looked up and smiled. He pressed something under his desk, and his office door slid open. He stood and walked toward them.

"Jason, I'm delighted to see you." Rick directed Gregor to push the chair toward the sitting area. "Can I help you into a more comfortable seat?" Rick reached for Jason's elbow.

"Uh . . . sure." Jason lifted himself to standing, letting Rick hold his arm. Jason played up his limp and shuffled to a plush purple chair. He plopped onto the cushion. Gregor rolled the wheelchair away and left the room.

Rick sat in a chair to Jason's right. "Dr. Carrington told me you were doing quite well, but I'm happy to see your progress for myself. You're something of a miracle."

Jason shifted in his seat. "Oh, I don't know. Maybe the break wasn't as bad as everyone thought."

"Had I not seen it with my own eyes, I could be persuaded to that point of view," Rick said. "But instead, I am gobsmacked."

"Uh, sorry?"

"Ah, yes. That is, I'm astounded," Rick said.

"Weird word, gobsmacked." Jason shifted from one hip to the other. "But I guess it's a good word to describe the whole weird thing that happened in Sewell Hall."

"We are proud of our processes and procedures, and I'm glad you were able to experience a special event first hand." Rick smiled.

"You mean you're glad I got my leg smashed?" Jason faked a laugh trying to cover a flash of anger in his voice.

"I was happy to see you step up and own your mistakes." Rick's eyes narrowed. "We must do our best for the League as the League does its best for us."

Jason leaned back. "Right. Yeah."

Rick slapped his knees and Jason jumped.

"I had a lovely visit with Zachary yesterday," Rick said.

"You did?"

Rick raised an eyebrow. "You didn't know?"

"He said something about it, but I didn't think it was a done deal. Plus it was work stuff." Jason shrugged like the topic didn't interest him, but he hoped to hear good news from Rick.

"I suppose for a fourteen-year-old young man such as yourself, 'work stuff' as you call it, might indeed be boring," Rick said. "But I found it quite enlightening, and I'm even more impressed with Zachary than I was before."

A woman walked in with a cart. The scent of French fries wafted through the room.

"Ah," Rick said. "Here's our breakfast."

The woman set food on the coffee table. Each plate had grilled trout, baked eggs with spinach and a cheesy sauce, and a bowl of kiwi and raspberries. She added glasses of ice water, and a pot of tea with two teacups. A large basket of fries sat between the plates for Jason and Rick to share.

"A bit of an untraditional breakfast, I know. Especially for an American," Rick said. "But I hope you find something to your liking."

Jason's mouth watered. "It all looks good to me."

"Excellent. Now as I was saying, Zachary and I did indeed have a conversation about work, specifically about his new position with the League. He came to me with ideas about how to improve things and do even more for our League family." Rick cut off the tail of his trout and ate it.

"Uh . . ." Jason watched the fishtail flick as it was pulled into Rick's mouth. The crispy edges crunched. *Gross.* Jason's appetite waned.

"Uh, he had good ideas?" Jason put a handful of fries on his plate.

"The whole conversation made a great impression on me," Rick said. "I hung on Zachary's every word and couldn't be happier that he requested time to speak with me."

Jason swallowed a bite of egg. "That's cool."

"Yes," Rick said. "I finally understand what your mother saw in him."

Jason stopped mid-chew of a slice of kiwi. He forced the fruit down. "My mom?"

Rick skipped over the question. "Della tells me you stopped by for a chat last night."

Clamminess set into Jason's skin. "I . . . uh . . ."

"Please." Rick leaned back in his chair and sipped his tea. "Do try to convince me that my daughter is lying about you visiting her residence last night."

"Your . . . daughter?" Jason's stomach rolled.

"You seem genuinely surprised," Rick said.

"Yeah, I'm surprised," Jason said. "Because it's not true."

"Really? The thought's never crossed your mind?" Rick asked. "You've never noticed Della is so very different from Kyle?"

"She's not different, from me or Kyle." Jason clenched his fists.

"And yet, she is." Rick walked to a cabinet and removed a small photo album. He set it on the table in front of Jason. "Take a look."

"I'm not looking at some stupid fake pictures." He stood. "Me and my dad and Della are leaving." Jason didn't dare mention Colette.

"You're staying right here with me, where you belong," Rick said. "Sit."

Jason spun on his heel and moved toward the door. Gregor stood on the outside looking in, his arms crossed. Jason's hands fired. Gregor morphed into a Yeti, the same one who'd crushed Jason's leg. Jason lifted his arms, ready to fight, blue light lasering around his hands.

Sparks crackled behind Jason and he pivoted. He kept one hand aimed at Gregor and directed the other toward Rick.

Rick had a ball of blue in his hand. "Guard too, remember?"

Jason glared. "I'm taking my family, and we're leaving."

"You really think you can fight your way out?" Rick asked.

Jason said nothing.

"Let's say you somehow get out of my office, away from me and past Gregor. Then what, Jason?" Rick asked. "Do you think you can get to your sister? And how will you find Zachary?"

"What did you do to my dad?" Jason's jaw tightened. *I just got him back . . .*

"Not to mention dear old Uncle Alexander. Written him off for dead, have we?"

Pounding racked Jason's head. "I . . . I will—"

Rick leaned forward. "You will sit. And you will listen. You have no other choice."

Heat burned through Jason's body.

"Now, Jason."

Jason stared at Rick. His mind searched for options, for action, for something.

I have nothing.

Jason powered down and dropped back into his chair.

"Good man. I knew you'd come to your senses," Rick said. "Now, have a look at the photos."

Jason yanked the book off the table and opened it. On the first page was a picture of Rick with Jason's mom holding baby Della. The caption underneath read: *Welcome to our baby girl!* Acid rose in Jason's throat. He turned the page.

On the left was a picture of Rick in front of Jason's old house in Colorado.

Where was Dad? And me and Kyle?

Rick was holding Della who was wearing a white dress with big sunflowers. The caption read: *Daddy and Della, age one.* On the right side of the album was Rick standing next to a pony with Della on the pony's back. *Daddy and Della, age two.*

"No, this can't be right . . ." Jason flipped the page. There was a picture of his mom with Della at age three, then age four. The next page had pictures of his mom with Rick, at the Tower of London, kissing. Then holding hands in front of Buckingham Palace. "No. This is wrong." Next was a picture of Jason's mom smiling at Rick while he stroked her face. The picture was taken two years ago.

Jason flung the book across the room.

"Careful, now. Those photos are a treasure to me," Rick said. He left the album lying on the floor.

"I guess you'll have to print up another book of fake photos." Jason slumped in his chair.

"Thankfully, I have digital copies. But I promise, those are one hundred percent genuine," Rick said. "Your mom and I were, shall we say, very close."

"You lie." Jason sputtered the words. But he remembered the coin. It didn't help Della.

"I speak only the truth," Rick said. "If you'd continued to the end of the album, you'd know that."

"I'm not looking at that thing anymore." Jason crossed his arms.

"One page, at the end of the album." Rick nodded. "Get it."

Jason didn't budge.

"Knowledge is power," Rick said. "Plus, it saves me the trouble of inviting Gregor in to . . . assist you."

Jason's mouth twitched. He shoved himself to standing and picked up the album, opening it to the back. He pulled out a piece of folded paper in a plastic sleeve. Bold type at the top of the page said, "Probability of Paternity: 99.9998%." Below that it listed Name of Child: Della Lex. Name of Mother: Adrienne Lex. Probable Father: Sewell Kendrick.

Sewell Kendrick? Jason's head spun.

He wanted to yell, to throw a punch, to run. He looked at Rick.

Rick . . . Kendrick . . . Sewell Kendrick . . . the "great man" Mom talked about.

A closed-mouth smile widened on Rick's face.

Jason crossed the room and fell back into the wall. Anger tornadoed through him.

"It's been such a joy to have both you and your sister here, to be able to finally spend some time together," Rick said.

Jason shut his eyes and kept them closed.

"I'm looking forward to doing more of that." Rick refilled his teacup.

"You tried to kill my brother." Jason's muscles twitched.

"That was your mother's doing, not mine," Rick said. "She should have followed my instructions."

"And when I tell Della that, do you seriously think she is going to stay here with you?" Jason opened his eyes and stared at Rick.

"Of course. I'm her father," Rick said. "And now that her mother is gone, her care falls to me."

"She won't believe you," Jason said. "She won't want to stay."

"She already believes me." Rick stirred sugar into his tea. "You talked to her."

"Serum-Della doesn't count," Jason said.

"A girl knows her father." Rick picked up two French fries and bit into them. "Don't you like the chips? Better eat up, they're getting cold."

Jason rolled his eyes.

"More for me then," Rick said.

How is this happening? How did we end up here?

"Wait," Jason said. "Did you do something to Della to get Dad to bring her here?"

"Your mother took care of that for me." Rick sipped his tea. "She started Della on small doses of one of her plant concoctions, resulting in Della's symptoms of anxiety and depression."

Jason slid down the wall.

Mom hurt Della.

"Why not kidnap her or something? Why poison her?"

"With the illness, your mother could justify bringing her for treatment, whereas a kidnapping would never allow us peace," Rick said.

Peace. Right.

"After your mother's loss, I directed the request to Zachary. He could hardly deny Della treatment." He swallowed a bite of the trout's head.

"And when me and Uncle Alexander showed up . . ."

"Your uncle was a bit of a glitch, but we handled it," Rick said.

"By attacking us and making Bartie look like a bad guy," Jason said.

"Bartie was a danger to the League." Rick took a drink of water.

"You mean he was a danger to you. Because he was figuring out you were behind all of this." Jason waved his hand. "And that you're trying to destroy the Rampart and eliminate humans, right? Is that still part of the plan?"

"*Pshaw.* I'll only eliminate those not on the serum."

A chill crept up Jason's spine. "What are you talking about?"

"The serum. We're working on aerosolizing it for mass distribution," Rick said. "That means health and happiness the world over."

Oh no . . .

"It's still about twelve months from completion, but it's coming soon enough. And since we'll have the global serum in place, the Rampart stays. I'll issue directives that will stop climate change and restore the planet." Rick ate the rest of the trout's head. "And the small segment of the population immune to the serum will be made donors or eliminated."

"What about my dad?"

"Zachary is back on the serum as we speak," Rick said. "I thought he might be immune since he somehow purged it from his system, but the reports I've received so far tell me he's absorbing the doses like a sponge in water."

Jason dropped his head into his hands.

"Oh, come now," Rick said. "That's much better news than elimination due to immunity."

"How did you know?" Jason asked.

"JaS units scan residences every night, whether they're assigned to clean or not."

Jason nodded once. *Everything's lost. Dad, Della, Uncle Alexander . . . all lost.*

"What I don't know is how Zachary purged it from his system in the first place," Rick said. "Any ideas about that?"

Jason shook his head. "Nope."

"Hmm . . ."

"What?" Jason jerked his head up. "You're the one that knows everything."

Rick leaned back in his chair. "Yes, well, after a few hundred years of building this, I should know everything. Yet I still encounter setbacks, and that irritates me."

"A few hundred *years*?"

"Believe me, I would have done this long ago but for capturing the rest of the Encantado. We're a clever and sneaky bunch."

Jason's eyes fixed on Rick. "We?"

"That's right." Rick removed his hat revealing the blowhole in his forehead.

"God, you're an Encantado, too." Jason pinched the bridge of his nose. "So all the dolphins in the tanks . . ."

"You know about that? My but you and Raymond were busy," Rick said.

Maybe he doesn't know about Colette.

"That system is one of my greatest accomplishments." Rick held his arms wide. "We utilize water from the Thames, processing it on the intake as well as before we flush it back into the river. Keeps my family members healthy, relatively speaking, and keeps our use of the Thames hidden from anyone who might care."

"The dolphins are your family members?" Jason asked.

"Most are," Rick said, "though there are a few from remote waters I met for the first time when they came here."

"And you're draining them, your own family, just to make serum," Jason said.

"Serum, yes," Rick said. "But they're more powerful than that. I discovered how to distill their combined command of mind control and shape-shifting into a special serum just for me. Not only does it enable me to direct anyone on the serum to do as I wish, I can also maintain human form indefinitely." Rick laughed. "And I must say, living this way is brilliant. Much better than short dashes out of the water during the night only to be forced back into the drink at dawn."

"You said you worked with my Grandpa Tate."

"Indeed I did," Rick said. "By that time I'd already created my serum and lived as human. I gave myself Guard powers by siphoning it off others and synthesizing it for myself."

"Did you steal it from Grandpa Tate?" Jason asked.

"That was the plan," Rick said. "But he figured out what I was working on. He was going to report me to the League."

"So you . . . you . . ."

"Killed him? No," Rick said. "That was your mother's doing. It was a great testament of her love for me."

"My mom . . . my mom killed her dad?" Nausea surged through Jason.

"She believed in our mission. It was the right thing to do."

Jason shook his head. "No. No, it wasn't." He thought of Grandma Lena, how sad she was when she talked about losing Grandpa Tate.

"Consider the bigger picture," Rick said. "Eliminating Tate allowed me to continue my work."

"When I saw you in there . . ." Jason thumbed at the door leading to the room with Rick's hospital bed.

"Receiving my daily treatment," Rick said. "I still regret my over-reaction to your presence. No hard feelings, I hope."

"Hah. Right." Jason rubbed his hands down his face and stared at nothing. "So now what? You hook me back on the base serum? Get me under your control?"

"Ah, well, I'd much rather we avoid that. I prefer having a relationship with the real you," Rick said. "And with you on my side, I'll be able to wean Della off the serum and we can be a family."

"You might as well pump serum into me right now because none of that is going to happen."

"You need time to process, but I think you'll change your mind," Rick said. "After all, Zachary's life depends on it."

"What are you talking about?"

"I don't need Zachary, and in fact, he's a liability until I figure out how he offset the serum." Rick sipped his tea. "He has no power, so he can't contribute to the greater good as a donor. But I'll keep him here, alive, as a favor to you." He set the cup on its saucer. "And I'll remind you, too, that our dear Della will forever be on the serum if you don't do your part."

"So I become your new BFF and have to hang out with you or something?"

"Oh dear, have I not been clear?" Rick asked. "Well, it seems I should have shared all of the documentation at the same time." He walked to the cupboard and retrieved a second photo album. "Della is not the only child I fathered with your mother." He dropped it in front of Jason.

"Son."

NINETEEN
Just Like Them

The room spun. Jason picked up the photo album and skipped straight to the back page. He pulled the paper out of its plastic sleeve.

The statistical probability was the same as he'd seen on Della's DNA results: 99.9998%. The only difference between her results and his was the Name of Child. This form said Jason Lex.

This can't be real ... the coin ... I saw its true form like Dad did. Jason scrunched his eyes shut as tight as he could squeeze. *But so did Uncle Alexander and Colette. The coin doesn't prove anything.*

The sound of Rick's voice came closer and a hand gripped Jason's shoulder.

"Settle down, son," Rick said. "Settle down."

"I." Jason sucked in air. "Am not." He snatched another gasp. "Your son." He shook off Rick's hand and stood.

"I know this comes as a bit of a shock," Rick said. "But you have proof positive right there in your hand."

Jason crumpled the DNA results and triggered his blue flame, burning the sheet to ash.

"Lovely parlor trick." Rick picked up both photo albums and set them on the coffee table. "But it doesn't change the facts."

Jason swallowed hard. He tried to center himself like Uncle Alexander had taught him.

"I am your father, you are my son," Rick said.

Jason's attempt at calm failed. "Stop saying that."

"Fine," Rick said. "You need some time to process everything. I understand."

"I want to see my dad," Jason said.

Rick *tsked*. "I am your father. You will call me Father, you will call him Zachary."

"No," Jason said. "I won't."

Rick crossed his arms. "I have been a patient man. I spent years building everything you see here, making the League the tremendous organization it is today. And I spent years watching another man raise my own flesh and blood. The day has finally come where I will have my children by my side. And you know what?" Rick slammed his fist into the wall. "I'm done waiting, so let me make this simple for you. Do as you're told, and Zachary lives."

"I—"

"Not open to negotiation," Rick said. "Do as you're told, and Zachary lives."

Jason swallowed hard. "You'd kill him? Just like that? How would you explain his death to the rest of the League? Tons of people know he's here, and he's supposed to be starting his new job. You can't kill him."

Rick laughed. "I'd hardly have to." He returned to his chair and poured another cup of tea. "Should you fall out of line, someone in the League will report Zachary for a violation. Should you continue to be a problem, Zachary will be accused of another violation." He stirred in a cube of sugar. "And should there be a third violation, well, you know what happens then."

"You can't . . . you can't make things up. Someone would know the violations weren't real." Jason's mind spun.

"I don't have to make anything up." Rick tapped his temple. "With the combined power of my Encantado, I can direct Zachary to commit violations in view of others." He sipped his tea. "Then I would nudge the Governess with my thoughts and she would perform the nasty business of recommending punishment. The Advisors would agree, the crowd would approve, and all would be right with the world."

"But . . . you can't," Jason said.

"Oh, but I can. Would you like proof?" Rick asked. "Shall we go ahead and get that first pesky violation onto Zachary's record right now?" Rick closed his eyes. "I hope his punishment doesn't interfere too much with his new job. It'd be a shame to see his job performance suffer from the get go."

Jason rushed over and grabbed Rick's arm. "No. Stop."

Rick opened his eyes. "Pardon me?"

"Stop. Please."

"Not quite getting the full message, son." Rick closed his eyes again.

"Stop, please . . . Father," Jason yelled. His hands heated and he forced them dormant, though he wanted to hurt Rick.

Rick opened his eyes. "Done. Now was that so hard?"

Jason looked down at the floor and shook his head. Acid burned in his belly.

"I'd like verbal confirmation," Rick said.

"No, it wasn't hard." Jason clenched his teeth.

"No . . ."

Jason bit the inside of his lip. "No . . . Father."

"And do you understand how the situation with Zachary works?"

"Yes, Father."

Rick clapped once. "That's my boy. It's good to have you home."

Jason's eyes watered. He kept his focus on the floor.

"Gregor will take you to the residence. Your schedule is free for the rest of the day, and I'll see you at dinner," Rick said.

Jason looked at Rick. "I'm going to your residence?"

"For now you'll be with Della." Rick sat. "She hasn't been sleeping well since her treatments, so we adjusted her daylight hours. She should be waking about now as we're trying to get her back on a normal schedule, especially since you'll be living with her. Don't need both of my children on odd hours."

Jason cringed. Rick waved at the door and Gregor entered with the wheelchair.

"Can someone else take me there?" Jason asked.

"I trust Gregor to take good care of you," Rick said.

Jason plopped into the wheelchair.

"By the way, you made impressive work of the brick wall. Well done," Rick said. "How long did it take you before you landed on literally hitting the brick wall?"

"I don't know, maybe twenty minutes," Jason said. He wondered how he'd adjust to this new way of life.

"I thought I was quite clever with that trick, but of course my own clever son would be the one to figure it out." Rick smiled. "I'm proud of you."

"Whatever." Jason grabbed onto the wheels and pushed toward the door.

"Stop."

Gregor halted Jason's forward motion.

"I paid you a compliment," Rick said. "I demand a respectful response."

Jason said nothing.

"Don't test me." Rick crossed his arms.

Jason clenched and unclenched his jaw. "Thank you . . . Father." He gagged on the word. It was like drinking curdled milk.

"I'll see you at dinner, son. Gregor, he's ready to go."

Gregor pushed Jason out of the office, away from the man he had to force himself to think of as his parent, as his dad.

✳✳✳

Gregor stopped the wheelchair outside the front door of Jason's new residence. The door was about ten feet tall, arched at the top, and carved from dark wood. A brown metal lever served as the doorknob. Jason's crutches were leaning against the wall.

"Della's suite is upstairs to the left, your suite is to the right," Gregor said.

"Great," Jason mumbled. He stood and shifted his weight onto his crutches. He opened the front door, went inside, and closed the door on Gregor. He set the crutches aside.

He was in a large living room that flowed to an outdoor patio in the back of the house, with steps leading down to the expansive yard he'd seen the night before. But there were no elephants, giraffes, or any other animals out there now.

Inside was a giant screen television with four reclining chairs facing the screen. Each chair had a mini-refrigerator built into one armrest and storage space in the other. A line of video game controllers sat on the coffee table. Jason dropped into one of the chairs and in its refrigerator found a can of lime-flavored soda, the same brand Dad always bought. "No calories, no sodium, no artificial sweeteners," Dad always said. "Soda goodness without the badness." Jason smiled for a moment, thinking about how dorky Dad could be.

His heart hurt. *Ex-Dad* ... He returned the can to the armrest and stood. Even if Rick was lying about everything, he had all the power. *It's either ex-Dad or dead Dad.*

Jason scanned for cameras even though he knew there shouldn't be any in a residence. All clear. He hoped there weren't hidden cameras. Then again, he wouldn't be stepping out of line.

On the other side of the room sat a couch, love seat, and two chairs with ottomans. A palm tree shaded one end of the couch from sunlight streaming through the skylight above.

Real shade from fake sunlight.

Della walked into the kitchen just past the sitting area. "Good morning."

"Yeah, uh, good morning, Dell." Jason hugged her. Her return hug was light and formal.

He sat on a barstool at the kitchen island. "Sleep okay?"

"My sleep patterns have improved." She took a box of cereal from the pantry. "Father said I would fall asleep fifteen minutes after he left, and I did."

"You were here all by yourself?"

"I follow procedures and no harm comes to me." Della poured milk on her cereal.

"Right. And what about food? Do you always eat cereal?" Jason asked.

"Lunch and dinner arrive at noon and five, unless Father invites me to join him," Della said. "He will also invite you now that your status has been upgraded."

Jason rubbed one eye. "Can't wait."

"Our Father is a great man." Della crunched a bite of cereal. "But he says we are his greatest creations."

Not saying a lot from a freaking psycho. "Do you really believe he's a great man, or are you saying what he told you to say?" Jason asked.

"He is a great man. He takes care of me," Della said. "He wants great things for me."

"Yeah, but . . . oh never mind." Jason pressed the heels of his palms into his eyes. *There's got to be a way to get out of here, or at least get her out of here.* He looked up at Della. She was staring at him.

"Father told me you are no longer in the medical unit," she said.

"Nope. I'm your new roomie," Jason said.

"You no longer have to wear those clothes." She took another bite of cereal.

"These are all I have." Jason pulled on the slack in his top and released it.

"You are a member of the League, and a permanent resident," Della said. "So now your wristband matches mine." She held up her arm.

Jason glanced at his band. It was black.

"As League residents, we are supplied with everything we need, including clothes."

"Oh, so I bet procedure states I have to change my clothes so I don't look like I escaped from the mental ward or something," Jason said.

Della nodded. "It is procedure."

"Not worth rocking that boat." Jason headed toward the stairs. "I don't want to upset Father." Jason used air quotes around Rick's new title.

A moment later he walked into his suite. He had a king-size bed and a desk with a computer. He tapped the mouse and checked the screen.

Figures. No internet connection.

In the next room sat a chair and reading lamp surrounded by built-in bookcases. Another room had a mini-theatre with a television and gaming systems. *Maybe I can just zone out in here and ignore everything.*

Jason had his own bathroom with a shower, a separate tub, two sinks, and a toilet in a separate nook. A walk-in closet at the other end of the bathroom was full of clothes and shoes and jackets.

"What the . . . who needs all of this?" *Rick really believes I'm staying forever.*

Jason thought about Dad—Zachary—drugged up on serum somewhere, and vulnerable to Rick's threats. *Who am I kidding? I'm not going anywhere.*

He put on jeans and a red T-shirt, and slipped on a pair of canvas shoes. All of it fit perfectly. He walked into his library and paced past the shelves. He pulled a book at random, read the title, tossed it on the chair. Jason grabbed another one, read the title, and threw it against the wall. He tried to calm himself, but his mind wouldn't rest enough to let him focus on anything but the idea that he was Sewell Kendrick's son.

How could Mom do this to us? To Dad?

Jason shook his head. "Zachary. I have to call him Zachary."

And how did I never know? How did . . . Zachary . . . not know about Mom and Rick?

Jason ran memories through his mind, trying to find clues or signs, something he should have noticed, but he found nothing. He punched a fist into an armrest of the chair.

None of this can be true. I'm not like them. They kill people. I would never—

Uncle Alexander flashed in Jason's mind. Everything else blanked.

I helped Uncle Alexander die . . . I don't even know for sure that's what he wanted, but I did it anyway. I am like them.

He rubbed his hands through his hair.

I am like them . . .

He stood and went back downstairs to check on Della. He needed to think about something else.

✳✳✳

Della lay on a lounge chair under an umbrella on the back patio. Jason sat on a chair next to her.

"What's on your schedule today, Dell?"

"I have treatment," Della said. "The assigned staff person will pick me up in five minutes."

"More treatment? How much longer until you're done?" Jason asked.

"Father says he wants me to achieve the best possible outcome, and it will take as long as it takes." Della clasped her hands in her lap.

"What do you do when you're in treatment?" Jason scooted back on the chair. "Is it like, lots of talking and stuff?"

"There are games. And talking," Della said, "but mostly games. And I get my serum."

"It's kind of annoying to take serum pills every day, isn't it," Jason said.

"I only sometimes take pills. Most of the time they give me liquid serum."

"Why—"

The doorbell rang.

"That's for me. See ya later." Della hopped off the lounge and was gone.

✻✻✻

The doorbell rang again at noon, only a short time after Della left. Jason opened the door and found a basket with a sandwich, chips, and a green salad. He ate lunch by himself on the back patio.

He spent the rest of the afternoon exploring the residence, trying to convince himself this was nice, this was good, this was home.

He failed.

What about Shay? What about Grandma Lena and Sadie? What will they think about us never coming back?

Jason throttled back a sob.

I have to be strong. And I have to . . . I have to be here. At least I'm here with Della. At least I can be a good big brother.

A little before five, Jason wandered from cupboard to refrigerator trying to find something he wanted to eat. Everything seemed bland and boring.

A few minutes later, Rick walked in without knocking or ringing the bell. Three people trailed him into the kitchen. They unpacked roasted chicken, mashed potatoes, steamed broccoli, and brownies, and then departed.

"Hello, son." Rick patted Jason on the back. "Hungry?"

"Not really," Jason said. "Where's Della?"

"Your sister is still in treatment," Rick said. "And please use the term 'father' when speaking to me."

Jason's mouth dropped open. "Seriously? Like every sentence? Father?"

"Not all sentences, but often. You need the practice, and we have many years to make up for."

"Whatever you say, Father." Jason's tone was sharp and made the term sound more swear word than term of endearment.

"Hmm." Rick side-eyed Jason. "Chicken?" He plopped a chunk of chicken on a plate and slid it in front of Jason.

"Why is Della still in treatment?" Jason couldn't force himself to say "father" again.

Rick didn't press. "She is a special case and requires personalized care."

Jason sliced off a bite of chicken. "She's been there since eleven this morning."

"She's receiving the best of care," Rick said. "She'll be home later."

What kind of treatment takes all day?

Jason watched Rick swallow three bites of chicken.

"What?" Rick asked.

"I'm surprised you're not eating fish." Jason scooped potatoes and broccoli onto his plate.

"Fish is my first choice, but I've acquired quite the eclectic palate having lived as human for so many years," Rick said.

"Yeah. Chicken is super eclectic." Jason popped a bite of broccoli in his mouth.

Rick took a drink of water. "I understand you're still getting used to things around here, but I'd appreciate a better attitude."

"What attitude?" Jason asked. "This is me being me, *Father*. Teenager, remember? It's part of the package." He ate another piece of broccoli.

Rick set his fork down and leaned back in his chair. "Do you think that if you annoy me enough, I'll tire of you and let you return to your old life? What life do you have to go back to, hmm? Your mother is dead, largely thanks to your inability to save her, I might add. And Zachary isn't your father. Once he knows that, do you really think he'd want you back in his home?"

Jason swallowed and stared at Rick.

"Same goes for your sister. Zachary doesn't want someone else's children, especially children who are a constant reminder of his dead wife's betrayal," Rick said. "And frankly, I can't blame him."

Jason swirled potatoes around his plate.

"It seems to me your best option is to give this a go."

Jason didn't respond.

"Do you have something to say?" Rick asked.

"No . . . Father." Pressure built in Jason's chest.

"Very well then," Rick said. "I expect that to mean you're fully on board."

"Yes, Father." Jason pushed away from the table. "I'm tired. I'm going to my room."

Jason slammed his bedroom door.

What Rick said made sense. *Even if we could leave, Dad wouldn't want me and Della around. Why would he?*

Jason flopped onto his bed. He yelled. He pulled a pillow hard onto his face. He wanted to block out everything.

A ding sounded from the desktop computer and Jason glanced over. A pop-up box flashed on the screen. He walked over to read the message: *Nice night for a walk in the garden.*

The message didn't indicate who'd sent it except for the tag "User 1017."

Della? Or Colette . . .

A few hours later, Jason wandered over to Della's room. It was empty.

How can she still be in treatment?

He went downstairs. Rick was long gone, the kitchen was clean, and leftover dinner was in the refrigerator. Jason grabbed a brownie and ate it in four bites as he walked outside.

A light breeze rustled leaves, and a golden moon hung in the sky. If he hadn't seen that sky as daylight when he knew it was night, Jason wouldn't have believed what he saw now was a projection. He crossed the patio and went down to the lawn. He watched where he stepped to avoid a mess of elephant or giraffe poop on his shoes. But the grass was clear of stinky surprises. He continued down the slope.

"Hey." A whisper of voice floated through the hedge. "Jason."

He ducked through the gap where he'd entered the yard when he'd talked to Della the night before.

Colette flung her arms around his neck. "You saw my message." She released him and jumped back. "Oh, sorry."

"No, that's okay," Jason said. "That was, uh, that's okay."

She walked away from the gap and sat on the ground, gesturing for him to follow. "What happened? What are you doing here?"

Jason told Colette everything that had taken place since he'd last seen her.

"So that's it," Jason said. "New dad, new house, new life."

"You can't stay here," Colette said.

"What choice do I have? I don't want Rick to hurt my dad. My ex-dad." Jason picked at a blade of grass. "Plus, Dad, I mean Zachary, will hate me when he finds out everything."

"What your mum did is not your fault. He'll know that."

"But the report said he's not even my dad," Jason said.

"Are you certain?" Colette asked.

"DNA doesn't lie." Jason rubbed his forehead. "Besides, it's more than that. I'm just . . ."

She touched Jason's arm. "What is it?"

"There are things that are wrong, that are bad," Jason said. "Really bad."

"I know, but we can't give up," Colette said.

"You don't get it. There's nothing to give up. There's nothing that can be fixed."

"Yes, there is. There's still the serum. I've got—"

"It doesn't matter," Jason said. "My parents are bad people and I'm just like them." He stood. "You should stay away from me."

Colette jumped up. "What are you talking about?"

"I hurt people. My brother got hurt because of me, and Della, and then there's your dad." Jason moved toward the gap in the hedge.

Colette followed. "You're not making any sense. You didn't hurt my dad."

"Don't come here again," Jason said.

"Talk to me," Colette said. "Tell me what's going on."

Jason stopped in the gap before heading into the yard. The empty swing swayed in the wind. He turned to Colette. "I killed my mom, I killed my uncle. Stay away."

TWENTY
Son

Jason rushed into the house, never looking back at Colette. He had to ignore how he felt about her. He had to accept who he was or his dad would die, too.

He checked on Della, but her room was empty. He went to his suite, changed into pajamas he found in his closet, and plopped onto a chair in his TV room, determined to block everything out. He clicked on the television.

The League of Governors emblem flashed on the screen then switched to an image of a mountain stream glinting in sunlight. A message on the left said, "Good Evening, Jason Lex."

God, they're everywhere.

The next line on the screen said, "Your schedule for tomorrow has been updated. Prepare for departure from your residence at eight a.m."

Jason's wristband vibrated. The same digital message scrolled across the band.

"That's new," Jason said.

After a few minutes of clicking through channels and finding nothing to watch, Jason walked to his bedroom. The same message about his schedule flashed on the computer screen.

"I've got it already. Jeez." Jason was disappointed the message wasn't from Colette. *But that's good. She needs to stay away from me and I need to stay away from her.*

He set the alarm on his phone and climbed in bed.

Della wasn't home when Jason got up. He didn't like not knowing where she was. But he didn't like a lot of things these days.

He dressed and was putting his cereal bowl in the sink when the doorbell rang at eight. Jason grabbed his crutches and opened the door. Gregor stood on the stoop.

"This is a sucky way to start the day," Jason said.

"My assignment is to take you to your father," Gregor said. "You are spending the day with him."

"Wow. That means starting the day with you is not even going to be the suckiest part of my day." Jason crutched over to the electric transport cart Gregor climbed into. It was painted dark green, and the League of Governors emblem embellished the nose.

A few minutes later, Jason hobbled into Rick's office. He wore black dress pants with red suspenders, a plaid shirt, red bowtie, and the same fedora.

"Good morning, son." Rick tilted his head. "Still on the crutches?"

"Yeah. Smashed leg. Huge pain. Remember?"

"Again with the attitude?" Rick asked.

Dad flashed in Jason's mind. "Sorry. Uh, sorry, Father."

"Thank you," Rick said. "You weren't using crutches when I saw you at dinner."

Jason's mouth dried. *Crap.*

"I was trying it out, to see if I could manage the pain," Jason said. "But it was stupid because now my leg hurts tons."

"Hurts tons, does it?" Rick rolled his eyes. "English lessons will be added to your schedule. This American-speak will not do."

Whatever.

"In the meantime," Rick said, "I have a delightful day planned for you. A boy should know what his father does. Experience and learn leadership skills first hand."

Right. Because mind control equals leadership skills.

"Don't you agree, son?"

"Yes, sir. I mean, Father." Jason shifted his weight to relieve pressure on one armpit. "And daughters should know too, so is Della coming?"

"She is in treatment today," Rick said.

"Seriously, what kind of treatment takes every minute of the day?" Jason asked.

Rick picked up a portfolio from his desk. "Della is a special case."

"Maybe you should take her off the serum and let her be herself." Jason's hands tingled. He forced them to cool.

"I'd hoped for that," Rick said, "but since your visit with her in the garden, I'm afraid she's had a bit of a backslide."

"What kind of backslide?" Jason asked. Heat faded from his face. "Father?"

Rick sighed. "If you are to learn the ways of the League, you should know the truth about your sister." He gestured to a chair. "Sit."

Jason crossed the room and eased himself into a chair facing Rick's desk. He placed his crutches on the floor.

"When Della arrived, our first priority was to purge from her system all remnants of the drugs your mother had administered," Rick said. "The formula your mother used should have had no long-term effect on Della, and we could have let her body clear the concoction on its own, but I didn't want to leave it in her system any longer than necessary. Call it a father's love."

Crazy father of the year award for him.

"Did it work?" Jason asked.

"Yes. But we discovered other problems," Rick said.

"Like what?"

Rick pursed his lips a moment. "It seems she has a chemical imbalance in her brain, much like your mother."

No, she can't be like Mom. "But Mom wasn't ... I thought maybe you ..."

"You thought I controlled your mother? Hardly," Rick said. "When I met her, I hadn't amassed the power of mind control that I have today. Like all Encantado, I could influence a human's thoughts for a short time, but I couldn't sustain it. That's why I had to work my way up the League ladder like everybody else." He leaned against the edge of his desk. "I thought your mother had a wild, independent spirit, and she most certainly did. But it wasn't long before I discovered it was more than that." He crossed his arms. "I could see her erratic behavior increasing, her choices becoming more radical."

"Like deciding she should kill Grandpa Tate."

"Exactly like that. You understand," Rick said.

"But you let her do it," Jason said. "You knew she was erratic or whatever and you didn't stop her."

"In my defense, I did encourage her to take the serum," Rick said. "Our early batches soothed the brain and reduced anxiety. It would have been perfect for her." He walked around and sat in his desk chair. "But she refused, and I supported her decision."

"Because you're—"

Rick's eyebrows arched.

Jason swallowed. "Because you cared about her, Father?"

"I did indeed. And she cared about me." Rick's eyes narrowed. "As I mentioned to you before, the actions she took demonstrated your mother's love for me."

"And Della is . . ." Jason said.

"Ah yes, our dear Della." Rick sat back in his chair. "Her condition is far worse than your mother's. Without the serum, her energy plummets, her sadness soars, and she's inclined to do herself harm."

"She wants to hurt herself?" Confusion swirled through Jason's mind. He'd never seen any sign of that kind of behavior from Della.

"More than simply hurt herself, I'm afraid," Rick said.

"That doesn't make any sense." Jason shifted in his seat.

"Regardless, we continue to work with her. We'd created an enhanced serum that kept her balanced, but your little garden rendezvous triggered a reaction," Rick said. "She's spiraling."

Why would my being there make her feel bad?

"You understand now why you haven't seen her, and why you likely won't see her for some time," Rick said. "The best of my team are working with her around the clock."

Jason lowered his gaze to the floor. *I can't even take care of my little sister.*

Rick leaned forward. "We will get her better, son."

Jason looked up. "Yeah, please...please, Father." *Though you haven't done it so far.*

"You have my word," Rick said. "We will be a family."

Jason stifled a cringe. "Why didn't...why didn't my mom leave Da—Zachary to be with you?"

Rick smiled. "We talked about it, and it would have happened eventually." His smile faded. "But for the time being, her presence was required in Salton. Little did I know her plan would fail and she would be lost to me forever."

The door to Rick's office slid open. Rick stood and waved at Jason to do the same.

"Governess." Rick crossed the room and took the Governess's hands in his. She wore a gold brocade gown with wide sleeves and a rope belt around her waist. Her swirling red hair piled on top of her head reminded Jason of a soft-serve ice cream cone.

Rick air-kissed the Governess's left cheek, then right.

"Director Shannon, I was delighted to receive your invitation this morning." The Governess switched her gaze to Jason. "What wonderful news."

Jason hopped on one leg and held the back of his chair for balance.

"Yes," Rick said. "I was overjoyed to learn the news myself when I saw the DNA results. And if I may make it official, Governess, let me introduce you to my son."

God, is this ever going to stop?

The Governess walked up to Jason and air-kissed both cheeks. "What an honor it is to have you with us at the League, Jason."

"We actually met already...your Governess." Jason raised one eyebrow at Rick.

"But not in this capacity," the Governess said. "You must be thrilled with the honor bestowed upon you."

"I don't—"

Rick stepped to Jason's side. "He does not yet know of the honor, Governess. I saved that news for you to deliver. After all, it is momentous and should rightfully be conferred by you." Rick bowed his head.

The Governess placed her hand on her chest. "That is so nice of you. I would have never thought . . ."

Rick looked up. His eyes narrowed at the Governess.

"Pardon my momentary distraction," the Governess said. "As the Principal Governess, I have much on my mind, always working to ensure our League family is well taken care of. But back to the situation at hand, this grand moment."

Jason looked from the Governess to Rick and back to the Governess.

"Jason." She reached for Jason's hand and he jerked back. "Please."

He inched his hand forward and placed it in the Governess's but stayed alert and ready to yank his hand away if she decided to order another punishment.

The Governess put her other hand on top of Jason's. "The League of Governors hereby recognizes you as son of Rick Shannon, an Advisor to the Principal Governess. As such, you receive the rights and privileges bestowed upon the children of The Advisors, and will succeed your father on the Council of Five at such time succession is warranted."

What?

"Congratulations and welcome to The Hierarchy." The Governess released Jason.

His hand stung and he shook it. He looked down. A tattoo of the League emblem had been etched onto the back of Jason's hand. "Hey!"

Apparently, she does have powers.

Jason blew on the mark. The stinging abated. "What did you do to me?" He gaped at the Governess.

"You have received the gift of The Hierarchy," the Governess said. "Each Advisor and each Advisor's heir wears the mark."

Rick raised his hand. His mark glowed then disappeared. "With healing, your mark will be hidden unless required."

Jason shook his hand and blew on it again though the pain had already resolved.

The Governess turned to Rick. "Congratulations. It's wonderful to see the bloodline continue."

"Thank you, Governess," Rick said. "And once the documentation is approved, the Kendrick name will be restored as well."

They know his real name?

"It's a shame your grandfather changed his name in the first place," the Governess said. "The Kendrick family is an important part of our history. And now it will be an important part of our future, with not only one Kendrick but three."

"Indeed," Rick said. "It will be an honor for my family to be known as Rick, Della, and Jason Kendrick."

Jason forced himself to stay quiet.

"I'll take my leave," the Governess said. "We'll do the public ceremony once the official name changes are complete."

"Thank you, Governess," Rick said.

The Governess left Rick's office.

"I am not changing my name." Jason's nostrils flared.

"Nonsense," Rick said. "You are a Kendrick. You will have the Kendrick name."

"And are you changing your first name back to Sewell?" Jason asked. "Because Rick Kendrick is kind of stupid sounding."

"Sewell Kendrick shall forever be my grandfather's name," Rick said.

"Obviously they don't know you're the same guy," Jason said.

Rick shook his head. "Nor do they need to know."

"What if they found out?" Jason asked. "What if I accidentally let it slip?"

"First, no one would believe you," Rick said, flicking his hand in dismissal. "And second, Zachary would soon have a not-so-accidental incident befall him."

Jason dropped into the chair. "So what are you, like, immortal or something?" He stared at the ceiling.

"Not quite immortal, I'm afraid," Rick said. "I have the longevity of the Encantado multiplied by the thousands of dolphins you saw, so I won't be kicking the proverbial bucket any time soon." Rick crossed his arms. "But not to worry. When the Governess moves on, I will become Principal Governor and your position will be elevated to Advisor."

So that sucks.

"How do you keep living? Do you regenerate like Dr. Who?" Jason asked.

"My process is not quite so spectacular," Rick said. "I simply shift to a face of my choosing and embellish it with age as needed. Though I do loathe the aging part. Regardless of my form, my life force is the same. If my current life force is extinguished, I have a ready supply to fill the gap. And I have more on the way in the nursery."

"You have . . . baby dolphins?"

"Of course. Have to think of the big picture." Rick scanned his computer screen. "The baby Encantado are raised in a large tank, free to frolic and play until full grown. Then they're moved to individual tanks. They get quite fussy when that happens but soon realize there's nothing to be done about it." He looked at Jason. "Does that remind you of anyone?"

Jason said nothing, remembering the endless rows of tanks.

"I asked you a question," Rick said.

Jason sighed. "No, Father, it doesn't remind me of anyone."

"Hmm," Rick said. "I wish I could say I believe you this time. You will accept you're a Kendrick."

I'm accepting that you're horrible.

"As such, I have an assignment for you," Rick said.

Jason looked at Rick and waited.

"I'd like you to call your grandmother."

Jason scooted up in his seat. "I can call Grandma Lena?"

"You can and you will," Rick said. "With my guidance."

"Meaning I can't tell her anything about what's going on," Jason said.

"On the contrary." Rick tipped up the brim of his hat and the bottom edge of his blowhole peeked out. "You'll deliver the news of Zachary's employment, and your decision to stay here."

"That won't work. She's going to want to speak to my— to Zachary . . . Father." Jason rubbed the Hierarchy mark, wishing it would disappear.

"You follow the script, and everything will go well," Rick said. "I'd call her again myself, but she's tired of talking to me and insists on speaking with someone in her family. That woman is persistent."

"Yeah, she is," Jason said.

"So let's go over key points," Rick said. "The first thing you need to know is that she visited the League about a week ago."

"What? Why didn't I get to talk to her?" Jason's heart pattered.

"Ah, but you did." Rick leaned back, his hands behind his head. "Well, a copy of you did."

"A shape-shifter." Jason slumped.

"He's both a shape-shifter and a mimic. Quite remarkable, really," Rick said. "Almost fooled me, and I was the one who arranged it. He doesn't know enough about your history to maintain a longer conversation, but for a hug and a hello, he was brilliant." Rick lowered his arms and crossed them over his chest. "Lena also visited with Zachary and Della, and your uncle, poor dear. She was quite upset to see her son in that condition."

Jason pressed the heels of his hands into his eyes. *I saw her talking to Dr. Carrington in the atrium. I should have yelled louder. I should have run faster.*

"He's still with us by the way, your uncle," Rick said.

Jason looked at Rick. *But how?*

"I notice you don't visit him anymore," Rick said, "and you haven't asked about him. Why is that?"

Jason shrugged. "I can't deal."

"You've seen death before. This isn't so different from the loss of your mother."

Except that Uncle A's good, and she wasn't.

"Everyone told me he's given up," Jason said. "I don't want to watch him die."

"Yes, quitting is an ugly quality in people," Rick said. "I agree with you there. Best to be done with him."

Be done with him. Like he's a ratty pair of shoes.

"Right, Father," Jason said. "I'm done with Uncle Alexander." His stomach pinched.

They spent the rest of the morning reviewing what Jason would say to Grandma Lena. It was the middle of the night in the US, so they'd call her later that afternoon. While he recited Rick's key points, Jason racked his brain to figure out things he could sneak into the conversation, hints he could drop that Grandma Lena would notice and Rick wouldn't. But based on everything Rick knew about Jason's family, hint-dropping would be tricky.

I have to figure out something. This is my only chance to get a message to someone on the outside.

Rick ordered lunch for them to be served in his office. After they ate, he took Jason to a meeting with division heads in the department of health services. Jason listened as they worked through the agenda, with one attendee after another agreeing with Rick's directives.

Jason's head bobbed and he snapped it up. He searched the room to see if anyone caught him falling asleep.

All clear.

"And our last item for today," Rick said, "is the discontinuation of JaS units older than three years. I move that we initiate replacement of said units effective immediately. All those in favor?"

"Aye," said most of the attendees.

"Any opposed?" Rick didn't wait for a response before noting the vote on his tablet like he had for all the previous votes on the agenda.

"Sir, I do have a question." A woman at the far end of the table had her hand up.

A bump of energy lifted Jason's drowsiness. No one had spoken up before now.

Rick's brows furrowed. "A question?"

"Yes," the woman said. "If the units are still fully functional, why spend the money to replace them?"

Rick's eyes narrowed. "Why do you think we need to replace the units?"

She stared at Rick a moment. "It makes sense to replace them so our department is equipped with the best the League has to offer."

"Exactly," Rick said. "The motion passes. Our meeting has ended." He watched the woman stand, gather her things, and leave the room.

"That was . . . interesting, Father," Jason said. "Can I call Grandma Lena now?"

Rick didn't answer. He was staring at the conference room door.

"Hello?" Jason snapped his fingers. "Phone call? Father?"

"Hmm? Oh, right." Rick checked the time. "Yes. Let's make that call."

Jason followed Rick as they made their way to his office, stopping often so he could introduce Jason as his son to anyone he deemed worthy. Everyone Jason met congratulated Rick and shook Jason's hand, saying, "Wonderful news. Welcome to the family."

All except one.

A man stepped in front of Rick and Jason. "Director Shannon, I heard the news." He reached out an orange-clawed hand. It morphed to human.

Kappa.

He shook Rick's hand. "How delighted you must be to have your son by your side."

"Yes. Quite." Rick didn't smile.

"And you must be Jason. Welcome to the family." The Kappa embraced Jason.

"Uh, yeah. Thanks," Jason said. *He's super friendly.*

The Kappa released Jason and smiled.

Rick zeroed his gaze on the Kappa's face. "You have work to do."

The Kappa paused a moment. His smile dropped. "I have work to do. I am happy to serve the League." He turned and walked away.

Weird.

Rick watched him go.

Jason noticed a couple of people nearby had interrupted their work to observe the exchange between the Kappa and Rick. One of them was Colette. She returned to her tasks.

"We should go, Father." He said it loud enough for Colette to hear him. He wanted her to believe he was team Rick. He wanted her to stay away.

He wanted Colette to be safe.

A couple of minutes later, Jason and Rick sat next to the speakerphone in Rick's office.

"You have all the key points at the ready?" Rick asked.

"Yes, Father."

"And you understand the consequences should anything be off the mark?"

"Yes, Father." Jason's mind raced. This was it. This was his one chance.

Rick dialed the number.

After a few seconds, Grandma Lena's phone rang. "Hello?"

"Lena, it's Sewell calling from the UK," Rick said.

Sewell? Jason thought for a moment. *Oh, Grams only knows Rick as he was when he first started at the League.*

"Good morning," Grandma Lena said. "Or I guess good afternoon is more appropriate for your time zone."

"Indeed," Rick said. "It's a bit after two p.m. here. I hope I didn't ring too early?"

"Not at all. Even after all these years, I'm still a morning person. I've been up for hours," Grandma Lena said. "Nevertheless, since seven a.m. is an odd hour for a phone call, I did hope this was a call from the UK. But no offense, Sewell, I wasn't wishing for a call from you."

Rick rolled his eyes but put a smile in his voice. "Perfectly understandable, which is why I haven't called alone. Jason's here, and he'd like to speak with you." He nodded at Jason.

"Hi, Grams." Jason wished he could crawl through the phone and hug her and never let go.

"Oh, Jason. It's so good to hear your voice after nothing but emails," Grandma Lena said. "How are you?"

Emails? "I'm fine, Grams. I'm good."

"Are you eating? Are you feeling better?"

Jason looked at Rick. He gestured for Jason to answer.

"I'm a lot better. And yes, I'm eating," Jason said. "Except for, like, Brussels sprouts. Still hate those."

"And how is your sister? And Zachary?" she asked.

Rick scratched out the word "treatment" on a piece of paper.

Della is doing okay. She's better than she was, but she still needs more treatment."

"Oh dear . . ."

"But I have good news about Dad. He has a new job." Jason's tongue wanted to stick to the roof of his mouth.

"My goodness. He's been job searching all the way from London?"

"Um, not really. It's just that everyone at the League really likes him, and they offered him a job here. So we're staying. And they can keep helping Della and we'll be together. Isn't that so great?" Jason glanced at Rick.

He held up his hand, indicating Jason should slow down.

"Well, I . . . you mean you're not coming home at all?" Grandma Lena asked, her voice quivering.

"Dad's already started his new job. And he's happy. I think he was bored with his old one," Jason said. "That's what he said anyway."

"Oh," she said. "I didn't realize he was that unhappy. I'd like to speak to him."

Jason was ready for that comment. "He wants to call you, but he's super busy with his new job, so don't expect a call until things settle down for him."

"I've left him a few messages already. I knew he had a lot to deal with over there, and now it seems there was even more happening than I knew. I assume your phone plan will be upgraded soon so I can reach you as well?"

Rick nodded.

"Yeah. Soon," Jason said. He wondered how Rick would deal with that lie. Grams wouldn't accept not hearing from her family for long.

"And what about Shay? Do you want me to send her over?" Grandma Lena asked.

Jason looked down and rubbed his eyes. "No, Grams, she should stay with you. It would be too hard for her here." Jason's heart ached knowing he'd never see his dog again. "And even though Sadie's allergic, she'll offer to take Shay. But don't let her, okay?"

"Of course not, dear. I'll keep Shay here with Finn. They need each other without you and your uncle around." Grandma Lena sniffed. "Sewell, are you still there?"

"Yes, Lena," Rick said.

"How is my son? Any improvement?"

"I'm afraid not," Rick said. "As we discussed when you were here, there is nothing to be done."

"Yes, well, I'm not giving up hope yet," she said. "I've seen a miracle or two in my day. No reason to think one can't happen for Alexander."

"We are all praying for him and continue to provide the best of care," Rick said.

"Jason?" Grandma Lena said.

"Yeah, Grams."

"Sadie has a few things she needs to talk to you about. Things that aren't my place to share. Please call her as soon as you can. You'll want some privacy for the conversation."

"Is she okay?" Jason asked.

Rick glared.

"You need to talk to her. Promise me you'll call her soon," Grandma Lena said.

"Uh . . ."

Rick mouthed the word yes.

"Yes. Yes, I promise," Jason said.

"All right," Grandma Lena said. "I'm going to let you get on with your day, and I'll start making arrangements for Kyle to join you."

"Oh right. Don't do that." Jason had forgotten to deliver Rick's point about Kyle. "Dad says he wants Kyle to stay with you so he can finish the school year there."

Sorry, only Kendrick children allowed. Kyle will be safer at home anyway.

"I guess that makes sense," she said. "And he and Brandon are getting along well, so neither of them has to worry about hanging out with me too much." She chuckled.

I totally forgot Brandon might be in Salton.

"How long is—"

Rick held up his hand.

Jason licked the dry skin on his lips. "I mean, look how long we've been on this call. I should go."

Rick nodded.

"Tell everyone I said hey," Jason said. "And Grams?"

"Yes, dear?"

"I love you. And everybody," Jason said.

Rick rolled his eyes.

"Love you too, Jason. You take care of yourself and we'll talk soon."

"Okay. Bye," Jason said.

Rick pressed a button and the call disconnected.

Jason rubbed his temples.

"Oh, you must be joking," Rick said. "It was a simple phone call."

"I miss her. I miss everyone. I miss home," Jason said.

Rick pressed his lips tight. "I'll let those comments pass because speaking to your grandmother churned up old feelings," Rick said. "But I suggest you buck up and carry on. Because if you don't embrace your life as my son, with the mark of The Hierarchy and all it entails, it won't only be Zachary who suffers. Do you understand me?"

Goosebumps pricked on Jason's arms. "Yes, I understand. Father."

"Good," Rick said. "And don't make me remind you again, or we'll be dining on fried Shay."

Adrenaline spiked and a burn zipped up Jason's spine.

He fought it down, forced it back. He had no choice.

"I understand, Father."

Jason thought about the clues he'd dropped for Grandma Lena. That he hated Brussels sprouts, that Dad was bored in his job, that Sadie was allergic to Shay. Grandma Lena hadn't reacted to any of them. Jason hoped it was because she'd missed them, not that she'd caught them and didn't let on.

Jason realized now that if Grandma Lena figured out something was wrong and tried to help, he'd just sentenced everyone he cared about to death.

TWENTY-ONE
Heir Kendrick

Rick arranged Jason's schedule so they spent the full day together, from breakfast through dinner. At lunchtime, Jason met with an English tutor in Rick's office. The lesson included how to use the past participle of get with emphasis that one should say "I've not got" rather than "I haven't gotten."

When the tutor asked Jason to use the past participle of get in a sentence, Jason said, "I've not got any interest in this subject."

"Correct," Rick said from across the room. "Or another example is I've not got any news about your lost dog."

Jason nodded and refocused on his lesson.

Five more days passed, all of them spent with Rick, either in his office or attending meetings and lunchtime English lessons. At Rick's direction, Jason traded his T-shirts and jeans for dress shirts and pants, which he now had to refer to as trousers. He no longer used his crutches or wore his passport holder, but he always had the Lex coin in his pocket and sometimes rubbed his thumb over the design.

Rick continued to introduce League members to Jason as his son. Jason fell in step and replied to everyone how honored he was to be there, and how proud he was to serve the League. When he was out with Rick, Jason scanned the people around him hoping to catch a glimpse of Dad or Della, but he never saw them. Jason hadn't seen Della since he first moved into the residence. If she was ever home, it wasn't when he was there in the evening. He asked Rick about visiting her and Rick told him it wasn't a good idea.

Colette sent a few messages through the computer asking Jason to meet her, but Jason didn't respond and he avoided the backyard. He spent his free time learning about the history of the League and memorizing League procedure.

✳✳✳

Jason arrived at Rick's office precisely at eight a.m. as he had the past six days, ready for another day as Jason Kendrick.

"Excellent. You're here," Rick said. "We have a big morning ahead of us. It's an important day."

"Why is that, Father?" Jason asked.

"A case is being brought before the Council of Five. You will join me in the Council meeting and begin your training as a future member of The Advisors." Rick picked up his digital tablet and tucked it under his arm. "Let's go."

"Right now?" Jason eyed the usual breakfast spread at the far end of Rick's office. "I haven't eaten anything." Jason no longer skipped meals or cut back on calories. He needed good food to keep healing, to get stronger.

"No time to waste," Rick said. "Grab something you can eat on the way."

Jason snatched a bagel and smeared it with butter. Better than nothing. He followed Rick out of the office.

They hurried through the halls of the medical unit. As they passed one of the nurses stations, Colette caught Jason's eye. She opened her mouth as if she wanted to say something but didn't. Jason kept walking. He missed seeing Colette. He missed talking to her. But she was better off keeping her distance.

Jason and Rick continued out of the medical unit and into a hallway with a sign directing them to the League Overground.

"What is the League Overground?" Jason asked.

"The Tube." Rick's pace increased. "And we must hurry or we'll miss our train."

Jason scurried to keep up. "The Tube as in, like, the subway?"

"Proper English, Jason."

"Sorry. I meant to say, do you mean the Tube as in the London subway system?"

"Precisely," Rick said. "But as we are traveling over ground rather than underground, our section is the League Overground."

"Seems like it would be simpler to say we're driving if we're going over ground," Jason said.

"But that would not be exactly correct."

Rick turned onto a platform next to train tracks reaching left and right into open sky, then disappearing into the air, much like the elevator cables Jason had seen at The Tower Residences. A moment later wind whooshed into the space. A horn sounded and a three-car train halted in front of them, its doors open. "This is the train to the Palace of Westminster," a recorded voice said. "All aboard for departure."

Jason and Rick boarded the train and the doors zipped shut. The train lurched forward. In a few seconds they were high above London, the walls and ceiling of the train transparent. Jason tightened his hold on a metal pole.

At least they didn't erase the floor.

"Are we over the river?" Jason asked.

"We were, and we will be again when we cross the Thames a second time," Rick said.

Jason gazed at the sights of London. They'd just passed Tower Bridge, and the London Eye was ahead in the distance. To its left was London's iconic clock tower.

"Oh, there's Big Ben." Jason pointed at the tower.

"The bell inside the clock tower is Big Ben," Rick said. "The tower itself is the Elizabeth Tower."

"Yeah, but—"

Rick pursed his lips.

"Right," Jason said, fingering the coin in his pocket. "Thank you for the information, Father."

"You're very welcome," Rick said. "And now I have a question for you."

"Yes, Father?"

"What is the meaning of that coin?"

A wave of vertigo swept over Jason. "Coin?"

"Don't be coy," Rick said. "The half dollar in your pocket. I saw it in your things when you first came into the League, and you showed it to your sister the other night like it was something special. What is it?"

"It's nothing," Jason said.

"Let me see it." Rick held out his hand.

"It's just a coin." Jason pinched the Lex coin between his fingers.

Rick kept his hand out.

Jason took the coin from his pocket and placed it in Rick's palm, Lex side up.

Rick shut one eye and squinted at the coin with the other. "Hmm." He turned it over. "As I thought."

"You thought . . . what, Father?" Jason swallowed.

Rick handed the coin back to Jason. "It's a worthless half dollar, other than the fifty cents it symbolizes, of course. I thought perhaps it was minted in silver, and I'd missed it the first time I examined it."

Jason's shoulders relaxed. "It's a good luck charm." *He didn't see the Lex design.*

"An interesting choice." Rick stood and moved toward the door. "Here we are."

The train stopped and a platform appeared. On the far wall were the words "Palace of Westminster."

Jason breathed deep and silently exhaled. "Are we meeting with Parliament?" He remembered reading about the houses of Parliament, and that they met in the Palace of Westminster.

"Thankfully, no," Rick said. "Today is League business only."

Jason followed Rick across the platform and through a series of doors and hallways. He stopped and faced a place on the wall where the surface changed from drywall to what looked like aluminum sheeting about six feet wide. There was no window, and no handle to indicate it was anything other than a wall.

"Consiliarius," Rick said.

A circle of orange light shone out of the wall and around Rick's face. It widened and swept down Rick's body and back up to his head. A second later the silver wall dissolved like dry raindrops falling to the floor.

Cool.

They stepped into a semicircular room with black carpet and five wooden doors. Each had a large brass plate but again, no handle or doorknob. The brass plate on the first door said First Advisor. Rick placed his hand in the center of the wood and the door opened.

Not as cool as the dissolving door, but still cool.

Jason followed Rick into a room that seemed part bedroom, part office. A desk sat at one end and a sitting area with a chaise lounge at the other. The carpet was beige, and dark wood carved with a row of circular bullseye-like designs spaced a few feet apart covered the walls. Opposite the door was a large armoire next to a full-length mirror. A crystal chandelier hung from the ceiling.

"That consilly word you spoke," Jason said. "Was that magic?"

"Nothing quite so dramatic," Rick said. "It's biometrics, voice recognition technology with a body scan. The word, consiliarius, is Latin for advisor."

"And the handprint—that was biometric security too?" Jason asked.

"Very good, son." Rick smiled.

I'll have to tell Sadie I really was listening when she talked about this stuff.

He swallowed hard. It would be a long time before he talked to Sadie again, if ever.

"Put this on." Rick handed Jason a white robe with a black sash for the waist.

"A bathrobe?"

"Hardly." Rick shrugged into the same black cloak and hood Jason had seen him wearing in Sewell Hall. He removed his hat and put on the silver headband.

Jason pulled the white cloak over his clothes and tied the sash.

I feel like a dork. Or an altar boy. Or a dorky altar boy.

Rick straightened Jason's shirt collar underneath the cloak. "Good. Let's go."

Jason turned toward the door, but Rick went the opposite direction and stepped up to the wall next to the mirror. He placed his hand on one of the circle designs. "Beatus."

A panel of wood slid open.

They walked into a glass room, bright with sunlight. Birds flew by and clouds floated overhead. A semicircular table of green stone flecked with gold sat on one side of the room, with five green leather chairs along its curve. The Principal Governess sat in the center. Through the window directly behind her loomed the spire of Elizabeth Tower.

"Welcome Advisor Kendrick, welcome Heir Kendrick," the Governess said.

Has my name been changed already? He pressed his hand into his thigh where the Lex coin sat in his pocket.

Rick directed Jason to a row of benches positioned at a ninety-degree angle to the stone table. Rick took his seat in the first of the leather chairs. Within a few minutes, all of the Advisors had arrived.

"The meeting of the Council of Five will come to order," the Governess said.

The statement seemed odd to Jason since the room was already silent.

"We are called together to address a first transgression of League member, Charlie Harris." The Governess read from a tablet in front of her. "Charlie Harris is accused of conspiring to influence League members to work against League procedure and disrupt the harmony and value of life at League Headquarters." She set the tablet down. "Bring in the accused."

A section of the floor slid open and a platform rose into the room. Standing in the center of the platform, his eyes wide and his mouth gaping, was the Kappa who had greeted Jason with a hug a week earlier.

Oh no.

"Charlie Harris," the Governess said, "do you understand the charge against you?"

Charlie hooked his human fingertips together and drew his hands close. "No, your Governess, I don't." His bottom lip quivered. "I am honored to serve the League."

"You deny engaging in conversations outside of protocol with other League members during dedicated League hours?" the Governess asked.

"I might have asked a coworker how their new baby boy was doing," Charlie said.

"Such conversation is prohibited during dedicated League hours." The Governess tapped something on her tablet. "And scans by your JaS unit indicate your serum levels have dropped."

"I take my serum every morning, like clockwork." Charlie wrung his hands. "I'm honored to serve the League."

Jason's heartbeats increased. *The pills ... the serum is wearing off. That woman in the meeting, Charlie hugging me ... they're waking up.*

"A secondary scan was conducted by another JaS unit and the findings are confirmed. Let the record show Charlie Harris has conspired against the League as noted in the charges brought against him," the Governess said.

But this isn't what was supposed to happen. I didn't want anyone to get in trouble. Jason squirmed in his seat.

"As punishment, I recommend the removal of the left hand of Charlie Harris, in Kappa form," the Governess said.

Charlie dropped to his knees. "Please, your Governess, there's been some sort of mistake." He pressed his hands together as if in prayer. "I love the League. I want to serve the League. Punishment is not warranted."

"And now you question the Council of Five?" The Governess glared.

Charlie bowed his head. "I apologize, I apologize. Please, I beg your forgiveness." He looked up. "I want nothing more than to serve the League. With great humility, I ask you to spare my Kappa claws as they are key to my power to heal, and to help my fellow League members."

"You will lose only one, and be fully restored when your left appendage regrows," the Governess said. "Until such time, your workload will be reduced, and your salary and other benefits will be adjusted to reflect your lesser contribution to the League."

Oh god, they can't do this. It's not Charlie's fault. Jason stared at Rick, trying to get his attention, but Rick's gaze stayed fixed on the accused.

"What say you, Advisors to the Principal Governess? Do you agree with the punishment of Charlie Harris as I've outlined?" the Governess asked.

From right to left, three of The Advisors agreed with the Governess. She then called on Rick.

Rick stood. "As always, you have provided wise council, Governess." He nodded in her direction. "And it is with great pride that I request my heir to The Advisors honor me and the Council by delivering confirmation of my agreement with the recommended punishment." He gestured for Jason to join him at the table.

Jason rose and inched across the room. Charlie muttered to himself, most of the words unrecognizable to Jason except for a mention of family and suffering.

What am I going to do? I can't let this happen.

He arrived at Rick's side, and Rick put his arm around Jason's shoulder. "Please, son, confirm my agreement."

"I don't know the official words," Jason said.

"Don't worry about the formality," Rick said. "A confirmation in your own words is acceptable."

Jason leaned close to Rick and whispered. "Does he really have to be punished like this? Can't we give him a warning or something?"

Rick whispered his response. "This is protocol. This is procedure. When one doesn't follow procedure, one might find themselves, or those they care about..." He paused a moment. "In dire straits. Now go ahead, son."

Jason looked at Charlie. He had his arms crossed and his hands tucked into his armpits. His gaze was fixed on the floor.

Jason had to say no. He had to speak up and tell the Council he disagreed. "As an heir to The Advisors, I have to—"

Rick clamped a hand on Jason's wrist and squeezed. "Dire straits." He seethed the words.

Grandma Lena, Della, Sadie, Shay, everyone flashed in Jason's mind. He cleared his throat and forced his mouth to form the words. "As an heir to The Advisors, I confirm my father's agreement with the punishment outlined by the Governess."

Charlie cried out and dropped his face into his hands.

Jason twisted his wrist out of Rick's grip and stared ahead at nothing.

TWENTY-TWO

Exit

Jason limited his interaction with Rick for the rest of the day. He answered Rick's questions, he performed assigned tasks, and he sat through his English lesson, pretending he couldn't be more interested. When he returned to his residence that evening, he went straight to his room and slammed the door. He threw his shoes at the wall.

Everything sucks.

Jason removed the Lex coin from his pocket, pitched it onto his desk, and crashed on his bed. He wished he could go back in time and change everything. He wished he'd never left Salton. He wished Della had never had problems.

He wished his name was still Jason Lex.

A message pinged onto his computer screen. It was from User 1017. Colette. "DON'T ignore. She isn't in system. Something's wrong."

The hairs on Jason's arms rose.

He replied. "He says she's in treatment."

"She's been deleted," Colette's reply said.

He had to find out about Della. But Jason wouldn't see Rick again, wouldn't be able to talk to him, until tomorrow.

"Shit." Jason paced his room. "Why did I believe he cared about Della?"

The computer pinged. "Are you still there? What can I do?"

"Nothing," Jason typed back. He turned the computer off.

He went to Della's suite and searched, looking through drawers and closets and under the bed for something that might give him a clue about where she was. He flipped on her television and a message appeared. "Good evening, Della Kendrick. Your schedule has been updated. Prepare to leave your residence at four a.m."

Jason checked the time. Nine p.m. If she was assigned to leave the residence at four, she had to come home first, didn't she?

Jason parked himself in one of the lounge chairs on the main floor and waited, wondering if Della would show, adrenaline keeping fatigue at bay.

At one a.m., the front door opened and Jason jumped from his seat. Della walked in.

"Della!" Jason rushed over and moved to hug her. She stepped back and Jason stopped.

"Procedure says you should be sleeping." Della walked toward the stairs.

"I haven't seen you in a while, and I wanted to wait up for you," Jason said. "See how you're doing."

"I'm fine, but Father says you may cause me to backslide. Goodnight." She started up the stairs to her bedroom.

Jason followed. "Wait, I just . . . what have you been up to?"

"I've been in treatment."

"And you like it? Treatment?" Jason asked.

"Father says it is the best thing for me." She opened her bedroom door. "I must get ready for bed now."

Jason hurried into her room before she could shut the door. "I thought we could hang out for a bit, ya know? Talk about stuff?"

Della set her phone on her desk. "I don't have anything to talk about." She stepped into her walk-in closet.

"Not even, like, baby animals or anything?"

"Those weren't real," she said from inside her closet. "Father created them for me to play with in the sunshine because I'd been good."

In the sunshine? "You don't get to play in the sunshine whenever you want?"

"I am in treatment." Della walked out of her closet. "I must brush my teeth now."

Jason heard the water turn on. *No wonder treatment has caused the weird sleep patterns—they don't let her off treatments long enough to have a normal day.* He glanced over at Della's phone. Jason grabbed it, opened it, and set an app so he could follow Della's movements. *With the internal Wi-Fi and GPS, this should work.* He replaced the phone in its spot.

Della walked in. "I must sleep now."

"You got it, Dell." Jason stood. "Maybe I'll see you tomorrow?"

"My day is full, and I don't want to risk backsliding." Della climbed into bed. "Please turn off my light."

"Yeah, okay." Jason flipped off the light. "Sweet dreams."

He returned to his room and opened the tracking app on his phone. A green dot labeled Della blinked next to Jason's red one. "Yes." Jason pumped his fist.

He set his alarm to be certain he'd be awake before Della left at four, but he only dozed in the few hours that passed. He peeked out his door when he heard her going downstairs. He watched from a top step while she ate cereal then put her bowl in the dishwasher. And he eyed his phone when she went out the front door with someone from the League. Her green dot moved away while his remained stationery. A few minutes later, hers stopped. It was four-fifteen.

Jason wriggled the wristband off his wrist. He hung it under the bulb of his desk lamp, knowing it probably wouldn't maintain an accurate body temperature reading, but maybe he'd get lucky. And it was better than having his wristband reveal he was out.

It was still dark. Jason hoped cameras outside the residence wouldn't pick up his image, but he knew that was more wishful thinking. He didn't care. He needed to find out what was happening to Della.

Jason followed Della's dot to a section of the League that looked like a medical unit, but it was not the one he knew. He walked through double doors into a lobby where a guard sat at a desk. The guard looked up. Jason's mind raced trying to find something to say to prevent the man from sounding an alarm.

The guard stood. "Greetings, Heir Kendrick. If you need anything, please let me know. I am happy to serve the League."

"Uh . . ." Jason composed himself. "Thank you. Good work." Jason waved his hand. "Please, continue with your assignment."

The guard sat and returned to whatever he had been doing. Jason moved through the lobby toward Della's dot.

Okay, that didn't suck. At least one good thing has come out of this Kendrick crap.

A moment later, his and Della's dots had almost merged. Jason turned toward the closest door and went inside. It was a room much like the first room he'd been in at the League, except the bed had a curtain pulled around it. Jason crept close and peeked through the gap. He gasped and yanked the curtain wide.

Della wore a hospital gown and lay on a metal table, her arms wide, her legs splayed, with each limb strapped down. IV fluids flowed into each appendage with one receiving purple fluid, one golden, one pink, and one clear. Her head was clamped into a brace and a drill hovered above her forehead. Her eyes were open.

Jason rushed to her side. "Della?" He fiddled with the strap holding her arm. "We need to get out of here."

"No." She didn't fight her bindings. "It's time for my treatment."

"What treatment?" Jason asked.

Voices sounded outside the door. Jason ducked through the other side of the curtain.

"This is the final experiment. All others have failed," a man said.

Experiment?

"I don't expect this one to produce positive results either, I'm afraid." It was Dr. Carrington's voice. "But we must give it our best, for Della, and for Director Shannon. Isn't that right, Della?"

"Yes," Della said. "I want to be the best for my father."

"And what does it mean to be the best, Della?" Dr. Carrington asked.

"To be the best, I must have powers, like my father," Della said. "Without powers, I am not one of my father's greatest creations."

"That's right," Dr. Carrington said. "Good girl."

What? He's trying to force powers on her?

Jason saw Dr. Carrington's silhouette turn toward the man. "Before we commence with Encantado, I'd like to do one more review of the previous power inductions and analyze their failure points. Maybe we'll discover something that gives us a better chance at succeeding."

"And if we don't?" the man asked.

Dr. Carrington didn't say anything, but through the curtain, it looked like she shook her head.

"I'll order tissue harvest and incineration," the man said.

Incineration? Hell no. Jason's hands fired blue. He clenched them tight.

"Yes, very good," Dr. Carrington said. "Della dear, we have a few more items to take care of before we start, and then we'll give you the power of the Encantado with a blow hole to match your father's. Won't that be lovely?"

"Yes," Della said. "I want to make my father proud."

"Start the Encantado serum," Dr. Carrington said. "By the time we finish our review, her body will be flooded and we can start the rest of the process."

"Very good." The man moved toward one of Della's IVs, then followed Dr. Carrington out of the room.

Jason hurried back to Della. "We have to go." He removed the tape around one of the IVs, clamped off the fluid and pulled the IV out of Della's arm. Nothing horrible happened. He pressed gauze on the spot and taped it in place. *I guess I did learn something after watching them do that to me.*

"Ow, that tape hurt," Della said. "Leave me alone."

"Not gonna happen." He removed another IV, then moved toward one of Della's legs where the pink serum was attached.

"I can't go. I have to stay for treatment."

"This isn't treatment, Dell," Jason said. "They're messing with you." He removed the last of the IVs.

"But I want to stay. I want to be . . . like . . . Father and make . . ." Della's words slurred, then her eyes shut.

Jason patted her face. "Dell?" She didn't wake. *Maybe that's better. This way I don't have to force her to go.*

He released the bindings and shoved the drill aside. He scanned the room for a wheelchair but found none. Even if there was a chair, where would Jason take her?

Maybe . . .

Jason crossed to the metal cabinet that matched the one he had in his first room. He slid the cabinet forward. In the wall was a hatch door.

Yes.

He opened the door and raced back to Della. He wriggled her wristband off, tossed it onto the table, and scooped her into his arms. Jason carried her to the passageway entry and climbed through backward, easing her body into the gap and down the steps, setting her on the floor. Jason returned to the room, grabbed Della's phone and disabled the network connection, and returned to the hatch. From the top step, he pulled the cabinet back into place and closed the hatch door behind him.

Jason heaved Della over his shoulder. *Jeez, when did ten-year-olds get so heavy?*

He wound his way through the passages, hoping he was headed in the direction of his residence. He turned a corner and found himself near the dolphins, a steamy window running along the wall next to him. He was close now. He remembered how to get to his residence from that section.

Jason shifted Della's weight and moved forward. The passage was longer than he expected, and he struggled under his load. He was still heading toward the entrance when Jason found a door to another room. The sign said Utility Room.

Maybe hide her in here, at least for a little while.

He lowered to his knees and eased Della to the floor. He stood and tried the lever on the door. It was unlocked.

The room was large. To Jason's left were steps up to a metal catwalk that crossed over several rectangular pools. Pipes zigzagged across the ceiling, running between pools and connecting to large tanks on the right side of the floor. A sign hanging above the tank closest to Jason said "From Thames." A sign hanging above a tank at the far end said "To Thames." There were no cameras that he could see.

This is the water treatment facility for the dolphins' tanks.

Jason pulled Della into the room and leaned her in a corner. He walked to the farthest tank. A gauge showed the tank was empty, and a digital readout underneath said, "Next flush 1800." *Not until six p.m.*

Jason opened an access panel. A large pipe flowed into the tank from above, drained straight down for a few feet, then angled into a tube that reminded Jason of slides he'd seen at water parks. The tube had a built-in metal ladder, and both the ladder and the sides of the tube turned transparent after a few yards, making it invisible to anyone outside the League. At the far end of the tube glowed a twinkle of light, like sunlight reflecting off water.

"We can get out this way before the next flush. We—"

Jason caught himself. Dad was still here somewhere and Jason couldn't leave him behind. Rick would hurt him. And maybe Uncle Alexander too, if he was still alive.

But Della and Colette, they can go. And maybe Rick'll never know I helped them. Jason's heart pounded. *And if he figures it out, well, I'll think of something.* Truth was he knew Dad would want him to get Della out, even if she wasn't his daughter.

Jason checked the time on his phone: five-twenty a.m. He had plenty of time before he was supposed to report to Rick's office.

He opened Della's phone and wrote a message on her notes app in case she woke up: "Wait here. I'll be right back. Jason." He left the app open so it would be the first thing she saw if she looked at her phone. He tucked it into the palm of her hand.

Jason hurried back to his residence and turned on his computer.

Please be there, please be there.

He opened the last message from Colette and replied: "You there? Need help."

The cursor flashed on the screen. Jason paced the room and checked the screen again.

Nothing.

He used the bathroom, washed his hands and checked the screen again.

No message.

C'mon . . . please see this.

He hurried into his closet and changed his clothes for another day with Rick. A ping sounded from the other room and Jason rushed to his computer.

"I'm here," the message said.

Jason typed directions to Della and asked Colette to meet him.

A few minutes later, he was back in the Utility Room. Della stirred in the corner.

He hunched next to her. "Dell?" He squeezed her hand. "Can you wake up?"

Della mumbled something and her head rolled from side to side.

"C'mon, Della. Wake up." Jason patted her cheek and Della mumbled again.

Colette walked in and he stood. She hurried over and hugged him, and Jason hugged her back.

Colette released her hold. "I'm glad you're okay."

"I'm fine." Jason turned away and scrambled to say something else before she asked more questions. "I have a way to get you and Della to safety." He showed her the tank with its ladder exit to the Thames.

"I had no idea this was even here," Colette said.

"Rick mentioned it when he was telling me about the dolphins, but I didn't think about it being a way to get out," Jason said. "That was stupid of me."

"But why would you? I would have thought they used small pipes like under sinks and stuff," Colette said. "I never would have imagined something like this." She scanned the room.

"I guess," Jason said. "At least we know about it now."

"Is it time for my treatment to start?" Della rubbed her eyes.

Jason walked over and kneeled next to her. "Uh, yeah Dell, it is time for your treatment. But first Colette has to take you to the treatment area." He shrugged at Colette.

She nodded and stepped next to Della. "Let me help you up, and I'll escort you to your treatment."

Colette and Jason hoisted Della to her feet. "I'm kinda dizzy," Della said.

"Why don't you sit right here for a minute." Colette guided Della to the first of the catwalk steps. "As soon as you feel better, we'll go, okay?"

"Okay," Della said. "I don't want to be late. Father would be disappointed."

"No, we wouldn't want that," Colette said.

Jason waved Colette to a spot farther away from Della. "When you get out, call my grandmother. I'll give you her number." He gestured for Colette's phone. "Is this water-resistant?"

"Supposedly," Colette said.

Jason entered Grandma Lena's number into Colette's contacts. "She's in the US, but she'll know what to do to help you guys."

"Fine, except we're not leaving without you," Colette said.

Jason handed over her phone. "You have to. I have to stay for my dad."

"But it's—"

"Rick said he'd hurt him. And he'll also hurt everyone else if you try to send help. So you have to leave, and you have to stay away. And tell my grandmother that, too."

Colette bit her lower lip. "You're not safe here."

"I know what I need to do. I can handle it." Jason thought of more people he might be forced to hurt as a member of the Council and his chest tightened. "And maybe I can stop him from making more serum. He's making enough to hook everybody on it."

"Everybody *is* on it," Colette said.

"No, like in the whole world everybody."

Colette gasped. "Oh my god."

"Yeah," Jason said. "Rick said it'll still take some time, but maybe I can do something before then."

"I feel better," Della said. "We should go now."

"Great, Dell." Jason noticed her face had more color, and her eyes weren't as glassy. "Let's get you on your way." He directed Della toward the tank with ladder access to the Thames. "Climb down the ladder. Colette will be right behind you."

Della's brow knitted. "I've never had to climb down a ladder for treatment."

"This is a new treatment," Jason said. "You know how we like to be thorough and try everything to make sure you're getting the best care, right?"

"The League provides us with the best treatment," Della said.

"Exactly. That's what we're doing now." Jason helped her into the tank and onto the ladder.

"I am grateful for all that the League provides."

"I know you are, Dell," Jason said. "That's really good." He turned to Colette and offered a hand to help her into the tank.

"Are you certain you won't come with us?" Colette asked.

Jason shook his head. "I can't."

Colette paused. Her eyes teared. "Thank you." She kissed Jason's cheek and scurried onto the ladder. "Go ahead, Della, I'm right here."

Jason watched them move down the ladder until they entered the transparent part of the tube and disappeared.

An hour later, Jason entered Rick's office.

"Good morning, son," Rick said. "Breakfast is ready for you, as always."

Jason made his way to the assortment of eggs, breads, and cheeses. "Thank you, Father. I'm starved."

"By all means, help yourself to a hearty breakfast. Far be it from me to deny sustenance to a growing young man," Rick said. "And when you're finished, I have quite the treat for you."

Butterflies fluttered in Jason's stomach. "What would that be, Father?"

"No, no." Rick grinned. "It's a surprise. One that I think will make quite the impression."

Jason loaded his plate with food and watched Rick from across the room. He made phone calls, scheduled meetings, met with people and cryptids who dropped by with health services business to discuss. Nothing in Rick's behavior made Jason more wary than usual. Maybe he didn't yet know about Della disappearing.

Jason's nerves settled into curiosity. He cleared his plate. "I'm ready when you are, Father."

"Excellent," Rick said. "Let me summon a transport."

They left Rick's office and stepped into an electric cart driven by Gregor. They traveled through the atrium, past the Tower Residences, and soon arrived at a one-level building made of gray cinderblocks.

"I'll see you after your assignment, Gregor." Rick stepped out of the cart.

Jason followed Rick into the building. It smelled like mothballs. "What is this place?"

"This is where we treat our very special cases," Rick said. He waved his wristband and a heavy door clunked open.

Jason's pulse surged. "Special cases? You said Della was a special case."

"I did indeed. I'm glad you brought that up." Rick opened another door and they stepped into a room with a two-way mirror.

It reminded Jason of interrogation rooms he'd seen on police shows. On the other side of the window was an empty room.

"Della was indeed a special case. And apparently she developed the power to make herself disappear." Rick stared at Jason.

"What?" Jason tried to sound shocked. "What happened to her? How did you lose her?"

Rick laughed. "Well played, Jason. If I didn't already know exactly what happened to her, I might have actually believed you to be innocent."

Chills raced up and down Jason's spine. "I don't know what you mean."

"You know most of what I mean." Rick placed his hand on Jason's shoulder. "But let me fill in some blanks for you.

Sit." He shoved Jason into a chair and leaned against the window. "Believe it or not, son, I haven't yet come to fully trust you."

"That's not—"

"Silence." Rick held up his hand. "Ever since your noble act at Sewell Hall, I've kept a close eye on you, and your friend, Colette. Your wristbands were adjusted to our highest level of tracking, so even the slightest digressions were noticed."

Sweat beaded Jason's brow.

"First I discovered your friend Colette had an app that she believed disabled her wristband's tracking. But lucky for me, the upgraded tracker was impervious and I was still able to watch her every move."

Oh no, oh god no.

"And then I discovered she spent a large amount of unauthorized time in one of our computer labs and routed a communication module to her residence computer," Rick said. "She's got quite the talent when it comes to technology." He picked at a cuticle. "It's a shame, really. We could have used someone with her skill set."

"Maybe she—"

"Silence!" Spittle sprayed out of Rick's mouth.

Jason scrunched his eyes shut.

"You will look at me when I talk to you," Rick said.

Jason blinked his eyes open. He called his power to start building in his hands.

"I saw she sent you several messages, son." He swiped bits of saliva off his lips with his tongue. "And I was heartened to see you ignored them."

Jason said nothing.

"And then, you didn't." Rick crossed the room and pushed an intercom button by the door. "Hold until my signal."

"Yes, First Advisor," came the response.

Shit. They used his Council title.

"After I saw you'd responded, I checked your data," Rick said. "You might think you were clever to leave your wristband behind, but as I mentioned before, I didn't trust you. Before we moved you into your residence, I had trackers implanted in your shoes. Unless you go barefoot, I know where to find you."

Jason tipped his head back and looked at the ceiling. *I'm screwed.*

"To make a long story short, I know where you took Della, and I know Colette met you there." He raised one hand and ignited it with the blue flame of the Rampart Guards. "And I know you think you'll fight your way out of here, but please." Rick launched a bolt at Jason's feet.

Jason scrambled back, knocking the chair to the floor. A hole smoldered where the bolt hit.

"I suggest you rethink that plan," Rick said.

The muscles in Jason's legs shook. He shoved his hands in his pockets.

"Oh, and one more thing I know that you do not," Rick said. "The flush schedule for water to the Thames was revised this morning and occurred approximately one minute after you left Della and Colette in the exit tank."

What? Jason collapsed to his haunches and his vision blurred.

"They were washed away, like so much excrement," Rick said. "And if by some chance they did survive their express trip into the Thames, members of the League were waiting for them on the other side."

Della . . . Colette . . . they're dead.

Rick pressed the intercom button. "Go ahead."

"Yes sir," the voice on the other side said.

Rick yanked Jason to his feet. "Time for your surprise." He shoved him up to the window.

Gregor and another man rolled a gurney into the empty room. A body lay strapped to it, draped with a sheet. The men tipped the gurney up and turned it so the body faced Jason and Rick.

No, no, no. Jason turned away from the window. Air wheezed in his throat.

"Come now." Rick jerked him back. "You don't want to miss the big reveal."

Jason swallowed hard and watched through the glass.

Rick knocked on the window and Gregor pulled the sheet off the face.

The head lolled forward. Gregor grabbed it by the hair and wrenched it back. The face was puffy and bruised, the eyes swollen shut, the lips cracked and bloody. But Jason recognized him instantly.

Dad.

TWENTY-THREE
Lex

Jason pounded his hands on the glass. "Dad!" He spun toward Rick. "You killed him!"

Rick's hand flew to his throat, feigning shock at Jason's words. "I am offended." Rick waved Gregor and the other man into the room. They stood behind Jason.

"I mean really," Rick said, "what good would it do me to show you a dead Zachary, hmm?"

Jason breathed hard. Voltage sizzled inside his clenched fists.

"I will say it's been quite interesting getting to know a little about Zachary." Rick pulled a chair over and sat. "After he purged the serum, we immediately dosed him intravenously and would you believe it had zero effect?"

The serum didn't work?

"I asked you a question," Rick said.

Jason focused on Rick. "No, I can't believe it had zero effect," he sniped.

"Neither could I," Rick said. "So we overdosed him. Should have killed him. But again, zero effect."

The Lex coin vibrated. Jason shoved his hands in his pockets and hid the movement.

"So we started experimenting," Rick said. "We injected different serums. We mixed serums and injected those. We even injected flu virus, small pox, and Ebola. And Zachary purged every one."

Jason fought to keep his hands cool. "You're an asshole."

"That's hardly any way for a boy to speak to his father." Rick stood.

"Are we really still doing that?" Jason asked.

"I admit I'm more than a little disappointed in how things have progressed." Rick sighed. "But facts are facts, and you are my son."

"Maybe in crazy-land but not in my world," Jason said. "So you might as well kill me and my dad because I'm not playing this game anymore."

Rick rushed Jason, stopping with his face inches from Jason's. "I am your father."

"Screw you." Jason kept his eyes fixed on Rick.

A flat smile crept onto Rick's face. "Let's see about that, shall we?" He crossed the room and leaned against the wall. "Take Jason to—"

A moan sounded from the other side of the window. Dad's head rolled to the other side.

"Dad," Jason yelled and slammed his hand against the glass.

Rick took two quick steps toward Gregor. "What the hell is wrong with you? I told you to induce coma."

Gregor's eyes widened. "I did, sir."

The coin's vibration ramped and Jason gripped it in his fist. Dad raised his head.

Rick pointed at the men. "Take him back to the lab." He crossed his arms and watched as the men rushed into the other room and rolled Dad out.

Jason dashed into the hallway. He rushed to the gurney before the men could block him.

"Dad?" He grabbed Dad's hand and pressed the Lex coin into his palm. "It's Jason."

Dad's eyes sprang open. "Jason. Jason you have to get out. Get your sister out."

"I know—"

Rick yanked Jason backward. The coin clattered to the floor and Rick picked it up. "You and your bloody lucky coin," Rick said. "Look at you. Look at Zachary. You still believe this coin is lucky?"

"So what if I do?" Jason held out his hand. "Give it back."

Rick dropped the coin into his pocket. "I don't think so. It's now mine. And all I am is fifty cents-American richer because there's no such thing as luck. Success is earned through hard work."

Jason kept his arm extended and jutted his chest. "Give—It—Back."

Rick laughed. "Or what? You'll glare at me?" He turned Gregor. "Your partner can return Zachary to the lab. I want you to take Jason to his cell."

Jason dropped his arm. "What are you going to do? Experiment on me now, too?"

"Perhaps," Rick said. "But we'll have to see what the Council mandates."

"You run this whole freak show," Jason said. "Why bother with the Council?"

A questioning look crossed Gregor's face.

"And deny our League members the honor of observing our justice system in action? That would hardly be fair," Rick said. "Though it would be interesting to learn how you fought through the doses of serum you did receive. Especially because the anti-serum we found on you shouldn't have worked. At least not as well as it did." Rick snapped his fingers. "Oh, I know. It was probably your lucky half dollar." He scoffed.

Rick gestured to Gregor. "Take him away."

Gregor seized Jason by the shoulders and pushed him forward.

"I'll see you later today in Sewell Hall, son." Rick grinned.

✳✳✳

Gregor ordered Jason to strip to his boxers and put everything in a plastic bag, including his phone. He tossed an orange jumpsuit into the cell. "Put this on."

"No matching orange shoes so you can track me if I escape?" Jason asked.

"You won't escape," Gregor said.

Jason scanned the cell made of cinder blocks and metal bars. "For once, I agree with you." He plopped onto a rickety cot. "When do we leave for Sewell Hall?"

"Two hours." Gregor walked away from Jason's cell, then returned. "What did you mean when you said the First Advisor is running the show?"

"Huh?" The question was outside serum-norm. *The effect of the pills is still wearing off.*

"Rick is in charge," Jason said. "He tells the Governess and the rest of the Council what to do."

"That's not possible. It's not procedure."

Jason shrugged. "I saw it myself when I joined the Council as his heir." He held up his hand where the mark of The Hierarchy was still visible. "Rick made all the decisions." Jason didn't think he should try to explain the mind control part.

Gregor shook his head. "It's not procedure."

"But it happened," Jason said. "He'll do the same thing at Sewell Hall today."

"It's not procedure." Gregor walked away.

Jason collapsed onto his back. *How did this all get so messed up?*

His chest wrenched as he thought about Della and Colette being swallowed by water. And Dad being tortured by Rick all this time, when Jason thought Dad was safe.

I thought I was doing the right thing. But I made everything worse. Even Uncle Alexander . . .

Jason forced back tears and sat up. Whatever punishment Rick had planned, Jason would take it. He wouldn't show fear; he wouldn't show weakness. He'd be brave.

He'd be a Lex.

✳✳✳

Gregor and three other men escorted Jason to Sewell Hall. In a room below the floor of the hall was a wooden chair carved with tentacles. Gregor instructed Jason to sit. The tentacles animated and wrapped Jason's calves, his arms, his waist, and his neck. Jason struggled for air.

"Anything to say?" Gregor asked.

"Maybe a little looser? This thing is choking me."

Gregor tapped the tentacle at Jason's throat and the tension eased. "Anything else?"

"Nope."

Gregor picked up a jar and brushed a paste onto Jason's lips.

They zipped together and sealed tight.

"Hmm. Mmm mm hmm!" Jason couldn't speak. He thrust his tongue forward and found no gap, not even a seam where his lips had knit together. He jerked against the restraints. "Mmm!"

Gregor painted paste on Jason's neck and his voice silenced. He willed himself to make some kind of noise, even a squeak or a chirp. But there was nothing.

Jason slumped.

Sounds of the crowd increased as they filed into the hall above them. A few minutes later, applause arose.

"Thank you all for coming here today for this special event," the Governess said. "We appreciate your attendance."

"It is our honor to serve the League," the crowd said in unison.

Sounds familiar.

"As you know, the League provides you with everything you need. The best work environment, delicious and nutritious meals prepared by world-renowned chefs, comfortable homes, excellent schools, the pinnacle of medical treatment whenever required."

Rick seriously can't think of something new for her to say?

"You know what the League does for you every day because you see it. You experience it," the Governess said. "And you appreciate it."

"We appreciate all that the League does for us," the crowd said. "We are happy to serve the League."

"But sadly, there is one among us who does not appreciate the gifts of League membership," the Governess said. "Bring in the accused."

The floor above Jason opened and a platform lifted him into Sewell Hall. The Governess and The Advisors were to his right, and the same tarp that concealed Raymond during the last event at Sewell Hall was in place at Jason's left.

Dad.

"I present Jason Kendrick," the Governess said. "Heir to First Advisor, Rick Kendrick."

A murmur rose through the crowd.

The Governess raised her hands overhead and silence returned.

"Jason Kendrick committed the highest possible offense—treason against the League of Governors." Many in the audience gasped, some even cried out. The Governess silenced them again. "As he is an Heir, and bears the mark of The Hierarchy, punishment will be severe and it will be swift."

Jason's hands heated.

"And given his circumstance, it is the First Advisor, his father, who will render and deliver punishment unto Jason Kendrick."

Jason's pulse throttled. He strained against the bindings and the tentacles tightened.

Rick stood and removed his hood. His headband glinted. "Raise the tarp."

The pulleys engaged and the tarp flew up. Dad blinked against the sudden light. He looked better than he had earlier, but he was tied to a pole, his arms bound behind him. He wore orange pants and his chest was bare.

"This man, Zachary Lex, is a false idol." Rick pointed at Dad. "He corrupted my son against me, and now my son is lost. He's unable to free himself of this man's power, and though we made every effort to save my heir, it is with great sadness I confirm my son is near to being unredeemable."

Jason rocked in his seat and the tentacles clamped down, threatening the circulation to his legs. His calves throbbed.

"As such, we have two punishments to deliver today, to protect the League and ensure our membership is sound." Rick turned to the Governess. "I order first the public vivisection of Zachary Lex."

The audience gasped.

"Not only is it apt punishment, it may also reveal how this man manipulates our people, and casts off the effects of our serum designed only to bring peace and happiness," Rick said. "It is also important for my son to see his false idol reduced to nothing. Perhaps then he can be saved."

"And if he cannot be saved?" the Governess asked.

"Governess, regardless of the crimes he has committed, he is my son. I have dispatched a League jet with a team to retrieve and deliver to us those loved ones outside the League who are closest to him: his grandmother, friends, even his dog."

What? No!

Rick glared at Jason. "Perhaps they can yet convince him to choose the right path."

Jason fought and the tentacles wrenched down. His airway closed to a hiss.

"And if they cannot," Rick's voice crescendoed, "he will be ended."

"As you wish," the Governess said.

Voltage amped in Jason's hands and traveled up his arms.

Rick ordered Gregor to bring him a package. Gregor stepped forward and opened a rectangular black box.

Fire raced up Jason's spine.

Rick removed a long, thin blade and held it above his head. "The Sword of Kendrick. Righteous, and holy."

Jason's legs burned.

Rick walked over to Dad and held the point of the blade at the base of Dad's neck. "We will start with the entrails."

Jason closed his eyes and focused his mind.

"And we will finish with the heart." Rick dragged the blade across Dad's chest, nicking the skin and leaving a thin trail of blood.

Jason pried his lips free. "No!"

His body erupted in blue flame. The tentacles burned. The chair incinerated and Jason launched. He fired bolts and freed Dad's bindings. Rick scuttled backward. Jason thrust himself between his dad and Rick.

Guards, including Gregor, morphed to Yeti and rushed toward them. Jason burned the floor, encircling his position with fire. The Yeti halted.

Jason kept his powers at full force.

"Is there a plan I should be aware of?" Dad whispered.

"Nope," Jason said. "Just fight."

"I can do that," Dad said. "I've got your six."

A roar arose from the crowd. Jason couldn't tell if they were shocked or excited or angry. Or maybe all three.

"Silence," Rick ordered.

The crowd hushed.

Rick turned to Jason. "This is foolish."

"Maybe," Jason said. "Or maybe it's an opportunity."

"An opportunity for what?" Rick maneuvered himself behind Gregor. "To show off your fancy Guard upgrades? They're quite impressive."

And surprising.

"I was thinking it was more an opportunity for League members to see how they're being manipulated," Jason said. "By you."

"Bollocks," Rick said.

"You made the serum, and you're using it to control everyone." Jason watched the movement of the crowd and other guards in his peripheral vision. "If League members stop taking it, you're finished."

"Hardly," Rick said. "And if you think anyone will remember this stunt of yours, forget it. I'll wipe their memories before they leave the room." Rick leaned on the hilt of the sword.

Murmurs rose from the crowd.

"In fact, I'll do it now." Rick closed his eyes a moment and the crowd stilled. "Done. As easy as that." Rick opened his arms wide. "If you think you can fight against everyone here, from the guards to our loyal League family, you're more naive than I ever imagined."

Jason scanned the audience. Everyone stared at Rick.

"Guards, seize them," Rick said.

Six Yeti rushed Jason and Dad, morphing into birds and flying over the flames. Jason cremated two midair. One landed in Yeti form and Jason seared its leg, sending it thundering to the floor.

Dad front-kicked another in the gut. Jason turned and burned a hole in its chest, and the fifth dodged Jason's bolts but ran when it caught its paw in the flames. The sixth grabbed Jason from behind. The heat from Jason's body singed the guard to ash.

No one else attacked.

Gregor remained next to Rick.

"What are you doing?" Rick asked. "Take the rest of your team and stop them."

"It's true," Gregor said. "You are controlling us."

Rick narrowed his eyes and locked onto Gregor's. "You are loyal to me. You are loyal to the League."

"To the League, yes," Gregor said. "To you, no."

Rick summoned his Guard power and ripped into Gregor's chest.

Gregor gulped, dropped to his knees and fell forward. Blood flowed from under him.

"Defy me and receive worse," Rick said to the remaining guards. "Apprehend them!" He pointed at Jason and his dad.

Humans and cryptids yelled and rushed forward. Jason fired bolts and launched flames. He ducked punches. He blocked for Dad. After a couple minutes, two Kappas joined their side.

Orange claws of the Kappas sliced through attackers. An Ahool swooped and picked off more threats.

Yes. We need all the help we can get.

Five Yeti moved in. "We fight with you. For Gregor." Jason nodded and returned to the battle. A Sasquatch stood back-to-back with Dad and delivered blows. Three Black Shucks raced in, teeth bared, and ripped the calves out of advancing fighters. Another Ahool snatched an attacker and flung the person into a wall.

Dad wailed and Jason spun, his hands at maximum power.

Dad's arms were burned and limp at his side. He was on his knees. Rick had him by the hair, the Sword of Kendrick at Dad's throat. Hundreds of League members stood behind him, their arms crossed, their gazes fixed on Jason.

"Stop this or he dies," Rick said.

"You'll kill him anyway." Jason kept his power sizzling. The fight continued behind him. "You'll kill us both."

"Perhaps not. But if you keep fighting," Rick said, "it's guaranteed. And the rest of your family and friends die, too. But if you stop now, I'll spare those I've sent for."

Smoke rose from far behind Rick's followers. *What the hell?*

"And you spare my dad," Jason said.

"No promises." Rick yanked Dad's head back. "He's been a thorn in my side for a very long time."

The crowd behind Rick parted at the back. More smoke billowed around them.

Jason eased up on his power for Rick's benefit but remained alert.

"Jason, no," Dad said.

Rick summoned his power and pressed his hand to Dad's scalp. Dad howled.

"This is between me and my son," Rick said.

"Okay, okay," Jason said. "Stop hurting him. What do I have to do?"

The parting of the crowd grew wider and moved closer. Smoke wisped toward Jason. His core reignited.

"Serve me," Rick said. "Without powers, my daughter was worthless. I must have a righteous heir ready to assume the role of First Advisor when I become Principal Governor. You and I have much to repair between us, but serve me well and in time you will be exalted."

The crowd behind Rick continued to step aside without hesitation.

Jason hooked his hands near the small of his back and maxed his power. "So you want me to be what? Your slave?"

The sound of fighting died down, but Jason didn't dare take his eyes off Rick.

Rick craned his neck. "Ah, you'd better act fast. My offer is rescinded if my forces defeat your traitors, and that seems to be happening as we speak." He jerked on Dad's head again. "And really, acting as my slave, as you call it, is a small price to pay for the lives of your friends and family."

Jason grinned. He kept his focus on Rick, careful not to entice him to turn and see what was coming.

"You think this is funny?" Rick asked.

"Not funny," Jason said. "I'm happy."

"Ah, very good," Rick said. "It pleases me that you're happy to return to my—"

A blade sliced through Rick's skull. Its point thrust out his blow hole. He crashed to the ground, thrashed, and was still.

"Gotta say, I've never been more excited to see you, Uncle Alexander." Jason extinguished his power and rushed forward to help Dad stand.

"Ditto," Dad said.

"Happy to be seen." Uncle Alexander smiled.

Bartie ran up and Jason's jaw dropped.

"The anti-serum gas has been fully distributed and folks are recovering nicely," Bartie said. He noticed Jason. "Jason, my boy, jolly good to see you."

"And you, too." Jason looked from Bartie to Uncle Alexander and back to Bartie.

"I'm off to check on Elizabeth, see if she needs any help with our other mission." Bartie hurried away.

"Elizabeth? His wife? How? And you?" Jason couldn't set his mind on a single question.

Uncle Alexander put his arm around Dad's waist. "I'll explain everything. But let's get your dad to a Kappa."

The fighting stopped. They walked Dad to a chair and eased him down, and Jason and Uncle Alexander sat next to him. One of the Kappas from the battle hurried over to help. She hovered her clawed hand over the burns on Dad's arms and scalp and the wounds healed. The bruises on his face faded. "I'm sorry, I can't restore the hair, but it will grow back."

Dad chuckled. "I always thought it would be cool to shave one side of my head. Now I get to try it." He shook her clawed hand. "Thank you."

"You're welcome." She moved on to the next injured League member.

"Wait, what about all the other injuries you had this morning?" Jason asked. "I thought you were down for the count."

"The coin helped with that," Dad said. "Gave me a jumpstart."

"The coin." Jason jumped up and ran to Rick's body. He searched his pockets and found the Lex coin. It turned green in Jason's hand. He showed Dad and Uncle Alexander. "I'm guessing green is a good thing?"

"Very," Dad said.

Jason handed it to Dad.

Dad held up his hands. "Nope. Like I said before, that coin belongs to you."

"Okay..." He dropped the coin in his pocket and scanned the hall. Bodies and body parts littered the floor. The air smelled like burned fur. "Can the Kappas fix everyone?" Jason asked.

"The wounded, yes," Uncle Alexander said. "But they can't restore the dead."

"That totally sucks." Jason turned to his uncle. "And what about you? Did a Kappa fix you? After I...?"

Uncle Alexander put his hand on Jason's knee. "You fixed me, Jason."

"But how?" Jason wiped his hands on his pants. "I thought I killed you."

"Killed him?" Dad asked. "What are you talking about?"

"It's okay," Uncle Alexander said. "Both of you can relax. Jason did exactly as I asked."

"You didn't want to die?" Jason asked.

"Not at all. The gold serum they had me on was specialized to preserve my appearance and enable some movement while they drained me of my Guard powers," Uncle Alexander said. "The other donors, like Bartie and his wife Elizabeth, didn't have that luxury."

Jason remembered seeing Bartie and the others in the donor room. They were like rocks in their beds.

"Rick wanted you to have hope for my recovery, and keep you here until he could control you with the serum. But that never happened. How did you escape it?" Uncle Alexander asked.

"I had help . . . really good friends who helped me." *And they're both gone now. And Della . . .* A lump formed in Jason's throat.

Dad put his arm around Jason's shoulders and squeezed.

"Well, I have to say, I was so damn proud of you when you figured out the Morse code," Uncle Alexander said.

"Hah. Thanks. And I'm damn proud of you for not making me kill you," Jason said. "But what did I do?"

"After you adjusted the IVs, I woke up. I was able to operate at night without discovery. I adjusted my IV sensors to avoid arousing suspicion, and I was able to get to the donor rooms and start diluting the poisons. Slowly but surely, they started to wake up, too."

"And they're all okay?" Jason asked. He remembered Raymond saying the donor process was a death sentence.

"Not all," Uncle Alexander said. "But many. And with the first to wake, like Bartie, we devised a plan. We looped cameras so we wouldn't be seen. We diluted liquid supplies of serums and would have done the same to the pills, but they were already inert."

"Oh." Jason raised his hand. "That was me and . . ." His enthusiasm faded at Raymond's memory. "That was me and Raymond, one of my friends. He's gone now." Jason swallowed hard.

"I'm sorry," Uncle Alexander said. "He was clearly a good person."

Jason nodded. "He was. He saved me."

Dad squeezed Jason's shoulders again.

"Keep going, Uncle Alexander." Jason wiped at moisture threatening to escape his eye.

"We found an empty lab and created an anti-serum. We used Rick's methods for aerosolizing the serum, doing that for the anti-serum instead. We weren't one hundred percent certain it was ready, but when we heard a Sewell Hall event had been added to the schedule, we decided to inject the anti-serum into the air conditioning system." Uncle Alexander patted Jason's arm. "Thanks to the work you and Raymond already did, the anti-serum worked."

"But the crowd behind Rick..."

"They'd likely been on the serum longer, so were slower to respond to the antidote," Uncle Alexander said. "We anticipated that, and released anti-serum smoke bombs, if you will."

"Nice." Jason high-fived Uncle Alexander.

"It was a long time coming," Dad said, "but this whole thing goes in the win column. Now we need to find your sister and get out of here."

Jason's heart sank. "Oh, uh..."

"Don't tell me you want to stay longer?" Dad stood.

"No, it's not that...it's just...there was kind of an accident." Jason bit his bottom lip to stop it from quivering.

"Jason," Uncle Alexander said, "you don't mean—"

"Dad!"

Dad turned toward the voice. "Della!" He rushed forward, scooped Della into his arms and spun her around. He set her down. "Are you okay? Let me look at you."

"Della?" Jason whispered the word. There she was, alive and well, hanging onto Dad. Bartie and a woman stood behind them. Jason didn't see Colette.

"That's really her," Uncle Alexander said. "She didn't die in the flush. We had a team waiting, led by Elizabeth. Let me introduce you." He stood.

Jason followed. "And Colette?"

"She's fine as well. She's here somewhere."

A laugh gurgled out of Jason's throat. He thought he sounded like a crazy person. "Yeah. Yeah, I want to meet Elizabeth." Jason rushed forward and fast-hugged Della. "I'm so happy to see you, Dell. Hah. You don't even know." He released her and immediately flung his arms around Elizabeth. "I'm Jason. Thank you for saving them."

"Oh, my. Yes." Elizabeth hugged him back. "It was sincerely my pleasure. But I don't deserve all the credit. I had help." She stepped out of Jason's hug and gestured to someone behind her.

There stood Grandma Lena, with Colette by her side.

Jason scuttled forward and hugged Grandma Lena, then hugged Colette, then hugged Grandma Lena again. He stepped back. "What are you doing here?"

Grandma Lena smirked. "You don't think I'd let my family go down without a fight, do you?"

"You knew we were in trouble?"

"I suspected, and my phone conversation with you confirmed it," Grandma Lena said.

"You got my clues," Jason said.

"Yes I did, and they were quite clever," Grandma Lena said. "Clearly you take after me."

"Hey now," Dad said, laughing. Della stood next to him.

"What about you, Dell?" Jason asked.

"What about me?"

"Are you hugging back today?" Jason asked.

Della made a face. "Yes, I'm hugging back today. I just wasn't ready a minute ago." She walked over to Jason.

"Well, last night you were all standoffish—"

"I know. Shut up." Della wrapped her arms around Jason's waist. "I'm sorry."

"Not your fault, Dell." Jason mussed the top of her head. "I get it."

She batted at Jason's hand. "Seriously with the hair again? Already?"

"Some things never change." Jason took Colette's hand in his and squeezed.

Colette smiled and squeezed back.

TWENTY-FOUR
Going Home

Jason scanned the scene in Sewell Hall. "As much as I'd like to bail and go home right now, we should help get things straightened up."

Dad nodded. "I agree. Let's get to work. But first, Jason, can I talk to you for a moment?"

"Yeah. Sure." Jason released Colette's hand.

"I'll go get some cleaning supplies," Colette said.

Jason walked over to his dad. "Is Della really okay?"

"In time," Dad said. "The anti-serum is helping her, but considering what Rick's people did, we'll need to keep working with her for a while. At home."

"I like the home part for sure," Jason said.

Dad drew him further away from the group where they wouldn't be overheard. "Son, I know about your mom, and about the DNA reports."

Jason swallowed hard. "Dad, I mean—"

"Stop right there," Dad said. "I know what Rick said, I know what those pieces of paper said, but I don't give a rat's ass about any of that. You are my son and Della is my daughter. Period."

Relief washed over Jason like cool rain on a hot day. He stared into his dad's eyes. *Lex. I'm Jason Lex.*

"You hear me?" Dad grasped Jason's shoulders. "You are my son. Got it?"

Jason blew out a breath. "Yeah, Dad. Yeah, I've got it."

Dad pulled Jason into a tight embrace. "Good." He released him. "Now we're going to do two things. First of all, we're not telling Della about any DNA tests. It seems like she's not remembering much, and anything she does recall we'll say was a trick of the serum, okay? I don't want her to have to deal with anything as heavy as wondering who her parents are."

"Yeah, okay," Jason said.

"And the second thing we're going to do," Dad said, "is get our own DNA tests done. Alexander says he can do them himself using one of the labs here. But as far as I'm concerned, Rick fabricated the whole thing."

"But why?" Jason asked. "Why us?"

Dad sighed. "Because he had an obsession with your mother, and she with him. He was the one she left us for, he was why she tried to destroy the Rampart."

Jason was surprised at how much Dad had figured out already.

"I'd suspected something was going on when she traveled to London, but I never saw any proof," Dad said. "Or maybe I didn't want to see it." He ran his hand through what hair he had left on his head. "Maybe he wanted to hold on to her through you and Della. Who knows? But we'll learn the truth, and we'll deal with it, and we'll move forward *as a family.*"

Ripples rolled through Jason as he thought about another DNA test that might confirm he was Rick's son.

"We'll get through all of this." Dad gripped Jason's shoulder. "And you're strong. You're one of the strongest people I know. You're a cornerstone of this family and I'm extremely proud of you."

Jason stood tall. "Thanks, Dad."

Dad smiled. "We'd better get back before everyone else thinks we're slackers." He winked.

Jason laughed. "Yeah, we're totally slackers."

✳✳✳

A few hours later, the group sat down to dinner at a large round table in the Italian wing. Colette sat on Jason's right, with Grandma Lena on his left. Filling out the rest of the seats were Uncle Alexander, Dad, Della, Bartie, and Elizabeth.

"We believe we've rounded up Rick's supporters, including Dr. Carrington," Bartie said. "They'll stand trial once a new Council of Five is sworn in."

Uncle Alexander smiled. "And with you and Elizabeth at the helm, I'm certain the League will be restored to its former glory in no time."

"My darling Elizabeth gets the hard job." Bartie patted Elizabeth's hand. "But she will excel as our new Principal Governess."

"Seriously?" Jason asked. "You're the new head honcho?"

"Indeed," Elizabeth said. "The removal of Rick's supporters moved me up the line of succession, and here I am. Never in my wildest dreams did I expect such an honor."

"And such a burden," Bartie said.

"Yes, but with you by my side, it will be that much easier." Elizabeth kissed Bartie's cheek.

A waiter brought bread, olive oil, and balsamic vinegar to the table and said he'd return in a few minutes to take their orders.

Jason popped a hunk of bread into his mouth. "Uh mmm ssh hngrr."

"Chew and swallow first, talk second" Grandma Lena gave him a look that said Jason should know better.

He swallowed. "Sorry. But I am so hungry." Jason looked at Bartie. "Wait—Uncle A said you'll both be in charge?"

"I'm replacing Rick as director of health services," Bartie said. "I want to ensure our members are well taken care of, with the most urgent business being the healing and release of all the so-called donors, including the Encantado in captivity. We've already started to reverse what's been done to them, but I'm sad to report not all can be saved. Regardless, we'll do our dam—" He glanced at Della. "Er, our darndest to help as many as we can, and return them to their homes."

"I'd love to work on that project," Colette said.

"That's a grand idea." Bartie looked from Colette to Grandma Lena. "But I think someone has other plans for you."

Grandma Lena turned to Colette. "It's more of an idea than a plan. But we'd love to have you return to the States with us and stay for as long as you like. Take some time to recover, and let us take care of you."

"That would be totally cool," Jason said. "I mean if you want."

Colette's face brightened. "I ... are you ... are you certain? I wouldn't want to be a bother."

"You wouldn't be, not in the slightest," Grandma Lena said. "We'd love to have you. All of us, including Sadie. And the dogs always like having another person around to love on them."

"Yeah, you'll get to meet Shay and Finn," Jason said. "And you could help me train like Sadie does. You and Sadie will totally hit it off, and her grandma's really cool, too."

Grandma Lena paused a moment. "Everyone would be delighted to meet you, Colette. I hope you'll think about coming home with us."

"I don't have to think about it," Colette said. "I feel so lost here at the League without my parents ... I can't imagine it ever feeling normal again. Maybe that will change over time, but right now ... I'd love to go to the States with you."

"Then it's settled," Grandma Lena said. "We'll make the arrangements."

The waiter returned and started taking everyone's orders.

Jason leaned into Grandma Lena. "Sadie's going to really like Colette."

"I'm sure she will," Grandma Lena said. "But Jason, Sadie's going through some challenges right now. I know you've been cut off from communications, and she knows that, too. But she's still going to need you when you get home."

"What's going on?"

"We'll talk about it later," Grandma Lena said. "Right now, let's focus on this moment, and this celebration, okay?"

Jason nodded. "Yeah, okay." A knot formed in his chest. "But is Sadie all right?"

"She's fine. And she'll be happy to see you." Grandma Lena turned to the waiter asking for her order.

Sadie's okay. We'll be home soon. It's all good. Jason scanned the faces of everyone laughing and chatting around the table.

It's all good.

Dad's voice snapped Jason's attention back to the conversation. "And then Jason transformed into a blue fireball, and that confirmed it for me."

"Confirmed what?" Jason asked.

"The legend about the Lex coin," Dad said. "One of the stories passed down in our family was about a Lex coin that searched for a particular Lex descendant, one worthy of the power the coin held. My parents used the story as a tool to keep us kids on our best behavior so maybe the coin would find us one day. I thought it was a story you tell children, like Santa's elves are watching so you'd better be good." Dad chuckled. "I mean, we never believed any of the coins existed, much less one that basically had something like a naughty and nice list."

"You turned into a blue fireball?" Colette asked.

"Sort of, I guess." Jason knew he'd found more power but didn't realize his whole body had been fiery. "But what power does the coin have? And why could some people see the real coin and others couldn't, like Rick?" *And Della. But I'm not saying that in front of her.*

"I don't know much about the power or the coin— nobody does," Dad said. "With Alexander's help, maybe we can learn more."

342

"I'll dive into researching it when we get home," Uncle Alexander said.

Dad put bread on his plate. "But the story says the coin chooses a descendant based on integrity of character and soundness of judgment. I'm feeling a bit bad I didn't qualify." He laughed. "But I'm not at all surprised that you did, Jason."

"I don't know about that," Jason said. "Maybe the coin has a glitch or something." *Or I'm a Lex, through and through . . .*

"Hardly," Bartie said. "After what I've seen from you, I'd choose you without question."

"Agreed," Dad said. "And I suspect the coin displayed its true form or hid it, based on how it read your instincts and trust in the people around you."

I didn't trust Della?

"As well as how the coin read those people around you, and their intentions toward you." Dad took a sip of water.

Or my gut knew Della wouldn't keep the secret that she'd seen me.

"Does that mean the coin is alive?" Jason asked.

"Perhaps," Uncle Alexander said. "The coin could be infused with a spirit or some other entity, a guardian angel if you will. Or it could simply be ancient magic."

"So Rick never knew what it was," Jason said.

"No. Very few people have heard of the Lex coins, and those that have heard of them thought they were only stories," Uncle Alexander said. "The only reason I've heard anything about them is because I've studied your family as much as my own." He dipped a piece of bread in olive oil. "And even if Rick had suspected, the coin never revealed itself, so he would have dismissed it."

"Well, the coin helped Dad get better, so maybe it's really Dad's coin," Jason said.

"I think you, using the coin, helped your dad get better," Uncle Alexander said. "In that moment, the coin knew your intentions and moved to make that happen."

Wow ... healing power?

"And that's why Dad came out of the serum fog when I threw the coin at him, because I wanted him to."

"Exactly," Uncle Alexander said.

"If I'd put the coin on your chest or something," Jason said to Uncle Alexander, "would that have woken you up a lot earlier?"

"Maybe," Uncle Alexander said. "But that's neither here nor there."

"Why didn't it fix everything from the beginning?" Jason asked.

"I suspect you have to do your part. You have to be healthy, strong," Uncle Alexander said.

"Great," Jason said. "One more thing watching to make sure I eat my vegetables."

"Which reminds me," Uncle Alexander said. "I told you so."

"Yeah, okay. You were right," Jason said. "I now eat plenty of everything, and I get rest, and I even do my deep breathing stuff."

"And you'll learn more Morse code."

"Yes, Uncle A, I'll learn more Morse code." Jason smirked. "And speaking of eating plenty of everything ..."

Three waiters approached and loaded the table with pasta, salad, and more bread. They poured champagne for the adults and sparkling cider for Jason, Colette, and Della.

Bartie raised a glass. "I hope you don't mind, but it seemed appropriate to mark the occasion with something special. Would you join me in a toast?"

Everyone raised their glass.

"I'll keep it short and simple," Bartie said. "To the good guys—ladies and gents—defeating the bad."

"Hear, hear," Dad said.

Everyone echoed the sentiment and sipped their drink.

"And thanks again for saving Della and Colette," Jason said.

"It wasn't really us," Elizabeth said. "Lena contacted Nessie, and Nessie arranged the whole thing with her cousin who lives in the Thames. Though the original plan was for infiltration only. Little did we know she'd help us with a rescue as well."

"Nessie?" Jason asked. "As in Loch Ness Nessie?"

"The very same," Elizabeth said.

"And her cousin..." Jason looked from Elizabeth to Colette.

"Her name's Mathilda," Colette said. "And if I hadn't already been panicked about drowning, she would have scared the heebie-jeebies out of me."

"She was cool," Della said. "She lifted me right out of the water and Grandma Lena pulled me into a boat. Then she dove back down and found Colette."

"I don't know how long I was under water. One moment I was spinning, trying to get my bearings, and in the next moment I was zooming upward. Mathilda is a fast swimmer."

"Super fast." Della slurped noodles into her mouth.

"We got Della and Colette dried off and warmed up," Elizabeth said, "and headed back here. We had the easy part."

"I'm sorry I missed out," Uncle Alexander said. "It's been a while since I've seen Mathilda."

"You know her?" Jason asked.

"Certainly. I met her on one of my first trips to the League," Uncle Alexander said.

"Huh." Jason took another sip of his sparkling cider. "So am I the only one who hasn't met Mathilda?"

"Are you jealous?" Colette grinned.

"No. I mean, maybe a little."

"So am I, Jason," Dad said. "Next trip to London, you and I meet Mathilda." Dad gave a firm nod like it was a done deal.

"Cool, Dad. Though I'm not sure I want to come back super soon."

"I understand that," Dad said. "We'll play it by ear and come back when we feel like it."

Jason nodded and stabbed a chunk of lasagna. "Are we set to leave tomorrow?"

Grandma Lena looked at Dad. "I'm not sure we'll be able to get everyone on a flight as soon as tomorrow. Perhaps the next day?"

"We can do better than that," Elizabeth said. "We'll send you home on one of the corporate jets. No need to make any other arrangements."

"That is a lovely offer, Elizabeth," Grandma Lena said. "Thank you."

"Super cool," Jason said. "We're like rap stars or something."

Elizabeth laughed. "I suspect the amenities on our jets may not live up to rap-star standards, but you'll be comfortable."

"Do we get free snacks?" Jason asked.

"Free snacks, free meals, and free drinks," Elizabeth said.

"Awesome." Jason smiled.

***

Jason spent the early part of the next morning preparing to head home. He threw a few things in a bag—only what he needed for the trip. He didn't want the clothes or anything else Rick had provided for him. Jason wished he had the suitcase and clothes he'd brought with him from Salton, but those items were never returned.

The last thing Jason packed was the Lex coin. He examined it closely and wondered about the powers it held and what else there was to learn about it. *I'm really glad you showed up when you did, Lex coin.* Jason clutched the coin in his fist, then dropped it safely into the pocket of his passport holder which was back around his neck.

Jason and Della met Dad, Grandma Lena, and Uncle Alexander in the kitchen. Jason liked that they were all able to stay together in the residence assigned to him and Della.

Dad and Grandma Lena prepared breakfast of pancakes, scrambled eggs, and fresh strawberries.

Dad placed a full plate of food in front of Della.

Della hesitated. "I always have cereal for breakfast." She glanced at Dad then looked at her plate.

"Not anymore you don't." Dad pulled the chair out for her. "Unless you prefer cereal? I can take that plate back and get you a bowl and—"

"No." Della sat and pulled the plate closer. "This is good. I'm good with pancakes." She beamed.

"What time are we leaving?" Jason took a seat at the kitchen island.

"We're leaving for the airport at noon," Grandma Lena said.

"So I have time to see if I can find my phone? Gregor took it from me yesterday. I can use Della's phone to track it if it's still on."

"Yes, and I'll come with you," Dad said. "We can track my phone, too."

"I have a few tests to run." Uncle Alexander looked at Dad. "I'll meet up with you when it's time to head to the airport."

Jason knew what tests Uncle Alexander was talking about. He tried to push the thought out of his mind. He didn't want to think about what the DNA might confirm.

The doorbell rang and Jason hopped off his seat and headed to the door.

Colette stood on the porch. She gave Jason a hug. "Hi."

"Hey. I'm glad you're here." Jason pulled her suitcase inside the foyer. "Want some breakfast?"

"Sure. Thanks." Colette rubbed her hands together. "But I'm a bit nervous."

"It's nothing fancy. Just eggs and stuff." Jason moved toward the kitchen.

Colette grabbed his arm. "Not about breakfast. About leaving. About staying with your family, especially your grandmother. She's kind of amazing."

"Oh. Yeah, I get that," Jason said. "It's a big trip. But it'll be great. I promise."

"But your grandmother—"

"She's totally cool. She won't boss your around or anything, if that's what you're worried about."

Colette pushed a loose strand of hair out of her face. "It's not that. It's because she's, you know, got her special skills and things. I don't want to end up being in her way if she needs to use them or something."

"What do you mean?" Jason asked. "Like cooking? She's a great cook and I'm sure she'd teach you if you want. She makes really good chicken. Or . . . are you talking about something else?"

Colette paused. "Oh . . . no, I was talking about . . . right, I was talking about her cooking. Yeah, I'd like to learn more about cooking."

"Cool. She'll love that." Jason motioned toward the kitchen. "C'mon."

Colette followed him.

"Grams, Colette wants to learn how to cook," Jason said.

"Good morning, Colette." Grandma Lena gave Colette a hug. "I'd be delighted to show you a few things in the kitchen. Whatever interests you." She winked.

"Uh, thank you," Colette said. "That'd be really nice."

Grandma Lena looked at Jason with a grin on her face.

"What?" Jason asked.

"Nothing," Grandma Lena said. "I'm just happy."

Okay . . . but why do I feel like I missed out on a joke or something? Jason returned his focus to his food and finished his breakfast.

✳✳✳

After locating the phones, Jason, his dad, and Colette met up with the rest of the group and were ready to leave.

Bartie shook Jason's hand. "A pleasure, Jason Lex. A pleasure indeed."

"Thanks, Bartie. Great meeting you, too. And I'm really glad it wasn't you that tried to kill us."

"You and me both, young man. You and me both." Bartie slapped Jason on the back.

Jason reached out to shake Elizabeth's hand and noticed her ring. He flashed on what Bartie had told him and Uncle Alexander when they were at his home.

No . . .

He checked her left hand. Her ring finger was missing.

"They really did send Bartie your finger . . ." Jason gaped.

Elizabeth raised her hand, her absent ring finger leaving a gap. "A small price to pay compared to what happened to many of my colleagues. And the remaining four fingers seem quite capable of the job at hand." She chuckled. "See what I did there?"

Everyone joined her in the laugh.

"Honestly, I'm quite fine, Jason." She pulled him into a hug. "Even better than fine, thanks to you."

"No way I'm taking all the credit." Jason held his arms wide. "This was a team effort for sure."

"Agreed," Elizabeth said. "And you all have special status with the League from now on. I dare say your names are likely being entered into our history books as we speak."

Jason and everyone else bound for the United States finished their goodbyes and headed to the airport. Soon they were aboard one of the League's corporate jets ready for departure.

Finally.

Jason and Colette settled into a pair of cream-colored leather seats, and he opened cans of lime sparkling water for each of them. A minute later, Jason's phone buzzed, then buzzed again, and again, and again, and again. He removed it from his pocket. The messages icon showed forty-two new messages, many of which were from Sadie. He tapped the most recent message from a few days ago.

"Your grandmother says you're in trouble. Sorry about earlier messages. Hope you're okay."

Jason scrolled to the next oldest one in the list. "How do you just not respond to me? What kind of friend are you?"

He started to read another message, but the pilot came on the intercom and asked all devices be turned off or placed in airplane mode. Jason hesitated then switched off his phone.

"Is everything okay?" Colette asked.

Jason remembered Grandma Lena saying Sadie was having a hard time. "I think so. It'll be good to get home."

Colette squeezed Jason's hand. "If there's anything I can do to help, do let me know."

After about an hour in the air, Uncle Alexander asked to speak to Jason in the back of the plane where he sat with Dad. Della sat near the front with Grandma Lena.

"What's up?" Jason took a seat opposite Dad and Uncle Alexander. "Your uncle has the DNA results," Dad said.

Jason's stomach dropped even though the plane hadn't hit any turbulence. "Okay . . ."

"Jason," Uncle Alexander said, "it is with near one hundred percent certainty that you are Zachary's son. You are Jason Lex."

Jason fell back in the seat and pumped both his fists. Weight heavier than he'd realized, lifted and dissolved. "Best news ever." He sat forward. "And Della?"

A shadow dropped over Dad's face. He shook his head.

"What?" Jason flicked his gaze from Dad to Uncle Alexander. "She's not . . ."

"I was so sure the DNA results would prove you both to be my children," Dad said. "That didn't happen with Della, but it doesn't change anything I said before. She's my daughter, and she'll always be my daughter."

"And we're not telling her about the test results," Jason said.

"Right," Dad said. "We're not telling anyone else except Lena. As Adrienne's mother and Della's grandmother, I believe she has a right to know. But we're not telling Della, or your brother."

"Yeah, okay." Jason rubbed his hands down his face. "This is so weird."

"It's only chemicals," Uncle Alexander said. "What really makes a family is their love for one another."

"I know. I totally get it." Jason loved Della no matter what. "I still wish the result was different. But yeah, we're family. One hundred percent."

Dad patted Jason's knee. "That's exactly right. And nothing is ever going to change that."

Jason nodded. "I still don't get why Rick lied about my DNA."

"I can help with that," Uncle Alexander said. "I found several papers he'd written over the years about the preservation of bloodlines for heirs to the Council of Five. He'd been vocal about the belief that heirs must present with powers. Once he took his place on the Council, he instigated a change in the procedures stating that if an heir lacked powers, then the heir should be disqualified and a new bloodline selected for the Council."

"And Della doesn't have any real powers," Dad said.

"Right. Rick had his team working with her to draw out any power that might not yet have manifested," Uncle

Alexander said. "Those were her supposed treatment sessions when she first arrived. When that failed, they began tests and therapies in an attempt to create a power. But he needed a backup plan, so he falsified a DNA report and worked to manipulate Jason into assuming the role as his heir."

"Couldn't he have just changed the rules?" Jason asked. "He had the whole mind control thing going."

"He could have, and I suppose he would have if his plan didn't come to fruition," Uncle Alexander said. "But for whatever reason, he opted for controlling you instead. I suspect he felt slighted that the child he had with Adrienne didn't deliver the perfect heir, so he decided to steal you from Zachary."

"That guy sucked," Jason said. "I hope he's deep in some hole somewhere."

"Better than that." Uncle Alexander crossed his arms. "His body went into the incinerator. Fitting, I thought, considering how many humans and cryptids he'd sent there after robbing them of their gifts and their lives."

"Absolutely," Dad said.

"I still have that stupid Hierarchy mark." Jason looked at the back of his hand. His skin was smooth, clear. "Somewhere in there."

"It's unlikely the mark will surface," Uncle Alexander said. "Without cause, without Rick being alive, there's no reason for it to manifest. I doubt you'll ever see it again."

"Good," Jason said. "But if it does show up, we have to figure out a way to get rid of it permanently."

"You have my word," Uncle Alexander said.

After what felt like forever in the air, the drive from the airport to Salton, and the change in time zones, Jason followed Grandma Lena into her house at around seven-thirty that evening. Shay tackled him in the foyer.

Jason dropped to his knees and pushed the top of his head into her scruff. She wriggled and swerved to lick Jason's cheeks and eyelids and neck.

"I have missed you so much, Shay." Jason scratched her ears and her back. Shay mouthed Jason's wrist and fell onto the floor for a belly rub. "Good girl. It's so good to see you, you have no idea."

"I don't need a belly rub, but I'd love a hug," Sadie said.

Jason jumped up and hugged her. "Are you okay? Grandma Lena said things have been tough." He remembered he hadn't turned his phone back on since he'd slept on the plane and in the car, awake only long enough to move from one mode of transportation to the next. "I'm sorry I didn't get your texts."

"That's okay," Sadie said. "But I'm really glad you're back. For a while, I thought you'd bailed on me and decided to live in London forever."

"No way," Jason said. "I'd much rather hang out here."

"Wait—are you saying boring old Salton is better than London?"

It hadn't been that long since Jason had used those words to describe Salton. "Believe it or not, there is nowhere I would rather be than right here in Salton. You won't believe half the stuff I have to tell you about what happened over there," Jason said. "But first, how are you? What's been going on?"

"She didn't tell you?" Sadie asked.

"No. Grandma Lena thought it would be better if I talked to you myself."

"Okay. In a little bit," Sadie said. "You should say hi to everyone first." She gestured to Brandon.

"Bro, so good to see you." Brandon, Jason's best friend since before they'd moved to Salton, gripped Jason's hand and half-hugged him with a pat on the back. "Things got rough in London, huh?"

"You could say that," Jason said. "Lots to tell. But sorry I wasn't around when you got here. Are you staying for a while?"

"A couple more months at least," Brandon said. "Parents are on a long assignment."

"Cool. We can totally catch up."

Finn pushed her head into the back of Jason's leg.

He turned toward her. "Good girl, Finn." Jason scratched Finn's chest and she kicked a back leg indicating he had a good spot. "Did you take care of Shay while I was gone? Teach her a few new tricks?"

"She did a very good job with Shay," Grandma Lena said. "She probably has a few surprises for you."

"I can't wait." He looked at Sadie. "Mrs. C. go to bed early or something? Don't tell me—she has some crack-of-dawn beehive thing to do tomorrow, right?" Jason chuckled.

Before Sadie could answer, the front door opened to everyone else who'd arrived from London. There were greetings and hugs and plans made to get everyone together the next day for dinner and long conversations. But now it was time to get some rest.

Jason stepped forward. "But I wanted to talk to Sadie—"

"No, it's okay," Sadie said. "You guys are all exhausted, and one more day isn't going to hurt anything. We can talk tomorrow."

"Are you sure?" Jason asked.

"Yep, absolutely." She nodded.

"Okay. I'll come by your house," Jason said.

Sadie glanced at Grandma Lena then back to Jason. "I'll come to your house instead, okay? You'll probably still be tired, adjusting to the time change and everything. Text me when you're up, and I'll swing by."

"Yeah . . . okay," Jason said.

Everyone said their goodbyes.

Sadie dropped and scratched Shay's ears and kissed the top of her head. Shay wagged her tail and licked Sadie's cheek.

✳✳✳

After a short drive to their house, Jason and Shay went up to his room. He threw off his clothes and left them in a lump on the floor. He removed the coin from his passport holder and set it on his desk. It didn't glow, it didn't heat up, and it didn't show anything but the usual Lex design.

Movement outside caught his attention. He glanced out the window. The shadow of a large figure scurried along the sidewalk below.

What the—is that a . . . Bigfoot? Jason scrunched his eyes and looked again. Nothing was there.

"I'm so tired I'm seeing things." Jason climbed into bed, and Shay jumped up and snuggled next to him.

"Home sweet home, Shay." He scratched Shay's neck.

She licked Jason's forehead and sighed.

THE END

Continue the adventure with the second "book
two," *Chronicle Two - Sadie: The Clan Calling*

Or, if you've already read *The Clan Calling*,
read *Chronicle Three: The Forge of Bonds*

Reviews are greatly appreciated and they help other readers
discover books they would enjoy. It would mean the world
to Wendy if you took a minute to write a review of
The League of Governors.

PREVIEW

The Clan Calling

CHAPTER ONE

Sadie glanced at her classmates passing in the hallway. They had no idea how close they came to being wiped out, incinerated, erased. She heard snippets of their conversations about football games, and papers they had to write, about teachers, and where to go after school, about how gross the latest lunch was in the cafeteria. But no one mentioned Skyfish. Or the Rampart. Or that her best friend, Jason Lex, can shoot blue bolts of electricity out of his hands.

Totally clueless. Not exactly how she'd imagined ninth grade would be, but it was just as well. Her classmates would freak out if they knew who and what lived around them, hidden by the Rampart.

Sadie met Jason at their lockers. "From Mamo." She handed him an apple from her grandmother's garden.

"All this healthy stuff is going to kill me." Jason grinned, took a bite. "Tell her thanks, as usual."

"I will. And she'll be glad to hear you are actually eating what she sends." Sadie snapped her locker shut.

"Hey, if it's good, as in tastes good, I'll eat it."

Sadie and Jason headed to the lunchroom where Jason tossed the apple core in a trash bin near the door. They grabbed seats and Sadie unpacked her lunch. Jason pulled a protein bar out of his bag and peeled back the wrapper.

"Seriously, that's all you're eating?" Sadie asked.

"I had an apple."

Sadie rolled her eyes. She looked across the room. "Ugh. Here comes Derek Goodman."

Jason looked over his shoulder. His lip curled.

Derek sneered. "What are you looking at?" He and two of his friends stopped behind Jason.

"I was trying to figure out what smelled so bad," Jason said.

Derek sniffed the space above Jason's head. "It's you, the slimeball that beats up his own weakling brother."

Jason bolted out of his seat and stood inches away from Derek. "Take that back."

"Or what?"

Jason pressed his fists into his thighs. His chin jutted. "Take—That—Back."

"Not—Gonna—Happen. For all we know, you've done something to your sister, too. I heard she hasn't been in school for like a month."

Jason's knuckles whitened and he glared at Derek.

"Jason?" Sadie wanted him to take a breath, to take a step back. Given Jason's power, she knew this could get bad fast. For everyone.

Jason shook his head. "You're not worth it."

"No? How about now?" Derek shoved Jason into the table.

Jason sprang into a fighting stance. Sadie rushed to his side of the table.

"What's going on here?" Coach Martel grabbed Derek's shoulder from behind. "You. To the principal's office."

Derek moved toward the exit. Coach turned to Jason. "Are you all right?"

"Yeah. Fine." Jason straightened and relaxed.

"Okay. Good man." Coach patted Jason on the back. "Don't forget basketball tryouts are in a couple of weeks."

"Thanks, Coach."

Sadie doubted Jason would try out for the basketball team. He was focused on his training for the Guards. Maybe too focused.

Coach Martel nodded. "Now, if you'll excuse me, I have a problem to escort to the principal's office. Again." The last word he said under his breath.

Lunch period was almost over and most of Sadie's classmates left for their next period. Sadie stepped closer to Jason. "Della's still having a hard time?"

Jason wadded his trash and tossed it into the nearby bin. "Yeah. She's awake half the night, she starts crying at the weirdest times. She was playing fetch with Shay yesterday and lost it when Shay wouldn't drop the ball for her."

"Is there anything I can do?" The bell rang and Sadie picked up her lunch bag.

Jason looked at his hands. The skin on his palms was shiny and smooth, newly healed from being burned when he'd tried to save his mom. "Nah. Dad's trying to figure it out. Thanks, though." He turned toward his next class. "See you later."

"Yeah, see ya." Sadie spun on her heel and headed to Algebra. She didn't want to disappoint Mrs. Bauer by being late.

✹✹✹

After the last bell, Sadie exited the school and watched a few parents picking up their kids. Parent stuff reminded her that she was different. Sadie didn't have parents. But she had Mamo and that's what mattered.

She walked down the street toward home. In front of her house, a tall man with gray hair and matching beard smiled and nodded at Sadie, then eased himself into a red SUV. Sadie didn't smile back, or wave, or nod her head. She didn't know the man. And she knew pretty much everyone. Salton wasn't a big town.

"Mamo, I'm home." Sadie dropped her backpack in the foyer and headed to the kitchen. "Mamo?" The kitchen was empty. She dashed upstairs. Mamo was lying on her bed. Sadie tapped lightly on the open door. "Are you awake?" she whispered.

Mamo's eyes slitted open. "Yes, come in. Sit with me." Mamo patted the bed beside her.

"What are you doing up here?" Sadie asked.

"I thought I'd lie down for a few minutes."

"Are you okay?"

"Of course," Mamo said. "Just wanted to rest my eyes."

Rest her eyes? That's a new one.

"So you probably didn't see that man out front," Sadie said.

"What man?" Mamo cleared her throat.

"Gray-haired guy. He was getting into a car when I walked up."

"Must have been visiting a neighbor. You didn't recognize him?"

"No," Sadie said, "and it's weird he'd park in front of our house if he's visiting someone else. It's not like there are tons of cars parked on our street."

"Maybe he was drawn to the shade of our pine tree," Mamo said.

Maybe, except there was no shade when I saw him.

Mamo rubbed her temples. She grimaced.

"Are you really okay?" Sadie pressed the back of her hand against Mamo's forehead, like Mamo had done to her whenever she hadn't felt good. "Are you sick?"

"I'm fine, I'm fine." Mamo took Sadie's hand in hers. "Just a little headache."

"Again?" This was the third headache in two weeks, and Mamo never got headaches. She never got sick.

"It's nothing. I already feel it fading. Now tell me about your day. Everything okay at school?"

Sadie shifted to face Mamo. "Well, no Skyfish attacks or surprises from parents trying to destroy all of us, so that's good." Sadie chuckled.

"And how is Jason handling everything? Is he still doing all right?"

"Seems like it, but he spends so much time on his training for the Rampart Guards that we don't get to talk much. He barely eats at lunch now because he says he doesn't want to be too full for training. Oh—he said thank you for the apple."

Mamo pushed herself up to sitting. "Maybe I need to send food for him every day." She closed her eyes.

"I think you need to see a doctor. You're pale, and I can tell you don't feel good."

Mamo's complexion was pasty, almost gray. Her hand felt cool in Sadie's.

"Just a little flu bug, I think. No doctor necessary. Good food and good rest will fix me right up." Mamo pushed herself a little higher against the headboard. "Maybe you could bring me a cup of the veggie soup we made, and hot tea with some of our fresh honey. You know our honey fixes anything."

"Sure thing. I'll be back in a few minutes." Sadie rose and headed to the doorway. She looked back at Mamo. Her eyes were closed again and Sadie's throat tightened.

She prepared the food, including a serving for herself. It was early for dinner, but she wanted to be with Mamo. Homework could wait. She'd have plenty of time to get her work done before bedtime.

Sadie carried the tray into Mamo's room.

Mamo opened her eyes. "Smells delicious."

She set the tray on Mamo's lap. "Of course it's delicious. I'm a highly skilled re-heater of soup." She smirked.

"I've taught you well." Mamo took a sip of tea. "Mmm. Just what I needed. Now tell me about school today, boring as it was without any mayhem."

"Jason almost got in a fight with Derek Goodman. He was picking on Jason about the Skyfish attack, the one at school when it seemed like Jason tried to hurt Kyle." Sadie sipped her soup from a mug.

"Glad to hear it was only an almost fight," Mamo said. "And poor Derek."

Sadie's head jerked. "Poor Derek? What about poor Jason? Derek is so annoying bringing up stuff he knows nothing about, and he's such a jerk to everyone, even his friends. Of which he has maybe two, and I'm surprised he has that many."

"People like that usually act the way they do because of other things going on in their life. It has nothing to do with Jason, or you, or anyone else at school."

"I don't know about that," Sadie said. "I think he's just mean."

"Maybe you should talk to him sometime."

"Um, no thank you. I'd rather not go out of my way to ruin my day."

Mamo pressed into Sadie's hand. "Hmm, well, maybe you'll change your mind if the opportunity presents itself."

Not likely. Sadie changed the subject. "So what are we doing this weekend?"

Mamo pushed her bowl away and leaned into her pillows. "You don't have plans with your friends?"

"Well, sure, we talked about some things. But I wanted to check with you first."

"I can plan around you and your friends."

"Yeah, I know. But you and I are a team. Two for one and one for two, right?" She and Mamo had adopted their own version of the Musketeers' motto.

"Always, my dear. But I'm not sure how I'll be feeling this weekend, so go ahead and make plans with your friends. We'll adjust our plans later." Mamo's eyes scrunched.

Sadie touched Mamo's forehead again. "How can I tell if you have a fever?"

"I don't. I'm fine."

"You feel kinda warm to me." Sadie moved the tray off the bed. "I'm going to call the doctor."

"No, no. I'll be just fine in another day or two." Mamo shifted down into the pillows. "A little rest and I'll be right as rain and back in the garden with the beehives."

Mamo's breathing was short, shallow. It seemed like she hurt everywhere, not only in her head.

"If I tell the doctor your symptoms—"

"A couple more days, Sadie, okay? I just need to rest." Mamo closed her eyes.

"Okay." Sadie rose from the bed and picked up the tray. "I'll let you sleep. I'm going to water the garden and do my homework. Call if you need anything."

"Thank you, sweetheart. I don't know what I'd do without you."

I feel the same way, Mamo.

✳✳✳

Sadie woke early the next morning. She had a text message from Jason: "See you at school. Staying at Uncle A's. Dad and Della headed to London."

Wow. That's huge. Sadie didn't text back. They wouldn't meet up to walk to school since Uncle Alexander's house was in a different direction. She'd ask Jason what was going on when she saw him at lunch.

She climbed out of bed and got ready, then checked in on Mamo. She was sound asleep, resting comfortably. Even though she hadn't eaten much of her soup, she did drink her tea and her headache had improved. Sadie hoped it stayed that way. She left a note in Mamo's office and headed out.

✳✳✳

"Sadie, wait up." Vanessa Barnes dodged students and hurried to where Sadie had stopped in the hallway. She'd been friends with Vanessa since first grade when Mamo met

Vanessa's mom through home schooling connections. The girls followed the same lesson plan, went on home schooling field trips together, and both transitioned to public school when they were ten.

"Hey, Nessa," Sadie said. "Ready for the history test?"

"Yeah, I think so. I was up a little late studying, but I feel good. Maybe not bright-eyed but definitely bushy-tailed so I count that as a win." She flicked her brunette ponytail and grinned.

Sadie chuckled. "So I can count on getting a better score than you."

"Like that's new," Nessa said. "But I'll be a very close second, and I may just shock you one of these days and amaze you with my super-intelligence."

"You already do that, every day," Sadie said.

They dashed into Mr. Bond's History class. He was in room number seven, and he'd added two zeroes, cut from construction paper, in front of the number on his door. He drank water from a martini shaker during the day, and always included an extra credit question on his tests that had something to do with James Bond. He usually wore bow ties, but not with a tuxedo. More often than not, Sadie saw him in plaid shirts and brown corduroy pants. And his first name wasn't James. It was Bruce.

Sadie and Nessa sat in their assigned seats, Nessa's directly behind Sadie's.

"Welcome to History Headquarters, students. I trust you've trained for today's test and will score at least eighty percent correct lest you otherwise end up in the pool of sharks swimming beneath our floor." Mr. Bond straightened a stack of papers on his desk.

"Whatever." Stevie Harkness, one of the not-so-bright football players, tipped back in his chair, teetering on two of the four legs. "Like, bad guys have the sharks, not James Bond."

"Whoever's in charge of Headquarters gets to decide what's under the floor. I've also decided that you get to hand out the exams since you apparently enjoy trying to be helpful." Mr. Bond picked up the stack and waved it in the air. "Come and get 'em."

Stevie huffed and clunked his chair onto all four legs. He shuffled to the front of the room and snatched up the tests.

Sadie took her copy and flipped to the second page to see the extra credit question: In what country does the opening scene of the James Bond novel, Carte Blanche, take place?

Yes. Two extra points. Sadie mentally fist-bumped the air and wrote her answer: Serbia.

Twenty minutes later, Sadie stood to walk her exam up to Mr. Bond. She jumped when Stevie snorted, waking himself from a nap. The class laughed. Mr. Bond sighed. He'd seen that from Stevie plenty of times before.

Sadie returned to her desk and glanced at Nessa. Her head was down on her forearm. Sadie kicked Nessa's foot.

Her head popped up. "Oh my god," Nessa whispered. She shot a look at the clock.

"No talking, Ms. Barnes," Mr. Bond said.

"Sorry." She mouthed the word and started scribbling answers on her paper.

Sadie sat. *Jeez, she must have been more tired than she thought. She's never done that before.* Nessa's pencil tapped and scratched and whisked behind her. *Please let her have enough time to finish.*

The bell rang and Nessa ran her exam to Mr. Bond's outstretched hand. She retrieved her backpack from her desk and walked out with Sadie.

"What happened?" Sadie asked.

"No idea. I don't even remember feeling sleepy. I was taking the test and then I was in Nap-land. I'm so glad you woke me."

"Me too. How do you think you did?"

"No extra credit this time," Nessa said. "But otherwise I think I'm good."

"That's a relief. And you're feeling okay?"

"Totally," Nessa said. "Nothing like a good power nap in the middle of an exam to get the batteries recharged. Hah." She blew out a breath.

The girls weaved through the crowded hallway.

"Are we on for the lake this weekend?" Nessa asked.

"I think so. Mamo isn't feeling that great, so we don't have any set plans."

"Sorry she's sick. But if she feels better, bring her along. She's cool." Nessa skipped left to avoid a teacher coming out of her classroom. "And then we'll have a ride instead of needing to ride our bikes. Plus she brings the best snacks."

"She does have the food thing down," Sadie said.

"Here's my stop." Nessa peeked into the classroom. "Ooh, substitute teacher. French should be a cakewalk today. Or, I mean, *c'est du gâteau.* I think." She laughed. "See you at lunch?"

"Yep. I'll save you a spot."

"And I'll be there. Think maybe there'll be a Jason-Derek rematch? I was bummed I missed that yesterday."

"I really hope not," Sadie said. "And you didn't miss that much." *Especially compared to everything else you've missed.*

Sadie wished she could tell Nessa about the Rampart, the cryptids, the secrets. But she'd promised Jason and his family to keep her lips sealed. At least Mamo knew the scoop.

"Yeah, well, one of these days I'd like to see Derek get what he deserves." Nessa stepped into the doorway of her French class. "Later."

"Later." Sadie continued down the hall to English. She passed the janitor's supply closet, though Mr. Whitfield liked to call it his office.

"Good morning, Sadie," Mr. Whitfield said.

"Good morning. Office is looking good." Sadie smiled.

"Thank you. You know how I like a clean and organized space." He chuckled and pretended to straighten a pile of disheveled rags on the shelf.

"On top of it, as always." Sadie waved. "Have a great day, Mr. Whitfield." She continued to her next class.

As she rounded the corner, a woman she didn't recognize ducked into a classroom across the hall. She was slight, only a bit taller than Sadie. Her hair was dyed purple.

Huh. Another sub.

That didn't happen at Salton High very often, especially one with purple hair.

✳✳✳

Sadie hurried home after school. She dropped her backpack in the foyer. "Mamo?" She spotted her out the kitchen window.

Mamo was in the garden. She wore a straw hat tied with a royal blue scarf, khaki shorts, and a peach-colored T-shirt that said, "Ask me about the birds and the bees." She piled zucchini into the basket next to her.

Sadie stepped outside. "You're feeling better." She hugged Mamo.

"Right as rain, just as I said." Mamo looked up at the sky. "Which is exactly what we could use more of these days. This Indian summer won't let go."

"I'll water the garden after I do my homework," Sadie said. She nodded at Mamo. "I haven't seen that shirt in a while."

"You asked me not to wear it in public, so I tucked it away. But I figured it would be just fine for gardening."

Sadie felt her cheeks flush. "It was a little bit embarrassing when we ran into Mrs. Bauer at the grocery store.'"

Mamo laughed. "It's only meant to get people into a conversation about actual birds and bees and their importance to our food supply."

"I know. But we'd just had 'the talk.'" Sadie laughed too. "Anyway, that was years ago. Wear it wherever you want." Sadie paused. "But maybe when we're not together."

"Oh, you're really growing up." Mamo smirked. "Help me carry in the zucchini."

Sadie lifted the basket and they walked inside.

"You get after your homework. I'm going to slice some of these and we'll sauté them with onions for dinner. We're also having trout and salad. Sound good?"

"Sounds great." Sadie grabbed her backpack from the foyer. She returned to the kitchen for a glass of water.

Mamo was hunched over the sink but straightened quickly when she heard Sadie behind her. She turned toward Sadie. "Forget something?"

Sadie took a glass from the cupboard. "Just water." She placed the glass under the dispenser in the refrigerator door. "You okay?"

Mamo dismissed the question with a wave of her hand. "I was just stretching my neck. It's a little tight from too much time in bed. That's all."

Sadie nodded. "Okay." She went upstairs. She wanted to believe Mamo was fine.

But something nagged at Sadie's gut and wouldn't let go.

Continue the adventure with
Chronicle Two – Sadie: The Clan Calling

Or, if you've already read
The Clan Calling, read
Chronicle Three: The Forge of Bonds

ACKNOWLEDGEMENTS

So many people go into the creation of a novel, and I treasure every one of them. Each person mentioned here contributed and influenced this story in the best possible way.

Thank you, Jeffery Deaver, for your encouragement after reading a sampling of my work, and for validation when I shared my idea for two book twos—two completely different stories, one for Jason and one for Sadie, which occur on the same timeline. And thank you for the idea to have same scenes in the beginning and ending of both books from the respective characters' points of view. The conversation with you solidified my conviction to try something different, and I'm delighted with the results.

Thank you to these talented artists, experts, masters of their craft, who provided their respective services:

Lisa Miller: I've said it once and I'll say it again and again, her class, Story Structure Safari, is unequalled.

Steven Novak: The brilliant, and patient, designer of the cover, including the transformation of the Lex coin from an image in my head to one for all to see.

Steve Parolini: Who knew so many words could be cut to make a story stronger? This guy. The NovelDoctor is more like an elite novel surgeon.

Susie Brooks: Not only a smart and sassy copy editor but a dear friend as well.

Dale Pease: Talented interior designer who also has a gift of patience.

Brian Callanan: The man's got skills and brings the books to life with his audio narration.

Thank you Pikes Peak Writers—yours was the first writing conference I ever attended and I was overwhelmed and mesmerized. And thank you Rocky Mountain Fiction Writers for giving me the opportunity to give back.

Thank you to my Racca's critique group of Kim Byrne, Judy Logan, and Terri Spesock, who provide me with thoughtful and enlightening feedback even when I bombard them with pages. And thank you Racca's for the continued welcome at your restaurant, for a menu of deliciousness, and for sharing Marilyn with us. She's not only the best waitress but also a friend.

Thank you to my Tattered Cover critique group of Mark Lehnertz, Sue Duff, Chad Mathine, Bob Biniek, Matthew Woolums, and Todd Leatherman who are always supportive, helpful, and available when I need them. Can't ask for more than that.

Thank you to many more people who continue to support me from near and far. Please know how much I love and appreciate you. A few I must mention here are:

Kelly Hindley who is a beta reader, supporter, and has been a friend forever.

Dianna Cannon who wows me with her support, her feedback, and is the third member of the friends forever triumverate.

Meghan Mortimer who never ceases to believe in me.

Katie Terrien who proved to be a skilled beta reader, and is clearly the best mother-in-law in the world.

Corinne O'Flynn who listens when I'm frustrated and cheers as hard as I do when success comes.

Maggie who warms my feet under my desk.

Shea who makes me laugh every single day.

Boon whose history as a misunderstood pit bull mix (he's a lover no matter what) inspired me to make both Finn and Shay pit bull mix dogs.

A special shout out to two readers I met after writing THE RAMPART GUARDS—Yusuf and Maryam. It's been fun staying connected on Goodreads. Keep me posted on the Bigfoot hunting!

Most of all, thank you to all the readers out there, not only of this book but all books. Authors write books because we love the stories, but there's nothing like learning that others enjoy the stories, too. If you love a book, any book, I encourage you to write a review on your preferred bookselling site or sites and help that story be found by more readers. Plus, you'll delight your favorite authors, too.

All the best to everyone, and may you always be surrounded by golden Skyfish.

WENDY M. BARNHART
(Formerly Wendy Terrien)

International bestselling author Wendy Barnhart (formerly Terrien) received her first library card at age two, and a few years later started writing her own stories.

Her debut novel, The Rampart Guards (February 2016), earned a Kirkus starred review and was named to Kirkus Reviews' Best Books of 2016. Next in her series are main character Jason's book two - The League of Governors (August 2017), and developing character Sadie's book two - The Clan Calling (August 2017). Both novels are award winners. Chronicle three in the series (and the fourth physical book) is The Forge of Bonds (February 2020).

Wendy graduated from the University of Utah (go Utes!) and relocated to Colorado where she completed her MBA at the University of Denver. She focused her marketing expertise on the financial and technology industries until a career coach stepped in and reminded Wendy of her passion for writing. Inspired, Wendy leaped and began attending writers' conferences, workshops, and retreats, and the storytelling hasn't stopped since.

She serves on the board of Rocky Mountain Fiction Writers, and is a member of Pikes Peak Writers, the Colorado Authors League, and the Authors Guild.

Wendy lives in the Denver area and is a proud dog mom. She's team dark chocolate, a fan of technology, and believes every dose of nature nurtures the soul. Wendy is also committed to promoting pet adoption from rescues or shelters as the best way to bring home a furry family member. If you're in Colorado, you may even spot her "Adopt a Shelter Pet" license plates.

Learn more about Wendy by visiting her website:
wendymbarnhart.com

www.ingramcontent.com/pod-product-compliance
Lightning Source LLC
Chambersburg PA
CBHW051213120726
47905CB00004B/1097